THE TOUCH OF MURDER

A Veronica Shade Thriller

Book 4

Patrick Logan

This book is a work of fiction. Names, characters, places, and incidents in this book are either entirely imaginary or are used fictitiously. Any resemblance to actual people, living or dead, or of places, events, or locales is entirely coincidental.

Copyright © Patrick Logan 2023
Interior design: © Patrick Logan 2023
All rights reserved.

This book, or parts thereof, cannot be reproduced, scanned, or disseminated in any print or electronic form.

First Edition: May 2023

For Ashley.
It's the troughs that illuminate
the wonder of the peaks.

Prologue

SWEAT POURED DOWN THE MAN'S face, stinging his eyes. He kept his head down as he walked, making sure that the black hoodie he wore was pulled low. His movements were labored, a strange shuffle followed by a large step, followed by another shuffle.

Despite squinting, everything was too bright and aggressive, even with the hood casting a large shadow over most of his face.

"Hey, man, you okay?" a voice called out.

The man looked up and glimpsed part of a face, old clothes, gloves with holes in them. Despite squinting, everything was still too saturated, too real.

"Jesus." The stranger pulled back. "Get the fuck out of here, freak."

The man turned quickly, lowering his head once more. The streets changed around him; the sidewalk beneath his feet became cracked and broken, the walls were covered with increasingly thick layers of graffiti, and what little windows there were, were more broken than not.

His blood pumped hard in his ears, and his breathing was labored.

An alley—an alley appeared on his right, and he glanced down it. This proved to be a mistake.

Three men stood around a burning barrel, warming their hands. They all had scraggly beards and pockmarked skin, but the man barely noticed them. It was the fire that caught his attention. It was bright… impossibly bright.

He groaned and covered his eyes. His skin, his *face*, felt strange, clammy, thickened, somehow.

Like it wasn't his face, but someone else's.

He kept moving and his shoulder struck something, and a man cried out.

"Watch where the fuck you're going."

The man had prominent cheekbones that accentuated gaunt, hollow features, and sunken eyes. His cheeks, like those of the homeless men in the alley, were pockmarked.

"Sorry…"

He looked up and stared at the man… the *sinner*… he'd bumped into. Their eyes met, and the man in the hoodie's vision exploded with red splotches.

"Sinner," he whispered and then lunged.

**

The boy wasn't supposed to be out after dark. He was supposed to be sleeping. But he had the nightmare again, the one with the monster coming to tuck him into bed. When he had this nightmare, he was never able to get back to sleep—no matter the time, he knew he'd be awake until his father came in to rouse him for breakfast.

So, he snuck out, although leaving silently through the front door could barely be considered sneaking out. More like leaving without asking permission.

The City of Greenham looked different at night. The boy was amazed at how much a place could change when the sun set. During the day, it looked like every other city: tall gray buildings that the sun only occasionally managed to peek through, people in matching suits, cars… so many cars. At night, the sun was lost, the buildings went dark, and suits were exchanged for long coats or dirty rags.

The boy usually didn't travel far, but today, the nightmare chased him into an area he'd never been to before. The night also made everything look the same, and before long, he had a creeping suspicion that he was lost.

All the shadows were the same: long and deep.

I went this way, the boy thought. *I know I did.*

But with every step, things appeared even more foreign. There was a white tarp hanging from the girders of a building that was in the process of being renovated.

That, he didn't remember. The boy was about to turn around, head the other way when he saw a shadow through the translucent white tarp.

It was the outline of a man.

There was something familiar about the way the shadow moved. Something... *strange.*

He knew better than to talk to strangers, but the shadow was a good twenty feet away. The boy, even though he was small and thin, was fast. If the man tried anything, he could outrun him.

He knew he could.

The boy used the blade of his hand to push the tarp back, just a little.

The figure was indeed a man, his back to the boy. He was wearing a dark sweatshirt and his shoulders were hunched and rolled forward. With the tarp out of the way, the boy realized that the man was mumbling something under his breath. One word, over and over again.

What was it? Spinner? Dinner? Why was he talking about dinner?

The boy couldn't quite make it out, the man's voice was too low and gravelly.

Thinner?

There was something terribly unnatural about this scene, something wrong with it, and the boy knew he should leave.

Only, he couldn't.

It was like the time he'd watched "Friday the 13th" with his dad. His father had warned him that it was too scary, but he'd acted brave. Said he wanted to see it. When one of the campers had been stabbed in the stomach with the huge knife, he tried to close his eyes, tried to stop watching.

But he was compelled to see.

That single scene haunted his nightmares for weeks. But nothing he saw in that movie or any of the others compared to the scene before him now.

Grumbling and twitching, the man in the hood reached down and dipped his hand into something dark and wet. Then he put two fingers on the wall and started to draw.

The boy loved to draw, and he quickly realized that this was no image, but a word.

"Sinner."

That's what he had been saying all along.

"Sinner... sinner... sinner."

The man in the black hoodie turned and the boy realized he'd made another mistake, one of many this night.

The hunched form wasn't a man at all.

It was a monster. A real-life monster.

The boy's bladder let go and warmth spread across the front of his jeans.

"Sinner... sinner... sinner..."

The boy turned and ran. He was fast, but never in his life was he *this* fast.

And he would never be this fast again.

PART ONE: ANGEL

Chapter 1

IT WASN'T A HANGOVER... NOT *quite*. It was the mild brain fog you got when you had one drink too many and woke up not feeling one hundred percent. It would be gone by mid-morning, but even armed with this knowledge, you still wanted to lie in bed a little longer than usual.

This is exactly what City of Greenham Detective Veronica Shade would have done if it hadn't been for a soft purring sound by the side of her bed. She opened one eye and saw her adopted cat Lucy staring at her accusingly, the way only cats could.

"All right, all right," Veronica grumbled, swinging her feet over the side of the bed. "Hold your horses."

She walked quietly out of the bedroom loft and down the stairs. After grabbing a can of fancy cat food from the fridge and plopping it into a bowl, Veronica gave Lucy some fresh water. While the cat ate, she made coffee.

Veronica didn't mind the mild brain fog from drinking last night. In fact, she almost wished it would last a little longer. It kept her mind blank and stopped her thoughts from racing, bouncing from what could have been to what was in a vicious and nonsensical circle. But the hot coffee started to sharpen her wits, and as soon as she started thinking about anything of real substance, Veronica made her way back upstairs.

She showered with hot water in the en-suite bathroom. When she was done shampooing and conditioning her shoulder-length brown hair, Veronica turned the dial all the way cold. The icy water took her breath away, and she stood under the faucet for as long as she could manage. It felt good—it felt *damn* good. The first time she'd tried this, Veronica lasted only a few seconds. Now, she could stay under the water for upwards of a minute, soaking her face with the cool spray before allowing it to cascade over her back and the rest of her body.

When she was done, Veronica toweled herself off and stood in the doorway of her bedroom, her eyes falling on the man who still slept in her bed. He was handsome, with a well-defined jaw, which was covered in a neatly trimmed and expertly manicured dark beard. Despite his angular face, his features were somehow boyish, accentuated by the way his hair was splayed messily on the white pillowcase.

It wasn't the man's looks that Veronica had been initially attracted to.

It was his kindness.

Initially was also a stretch. She hadn't always thought of him in a positive light. Quite the opposite.

The man's eyes opened and when he saw her, a smirk appeared on his face.

"This isn't creepy at all. Not one bit," he said.

Veronica looked skyward as she pulled the towel from her body and used it to dry her hair.

"Now that's more like it."

"Now who's being the creep," Veronica shot back. She returned to the bathroom to finish her morning routine.

"Today's the big day, huh?" he called out.

Veronica looked at her face in the mirror, pulling the skin below her eyes down. She was slightly dehydrated from the drinks she'd had last night, but over the last six months or so, her skin had regained some of its color and elasticity.

"The big day," she agreed.

Veronica observed her body next. She'd put on a few of the pounds that she lost following her showdown with The Dollmaker. Her thighs were muscular, her shoulders just a little broader. Even her breasts appeared fuller.

In a word, Veronica Shade looked healthier than she had in a long time. And despite the clinging remnants of her hangover, she felt healthy, too.

"So, what's this guy's name? Should I be worried about him talkin' to my girl?"

Veronica chuckled.

"His name is Ethan Blake, and if the rumors are true, he's got a twelve-inch cock."

When there was no reply from the bedroom, Veronica wrapped a towel around her body and leaned out of the bathroom.

"You mean like this?"

The man was no longer in bed. He was standing beside it, completely naked, his arms out at his sides. His body was well-sculpted, muscular, and lean, like a runner's. And what hung from between his legs was equally as impressive.

"No," Veronica said, shaking her head. "You must have misheard. I said twelve inches not a twelfth of an inch."

"I'm a grower, not a shower." The man gestured toward the bed. "Come lie down and you'll find out."

Veronica rolled her eyes again and ducked back into the bathroom to finish applying a little bit of eyeshadow.

"You're just trying to make me late for work."

"Do you blame me? I mean, my girlfriend, the big shot detective, is getting teamed up with Ethan Blake who, apparently, has a lethal weapon for a penis. You know what I would give to have a partner with a twelve-inch cock?"

Veronica stopped applying her makeup.

"What?"

"I don't know—but a lot. Hell, I'd give a lot to work with a eunuch—anything beats working alone."

Veronica finished getting ready, then dressed in her daily attire: gray slacks and a white blouse with a flat front to hide the buttons.

Her boyfriend had since gotten back into bed and his body was covered by a thin sheet. The man wasn't lying, he was a grower all right.

"You know, if you're not happy at work, you can always look for a new job. Selling just a single pair of your fancy shoes would hold you over for months," Veronica remarked.

"Can't sell them, they're monogrammed," the man replied with a chuckle. "Besides, what would I do? Become a computer engineer?"

Veronica's suggestion had been offhand, but his response made her stop and think.

"Well, what is it that you wanted to do before getting into law enforcement?"

The man considered this for a moment.

"Honestly? I wanted to be a private investigator."

Veronica shook her head.

"No, I'm serious," he continued. "I'm good with people, and while I might not be as good as you when it comes to telling if someone's lying, I can read a person. I think I'd be good at it."

Veronica couldn't argue with that.

"I can see it now, PI of the year." The man raised his hand above his head as if imagining a marquee.

Veronica walked over and kissed him on the forehead. He tried to pull her down on top of his growing bulge, but she spun away.

"A man can dream, right? Unfortunately, there are no awards for internal affairs officer of the year. The best thing I ever got was a bag of steaming dog shit burning on my front porch."

"You mean *my* porch."

The man shrugged.

"Details, *shmetails*. Cole Batherson, internal affairs officer of the decade, how's that sound?"

Veronica smiled again.

"Why don't you just start by getting dressed so you still have a job?"

"Yes, ma'am."

On the way out, Veronica grabbed a coffee to go and pet Lucy one final time.

"Good luck with your partner and his huge cock!" Cole yelled from upstairs.

Veronica laughed, a real, genuine laugh. Like the weight she'd lost, this too had returned with time. Regrettably, so had the realization that, given her line of work, such moments of happiness were not meant to last.

Chapter 2

FREDDIE FURLOW WAS BREATHING HEAVILY, his thick chest heaving. He put his hands on his knees, drawing in huge breaths.

It was getting easier.

It wasn't *easy*—Freddie doubted that it would ever be easy the same way he doubted that he would ever enjoy exercising or running in particular. No, he hated running. Absolutely loathed it. But that was why he'd chosen it. After his heart attack, the doctors suggested walking on a treadmill set to a slight incline or using a stationary bike for cardiovascular exercise.

Those weren't painful enough. His penance was to run. And he hated it. But it was getting easier.

Freddie had made it two miles without stopping, his longest distance yet. No David Goggins-level feat, and he wasn't breaking any land speed records, either, but it was progress. Running every day—no breaks, not even on the Lord's Day of rest, Sunday—combined with a more balanced diet had resulted in him losing nearly seventy pounds in just under six months. And for part of that time, because of his recent coronary event, he was under doctor's orders not to do any exercise at all.

Still, Freddie was no specimen and had no illusion of ever becoming one. But Freddie's goal had never been to look good. He simply wanted to stay alive.

And now he had reason to.

When he first decided to punish himself by hitting the pavement, he did so aimlessly, sticking close to the parks near his home. But now, his route was different. It was specific. From his door to theirs, it was nearly exactly four miles. One day, he hoped to run there *and* back without stopping—a pipedream, but you never know.

Freddie raised his head and wiped sweat from his brow as he stared at the house. When he'd lived there, the door had been black. Now it was a deep burgundy. Susan had also painted the small front porch white, even though Freddie much preferred the natural look of the wood beneath. All in all, however, it looked pretty much the same.

It wasn't often that he spotted them inside—Freddie liked to run early in the morning, and Susan and their two sons, Kevin and Randall, were late risers. But every once in a while, he would catch a glimpse of his ex-wife's swirling blonde hair or see a shadow of someone standing in the kitchen like a ghost of his past.

Not much, but enough to keep him going.

And he would keep going. And then one day, Freddie might find himself on the other side of those sheer curtains.

This was about as likely as running eight miles.

But it wasn't impossible.

Freddie took a huge breath, filling his lungs to their capacity, straightened, then started to run again. Normally, after arriving at the house he once called his own, he would walk home. But today, he was determined to run all the way back. He made it about a mile before having to stop, but a mile today was a mile more than yesterday—a mile closer to redeeming himself for his past transgressions and turning his life around.

First stop, his health.

Next, came getting back to work.

Freddie Furlow had dedicated his entire life to law enforcement. He began as a rookie cop, training in Matheson, before moving around to different departments and different cities until he found his home in Greenham. There, he'd naturally progressed from boot to detective where, for a time, he'd been happy.

When Peter Shade had become his captain, his friend had tried to promote him on several occasions. And to Freddie's knowledge, at least twice these proposals had been approved by whoever signed the checks. But after the events that had sent his life into a spiral and his weight ballooning, he'd declined.

He didn't deserve a raise. Not after what he'd done. If anything, he deserved to be behind bars like the criminals he used to hunt.

Freddie sighed.

First health, then work.

Back to work—he *had* to get back to work.

But that might prove even more challenging than running. At least with running, you had a basis—everyone knew how to walk.

How do you escape demons that will never stop chasing you? Even if you could run from them, they were always just a step behind.

Just waiting for you to stumble so that they can pounce.

And devour you.

Chapter 3

VERONICA KNEW THAT IT WAS going to be awkward, but as a member of the Band-Aid generation, she believed in the importance of ripping the covering off quickly rather than suffering through peeling it back slowly.

She didn't hesitate before heading into the City of Greenham police station.

With her head held high, Veronica walked briskly up the stairs, trying not to think about Freddie. This soon proved impossible, however.

She had never seen a photograph or heard a description of her new partner Ethan Blake—like a crime scene, she wanted to go into this unbiased—but the process of elimination made him obvious.

And Ethan couldn't have been more different than Freddie.

Thin, with defined features. Freddie had a wealth of experience, and just looking at Ethan was enough for Veronica to know that this man did not.

"Detective Shade? My name's Ethan." He extended his hand. His grip was strong, but not too strong—he wasn't compensating for anything. This made her smile a little, remembering Cole's joke from earlier that day.

"Please, just call me Veronica."

Ethan had dark brown hair that was neatly styled with a part on the left-hand side. His jawline was pronounced, not as sharp as Cole's, but similar. His outfit was what tipped Veronica off to the fact that he was green: a classic light gray suit with a belt that matched his brown loafers.

Brown loafers... shoes that would give Ethan blisters after day one.

Anybody who had been a detective for more than ten minutes knew the value of function over style.

"Where are you from, Ethan?"

When her father, Peter Shade, had been forced into retirement, the department, with the oversight of the mayor, had looked outside of local jurisdictions for his replacement. Enter Captain Pierre Bottel from Washington, DC. Her father might have been police captain, but he was—*is*—a cop through and through. Pierre Bottel, on the other hand, was a politician masquerading as a captain.

Ethan Blake, the first detective hired or promoted by the department since Veronica herself more than a year ago, wasn't local either. If he had been, she would have known his name and his rep.

"Originally?"

Veronica started toward her desk, and Ethan respectfully fell in step with her.

"Sure."

"Arizona. But I was only born there; I didn't live there long."

Veronica stopped in front of her desk.

"That one's yours." Veronica indicated the desk across from her, the one that had once belonged to Freddie Furlow. It had long since been cleaned out, with her ex-partner's belongings either being placed into storage or having been delivered to him while he was on leave. "But I wouldn't get too used to it. We don't spend much time in the office."

Most of my time as a rookie was spent in Freddie's disgusting car full of fast-food wrappers.

"What did you do before being hired as a detective here in Greenham?" Veronica continued with what she hoped came off as casual conversation.

"Oh, yeah, right—well, I completed my police training in Oklahoma, but then I got a job as a trooper with the Oregon State Police."

Veronica, who was in the process of sipping from her travel mug, sputtered.

"Dammit."

Ethan quickly grabbed a Kleenex from a box on her desk and handed it to her.

"Thanks," Veronica said, wiping her face.

In many ways, Ethan Blake reminded her of Cole Batherson; they were both young, had a similar style, and while Cole was better looking, Ethan wasn't hard on the eyes.

"How long did you work as a state trooper?" Veronica asked, trying to keep her tone even.

This wasn't the question she wanted to ask. She wanted to ask if Ethan knew ex-State Trooper Steven Burns. She wanted to ask if they'd ever worked together. She wanted to ask why Steve left the State Police.

"Two years. Two years and then—"

"You came here," Veronica finished for him.

Ethan shrugged.

"I came here."

Veronica gulped her coffee, finishing what was left.

"Well, welcome to the City of Greenham, the drug abuse and overdose capital of the West."

Ethan clearly wasn't sure how to respond to this, so he just nodded.

The lack of reciprocation when it came to her career trajectory indicated that Ethan already knew about her past. Veronica actually found it refreshing that he didn't placate her by asking. Unlike Veronica, a man who wore an outfit as fancy as

Ethan did, and was that put together, clearly did his background research. And she knew exactly what her new partner would've found.

Greenham PD Officer Veronica Shade was promoted to detective approximately fourteen months ago. That made her one of the youngest detectives in the department. There were rumors that she'd only been promoted because her father was captain—thank you Ken Cameron—but any detective worth his salt would have seen through that.

Ethan would've also discovered that she brought down the Dollmaker, Gloria Tramell, a murderer, abusive wife, and neglectful mother. And no story would be complete without reading about or watching the video that still circulated online of the botched live TV interview with Marlowe Lerman. The one in which a mysterious caller revealed all of her secrets to the world, including the fact that she suffered from a rare condition called multimodal synesthesia, where sensory stimuli entered her brain and got mixed around like melted chocolate in a bowl.

There were more details, sure, but the practical man probably passed some, if not all of them, off as fantasy. He would have also learned of Dante Fiori, maybe even of Veronica's late brother, Benny.

Maybe, maybe not.

It didn't matter to Veronica—she was beyond caring what people thought. She was just here to do her job, one that she wasn't ashamed to say she was excellent at.

Veronica sat in front of her computer and opened her email. Across from her, she watched Ethan awkwardly lower himself into Freddie's chair... only to sink nearly to the floor. Freddie's girth had permanently damaged the springs in the chair.

As he struggled to adjust the chair's height, Veronica felt herself smiling.

There was one interesting email, some stranger reaching out after reading Cole's piece about her in the Times and being inspired. It was nice, but she didn't respond.

After a few minutes of Ethan doing nothing other than looking more uncomfortable than a nun at an adult cinema, she finally addressed him again.

"We mostly wait," Veronica admitted. "Wait until a case lands in our lap and then we move. And we don't stop moving until we solve it."

Just as she finished speaking, the door behind Ethan opened and Captain Pierre Bottel stood in the doorway of his office.

"Detectives Shade and Blake, can you join me in my office, please?"

Veronica stood and Ethan joined her.

"And this would be the case. Just follow my lead."

Once inside the office, the captain asked them to close the door. Ethan obliged.

"Welcome to Greenham PD, Detective Blake," Captain Bottel said.

"It's a pleasure to be here," Ethan responded.

Captain Bottel scratched his bald head then adjusted his wire-rimmed glasses. In his mid-fifties, the man was completely bald, and almost entirely hairless aside from a rust-colored mustache that Veronica was fairly certain he dyed on a weekly basis.

"Normally, I'm not in favor of throwing a new detective right into a murder investigation, but unfortunately, you are the only two available."

Veronica's interest was piqued. Since Dante Fiori, the most exciting cases she'd been given were robberies and assaults. Better than unarmed jewelry heists, but she would be lying if she said she didn't miss the excitement of something a little more… *substantial*. It wasn't as if serious crimes weren't being committed in Greenham—if anything, the opposite was true. All crime was up, from drug overdoses to break-ins, to murder.

"That okay with you, Detective Shade?" the captain asked.

"Yes, sir," Veronica replied. "Not a problem."

There was a folder on the captain's desk, and he nodded at it. Veronica took it and handed it to Ethan. They were starting to leave when Captain Bottel spoke up again. "Hopefully quick and easy with this one, detectives."

Veronica loathed euphemisms. All they did was confuse and obfuscate.

But in this case, the captain's meaning was clear.

"Quick and easy" meant to keep it out of the press. It also meant no more serial killers, and no more drama. Find out what happened, arrest the culprit, and move on.

But even though Veronica nodded in agreement, deep down, doubt began to creep in. After all, her name was Detective Veronica Shade.

She didn't know how to make things quick and easy.

It simply wasn't in her genes.

Chapter 4

"No, don't open that," Veronica warned. Ethan, who was in the process of opening the case folder, snapped it closed as if looking inside would break some unwritten rule.

Jesus, he's skittish, Veronica thought. She tried to remember her first day on the job, to recall if she'd been this nervous. She thought not, but Veronica was well aware that her memories weren't always the most reliable. *Then again, I had a decade-plus veteran to guide me through the first days. And my first case... what was it?* She couldn't remember. But she knew what it wasn't: a murder investigation. Captain Shade would have never allowed it.

"Sorry, I didn't mean to startle you," Veronica apologized. She wasn't prepared to be a mentor, but she also didn't want to make another enemy in the department, either. Been there, done that. Arresting fellow officer Ken Cameron had garnered her no friends. His murder, also tied to Veronica, made her even fewer.

"If you want to look at the case, by all means, be my guest. My personal approach is a little different, as you can imagine. I read what someone else has written and it biases me. Can't help it. I like to go in clean, open-minded."

Ethan said nothing—he just chewed the inside of his cheek.

"That's not going to work for me," she added.

Ethan made a face.

"What do you mean?" he asked.

"Look, my last partner and I, well, we had some..." Veronica sucked her teeth as she tried to come up with the right word, "—secrets, I guess. I don't want to start off the same way with you. If we're going to be an effective team, we should be able to speak our minds to each other."

Ethan still looked uncomfortable, and Veronica sighed.

"I don't like playing games either, Ethan. If you want to say something, just—"

"Do you want to avoid the crime scene photos because you think it will affect your synesthesia?" Ethan interrupted.

Well, that's one way to ask what's on your mind. Blunt, to the point of being rude.

But she'd asked for it and couldn't get mad because her partner had listened to her.

"Partly," Veronica admitted. She didn't like talking about her synesthesia, didn't like making it the focus like it had been on *Marlowe*, but at times, it was unavoidable. "But I also find that when you look at pictures that someone else took of a crime scene, you're tempted to try and find their angle, instead of investigating from scratch. You're apt to miss things that way. As a state trooper, I'm sure you developed methods of your own."

"Yeah, I did."

"Good."

Veronica waited to see if Ethan would open the folder. He didn't.

She placed her hands flat on the table and stood.

"Alright, let's get going then, shall we?"

They drove in silence through Greenham, making their way toward the city's seedier districts. Like most of Oregon, most of the West, hell, most of the Country, Greenham had a significant drug problem. It rivaled Portland in scope and per capita overdose deaths, despite having less than a fifth of its population. Overdoses were so common in Greenham that beat cops usually spent a grand total of five minutes at the scene before signing off on them. Detectives were rarely called in.

And the borough that their case drew them to now was in the worst area in all of Greenham: a wedge-shaped district sandwiched between the more affluent Meadowbrook and Cedar Heights. It was officially named Nettle Point, but everyone called it Needle Point.

She knew the approximate address of the crime scene and the police car parked by the curb offered something more specific.

Veronica got out of her car and was preparing to show her badge when a man with slicked black hair in a police uniform stepped out from behind a white tarp that hung from rotting scaffolding.

"Court," Veronica greeted the man with a grin.

"Detective Shade."

Court was young, even younger than Ethan by a few years.

"This is Detective Ethan Blake, first day on the job. Ethan, meet Officer Court Furnelli."

The two men shook hands and exchanged pleasantries.

"They finally got you out of the Greenham holding cells, huh?" Veronica teased.

Court performed a mock salute.

"Onward and upward."

"Good for you."

"How's Freddie doing?" Court asked.

"He's better, out of the hospital," Veronica replied with a shrug.

Even though she was at odds with her ex-partner, Detective Freddie Furlow, she still cared for the man. And while she may not have visited him in the hospital, she'd followed up to make sure he was doing okay.

After a massive coronary, Freddie had been hospitalized for two weeks before being released with a more-or-less clean bill of health. Cleaner, anyway.

"Yeah, I heard that. How's he doing? I heard he's coming back to work soon," Court said. He turned and gestured for them to follow him beneath the white tarp.

"Really?" The last Veronica had heard was that Freddie was on indefinite leave.

"Yeah, a couple of the fellas and I were talking, told me that he was doing really good. Lost some weight. A *lot* of weight. Might be back real soon."

That's why I didn't hear, Veronica thought. *Because it was chatter among boys. And the boys don't like me.*

Except for Court. Court had always been nice to her, even after the Ken Cameron debacle. He was a good kid, and a smart cop.

Freddie getting healthy, and losing weight, was good news. The heart attack had done what she never could: get the man to take his health seriously.

"Good, good," Veronica said absently.

Before stepping beneath the tarp, Court turned to look at both her and Ethan one last time.

"I should warn you," he said, his tone suddenly serious. "It's not pretty in here."

Veronica nodded, appreciating the man's warning, but she took it with a grain of salt. Like all rookie police officers, Court Furnelli had spent a year and change working in the bowels of the Greenham PD—working the holding cells. It was a bad job, the *worst* job, mostly consisting of cleaning up junkie puke. But that was a far cry from murder.

"Thanks."

Court pulled back the drape, and Veronica realized that she was very wrong. The scene before her was enough to bring bile to the throat of even the most hardened and seasoned detective.

And her new rookie partner Ethan Blake was anything but.

Chapter 5

"AN ANONYMOUS CALLER REPORTED HEARING strange noises in the wee hours of the morning," Court said. "Must have been hella strange for someone to send me out here."

Before stepping through the curtain, Veronica took a deep breath, then a second without exhaling. She had gotten so good at preparing herself for her synesthesia that it came second nature to her now. It had been her psychiatrist, Dr. Jane Bernard, who had first taught her this technique. It was simple, yet effective. Without it, there was the real potential of being overwhelmed.

It had happened before—it had happened in Steve's barn when Veronica had been exposed to Maggie Cernak's supposed suicide.

The cirrhotic glow seeping through the translucent white tarp now was a result of a weak yellow bulb affixed to the brick wall. But as the tarp was pulled back further, this quickly changed and how Veronica experienced the crime scene was very different from both Court Furnelli and Detective Ethan Blake. To this day, after countless hours of psychiatric sessions, of research, of delving deep into her subconscious with Dr. Bernard's help, Veronica still didn't know what about a crime scene tripped her synesthesia. All she knew was that the presence of either impending or recent violence caused her vision to explode into red, orange, and yellow splotches. It was as if someone had dropped watercolor paint from a great height and when it struck her eyes, it spread out. The more violent a scene, the more paint, and the more paint, the more opaque these colors were.

And this particular scene was one of the worst. Veronica felt like she was wading through fiery oil.

The victim sat in a weathered chair, his elbows on his knees, his head slumped forward and angled downward, almost chin to chest. He was completely nude, and his arms, wrists, and ankles were strapped with what appeared to be duct tape to the chair.

Dark stains covered his bare chest and thighs. Blood pooled at the victim's feet, congealed like loose Jell-O. The man was facing them, but with the way he was hunched over, Veronica could see that there was something very wrong with his back. Two large flaps of skin hung down and there was some sort of thick tissue, gray or purple, maybe, seeming to extend outward. The colors were hard to distinguish with her synesthesia firing on all cylinders.

Veronica shook her head, trying to lessen the effects. This didn't work, so she squeezed her eyes closed and then opened them again. A little better now.

Her gaze drifted upward and fell on a word written in blood on the wall.

All capitals, each letter about eight inches tall.

SINNER.

Veronica performed her double breath again. It wasn't just the scene, but a memory that gave her pause. The memory of Anthony Wilkes, a man she'd never met, but a man who had endured a tragedy similar to her own. He was dead from an overdose, and the word *MEENIE* was spray painted above the mattress upon which he'd expired. But while that had been an overdose, most likely accidental, the fate of the victim before Veronica now was anything but.

A strange gulping sound made her turn. Detective Blake was swallowing audibly, his Adam's apple bobbing frenetically as if trying to escape from his throat via any means necessary. He was incredibly pale—his skin nearly the same color as the tarp they'd just walked through.

"Go get some fresh air," Veronica instructed.

Ethan looked hesitant, and she thought she knew how he felt. He didn't want to embarrass himself in front of her, his new partner. The problem was, Veronica cared more about preserving the crime scene than Ethan saving face.

"Outside, now," she ordered.

The man nodded several times and then ducked beneath the tarp.

Veronica heard him gulping fresh air.

Jesus, he is green.

"Court, what the hell is that on his back?"

Veronica started to walk around the body, intent on getting a better look, but stopped when Officer Court Furnelli answered.

"I'm no doctor, Detective Shade. But I think... I think those are his lungs. Someone ripped his lungs out of the man's back and just... just laid them on his skin like wings."

Chapter 6

BEAR COUNTY SHERIFF STEVE BURNS splashed water on his face. The cold felt good against his warm skin. He pumped the hand soap dispenser, lathered, and then cleaned his cheeks and chin. Next, he ran his damp hands through his hair, which had grown long, making him look unkempt.

Having already washed most of his body in the restroom, and shaved his neck, Steve replaced his personal belongings, including a razor, toothbrush, deodorant, and hairbrush, in his cosmetic case. He donned his hat and ran his thumb and forefinger across the brim. Then he nodded and left.

On the way out, he passed Alvin Gentry, the concierge at the Matheson Arruvidia Inn. Steve thanked him by handing over a ten-dollar bill. Alvin took the money and made it disappear, assuring the sheriff that letting him use the restroom was no problem.

Steve left through the back door and headed directly for the employee parking lot. For an extra ten a week, Alvin overlooked him parking there. Although they'd never spoken about it, Steve was fairly certain that Alvin knew he was sleeping in his car. Evidently, that was free.

Steve opened the back door and pulled his blanket out. He folded it delicately, then fluffed his pillow and popped the trunk. No matter how many times he saw his clothing, meticulously organized by type, and neatly folded, it was still shocking to him. Maybe it was the dichotomy of having his underwear next to a police-issued shotgun that gave him pause. Or maybe it was the fact that it reminded him that he had been living out of his car for the past three months.

Or was it four?

Steve shook his head and pushed his pillow and blanket to the very back and out of sight, then got behind the wheel. His hand trembled so badly that it was difficult for him to put the keys in the ignition. Using his other hand to grasp his wrist and steady it, he eventually managed. Soft music filled the cab.

Steve always parked in the same spot, the furthest corner of the employee lot from the hotel. Even during peak hours, there were only ever a handful of cars, with most cleaning staff electing to take public transport. Now, at the crack of dawn, there was but one: Alvin's.

Still, Steve knew to be cautious. He also knew where all the security cameras were and made sure to stay away from their inquisitive eyes.

Confident that nobody was around, and he wouldn't be seen, Sheriff Steve Burns opened the glove compartment. This too was a shocking sight: a baggie with dirty-looking yellow powder, a bright red yoga band, a black spoon, a lighter, and of course, a small case full of hypodermic needles.

How long had it been since he'd transitioned from opioids to heroin? Three months? Four?

Steve removed all the objects and then took out a roll of fresh paper towels. He laid a sheet across the center console, then opened his shirt and teased his left arm out. If you looked closely enough and if you had experience with junkies, especially the kind who liked to keep their dirty little habit a secret, you might be able to notice the miniature holes dotting his flesh.

But that wasn't something you would look for in the Bear County sheriff.

Steve took one of the alcohol wipes he had borrowed from the local chicken joint and tore it open. He cleaned his skin, making sure to rub hard in all the crevices. Then, he wrapped the red band over his bicep and tied it tight. Boiling the heroin was second nature as was drawing the liquid into a clean syringe. The injecting part? That was more difficult.

For some reason, the human psyche had an innate fear of injections. It was irrational, of course. Consumption was the leading cause of death in the USA. Eating cheeseburger after cheeseburger was more apt to kill you than a needle. So was snorting cocaine or drinking a six-pack every night. But even Steve, who had done this routine on the daily, still hesitated.

The needle rested on his skin, and he inhaled deeply and waited. Two breaths later, he pierced his flesh, aspirated to make sure he was in a vein, then pushed the plunger all the way down.

Knowing he had only two seconds before the heroin kicked in, he removed the needle and placed it back in the case. Then he put everything else in the glove box.

Only then did he release the red band that had been clenched between his front teeth.

It hit him hard and fast.

Steve's eyes rolled back, and his lids fluttered, and he felt a surge of what could only be described as sheer pleasure. It undulated through his entire body, at first numbing, and then sending wave after wave of bliss to every cell. It was like the moment right before orgasm, that delicious tingly feeling. Only it wasn't restricted to just his balls.

It was everywhere.

It was everything.

Steve exhaled once, twice, licked his lips, and reveled in the feeling. Fifteen or twenty seconds later, he opened his eyes again. The world was vivid, the colors more vibrant, everything more obvious and meaningful.

Sheriff Steve Burns crumpled the towel and made sure that everything was cleaned up before triple-checking that the glove box was locked. Then he put his car into reverse, pulled out of the parking lot, and headed to work.

Chapter 7

LOOKING AT THE VICTIM FROM behind, Veronica thought Court was right.

The purplish organs that had been yanked through the man's back were more than likely his lungs.

His skin had been flayed and then it appeared as if his ribs had been broken near the spine and bent backward or pushed out of the way. After his lungs were pulled out, the ribs were replaced beneath them, which made the two purple organs look as if they were almost hovering above his back.

It was gruesome and horrible.

"What does it look like to you?" Veronica asked.

"As I said, I think it's his lungs. I've already called the coroner, and—"

"What about the medical examiner?"

Court nodded and averted his eyes from the body.

"Yeah, I mentioned the... *uhh*... the *condition* of the body to Kristin, and she said she was going to reach out to one of the medical examiners."

"Good."

Veronica cocked her head and looked at the victim's back.

"I think they're his lungs, too. But what does it *look* like to you?"

Court reluctantly examined the body again.

"Not sure."

Veronica took a step back and turned her head the other way.

Then she read the writing on the wall, which looked as if it had been written with two fingers, before turning her attention back to the victim.

To her, it looked like a macabre...

"Angel," she whispered.

"Excuse me?"

Veronica cleared her throat and stood up straight.

"I think they look like angel wings."

Furnelli made a strange sound.

"No, I'm serious. It looks like angel wings." Veronica pointed at the bloody writing. "Whoever did this made our vic pay for his sins and then turned him into an angel."

She was speaking off the cuff, much like she used to do with Freddie. Unlike her ex-partner, though, Court didn't challenge her. He didn't do anything—just watched and listened.

Veronica pulled a nitrile glove from her pocket but didn't slip it on. She just grabbed it and used it to lift the victim's chin.

Experience had taught her not to judge a book by its cover. However, the man's appearance—sunken eyes, gaunt cheekbones, pockmarked flesh—painted a fairly vivid portrait and Veronica had a good idea of what sins this man was guilty of. She also knew the cause of death and it had nothing to do with the display on his back. There was a ragged gash that ran from ear to ear, which explained the blood that soaked the man's chest, stomach, and genitals before pooling at his feet.

Veronica lowered his head and then grabbed the man's forearm. The tape holding his wrist to the chair was loose enough that she was able to turn his arm over enough to get a good look at the crook of his elbow.

His skin was peppered with purple dots, some fresh, some older, all confirming her suspicions.

Veronica looked around again.

The area was partially covered by the tarp, likely left behind from some long-abandoned renovation project. It was the perfect place for vagrants and junkies to stay warm and seek shelter and maybe even a modicum of privacy.

"Nobody saw anything?" she asked.

"Haven't asked yet," Court replied. "Was just waiting for you. *Buuuut*, you know Needle Point as well as I do. If they saw something, they aren't going to say anything."

Veronica sucked her teeth.

"We still have to ask."

Veronica walked back the way they'd come, slipping beneath the tarp and back onto the sidewalk. Even though the area that housed the body was vast, it was still somehow stifling.

Veronica took a deep breath, enjoying the sensation of fresh air filling her lungs. It was also good to clear the synesthetic hallucinations that marred her vision.

She looked right first, then left.

Detective Blake, whom she'd completely forgotten about, was leaning against the wall, his head down.

"You okay?"

The man swallowed hard.

"Fine."

No longer inundated by the coppery scent of blood, the only thing that Veronica could smell now was gasoline.

Detective Blake was lying.

He was also sweating.

Veronica blinked, trying to force the blue aura coming off Ethan into the background.

It didn't work.

So much for being rid of the colors, she thought.

With a sigh, she glanced right again, squinting hard.

"If we're going to ask, we should probably start with him."

"With who?" Court said, following her gaze.

"Wait… wait…" Veronica pointed. "*Him.*"

About a block down a face peered out from an alley.

"Excuse me a second," she said to Detective Blake. And then she broke into a jog when the person ducked out of sight.

Freddie never ran. Ethan looked like he did five miles every morning, but he was in no shape to go anywhere.

But Court was game. He wasn't as fast as she was, but it turned out that Veronica didn't need backup.

The man was trapped; the alley was a dead end. And one look at him, at his body which was shaped like a swollen bowling pin, and it was obvious that, unlike Dylan Hall, this man wasn't going to be scaling any walls. Not now, likely not ever.

He seemed strangely bewildered by his predicament and was pressing his hands against the brick as if searching for an invisible secret passage.

"Hi," Veronica said softly, encouraging the man to turn.

"Hey, you, arms where I can see them!" Court bellowed as he reached her side.

Veronica gestured for him to stand down and stay back as she took a handful of steps forward.

"Hi there, we just want to talk."

"Talk, talk, talk," the man mumbled, his back still to them.

Veronica continued to move deeper into the alley. The smell of gas was replaced by an astringent body odor.

This man posed no danger—nothing about him had triggered her synesthesia.

At least not yet.

"Yes, we just want to talk," Veronica repeated.

"Talk, talk, talk."

He finally turned, revealing wide, slanted, and upturned eyes, a patchy beard, a thick but shortened neck, and just a few wisps of hair on his forehead.

Veronica was no expert, but if she had to guess, this man had Down Syndrome or some similar condition. He wore a giant sweatshirt that Veronica thought might have been from Oregon University, but she couldn't be sure because it was smeared with some sort of brown grease or maybe blood.

"That's right, just talk." Veronica pulled out her badge. "I'm a police officer, and this is my friend Court. He's also a police officer." When Officer Furnelli did nothing, Veronica nudged him. "Show your badge," she said out of the corner of his mouth.

"Yeah, I'm a cop too." Court flashed his shield.

The man's eyes moved back and forth between the two badges.

"Star, star, star."

"Right," Veronica said. "Would it be okay if we asked you a few questions?"

"Questions, questions, questions." The man nodded with each word.

Veronica was so close to him now that she could smell urine as well as BO.

"Last night, did you see anyone in the tarped area?"

"Tarp, tarp… tarp?"

"Yeah, the white sheets hanging." Veronica mimed hanging. "Did you see anyone in there last night?"

The man hesitated, then nodded.

"Monster… monster… monster."

"Okay, you saw a monster. What did he look like?"

"Monster… monster… monster." He was becoming more agitated.

"Was he white? Black? Hispanic?" Court chimed in.

"Monster!" the man shouted.

Veronica held her hands out trying to calm him.

"Fine, a monster. That's good. That's helpful. Thank you. Just a couple more questions, okay?"

A nod, less enthusiastic than before.

"Did you maybe see a car in the area?"

"Car, car, car."

"Alright. Can you tell me anything about this car? What was its color?"

"Midnight blue, midnight blue, midnight blue."

"Okay, great. Midnight blue car. Now did it—"

"Star, star, star."

"Right. We're police officers. Is there anything else you can tell us about the car?"

The man scratched his left armpit and then smelled his fingers.

"Sleep, sleep, sleep." His voice dropped a few octaves, and he seemed to draw into himself.

Court's patience had expired.

"Did you see anybody with blood on them? Someone with a knife?"

"No, no, no!" Every 'no' was progressively louder than the previous. "Monster! Monster! *Monster!*"

The man was pressing himself against the brick wall, trying to put as much space between them as possible.

"What do you want to do?" Court whispered in her ear. "Bring him in for questioning?"

Veronica thought about it before shaking her head.

What would be the point? If they'd tried to cuff him, he might react violently. Even if they got him to the station without incident, Veronica doubted putting him in an interrogation room would get him to open up. On the contrary, he might never speak to them again.

Instead, Veronica pulled a twenty from her wallet and placed it on the ground.

"This is for you, okay? You were a big help. Use it to buy some food."

"Food, food, food."

Veronica pulled Court from the alley, and they made their way back to the crime scene. Detective Blake was in the exact same place as before, but he must have moved at some point; Veronica saw vomit on his fancy loafers and between his feet.

She frowned, wishing she had some water to offer her partner.

Or anything other than a disapproving look.

"Did the coroner say when she was going to arrive? We can't just leave the scene like this."

Veronica's phone chimed and she quickly took it out of her pocket.

"As soon as possible. Couldn't be more specific."

It wasn't an incoming call but an alarm. A single word appeared on the screen: *SHRINK*.

"Shit." Veronica raised her eyes. "I'm sorry, I have to go—I have an appointment. Detective Blake…" she was going to ask her partner to stick around and wait for the coroner, but reconsidered when she saw the state he was in. She looked at Court next, and was about to ask the same thing, but didn't have to.

The man nodded preemptively.

"I'll be here. I'll wait for Kristin, send you an update if she comes up with anything."

"Thanks, Court. I'll be back as soon as I can."

Chapter 8

WHEN IT CAME TO PSYCHIATRISTS, Detective Veronica Shade's approach was completely opposite to crime scenes.

She wanted to know every single detail about the person who would be analyzing her life before she ever sat down with them. That way, when they inevitably said those two cursed words, "I understand," she could reply, unequivocally, with "no, you don't."

This would quickly be followed up with, "You don't understand because your home was not invaded when you were a child by two psychopaths. You were not tied up beside your brother, mother, and father. You were not told to select which one, of the four of you, would leave the house alive. You did not select yourself, and you did not watch your family burn."

This, of course, made it very difficult for someone to actually treat her. Yet, Veronica was determined not to go back to her longtime psychiatrist, Dr. Jane Bernard. Not after discovering her decades of lies and deception.

The psychiatrist *du jour* was Dr. Simon Patel, a man of Indian descent in his mid-40s. He'd gone to all the best schools: Yale, Harvard, and even studied overseas at Oxford for six months. His specialty was soldiers with PTSD.

Seemed like a good fit and it started off well enough.

Veronica wasn't forced to wait in a cozy yet chic room with magazines available to read, the specific titles carefully curated. Nor was she greeted by an intentionally bland and nondescript secretary.

Dr. Patel answered the door. He was a short man with deep-set eyes and short dark hair that he probably got cut every other week.

"You must be Veronica?"

"And you must be Dr. Patel."

The man smiled warmly, an expression that reached his eyes.

"Just Simon, please."

Already on a first-name basis, are we? Let me guess, making the session seem more personal is a good way to get someone to open up?

There were two chairs in the room and a small, round glass table beside each. On one of them was a jug of water and a glass, both of which were clear.

Ah, a nod to transparency, am I right, Simon?

"Please, take a seat," the doctor encouraged.

Veronica asked which chair and he replied with whichever one she wanted.

Making me feel like I'm the one in control.

Veronica selected the chair closest to the water and sat. Dr. Patel occupied the other chair, crossed his legs, and rested an iPad on his lap.

"This is always the most awkward part, I must admit," Dr. Patel said with a slight grin.

Veronica resisted the urge to roll her eyes. After leaving Dr. Bernard, she'd seen five psychiatrists. They all had different tricks, but their goal was the same.

"Not awkward for me," Veronica remarked, shrugging. "Look, I don't want to come off as rude, but can we just skip all the preamble? I assume you've read my file, and I've read yours. So, why don't you go ahead and start asking the questions you want to ask and not waste any time?"

One of Simon's eyebrows rose in silent inquisition.

"You are right, Veronica, I have read your file. But rather than ask questions, I'd prefer to just talk. To have a conversation."

Veronica scowled.

More games. Okay, Simon, I can play, too. But something that probably wasn't in my file, is that if I play a game, I play to win.

"A conversation? Like we're friends?"

Another warm smile.

"Sure, if you wish."

"Okay. Well, when I talk to my friends, I can ask them anything."

A hint of gas in the air — Veronica didn't really have friends.

"Then feel free to ask me whatever you—"

"When's the last time you jerked off, Simon?"

To his credit, Dr. Simon Patel didn't balk at the question. To her surprise, the man answered.

"The day before yesterday. How about you?"

Veronica leaned forward.

"I can't remember. But I did get fucked last night."

No reaction from the man.

"I hope it was good."

"The *best*."

The scent of gas graduated to more than a hint.

"I'm glad."

"Are you?"

Dr. Patel sighed.

"Look, we can do this for the entire hour if you want. I'm getting paid either way. Or we can talk about something else, something that might be on your mind."

"I don't know what's on my mind, because it's a fucked-up place."

Dr. Patel sucked his top lip into his mouth and Veronica felt bad for not giving the man a chance. She also recognized that this was a pattern of hers, and the primary reason why she bounced from psychiatrist to psychiatrist. It wasn't that they weren't competent, it was that she never gave them a chance.

Because, inevitably, it would all circle back to one thing: forgiveness.

And Veronica didn't deserve it.

"Really?" Dr. Simon Patel shrugged. "Look, I'm getting paid for the session, and I suspect that, based on what already happened, it's going to be your last. If that's the case, if you want to sit here and say nothing, I'm okay with that too. If it makes it any easier, you can just tell me what you're thinking about right now."

Veronica peered into Simon's eyes.

"I was thinking about the crime scene that I just came from," she lied.

"You can talk about that if you want."

Want was the operative word.

What Veronica wanted was to be out of there. But if she left, Dr. Patel might reach out to Captain Bottel and inform the man that she had not completed her mandated psych session. If he did that, she could be suspended.

If the doctor told her to leave, however...

Based on their limited, yet graphic, interaction, Dr. Patel seemed like a tough nut to crack. But everyone had their breaking points.

"Well, today I took my rookie partner to a murder scene. The victim was naked, and his throat had been slit. Then someone stripped the skin from his back, broke his ribs, and tore his lungs out to look like angel wings."

"Interesting," Dr. Patel remarked.

"It's fucking disgusting is what it is."

"I'm sorry, of course, it is. But I find it interesting that you think they looked like angel wings." Before Veronica could add the bit about SINNER being written in blood on the wall, Simon continued, "Are you familiar with a blood eagle?"

"Never heard of it."

"Well, it was rumored that when Vikings captured an opponent in battle, they would tether their arms and legs to a table, cut their back open, snip the ribs, and pull their lungs out for display. This ritual was typically performed when the victim was still alive."

It sounded uncannily like her crime scene, although the lack of blood on the man's back suggested he was dead or very nearly dead when his lungs had been removed.

"Did they write 'SINNER' near the body in blood?"

"I doubt it. Vikings had their own unique beliefs—not sure if they even knew the word."

Veronica mulled this over.

Could the display be a blood eagle instead of an angel?

"From your file, I gather that you're not religious," Simon continued. "But it's worth noting that the thing about sin, at least in the catholic context, is that no matter how bad, it can be forgiven."

There it was.

Veronica bared her teeth.

You chopped dad's finger off with a knife, you fed your mother ice cream with bleach.

Some of Dante Fiori's last words. Words that were impossible to corroborate. The ramblings of a madman or insights shared with him by her brother?

If only my fucking mind wasn't so... so broken. *If only I could remember.*

Veronica clenched her fists.

Once a killer, always a killer.

"Veronica, are you okay?"

"No. I'm not." She nearly leaped to her feet. "This—this isn't going to work. I have to go."

"Veronica, please—"

"No!" she yelled. "There's someone out there who slit a man's throat and pulled their lungs out like a... like a blood eagle, and you want me to stay here and talk about *forgiveness*?"

"We can talk about—"

"Fuck you," Veronica spat and then left, no longer caring if Dr. Patel reported that she'd run off.

All she cared about was being out of there.

And finding whoever was responsible for this horrific crime.

Chapter 9

VERONICA WAS HALFWAY BACK TO the crime scene when her phone rang.

"Hello?"

"Detective Shade, it's Kristin." The woman on the phone sounded more tired than usual, which was saying something. Bear County coroner Kristin Newberry worked long hours at her day job as a lawyer and was typically exhausted whenever Veronica met with the coroner. She was also in her mid-sixties and had probably been working eighty-hour weeks since law school.

"I'm almost at the scene. I'll be there in ten."

"Right, I haven't made it out yet," Kristin said with a hint of guilt in her voice. "Officer Furnelli called, but I'm tied up right now."

This occasionally happened, especially if there was a big trial going on. But given the horrible fate of their victim, she would have assumed that Court had mentioned that expediency was key to avoiding prying eyes and potential panic.

Veronica heard the captain in her head.

...quick and easy with this one, detectives.

"The scene is pretty gruesome," Veronica said. "No, scratch that. It's downright horrible. The victim's throat was slit, and his lungs were pulled out through the back. I don't know what Officer Furnelli told you, but we're going to need your help and get a medical examiner in to look at the body."

"Right, no, he told me. I put a call in to Portland. ME should be there soon."

"Dr. Thorpe?"

"Yeah, Dr. Thorpe."

That was good. Veronica liked Kristin a lot and respected her even more. But the woman wasn't a medical professional by trade. While there was no doubt that the coroner had experience and insights that made her invaluable to the cases, she was mostly limited to blood tests and superficial inquiries. Autopsies and more specific testing required the services of a medical examiner, who was often a forensic pathologist. Dr. Julia Thorpe was a plump no-nonsense woman in her fifties.

Veronica liked her, too.

"Good." Veronica waited. She was unsure of why the woman had called. "Kristin, everything all right?"

"No, not really. I'm working that case for you."

"Dylan?"

"Yeah, Dylan Hall. Veronica, I've done everything I can… I've asked for stay after stay, trying to get the DA to offer a better deal. *Anything*."

Veronica cursed under her breath.

Dylan had been arrested after the Matheson police found him in possession of a kilo of heroin. A *kilo*. Veronica had confronted him about it, and he claimed it wasn't his.

He was telling the truth.

But with his track record, Dylan was looking at some serious jail time. And nobody but Veronica would believe that someone had set him up.

Despite his past transgressions, Dylan Hall was a good man. He'd acted as Veronica's confidential informant and had once even saved Freddie's life. He'd also groped Veronica while high, but that was something that they'd put behind them.

The true reason, however, why Veronica felt such a kinship and responsibility for the man ran even deeper.

Like Dante and her brother Benny, Dylan Hall had been one of the Renaissance Home boys.

He had been doomed from the start, but had somehow, beyond all odds, managed to turn himself from a junkie into a man who wanted to start over.

Until someone planted a kilo of heroin on him.

"The problem is his priors. DA doesn't even seem keen on pleading this one out—they might want to go to trial, and they *never* want to go to trial. With all the recent overdoses, I think they're looking for—"

"Where are you now?" Veronica interrupted.

"Matheson Public Jail."

Veronica looked out the window and then pulled a U-turn.

"Wait there—I'll be there in fifteen."

***

"A kilo's no joke, Veronica. It's not something they're willing to downgrade or sweep under a rug."

Veronica's eyes moved away from Kristin Newberry and to the one-way glass behind which sat Dylan Hall.

She'd seen the man at his worst; she'd seen the six-foot-nine man completely bald, running around in soiled underwear, his eyes so sunken that she could almost see the back of his head through his pupils. Veronica had seen Dylan coked out, then on the road to recovery. But she had never seen him like this.

Although he had hair now, short black stubble, and had put on weight, he somehow looked worse than ever.

Dylan Hall looked scared.

"The issue is, because he continues to claim that the drugs weren't his, even if he were to flip on someone higher up the totem pole, I don't think the DA would believe him."

Veronica knew that was what usually happened in these cases. The big, bad DEA just wanted to catch a bigger fish.

They'd trap a minnow, put that on a hook, feed it to a bass. Then they'd use the bass to catch a grouper. And up and up they went, hoping to eventually land a shark. It was like a twisted, aquatic version of the woman who swallowed a fly.

"There's nothing you can do?" Veronica hadn't meant to sound accusatory, but Kristin's reply suggested it had been taken as such.

"I've done everything I can. My expertise is corporate law, not criminal. I reached out to some colleagues, I've called in favors, and I've exhausted all resources. The DA isn't budging."

"Thanks, Kristin. I appreciate it," Veronica said, still looking through the glass. "Can I speak with him?"

"I was hoping that you would. If anyone can get him to flip, it's you."

Dylan was moving his hands from the tabletop to his thighs, to beneath his armpits, but couldn't seem to figure out what to do with them.

"I'll try my best."

The second she opened the interview room door, Dylan's eyes shot up.

"Veronica," he said in his harsh voice. "I didn't do this. They weren't my drugs."

Chapter 10

THE ROOM SMELLED OF MUST but not gas.

"I know they aren't yours," Veronica said as she sat across from Dylan. "But, unfortunately, that doesn't seem to matter as much as it should. Can you tell me what happened?"

Dylan stretched his fingers and then placed them down on the metal table. He was so tall and his arms so long that they nearly reached Veronica's side.

"What happened? What happened is someone framed me. That night you came over with your fat-ass partner? The cops roll in with the goddamn DEA. Kick my fucking door in. If you think it didn't close well before, imagine now. Then, get this, they find a kilo of smack in my house. A fucking *kilo*."

The more he spoke, the angrier he got.

Veronica remembered the night in question. She and Freddie had visited Dylan to ask him if he knew anything about the caller who had harassed her on *Marlowe*. He hadn't, but by sheer luck, Veronica had mentioned the song. That Dylan did know, and had led them to Renaissance Home, and eventually Sister Margaret.

"Let me ask you something, Veronica? You've been in my place. Did it look like I got my shit at IKEA?"

Veronica had to smirk. His idea of fancy was IKEA.

And no, it didn't. She was fairly certain that most of Dylan's belongings had come from less auspicious means—primarily dumpster diving.

"Right," Dylan said preemptively. "Hey, you know what a kilo's worth? A kilo of smack?"

Veronica shrugged. She honestly didn't know.

"If it's good shit? Seventy, eighty k. In my hands, I would chop that shit up six ways from Sunday and make four times that amount. And if I had that much cash, my entire goddamn house would be made of IKEA shit. Floors, ceilings, hell, even the walls would be put together with those little fucking wooden nub things."

The narrative made no sense. Even if Dylan was still in the game, which Veronica was certain he wasn't, no one would trust him with a kilo and he sure as hell couldn't afford it himself.

But it wasn't a bad idea to double-check.

"So, it wasn't yours?"

Dylan threw his hands up.

"No, it's not mine. Jesus Christ, someone fucked me over and set me up. That's what I've been telling that gray-haired broad, that's what I've been telling that bald dude who smokes enough cigarettes outside to kill everybody in the city. *It's. Not. Mine.* I've never seen it before. I've never touched it. Someone fucking framed me."

Veronica kind of wished it was his. It might've taken some persuasion, but she thought she would have been able to make Dylan give up his source.

But being out of the game as long as he had and seeing how rapidly things changed in the drug game, she probably knew more major players than Dylan did.

And Veronica hadn't worked a drug case in months.

"Veronica," Dylan's tone suddenly changed. "It's been almost six months in County. I can do County. But... shit, I can't do BCC or any big house. I fucking... I *can't*."

Dylan Hall had grown up in Renaissance Home, had seen horrible things, experienced even worse, and had been in and out of foster care his entire life.

Dylan Hall had been to prison more times than most people visited the bathroom, and yet he was terrified.

"I'm doing what I can." Her comment was lame, but she didn't know what else to say. "Hang in there." Veronica touched his hand briefly. It was clammy. "I'll figure it out."

Veronica left the room and rejoined Kristin on the other side of the one-way glass.

"He's not going to change his story," Veronica said absently. "The worst part? He's telling the truth. Someone framed him."

"With a kilo? That's an incredibly expensive frame job."

Veronica shrugged and Kristin sighed.

"It doesn't matter. If we don't do something soon, he's going away for a long time."

"What's a long time, Kristin?"

"Ten years on the low side. Most likely fifteen."

Veronica cursed.

Dylan wouldn't last fifteen years in Bear County Correctional. In Veronica's experience, there was a big difference when someone who was facing considerable jail time said they 'can't' do it compared with 'won't'.

Can't meant that they didn't want to.

Won't meant that they would do anything—absolutely *anything*—to avoid going inside.

As the two of them stared at Dylan, Veronica couldn't help but think about how her life could have been different if Peter had not been the first cop on the scene, or if he had decided to adopt a son instead of his daughter.

If either had been the case, Veronica would have probably been on the other side of the glass.

No, that wasn't right.

She would have been six feet under.

"I can stall for another week, maybe. Then we have to make a decision."

"Right."

Neither woman said anything for a minute.

"I guess I'm going to hit that crime scene now," Kristin said. "Dr. Thorpe should be there soon. Wanna ride with me?"

The last thing that Veronica wanted to do was go back to Needle Point. She had to figure out a way to get the DA to drop the charges against Dylan.

And she could only do that with a clear head.

"I might sit this one out."

"Sure, I get it. Anything I should know about this scene?"

Veronica licked her lips.

"Yeah, let me know if you see an angel."

Chapter 11

CROWDED SPACES AND VERONICA SHADE never got along. And, for some reason, restaurants were the worst. Maybe it was because a high number of patrons were on a first date, lying to try to impress each other, or maybe it was the old married couples, lying to keep their relationship alive. Whatever the reason, if Veronica found herself in a restaurant packed full of people, she would be overwhelmed by the smell of gas, ruining any enticing odors coming from the kitchen. Occasionally, she would see colors too, colors associated with impending violence. This always posed a moral dilemma for her. She couldn't rightfully go over to a man who was angrily shoving chicken Alfredo down his gullet as he glared at his demure wife who sucked back martinis like they were water and say, "Excuse me, sir, don't even think about it. Don't even think about hitting your wife tonight."

Cole, on the other hand, liked to go out and eat. He also liked crowds, although, for the benefit of them both, he typically chose restaurants that were off the beaten path and were often empty or close to it. And on the rare occasion that it was busy, he'd specifically request a table near the back.

Tonight, Cole had opted for a new Japanese restaurant. They ordered a sharing plate of sashimi, as well as some traditional sushi rolls and deep-fried octopus. Cole was deep into a tale about his most recent case. It had something to do with a missing bra, and judging by the expression on his handsome face, she expected that it was, at least to him, comical. But Veronica was having a hard time concentrating on anything he was saying. She kept thinking about Dylan Hall, thinking about him sitting in that cell, scared out of his wits about going back to jail.

It was no secret that the captain wanted her to keep her nose clean. That meant no interfering with other cases.

But fuck the captain.

Could she go to the DEA? Ask for a favor?

No, letting Dylan go wasn't a favor. That was something else. Something much bigger.

What the hell could she do, then?

"What do you think?" Cole asked as he snagged a piece of tuna between his chopsticks.

"What do I think?" Veronica repeated as a stall tactic.

Cole popped the fish into his mouth, chewed a few times, then swallowed.

"Yeah? You think I should have him arrested? Seek the death penalty?"

Veronica's eyes bulged.

What the hell was he talking about?

Did he move on from the missing bra?

"I don't…"

"Yeah," Cole said. "I think I'll suggest to the DA that they seek the death penalty. Aim high, am I right?"

Veronica was completely and utterly lost.

Cole ate another piece of fish, looked directly into her eyes, and then broke into a grin.

"The death penalty." He pointed at her with his chopsticks. "You should've seen your face, Veronica!"

"Sorry."

He shrugged off the weak apology.

"So am I. I'm sorry that the most exciting thing I've done in the last two weeks is hunt down a missing size E bra."

"I just—"

"This is my every day. Either I'm trying to catch a police officer stealing from the evidence locker or hunt down lewd pictures that a cop took of someone in lockup. A police-involved shooting? Forget it. They never give me those cases. It blows, Veronica. It *fucking* blows."

Cole often griped about his job, but he seemed more intense today. He wanted to vent but he was also seeking guidance. Unfortunately for him, Veronica wasn't in the right state of mind to offer much of anything. The good news was that she'd seen so many psychiatrists that she was capable of channeling them without so much as a second thought.

"When you were in basic training, did you ever think that you would end up in internal affairs?"

Cole laughed.

"*Helllll* no. I thought I was going to be a goddamn SWAT team leader in Los Angeles. I thought I was going to be—" he made a fist and thumped his chest, "—an alpha male, cracking heads, making the world a safer place."

"How did you get into IA, then?"

Veronica snagged a piece of sushi, her first, and popped it in her mouth. She took one bite and then stopped.

It was fantastic.

Cole looked at her a little strangely, and Veronica wondered if he'd told her this before. Probably. But Cole liked to talk.

That was one of the main differences between them. After her day was done, Veronica wanted to push everything out of her mind, whereas Cole felt compelled to discuss every little detail.

"I was roped into it, actually. Loaned out, a sort of internship, you know? And my first case? It was interesting as hell. Bribery in a small town, corruption, a mayor who was coercing local businesses to sell their buildings at a loss—it would have made an amazing book. And I liked it. I liked it because everyone involved was bad. So, I hopped on the IA train. But then…"

Cole let his sentence trail off.

Unfortunately, not everything was so cut and dry. Instead of chasing unequivocally bad men, Cole ended up harassing morally ambiguous characters who chose the lesser of two evils.

And the occasional underwear thief.

"You said this morning that you wanted to start a PI firm."

"Yeah, after my dream of leading a SWAT team died an agonizing death, sure."

"And what kind of cases do you think you'd be investigating then?"

Cole closed one eye.

"Oh, you're a sly one, aren't you? More underwear capers? Maybe. But at least there'd be the occasional action shots of some hot stepmom having an affair," Cole joked, miming taking photos. "But seriously, in IA, I just feel like I cause problems. As a PI, I'd be able to help people, you know? Cheesy, yeah, but true."

"I'm not sure I help people," Veronica whispered.

Cole sighed.

"No, you don't help people at all," he replied sarcastically. "Speaking of *not* helping people, how was your day? How's your new partner?"

Veronica pictured Detective Ethan Blake standing in a puddle of his own vomit.

She didn't want to talk about him. Didn't want to talk about the victim with the slit throat, either. Veronica just wanted to eat and drink and go home.

But she knew Cole wouldn't let her off that easily.

"He's green, young," Veronica said, pausing for a second to think of a way to steer the conversation in a different direction.

"But you'll be happy to know that he doesn't have a twelve-inch cock."

Cole was taking a sip of his beer and laughed midway through. It sprayed across the table and speckled Veronica's shirt.

She couldn't help but join in.

"It was ten and a half inches."

Cole growled at her.

"I'll show you ten and a half inches…"

***

Sex with Cole was good. It wasn't great, but that wasn't because the man wasn't well-endowed—although she doubted the ten-and-a-half-inch claim—or that he wasn't a conscientious lover. He was both. Sex with him was exciting, exhilarating, and Veronica liked everything about it.

The problem was that Veronica liked Cole, but what they had didn't feel like love.

It was too… orchestrated. Too normal.

Things had progressed at a reasonable pace since that day in the hospital, since reading the article that Cole had written about her. There was a vulnerability to the man that she was drawn to. And he was undeniably handsome.

They took things slow, went on a few dates, and even managed to hold out having sex for the first three despite the obvious tension and attraction. After the first month, their bi-weekly rendezvous became a nearly daily occurrence. By month three, he was sleeping over more often than not. At month five, he had started leaving clothes in one of the drawers instead of bringing a new set every evening.

Despite talking—*a lot*—and mostly about himself, Cole cared about her. He was kind, affectionate, funny, interesting... he ticked all the boxes.

But Veronica didn't love him. Maybe she would, in time.

But that night, like most nights after they had sex, when Veronica closed her eyes, she found herself not thinking about the man who lay beside her, but someone else entirely. Someone who was a bit older, someone who also wore a uniform. Someone whom she hadn't spoken to since the day she flushed his drugs and screamed at him to leave her house and never come back.

That someone was Sheriff Steve Burns.

Chapter 12

WHEN VERONICA DIDN'T SEE DETECTIVE Ethan Blake waiting for her with a coffee when she arrived at work like Freddie used to, she realized that she was going to have to train the man better.

But when she made her way upstairs and saw that his desk was empty and he wasn't there yet, Veronica thought maybe she should start with something more basic.

Like coming to work on time.

While she waited for Ethan to show up, Veronica looked at the folder that had been left on her desk. There was a sticky note on the front that read "From Officer Furnelli."

She smiled and opened the folder.

At least one of them took their job seriously.

Inside was a rap sheet for a man named Jake Thompson. One glance at the mugshot confirmed that it was the victim from Needle Point.

It was their angel.

Apparently, instead of cutting loose early as she had done, Officer Furnelli had taken the man's fingerprints and run them through the system.

Veronica wasn't sure if she should be happy or sad that her impressions of the victim turned out to be correct. Jake was in his mid-thirties and, judging by his extensive rap sheet, had struggled with addiction for a considerable number of years. Maybe since his late teens or even earlier.

He was frail and thin. On his last arrest, which was just over a month ago, Jake was listed as weighing just one hundred and fifty-four pounds.

And he was a sinner, all right.

Jake had been arrested on more than twenty occasions, all of which, at least on first glance, appeared to be related to the possession, use, or sale of illegal narcotics.

Veronica wasn't surprised to discover that the man's drug of choice was heroin. This, of course, made her think of Dylan Hall. Veronica had no idea who had murdered Jake Thompson, but she couldn't help but think that the victim could have just as easily have been Dylan.

Instead of sitting behind bars, the man could have been propped on a chair, his throat slit, his lungs pulled out his back.

"Detective Shade, could you come in here for a moment, please?"

Veronica raised her eyes from the folder.

Like yesterday, Captain Bottel was standing in his office doorway.

"Sure."

She entered her boss' office and closed the door behind her.

"What happened yesterday, Detective Shade?"

Veronica's first instinct was that Dr. Simon Patel had reported her. Her second thought was that this question had something to do with Detective Blake.

Early on in her law enforcement career, Veronica had learned the value of pauses. Not only did they give you a chance to select the right words, but they also gave the impression of being knowledgeable and confident.

Veronica had become an expert at pausing and was comfortable with silence.

Pierre Bottel, evidently, was not, as he broke first.

"I sent you and Detective Blake to investigate the murder in Nettle Point."

Veronica didn't hear a question, so she continued to remain quiet.

Captain Bottel sighed.

"Detective Blake quit yesterday."

Veronica's eyes bulged. Silence was no longer an option.

"What?"

The captain nodded.

"Called last night, left a message. Said, under no uncertain terms, that he was done. Out. Not coming back. Do you want to hear it?"

Veronica did not, but if it had been anyone other than the captain telling her this she would have insisted. It was unbelievable. Detective Blake had been sick at the crime scene, but that was understandable. After all, Jake's murder had been brutal, gruesome.

But quit? *Quit?*

Where the fuck did they find this guy?

"The thing that bothers me most," the captain continued, "is that you didn't know."

Veronica shrugged.

"I barely even—"

Bottel silenced her by raising his hand.

"Now, I know you had an appointment with Dr. Patel." It was his turn to pause, and Veronica fought the nearly irresistible urge to interrupt. "But afterward, you were expected to go back to the crime scene."

"I—"

There was a knock at the door, one that the captain had clearly been expecting because he immediately said, "Come in."

Court Furnelli entered, his eyes down.

Veronica couldn't help the growing feeling in her gut that she was being ambushed.

"Officer Furnelli, you were first on the scene yesterday, correct?"

"Yes, sir."

"Now, as I understand it, Detectives Shade and Blake arrived about an hour after you secured the scene."

"Yes, sir."

Yeah, definitely an ambush.

"After Veronica left for her appointment, what happened?"

Court licked his lips and glanced around nervously.

Veronica felt bad for him. He was just a rookie cop, and he was essentially being asked to rat on a detective.

"Captain, I just—"

Once again, Veronica was silenced with a wave. Oh, how she hated that. She clenched her jaw so tight that it started to hurt.

"Officer?" Bottel encouraged. "What happened after Detective Shade left?"

"Detective Blake started feeling ill. Said he needed to go lie down."

"And after he left, you were alone at the scene until the coroner arrived?"

Officer Furnelli cocked his head.

"No, sir."

This surprised the captain. It surprised Veronica, too.

"No?"

"No," Officer Furnelli confirmed. "About an hour after Detective Blake left, Detective Shade returned. She helped me fingerprint the victim."

The small office now reeked of gasoline.

"Detective Shade?" the captain asked.

"Yeah," she said. "I have the fingerprint report on my desk. The victim is Jake Thompson, in the system for possession."

Veronica suppressed a smirk. Clearly, this had gone differently than the captain had hoped. It was no secret that after the problems she'd caused the department not many wanted to keep her around. And the new captain wanting to be rid of the previous captain's daughter surprised no one.

Veronica knew that if Captain Bottel had it his way, she would have been relegated to indefinite leave after being on *Marlowe*.

Well, tough luck. I'm here to stay.

"Thank you, Officer Furnelli," the captain said reluctantly.

"Sir."

Officer Furnelli started to leave, and Veronica was about to follow, when the captain said, "Hold on a second, Detective Shade."

Court left and Veronica turned back to face her boss.

"Detective Shade, policy dictates that two detectives are required to work every case."

"What? What are you talking about? Until Ethan, I was working alone."

This made no sense.

"New policy," the captain said flatly. "And because of Detective Blake's resignation, I'm forced—"

"No way, I'm not getting off this case. I—"

"That's not what I was about to say." The captain raised his eyes over Veronica's shoulder and gestured for someone to enter. "And, no, I'm not taking you off the case. I'm partnering you up."

Veronica whipped around and saw a familiar, albeit very different, face.

"Welcome back, Detective Furlow," Captain Bottel said loudly. "I know I can count on you for not quitting on day one."

Chapter 13

SHERIFF STEVE BURNS PARKED HIS car in front of the Bear County headquarters, then checked again that his glove box was locked. He was about to get out when he spotted two people standing near the corner of the whitewashed concrete building. The first was a large man with thick lips and wide eyes: Chief Deputy Marcus McVeigh. The second was even bigger, with a bald head and a mustache. He was smoking a cigarette. This man, Steve didn't recognize him.

"Fuck."

He'd hoped to arrive first and not have to deal with anyone for a good hour at least.

Especially not McVeigh. As Steve was considering leaving, the deputy turned his head in Sheriff Burns' direction. The man squinted and then tipped his hat.

"Fuck."

There was no leaving now. McVeigh was already suspicious of him—if Steve left now, he might as well never come back.

And yet, he didn't get out of his car right away, either. Instead, he just watched and waited.

No cuffs—Deputy McVeigh didn't walk over to him with a set of handcuffs dangling from one finger and say, "Get out of the car, you junkie thief. You're under arrest."

When the bald man finished his cigarette and immediately lit another, Steve figured that that moment wasn't coming.

At least not today.

"Deputy," Steve said as he approached. He was surprised at how normal his voice sounded. He was surprised at how normal *everything* felt.

But that was the thing about 'normal'. Normal was as personal as your own style, your own brand. It was malleable.

Sure, people generally have an idea of what normal is, what constitutes normal behavior. But you'd be hard-pressed to find a more relative concept than normal. Not only did it differ from person to person, but it changed from day to day, moment to moment. One second, you're just someone working in a tower in New York City. The next, a plane strikes and everything around you is on fire. One day, you're attacked by a bear and prescribed opioids for the pain. Six months or so later, you're a fully functioning heroin addict.

What in the fuck.

Life was strange. Life was unpredictable. Life was anything but *normal*.

"Sheriff," McVeigh returned. "This is DEA Agent Troy Allison."

A cold sweat broke out on Steve's forehead.

Well, my new normal is about to include an eight-by-ten cell.

Everyone knew that cops didn't fare well in prison—just ask Ken Cameron, ex-city of Greenham PD police officer. But sheriffs? Oh, there was probably a special sort of hell reserved for sheriffs behind bars.

Steve would be lucky to make it through a single day.

"Heard a lot about you, Sheriff," Troy said between puffs of his cigarette.

He extended his hand and Steve thought that this was the moment that the man would pull the cuffs from behind his back and slap them on his wrist.

But he didn't.

Troy's grip was strong and tight.

"You all right? You look a little under the weather," McVeigh said.

Steve swallowed hard.

"I'm fine," he replied, but this time his voice betrayed him. His vocal cords were constricted. "What can I do for you, Agent Allison?"

"Not here—I was hoping we could go upstairs and have a little chat."

The cold sweat returned. That's why they were being friendly. They didn't want to make a scene. They didn't want to risk enraging a drug addict in front of everyone.

"Sure," Steve said so quietly that he wasn't sure the men standing but a few feet from him could hear. "Come with me."

***

Nothing that either Deputy McVeigh or DEA Agent Allison did after they entered the conference room assuaged Steve's fears that today was the day he would be thrown in jail. They both sat on one side of the round table, across from Steve who took a seat at the head.

And when Troy slid a folder across the impossibly long table, Steve believed that inside would be his arrest warrant and a litany of charges.

He didn't open it, just held it in his hand as he waited for the dreaded words to come.

"I have some disturbing news to share with you," Troy began.

Yep, here it is. Disturbing is a strange way of putting it but still, it—

"We've been tracking an influx of new product into Bear County."

Troy indicated the folder in Steve's hands.

"Open it," McVeigh said softly.

With shaking fingers, Steve obliged, still half-expecting that this is where the charade ended, that inside he'd see a still from the evidence room security footage of him stealing the pills. Or maybe from this morning, him shooting up in the hotel parking lot.

But no.

That was not his new normal... yet.

Instead, he saw a photo of a rectangular package emblazoned with a snake or worm devouring what could have been an eyeball or the earth. Most drugs in this quantity, a kilo or more, had their producer's insignia on them.

That's what Steve figured this was. Only, he had no idea what it had to do with him.

"Long story short," Troy continued, "several years back, the mayor of New York City was bringing in high-quality product from Colombia. He was eventually found out by a disgruntled cop, Drake or somethin', and he fled. The mayor is presumed dead and the product with that snake on it slowly died out. Until about a year ago. That's when it started showin' up again, this time in the Midwest. And then Matheson. We set up shop, tried to track it."

"Coincides with the increase in overdoses we've seen," Deputy McVeigh remarked.

"Yeah, someone's been cutting it with fentanyl. The problem is, nobody wants to flip," Troy said with a nod. "Usually, it's not that hard. These junkies are pussies—normally, we just squeeze a little, threaten them with jail time, and they can't snitch fast enough." When the man said "squeeze," Steve saw the man's large hands clench. "But not with these guys. Nobody's talking. *Nobody*. That's where I was hoping you could help."

Steve licked his lips and looked at Marcus as he spoke.

"Not sure how. We're doing our best to keep drugs out of Bear County, but it's a losing battle."

"*I'ma* be straight with you, Sheriff." Troy exchanged a look with McVeigh. "It's not Matheson that's the problem. We think these guys are workin' outta Greenham. The thing is, Greenham PD doesn't like nobody messin' around in their business. Completely blocked us out. But considering that Greenham is part of Bear County..." he let his sentence trail off.

The mention of Greenham brought Veronica to mind, of course—it always did.

And how he missed her.

How he'd fucked that up royally.

Just like with Julia before her.

"Sheriff?" McVeigh prompted.

"I'm open, especially if it means—" Steve had been absently turning the pages in the folder that Troy had given him as he spoke, and what he saw now shocked him into silence.

Troy lifted off his seat to get a better look.

"That guy there? He's the farthest up we've gotten so far. His name is Jake, but he goes by—"

"Bunky," Steve finished for Troy.

"You know him?"

"*Of* him," Steve said quickly. "Hangs out at Needle Point. Didn't know he was anything other than a low-level dealer, though."

Steve was truly shocked. Shocked and a little confused.

"To be honest, I'm not really sure what his role is in all of this. He's just the highest up we can get."

Steve nodded and he closed the file to avoid any more surprises.

"I can go down there and pick him up, bring him in for questioning. He has a history with Bear County."

"I'll go with you," Troy offered.

That was something that Steve definitely didn't want. Bringing your heroin stash to work in your car was one thing, sharing that same vehicle with the DEA was another, entirely.

"Let me check it out first—don't want to ruffle Greenham PD feathers. If Bunky's up to anything, I'll bring you in."

Steve put a hard stop to the conversation by standing and holding his hand out.

"Thank you for your help, Sheriff."

"More than willing," Steve said, feeling McVeigh's eyes boring into him. "We'll do whatever it takes to keep drugs out of Bear County."

Chapter 14

CAPTAIN PIERRE BOTTEL COULDN'T POSSIBLY have known what had transpired between Freddie and Veronica in the few days prior to his heart attack. And yet, she could've sworn, based on the way that the captain looked at her with that small grin just barely peeking out from beneath his mustache, that he was well aware of what went down.

And he'd teamed them up on purpose just to spite her.

Fuck you, Pierre. And fuck you, too, Ethan Blake.

"Detective Furlow will be taking the lead on this case."

Another dagger in her side, but this one didn't sting as deeply. Both Freddie and Veronica knew who wore the pants in their professional relationship.

"Great," Veronica said with a horrible fake smile. "Nice to have you back, Detective Furlow."

"Like I said," the captain interjected, "I want this thing done with quick and easy. You're dismissed."

Freddie opened the door and held his hand out for Veronica to walk through. Veronica held her head high as she left the office. She grabbed the folder Court had left on her desk, crumpled the sticky note, and put it in the trash, then walked to the stairs. When it became apparent that Freddie wasn't following, she looked over her shoulder.

"You coming?"

"Sure," he said hesitantly.

"We're going back to the crime scene," Veronica explained preemptively. "And even though you're the lead on this one, I'm driving."

***

"You look good, Freddie."

It was the best way she could think of to break the ice. The man might have said some horrible shit to her, but she still cared for him.

You could do real damage with just a few words, but it would take more than that to erase months of friendship.

And there was also the fact that she didn't have a choice.

"Thanks."

Veronica got comfortable behind the wheel.

"No, you look amazing. What's your secret?" When Freddie said nothing, she looked over at him. Then Veronica bit her lip and squinted one eye. "No, no way. No *fucking* way."

Freddie grinned.

"Yes, way."

"You? *Running*?"

"Me, running. Eating healthier, too."

Veronica gave the man a more intense up-down. Court had said that Freddie had changed, lost weight. But this... he must be at least fifty pounds lighter. He was still large, no doubt about it, but Freddie no longer looked like he was on death's doorstep. He looked like a man who liked to eat, not like a man who was trying to kill himself with food.

It was impressive. Six months had passed since his heart attack, and Freddie looked like a completely different man.

"I can't believe it. All those times I tried to get you to run, and you refused to listen... but a little medical issue and that's all it takes?"

Freddie chuckled.

She was trying, they both were. But it was awkward and uncomfortable.

"And... how have you been?"

"You know me, Freddie. A hot mess, as usual."

Once a killer, always a killer.

Dante's voice came out of nowhere and soured her mood, which was just starting to lift.

"Yeah, I know it." Freddie bit his lip and then he sighed dramatically. "Veronica, I just wanted to say that I'm sorry for—"

"No, we're not doing that," Veronica interrupted sharply. "We're not both going to sit here and say I wish I had, I wish I hadn't. Let's just move on, right?"

"Sounds good to me." Freddie dropped into professional mode, and Veronica wondered if she should've let him say his piece. When he remained quiet for the rest of the ride, she knew she should have.

As they approached Needle Point, Veronica updated Freddie on the case, including what Dr. Patel had described as a Blood Eagle.

When she was done, Freddie whistled.

"Yeah, some case to come back to, huh?"

"No wonder Dwight quit."

Veronica smiled and didn't bother correcting her partner.

"So, what are you thinking? Some vigilante trying to clean up Greenham?" Freddie asked.

"If that's their motive, they set up one hell of a scene."

They parked in front of a police cruiser, not Court's, and got out. The man behind the wheel lowered his newspaper, saw Veronica, frowned, then raised it again.

"Yeah, fuck you, too," Veronica grumbled. With Freddie at her side, she approached the tarp.

"It's behind here."

Freddie looked at the dilapidated scaffolding above, then leaned back and craned his head up and down the street.

"If whoever's behind this is really trying to scare people off, it would've made more sense to keep the body out here."

THE TOUCH OF MURDER 71

"Good point."

Veronica pulled back the sheet and stepped through it.

The chair was still there, but the coroner had since removed the body. CSU had even cleaned up some of the blood.

The word on the wall remained, however.

"Any witnesses?" Freddie asked.

"Sort of. A man with a severe... *uhh*... cognitive disability, I guess, said he saw a monster."

Freddie continued toward the word on the wall.

"A monster?"

Monster... monster... monster...

"Yeah. Also said that he saw a midnight blue car in the area. Not sure how much stock we can put in that, though."

Freddie nodded, letting her know that he'd heard, and then examined SINNER closely.

"Looks like this was made with someone's fingers? Any prints?"

"I doubt it—smudged like that you're not going to get any clean ridges. Haven't checked with Kristin, yet."

The sound of an engine approaching drew her attention and Veronica swept the tarp aside to take a look.

A midnight blue car was slowly making its way down the street.

"Hey, Freddie," Veronica said over her shoulder as she moved onto the sidewalk. "Blue car. Midnight—"

There was a star on the side of the vehicle accompanied by the words "Sheriff's Department."

"No way," Veronica shook her head. "It can't be him."

But as the car slowed even further, she got a glimpse of the man behind the wheel.

It *was* him.

What the hell is going on? First Freddie, now Steve? Have I traveled back in time?

Sheriff Burns looked drawn. Tired.

He parked in front of Veronica's car, clearly not realizing whose it was, and started to get out. Steve didn't notice her—how, she wasn't sure as she was standing *right* there—and instead, appeared to be assessing the area.

Then, as if spotting something terrible that only he could see, Steve squinted, craned his neck, and then recoiled.

What the hell?

Still without seeing her, the sheriff got back into his car and drove away.

"Who was that?" Freddie asked. He was right beside her now and Veronica jumped.

"Nobody," she whispered. "Nobody at all."

Chapter 15

IT WAS LIKE OLD TIMES. Freddie and Veronica, Kristin and Dr. Thorpe.

"Welcome back, Detective Furlow," Kristin said with a smile.

"Thanks. Captain decided to start me off with something light."

Kristin smiled. Dr. Thorpe did not.

"Victim's over here." The medical examiner led them to a gurney covered in a sheet. "Found morphine in his blood, heroin metabolite." This came as no surprise to anyone in the room. "Cause of death was exsanguination—he bled out from having his carotid artery and jugular vein severed. Weapon was a blade, nothing special. Sharp kitchen knife, I'll make a mold, just in case."

Dr. Thorpe pulled the sheet back, and even though Veronica was prepared for what lay beneath, she still felt her stomach tighten upon seeing it. Freddie's reaction was more verbal, but at least he didn't vomit.

"Those pinkish-gray things are his lungs." Dr. Thorpe lifted one of the organs with a gloved hand, using a squirt bottle to irrigate the tissue so that it didn't stick. Freddie inhaled sharply. "Ribs were crushed and pulled back to gain access to the lungs. The general lack of blood suggests that this was done post-mortem."

After what Veronica had been through, not much affected her. But seeing the gleam of white bone, of glistening connective tissue, and organ meat confirmed that she would not be eating again today.

"Any idea what was used to do that to the ribs?"

"Can't be certain, but if I had to guess, I'm thinking lock or bolt cutters."

Freddie cleared his throat.

"Dr. Thorpe, would this sort of mutilation require medical knowledge?"

"You're asking if I think a doctor did this?"

"Sure."

"No," Dr. Thorpe said simply. "The damage to the primary bronchi is severe. The left primary bronchi is almost completely severed. The aorta is stretched nearly to the point of tearing, as well."

"Meaning?"

Dr. Thorpe sighed as if this was all boring her.

"Meaning if I were to do this, it would have been much neater."

Veronica pursed her lips.

"Good to know." She was suddenly reminded of Dr. Patel's comment. "Either of you know what a blood eagle is?"

Dr. Thorpe cocked her head and Veronica could have sworn the woman smiled.

"Show them."

Kristin waved Freddie and Veronica over to a computer while Dr. Thorpe replaced the lung and covered the body.

"Check this out." Kristin pressed a few keys and a terrible image appeared on the screen.

"Shit," Freddie cursed.

The image was similar to the display in the alley, but there were significant differences. For one, the victims' skin and lungs were pulled back and out using thin ropes. The man's face was also twisted in agony. It didn't appear that his throat had been slit. If anything, it looked like the man was screaming.

"The thing is," Kristin said, "with a blood eagle, the victim is usually alive. It's a torture method."

"And our guy was dead because his throat was slit *before* his lungs were removed?" Veronica asked.

"That's right," Dr. Thorpe confirmed from behind them.

Kristin closed the image and opened a photograph from their crime scene.

"So, not a blood eagle, then?" Veronica asked, scratching the back of her head. They were missing something.

"I don't know about that, but it almost looks like an angel, doesn't it?" Freddie remarked. He tapped the word SINNER above Jake's head. "Like whoever did this wanted to punish Jake for his sins?"

Veronica was surprised.

"That's... that's what I said."

"It's not my first rodeo," Freddie remarked. "No ring rust, either, apparently."

"Right. What if... what if this was personal against Jake? Maybe we're reading too much into this and it's just a creative way to settle a score. What about next of kin?"

"Doesn't have any," Kristin said. "Not that I could find, anyway."

Veronica sighed.

"So, we might just have a vigilante on the loose, punishing sinners in the most sinful place in all of Greenham. And our unsub might be a Viking." She reconsidered. "A Viking monster. What the actual fuck?"

Veronica's final curse landed softly and went unchallenged.

"Well, thanks for your help. Dr. Thorpe, if the mold from the knife wound turns out to be anything special, please let us know. And hopefully," she looked at Dr. Thorpe then Kristin, "hopefully I don't see either of you two again anytime soon about angels or eagles or anything else that doesn't have at least two feet planted on the ground at all times."

***

There were few places that made Veronica feel as uncomfortable as the Matheson Public Library.

Both librarians—Gina Braden and Maggie Cernak—were dead because of her.

She felt like an imposter. And guilty.

She felt *incredibly* guilty.

Gina's replacement was a woman with raven-black hair and severe features who didn't look up from the book she was reading when they entered. Even when Veronica asked her to direct them toward reference material pertaining to angels and Viking rituals, the woman just grunted and pointed, her eyes never leaving the page.

They split up, with Veronica adamant that she look at the Viking material. She had enough of churches, orphanages, priests, and nuns to last a lifetime. Freddie didn't seem to mind either way.

It took Veronica a while to find any reference to a blood eagle and when she did, it was more of a history lesson than anything else.

One of the more famous uses of this method of torture involved King Aella of Northumbria who was murdered by the Viking warrior Ivar the Boneless. According to the story, Ivar wanted revenge for the death of his father, Ragnar Lodbrok, and had Aella captured and subjected to the blood eagle before killing him.

The traditional method involved tying a person down, spreading their arms and legs, then slicing along the spine with either a knife or a sword. Next, the ribs were broken with an ax, pulled back, and the lungs yanked out.

All while the victim was still alive.

They usually didn't survive for more than a few minutes.

But no matter how hard Veronica looked, she could not find any reference to sinners. Like Dr. Patel had told her, Vikings had their own complex belief systems, but there didn't seem to be anything analogous to Christian 'Sinners'.

Veronica spent the better part of the afternoon reading but felt as if she were wasting her time. Before she knew it, it was close to 6:30, and despite previous claims that she wouldn't eat again today, she was getting hungry.

"Any luck?" Freddie asked as he groaned and stretched.

Veronica closed the large reference book in front of her.

"Nothing. How about you?"

"Well, I learned more about angels than I ever wanted to. Did you know that the word comes from a Greek word that means messenger?"

Veronica did not and said as much.

"I also learned that the physical description of angels in the Bible is not the way we traditionally think of them. And they're nothing like that 'angel' we saw today. Apparently, they have human-like bodies, with wings, and four faces—a lion, an ox, an eagle, and a man."

"What?"

Freddie shrugged. Veronica had seen her partner do this a million times before, but now it was different, and it took a few seconds to realize how. Normally, this would send a shock wave down his many chins and into his belly. A dramatic, oversized gesture by an oversized man. Not anymore.

Now it was subtle.

And strange.

"Yep. Four faces."

"And one is an eagle?"

"Apparently. But that's where the similarities end. Could just be a coincidence... I dunno."

Veronica used the heel of her hand to rub both eye sockets and then her forehead.

"So, we've got a man who knows nothing about Viking mythology, limited knowledge of Catholic studies—"

"—who is so obsessed with cleaning up Needle Point that he's willing to kill for it—"

"—and our only witness saw a monster... but he can only manage a handful of words. I'm telling you, this is all messed up. It's like our unsub is deliberately trying to send us in different directions."

"Or he just doesn't know what he wants."

"What he wants is to kill people," Veronica corrected. "And we both know he's going to do it again."

"Yeah." Freddie paused. "You hungry? Wanna grab a bite to eat? I'd love to go to Daphne's, but the old ticker doesn't agree with it. I'm game for anywhere that has a healthy salad, though."

Veronica wasn't sure what was more unbelievable, the fact that her partner would turn down Daphne's or that he wanted a salad.

Even though she was hungry, Veronica still wasn't there yet with Freddie.

She declined.

"I'll see you tomorrow."

Veronica didn't want to go to dinner with Freddie, but she didn't want to go home to Cole, either. She wasn't in the mood to listen to him gripe about his shitty job.

After returning the books—the librarian *still* didn't look up—she went to a bar. An empty bar where she could be alone.

The first drink numbed her brain a little. The second numbed it even further.

The third she consumed while thinking about Steve.

What the hell was he doing there? What did he see?

Why did he run?

As was the usual case when she started to drink, eventually Veronica reached into her wallet and pulled out the photograph that she'd stolen from the orphanage. The worn, faded image of Dante and her brother, their arms over each other's shoulders. Neither boy smiling.

Forgive.

Veronica quickly swallowed two more drinks.

Fuck forgiveness.

When she eventually made it home, Cole was already asleep.

Veronica dreamed of neither angel nor demon that night. The nightmares were reserved for daytime now, apparently.

Chapter 16

THE MAN STUMBLED THROUGH THE streets, shuffling, and nearly falling with every step.

But, somehow, he managed to stay upright.

His breathing came in shallow blasts as if he was wearing a mask, and it was all he could hear in his ears. He could barely see, his eyelids felt coated in cement.

But he kept going.

A jogger passed on his left, and he lowered his head. This caused sweat to drip into his eyes, but he made no move to wipe it away. He didn't want to touch himself—his face... it wasn't his.

It was a monster's.

And it wouldn't matter anyway. His entire body was coated in sweat. Wipe some away, it just came back.

Eventually, he came to a large multi-story office building set back behind a parking lot.

This was it. This was the place.

Keeping his chin to his chest, he slid behind a small set of shrubs and waited.

Time passed. A thousand breaths, maybe more. Then the front door opened and a man in a suit stepped out. He was heavy-set and when he looked at his watch, he cursed, then picked up his pace as he crossed the parking lot. The man in the bushes rose and started after him.

Just as the businessman struggled to pull his keys from his pocket, he heard the man in the hoodie's breathing.

He turned.

"The fuck do you—"

The man pulled the hoodie back and the suit dropped his keys.

"What the *fuck*? Get the—get the fuck away from me!"

All the man in the sweatshirt saw was red—blooms and blossoms of blood everywhere. The businessman backed up but soon bumped up against his car. He tried to get his phone out but was even less successful at this than he'd been with his keys.

"Please, just—"

The man in the black hoodie jumped. His hands were swollen, but it took very little coordination to pull the knife from the center pocket of his sweatshirt.

Even less to plunge it into the man's throat.

It slid effortlessly through skin, fat, and sinew. The businessman's eyes went wide, and he tried to say something but managed nothing more than a wet gurgle on account of his windpipe having been severed.

But the man in the hoodie had no such problem.

He leaned in close and whispered in the businessman's ear, "Sinner."

And then he got to work.

PART TWO: DEMON

Chapter 17

"Jesus," Detective Freddie Furlow muttered, "I'm so glad I don't eat breakfast anymore."

Veronica shared the sentiment. In her case, she had skipped breakfast not because she was on a diet, but because she was hungover and couldn't stomach the idea of eating. But she did appreciate the coffee. That was one of the things she missed most: Freddie smiling and greeting her with a coffee outside the station every morning. Sadly, today didn't involve the station. It didn't even involve a full night's sleep. Veronica's phone started ringing around five and continued doing so until she answered at just after five-thirty. Cole, being the deep sleeper that he was, didn't even wake.

It was Officer Furnelli letting her know that there was another and that Freddie was already on his way.

By six, she was standing in front of the large parking lot of a multi-story office building in Meadowbrook, about three miles north-east of the location of the first victim. The setting was different, but the MO was almost identical.

There was no chair this time—the victim was lying flat on his stomach on the pavement in a pool of his own blood. As with Jake, his lungs had been removed and the shriveled organs were exposed on his back.

SINNER had been written in blood on the side of a black BMW, which, based on the proximity to the body and the set of keys on the ground near his outstretched hand, probably belonged to their vic.

Kristin, Dr. Thorpe, Freddie, and Court were already on the scene when Veronica arrived.

"Throat slit, just like the junkie," Kristin informed her.

"Do we have a name yet?" Freddie asked.

Kristin nodded.

"His wallet was on his person, cash still inside. Cooper Mills, forty-two, lives not too far from here."

Cooper's corpse was surrounded by fading embers—Veronica's synesthesia was firing, but not as intensely as it had been at Jake's murder scene. Maybe it was the booze or maybe it was because this murder had taken place in the open that muted her condition.

She didn't know.

As Kristin said more about Cooper, something about him being an accountant and working in the building behind them, Veronica bent down low.

What did you do? She wondered. *What the hell did you do?*

"Any idea on time of death?" Veronica asked, not taking her eyes off the body.

"Won't know for sure until we get him back to the morgue, but liver temp suggests four, maybe five hours ago. Somewhere around midnight," Dr. Thorpe replied.

Veronica finally looked away from Cooper and glanced around the parking lot, her gaze eventually settling on the building itself. It looked fairly upscale, which to Veronica meant that the people who worked there probably worked long hours.

"What are the odds that Cooper was the last person to leave this morning?"

"Not great," Freddie said.

"What are the odds that he was captured leaving on that security camera?" she asked, pointing at the device nestled just under the awning.

"Better."

"Let's go have a chat with security then, shall we?"

Court accompanied them to the front doors, telling them along the way that the security guard had found the body at around four forty-five and called it in.

"He still in there?"

"I don't think he goes very far," Court replied.

Veronica understood when she met the security guard in his office. He was ancient to the point of desiccation. Veronica was tempted to question the value of a security guard this old, but then she remembered that, up until recently, her partner had been a 350-pound man who got winded taking a piss.

But whereas the previous iteration of Freddie had been slow, he'd at least been competent. The same could not be said of the guard. It took the man so long just to boot up the computer that Veronica worried the two-week window before old footage was overwritten by new might expire.

"Do you mind?" she asked, leaning toward the keyboard.

"Company policy states that only security employees can touch the computer." He even spoke slowly.

"Right, well, we're going to have to make an exception this time."

As Freddie gently guided the man aside, Veronica attacked the keyboard. Within minutes, she found footage from earlier that morning, both from the foyer and outside the building. Cooper Mills was on both. He looked tired and in a hurry.

The camera beneath the awning was designed to capture people coming and going, not film the parking lot. Cooper left the building and then disappeared out of the frame before being attacked or making it to his car.

Veronica watched a little while longer, but the next person to appear was the guard at four thirty-nine 'rushing' inside the building, presumably to call the cops.

"Damn, there's nothing here."

"Maybe... go back to the outside camera for a second?" Freddie asked.

Veronica obliged and just before Cooper Mills exited the frame, her partner told her to pause the footage.

He leaned forward and pointed at the lower left-hand corner of the screen.

"Do you see that? Can you go frame by frame?"

Veronica could and did. And sure enough, she saw it.

It appeared to be the outline of a shoulder and a head, both covered in a black sweatshirt.

"Where did he come from?" Veronica asked.

"There are some bushes over there. Could he have been hiding in them?" Court asked. "You know what, I'm going to check it out. Gimme a second."

As they waited for Court to return, Veronica ran the footage forwards and backward trying to pick up any more clues.

"Looks like a man's build, no? Medium stature? Smaller than Cooper, that's for sure," Veronica remarked.

"I'd say so. And look at how he moves. Awkward, like he's drunk."

"High? He could be high. I'm—"

"So, yeah, I think he was hiding in those bushes. Grass is crushed there," Court said, returning to the security room. He was out of breath. "Was he waiting for him? Was our unsub waiting for Cooper, I mean? Like, was Cooper the intended target?"

Veronica looked at Freddie, who shrugged.

"Probably," she conceded. "If this was just a random attack, it would have been easier to stick to Needle Point. And Cooper is a big man. There had to be easier targets out there."

"But he was also distracted and in a hurry," Freddie countered.

"Yeah, maybe."

Veronica used her phone to make a copy of the recordings. Then she thanked the elderly security guard, who continued to mumble that they had broken company policy, and went back outside.

"I think I'm done here," Dr. Thorpe exclaimed. "If you're done, I'll get CSU to help me get the body back to the morgue."

"Go ahead," Veronica said. And then she remembered that the captain had put Freddie in charge. Her partner agreed.

"All done."

"Court, can you hold the scene until CSU finishes up?" Veronica asked.

"Sure thing."

"Thanks."

Freddie and Veronica walked back to the road.

"I can go alone if you want," her partner offered when they were out of earshot of the others.

Veronica sighed.

Part of her wanted to tell him, yeah, go ahead. You owe me. You owe me *big time*.

But that was petty.

And the truth was, if Freddie deserved to be punished, then she did, too.

"No, let's go together—let's go break the bad news to Cooper Mills' next of kin."

Chapter 18

SHERIFF STEVE BURNS WAS IN shock.

Of course, he recognized Jake 'Bunky' Thompson. How could he not?

After all, he'd met up with the man the night before.

Bunky was his supplier. This complicated things significantly, but Steve had come up with a plan that he hoped would straighten things out.

It was simple, but weren't those always the best kinds of plans?

Steve would play the undercover card, lie to Bunky, and convince him that all the heroin he'd purchased up to this point was in evidence.

And if Bunky didn't snitch, he'd go down.

DEA Agent Allison claimed that nobody was talking, but Steve could be persuasive.

What Steve would be able to get out of Bunky was another issue entirely. Steve had never seen the snake and eye logo on any of the man's product. Not once.

And the man's gear wasn't tainted with fentanyl. At least, he didn't think so. Fucking hoped not.

That was Steve's plan, but then everything changed when he spotted the Greenham PD cruiser. He got the fuck out of there as fast as he could. Then he'd placed a few calls.

Bunky was dead.

Murdered.

That, in and of itself, wasn't overly surprising. After all, the man worked a dangerous profession.

The way he was killed, though? Throat slit and lungs pulled out of his body? That was not an occupational hazard.

That was something almost ritualistic.

And Steve had been there.

Two things went through his mind, both incredibly selfish considering what had happened to Bunky. But self-preservation was a powerful motivator.

The first, was that it could have been him. He could have been brutally murdered.

The second was that he had been there and while Steve always made sure to be careful, his priority was to score.

And that could make you sloppy.

His heart was racing, and even though Steve had long since made up a set of rules to follow, primarily, one shot in the morning and one at night, none during the day, his eyes drifted to the glovebox.

If he was going down, then —

Someone knocked on his window and he jumped.

"Fucking hell."

He'd been so lost in thought that he didn't notice Deputy McVeigh approach. Steve rolled down the window.

"Sheriff Burns?"

"Yeah?" Steve's car was still running, and his hand instinctively went to the gearshift.

"I was thinking that maybe you'd want me to take this case. Sit this one out, you know?" The man's words sounded deliberate, practiced.

Steve's eyes narrowed; this was not what he'd expected. He knew Marcus McVeigh wanted his job, but he'd never been this direct before.

"What are you talking about?"

McVeigh averted his eyes, but his voice remained strong.

"Given the nature of the case, perhaps you wouldn't mind letting me take it on."

The sheriff's grip tightened on the gearshift.

"What do you mean by nature of the case?" Steve dared.

McVeigh knew he'd taken the drugs from the evidence locker—nobody else could have gotten that footage. He was holding on to it, waiting for his moment.

Steve was sure of it.

But the man couldn't possibly know about everything else. About sleeping in his car.

About using.

About meeting with people like Bunky.

Nobody knew that. And nobody ever would.

McVeigh stiffened.

"What did you mean by that comment, Marcus? If you have the balls to—"

A large figure appeared behind the deputy.

"Sheriff," DEA Agent Troy Allison said with a nod. McVeigh stepped aside. "Back already?"

"Jake Thompson's dead," Steve said flatly, wanting to get this out of the way.

Marcus McVeigh's eyes widened, his coup suddenly forgotten.

"What?"

"Yeah, murdered."

Steve briefly explained what he'd learned from Greenham PD about Bunky's death. With each word, McVeigh's eyelids retracted further while Troy's moved in the opposite direction. When he mentioned the lungs being pulled out, both men made identical faces.

"Damn it," Troy said. "There goes our *fucking* link."

"Any suspects?" McVeigh asked, more concerned about the brutal nature of the crime in Bear County than losing their tenuous connection to an expired New York cartel.

"No," Steve answered. "Nothing yet."

But there could be, right, Steve? There could be DNA left at the scene. A fingerprint? Didn't you take your gloves off when you were counting the cash for Bunky? A hair? Did you run your hands through your hair?

No, of course not. I dressed in black, hood pulled over my eyes. Parked my squad car far away. If anybody spotted me, I'd go with the tried and true: undercover.

"All right, well, Sheriff," Agent Allison said, lighting a cigarette. "Thank you anyway. Back to fucking square one."

Troy squeezed McVeigh's shoulder and started to walk away.

Undercover... undercover.

The word refused to leave his brain.

"Maybe not," Steve blurted.

Troy slowly turned, his head engulfed in a gray cloud of smoke.

Oh, shit.

Steve hadn't thought this through.

"Sheriff, maybe it's—" McVeigh tried to intervene, but Troy didn't strike Steve as the type of person who cared much for interruptions.

"What do you mean?"

Steve finally took his hand off the gearshift, flexed his fingers, and shut off his car.

"I'm not giving up, yet," he said, staring directly at McVeigh as he spoke. "I know this place, I know this area, I know this County. But I don't think the County knows me. I'm going undercover."

Chapter 19

"I DON'T KNOW ABOUT 'SINNER,'" Freddie said from the passenger seat of Veronica's car, "but Cooper Mills sure as hell was no saint."

He was on his laptop, pulling up the victim's rap sheet. Most of the charges that Freddie read off were white-collar in nature.

There were two noticeable outliers.

"Looks like he also liked to use his wife as a punching bag."

Veronica raised an eyebrow, encouraging her partner to continue.

"Twice, he was arrested for assault and battery, domestic. Both times the charges were dropped."

It made Veronica sick to her stomach to hear this. Unfortunately, it wasn't a unique tale. There was a considerable amount of confidence and courage needed to report one's spouse for domestic assault. When this happened, it was usually following an extremely volatile and emotionally charged period. After these hormonal inputs waned, the next day, for instance, regret would slowly set in. Fear and insecurity soon followed, especially because these characteristics had been indoctrinated into them by their abuser.

They refused to press charges and thus the cycle repeated.

"So, we have two victims from two very different walks of life. Both were 'sinners'—who isn't—and it's unlikely that there is a link between them. Can they be completely random?" Veronica mused.

Freddie shrugged.

"It didn't look random in the security footage. But I'm not sure."

Cooper and Molly Mills lived in a modern detached home in a quiet Meadowbrook neighborhood about ten minutes from his office. She passed a police car about half a block away—as per her instructions, the officer was to watch the home, but not enter—and then parked on the street.

Freddie, sensing her apprehension, offered to take the lead. Veronica didn't argue.

"All right, let's get this over with. You have a picture of Jake Thompson?"

Freddie did and handed it to her. She tucked it out of sight while her partner knocked on the door.

After about a minute, a thin, dark-haired woman peered out. Veronica had her badge at the ready, but she hadn't even fully raised it before the woman broke down.

TV—Veronica blamed TV. Watch enough cop shows and you came to believe that two stern-faced people on your porch with badges could only mean one thing.

And it was never good.

"Please," Molly begged as if Veronica and Freddie turning around and leaving would change the facts.

"Mrs. Mills, I'm so sorry to tell you this," Freddie said. "Your husband, Cooper, is dead."

"No," the woman sobbed. "Please, *no*."

Molly surprised Veronica by reaching out to her.

Veronica wasn't sure what to do. She remembered when she'd told Dahlia, Marlowe Lerman's handler, that her boss was dead. Marlowe had treated the mousy woman like crap, but Dahlia had broken down just the same.

So did Molly Mills.

Veronica embraced the woman.

"I'm sorry," she said softly into the woman's hair.

After thirty seconds or so, Molly Mills' sobs became silent tears and she pulled away from Veronica. Her face was puffy from crying, but Veronica thought she could see some bruising around her left temple that seemed unrelated to the woman's grief.

Cooper Mills' doing, no doubt.

Sinner.

"What happened?" Molly sniffed. "What happened to Coop?"

"He was killed," Freddie said, frankly. "Murdered."

"*No.*"

This reinvigorated Molly's sobs. She reached out again, but this time Veronica gently guided her hands away.

"I know it's difficult to talk right now," Freddie continued. He nodded at Veronica, and she pulled out the photo of Jake Thompson. "But if we want to find out who did this, we're going to need your help. Can you do that?"

Shock, ambivalence—good enough for Veronica.

"Have you seen this man before?"

To her credit, despite her condition, Molly took a good look at the photo.

"No, I don't know him. Do you think—"

"He's not a suspect," Freddie said quickly. "Have you ever seen your husband with this man?"

Molly shook her head.

"Okay, can you think of anyone who would want to hurt your husband?"

"No. No," she protested, "he was a… good… man… I don't understand. Why—"

Veronica could feel that she was losing her.

"Mrs. Mills, I need you to tell me the truth, okay?"

"I am! I—"

Veronica grabbed the woman by the shoulders.

"Did your husband take drugs? I'm not talking about smoking the occasional joint, but pills? Cocaine? Anything stronger? We need you to be honest."

The woman made a face.

"No."

Veronica inhaled deeply. She smelled no lies.

"Cooper never did drugs. He didn't smoke. He liked to drink, maybe a little too much. But not drugs."

Molly was telling the truth. It had been a long shot—Cooper Mills, despite his faults and transgressions was a wealthy accountant. It wasn't impossible to be a successful, functioning addict, but it was rare. And Veronica hadn't noticed any of the telltale signs of drug abuse on the man's corpse.

"How... how did Coop die?"

Veronica pictured Cooper lying on his bare stomach, his lungs torn from his back.

"He was killed with a knife, Mrs. Mills," Veronica said, hoping that this was sufficient.

It wasn't.

"But how? Was he stabbed or cut, or... I don't understand..."

Molly broke down a third time, and this was particularly difficult for Veronica to watch. Waves of thick blue smoke started to come off the woman's head and shoulders as her perspiration intensified.

"Sometimes it's difficult to make sense of things," Veronica said, her voice calm and even. "Sometimes bad shit just happens." She sighed. "We're going to find out who did this to your husband, Molly. And when we do, they will face justice."

In the back of her mind, Veronica heard a small voice.

It was a voice reminding her that when Veronica Shade dealt justice, it wasn't the same as other members of law enforcement.

Just ask Gloria Trammell.

And this voice didn't belong to her.

It belonged to Dante Fiori.

Once a killer, always a killer.

Chapter 20

"Like I said earlier, Jake Thompson was as high as we got up the chain with this new product." DEA Agent Troy Allison tapped the image of the snake eating the eyeball. "But, in Needle Point, this man," now he indicated the photo of a black man with a shaved head, ratty goatee, and a small upside down cross tattoo just outside and below his left eye, "usually runs the show. His name is Damien 'Toots' Blackwell. His top lieutenant is Kendrick 'Trigger' Holchester." Troy flipped to a third photo. Like Damien, Kendrick was also black, with an afro, and deep grooves around his mouth that appeared almost gray on his dark skin.

Steve recognized Kendrick—he'd seen him while scoring from Jake about a month back.

"I don't really understand why it has to be you," Marcus McVeigh said. Then, realizing how he sounded, quickly followed up with, "It should be a younger officer. I mean, someone could recognize you. I know you try to keep a low profile, but you were on the news with the dollmaker and the—"

"Look," Troy interrupted. He leaned on his elbows and stretched across the table. They were alone in the conference room, and the door and blinds were closed, but Troy felt the need to lower his voice, nonetheless. "I'm not sure if it's Bear County or Greenham PD, but there's some chatter about law enforcement being involved."

Steve's eyes narrowed.

Had someone spotted him? Did someone see him in Needle Point?

His plan was on the verge of cratering. Instead of solving his problems, maybe it was bound to add to them.

"Just chatter for now," Troy specified. "Unconfirmed, but… it's probably best if we keep it in-house if you know what I'm sayin'."

"I'll do it, then," McVeigh offered. "Let me go undercover."

Steve didn't know if McVeigh was so desperate to take his spot because of how it would play out in the press if they managed to overthrow this new cartel, or if he was aware of how deeply the sheriff's addiction ran.

If that was the case, was he trying to protect Steve?

"No." Steve shook his head. "It should be me. If anything happened to you while I was just sitting here…"

"The sheriff's right. To be honest, I doubt Toots or Trigger pay much attention to the news. And," Troy looked at Steve, "no offense, but if we dirty you up a little, you could pass as a junkie."

Closer to the truth than you can ever imagine.

"Been a rough couple weeks," —*months*— "but that settles it."

"Good."

Steve was having a difficult time getting a read on Troy. He seemed brutally honest and rough around the edges. Based on his limited experience with the DEA, this wasn't terribly uncommon. But there was something different about the man, too. Something the sheriff couldn't put his finger on.

"I think we should start tonight," Steve offered. When McVeigh looked like he was about to interject, he quickly added, "there might be someone out there hunting these guys—Jake was viciously murdered. Who knows, maybe while I'm trying to figure out where the drugs are coming from, I'll get a lead on whoever killed Jake."

"Right," Troy agreed. "I think this should just stay between us, too."

McVeigh held his hand out in protest.

"He can't go undercover without—"

"It's fine."

"No, this..." McVeigh sighed and lowered his voice. "This is fucked up."

"Yeah, well, you know what else is fucked up?" Troy asked gruffly. "Heroin laced with fentanyl that costs the same as a joint. A *fucking* joint. That's fucked up."

Troy held McVeigh's stare for a few seconds as if willing him to argue. When it looked as if his chief deputy was going to say something, Steve rose to his feet.

"That settles it. Nothing leaves this room." Steve paused. "How are we going to do this, Troy?"

The big man rubbed his palm across his scalp.

"Right. I mean, you'll probably meet Trigger, first. Man's a fiend for E. Maybe... maybe you bring him some E. Ask him to trade."

Troy was making it seem like he was coming up with this off the top of his head, but Steve wasn't buying it. He'd thought about this plan before. And that meant, more likely than not, they'd tried it before.

And, clearly, it hadn't worked.

That was what was different about Troy, Steve realized. The man lacked empathy. For the DEA Agent, it was about getting the job done, no matter the cost. And while others might look at this as a positive trait, not Steve.

Because Steve knew the danger of such a Machiavellian attitude. He'd seen it as a State Trooper. It started out noble enough, no breaking any rules, no deals, no compromising— just the job. But then you realized that you could be more effective by maybe stepping a little harder on a suspect's neck.

Before long you were banging down doors without a warrant. In months, maybe a year or two of accolade after accolade? You were on your path to becoming Wayne Jenkins in the Baltimore Police Department's Gun Trace Task Force.

A slippery slope if there ever was one.

But Steve was in thick.

"Sounds good," he said. "Then let's get some product to trade, shall we?"

Chapter 21

DESPITE VERONICA'S PROMISE, THEY HAD nothing.

Two bodies, a word written in blood, a video capturing some of their likely murderer, and a grisly MO.

They had all of that.

But they had *nothing*.

No motive, no suspect, no idea when their unsub would strike again. Veronica had spent a good hour on her computer trying to identify a link between Jake Thompson and Cooper Mills.

Again: nothing.

A career criminal involved in drugs and a sketchy accountant who liked to knock his wife around.

They didn't go to the same bars, stores, gym… *nothing*.

They lived fairly close to each other, about five miles apart, but in dramatically different settings.

Freddie wasn't having any luck either.

"Maybe it really was random," the man remarked. It was perhaps the fifth time he'd said this during the course of the day.

Veronica didn't want to believe it but was leaning in that direction despite the security footage from outside Cooper's office.

Random acts of violence, especially with this level of depravity, were exceedingly rare. And that made them exceedingly hard to solve.

Veronica knew from experience that even if a crime appeared random, it very rarely was. Even Bundy had a type.

But what did a skinny, malnourished drug dealer and an overweight tax accountant have in common?

Sinner.

That was it; they were both sinners.

Her phone rang. It was Dr. Thorpe.

"Tell me you have some good news for us, Dr. Thorpe."

Good news in the form of evidence. Foreign DNA, a fingerprint, anything.

"Unfortunately, not. Ran a tox screen on Mr. Mills—no alcohol or drugs in his system."

Veronica had suspected as much, but deep down, she'd been holding out hope that Cooper Mills was secretly buying drugs from Jake Thompson.

Secretly buying drugs...

This made her think of Steve and the pills that she'd found in his pants pocket and flushed. She contrasted how he looked then—red-faced, eyes wild—with yesterday when he'd strangely gotten out of the car at Jake's crime scene, only to get back in and drive off moments later—pale, withdrawn.

He couldn't still be using, could he?

This made Veronica feel guilty. Despite how things ended between them, she still cared for the man. And yet, she hadn't so much as checked in with him in months.

In turn, these thoughts spurred more guilt—guilt that she was with Cole and thinking about Steve. Not just now, either. But lying in bed after—

"Detective Shade? You still there?"

Veronica shook her head, trying to rattle thoughts of Sheriff Steve Burns out of it.

"Sorry, I'm here. You were saying?"

"I made a mold using the wound in Mr. Thompson's throat. Nothing unique about it, I'm afraid. One edge, likely a kitchen knife. I compared it to molds made from Mr. Mills' wounds. All I can conclusively say is that nothing rules them out as being the same weapon."

Veronica frowned, thanked the doctor, and then hung up.

"Nothing good?" Freddie asked.

"Nothing good," Veronica confirmed. "You're *sure* there's no link between their socials?"

"Can't find anything." Freddie took a bite out of the apple he was holding, which made an annoying squishing sound. It was a huge bite, and he was forced to chew dramatically. Juice ran onto Freddie's lips, and he licked it away. For some reason, this annoyed Veronica, and she wished that he still stuffed his face with chips and French fries. Somehow, that would be less disgusting at the moment. "Jake didn't have much, but he was on Instagram. I couldn't find anything closer than four degrees of separation linking the two."

"Check again," Veronica snapped. When Freddie raised an eyebrow, she toned down her request. "Please? There has to be a—"

The captain's door opened, and once again he summoned both Veronica and Freddie into his office. Normally, Veronica appreciated the man's desire for privacy. But now, getting up, walking to his office, closing the door, waiting for him to sit while they just stood there, twiddling their thumbs?

That was annoying, too.

Everything was annoying when you were going nowhere on a case.

"Detective Furlow, I'm going to need an update."

Freddie obliged, offering what little information they'd uncovered. He spoke of Molly Mills, the expected abuse, but noted that the woman's grief seemed genuine. He looked at Veronica as he hesitantly put forth the theory that these killings might indeed be random, that someone out there was obsessed with punishing sinners for their transgressions.

When he was done, Captain Bottel sat there, massaging the corners of his mustache with thumb and forefinger, smoothing it out.

Yeah, this was annoying, too.

"There's no way that these two men knew each other?" the captain asked after a pause.

"If they did," Veronica replied sharply, "we haven't been able to find any proof of it. I doubt they ever so much as passed each other in the street."

More stroking of his mustache. Veronica half-expected to see his fingers dyed brown when he finally pulled them away.

"I think we should go public."

Veronica had not been expecting this.

"You're joking."

Captain Bottel pressed his lips together.

"I thought you said... I thought you wanted this to be quick and clean? That's the opposite of going to the public."

"I know what I said," the captain replied, matching Veronica's tone. "But that was when we had one victim. Now, we have two. Somebody may have seen them together or noticed something unusual the nights they were killed. Maybe there was a car—"

Veronica suddenly thought of something.

"There was a witness at Jake Thompson's murder."

The captain made a face and Veronica knew what he was thinking.

Why didn't you start with this?

"*Sort of,*" she clarified. "A man with a severe mental disability said he saw a midnight blue car at the scene around the time of the murder."

And a monster. He saw a monster, too.

Veronica kept this bit to herself.

"Did he get a tag number? A look at the suspect?"

"Like I said, he has some severe disabilities. Saw a midnight blue car, but that's all I could get from him."

"Right, well, that doesn't exactly narrow it down." Captain Bottel straightened. "We're going public."

"I'm not going back on TV," Veronica stated, crossing her arms over her chest.

The captain held her gaze.

"Understood. Detective Furlow, set up a press conference for this evening."

Veronica had intended on staying quietly defiant, but her willpower wasn't what it once was. She'd expected to have a few days to come up with at least one suspect before they opened the gates to the zoo.

"This *evening*? Captain, we need more time. If we go public tonight, with nothing, the only thing we're going to accomplish is spooking this guy. If he leaves the state, we'll never find him."

Veronica read through the captain's silence. If their unsub leaves the state, then he became someone else's problem. Sorry, Molly Mills, the person who murdered your husband got away.

Ho hum, better luck next time.

"Give us another day," she pleaded. "Give us one more day to figure out who did this, and then we'll have the press conference."

"You know, Detective Shade has a point," Freddie said when it looked like the captain wasn't about to change his mind. "If we can come up with a suspect list, even a vague one, we can have eyes on them when we go live. That way, if they get spooked and make any rash moves, we'll be watching."

Veronica was grateful for her partner's support, but she was also perturbed that her pleading wasn't enough.

"I know how these things work, Detective Furlow." The captain snapped. "But I think we can hold off until tomorrow. In the meantime, what's the patrol situation like in Nettle Point? I don't want another victim on our hands by the time we go to the media."

"I'll double the number of cops circling the area tonight," Freddie said.

"Good. Now go get me a suspect, will you?"

Chapter 22

VERONICA OPENED THE DOOR TO her house, then closed it as quietly as possible. It was late, and she didn't want to wake Cole.

But she was also a little bit drunk after going to the bar again after work.

She dropped her keys.

"Shit."

As Veronica bent to pick them up, Lucy sauntered over, the bell around her neck tinkling softly.

"Shhhh," she said as she scratched the cat's back. "Quiet."

Veronica straightened too quickly, and she bumped into the closed door.

"Shit."

The lights flicked on, and she saw Cole sitting at the kitchen table. In front of him were a bottle of champagne and two glasses filled to the brim.

What the hell?

Thinking that this was a mirage of some sort, Veronica blinked rapidly.

Nothing changed.

"Cole? What the—what the hell is going on?"

The man appeared as confused as she was. He looked at the glasses, then the champagne.

"I tried calling like a dozen times, Veronica, but you never picked up. I must've fallen asleep waitin'."

Veronica brought a hand to her forehead.

"Did we—did we have plans or something?"

Cole grinned slyly as he picked up the two glasses and walked over to her on unsteady legs.

"I don't understand what's going on," Veronica protested. "I'm tired, Cole. It's been a long day, and—"

He pushed the glass against her chest, and she had no choice but take it.

"I quit," the man said simply. Then he clinked her glass, cocked his head, and sipped the champagne.

Veronica wasn't sure if it was the alcohol or if this scenario was just too bizarre to wrap her head around.

"You quit what? What the hell are you talking about?"

"I took your advice and quit. I'm out. No longer part of Internal Affairs, no more investigating whether or not Lieutenant Tim Brown stole rookie cop Miranda Smith's underwear from her locker and wore them for a five-mile run. I'm out."

When Veronica didn't say anything, Cole's grin reversed course.

"I thought you'd be happy for me. I'm thinking of starting a PI firm like we talked about." He took another sip of the champagne. "I think this is the point in the conversation where you say something."

Veronica blinked.

"You're not serious, are you?"

"Yeah, I'm serious. I quit. I couldn't handle one more day of IA."

Veronica finally raised her glass, but it wasn't to cheers Cole. Instead, she brought it to her mouth and downed the entire glass. She wasn't typically a champagne person, didn't like the way the carbonation tickled her throat, but this tasted like the good stuff. Not overly sweet or acidic.

"Cole, you can't just quit. Y-you *can't*."

Cole shrugged.

"I can. I *did*."

She knew that she was hurting his feelings now and that he was incredibly disappointed by her reaction, or lack thereof. But they hadn't discussed this, not really. You couldn't just decide in a day or two that you were going to just quit your job.

That's not how it was done.

Even though he was in IA, Cole was still a cop. He had to go through the same basic training Veronica had, and while boot camp was a far cry from Navy SEAL hell week, it wasn't fun. It was a commitment, physical and mental. You didn't graduate, become a cop... just to quit.

"Cole, like, why didn't you just transfer out of IA? You know, Greenham and Matheson are always looking for cops."

"Because I didn't want to. I want to start my own private investigation firm."

"But you spent all that time becoming a cop."

Cole shrugged.

"So? I'm young, besides, I made some connections that can definitely help. There's stuff I learned..." Cole let his sentence trail off. "Didn't you say I should try this?"

"No, don't do that," Veronica warned. "It wasn't my idea; it was *your* idea."

"I'm pretty sure we were lying in bed talking, and you said that I should just quit, that if I wanted to start a PI firm, I should just do it." Any hint of humor or enjoyment was gone from the man's voice now.

Veronica couldn't remember the exact exchange—the past few days had been rife with distraction—but that sure as hell didn't sound like her.

"I thought you'd be happy for me, Veronica."

"Then you thought wrong, Cole. This is a completely rash decision. Did you even think about how much it costs to become a PI? What about getting a license? Did you do any research at all?"

Cole put his glass down on the table and stared at her.

"I did my research. As an ex-cop, I'll have no problem getting a license. As for costs? It's about five hundred bucks in fees or whatever. I could set up shop right out of our—" he stopped himself, but Veronica knew what he was going to say.

Our home.

But it wasn't their home. It was *hers*.

"I'm sorry, I can't be happy for you, Cole. It's just... it's just... this is too much." *Everything* was too much. Too fucking much. "Please... I—I think you should leave."

Cole was aghast.

"*What?* What did I do?"

Veronica stepped away from the door.

"Yeah, please. You should go."

"What are you talking about, Veronica? I didn't mean to upset you, I thought that—"

"I'm sorry, Cole, please, I just need some time, okay?"

Cole made a face.

"Veronica, what did I do? I thought things between us were great. I get why you're concerned about this whole PI thing, but I've got some money saved up. It's not that big a deal. I left on good terms, too, so if things don't work out, I can go back."

Veronica felt guilt threatening to overwhelm her again. Cole didn't deserve this. She should be happy for him, nervous, sure, but also happy.

But she wasn't.

She was just annoyed.

And that was telling.

It wasn't fair for her to be with Cole, not now.

She liked him, but she didn't love him. But it was clear as day that Cole loved her. Even though he hadn't explicitly said it, she could tell. Veronica could tell every morning she woke up next to him and saw that expression in his soft eyes.

"I'm sorry," she said, staring at her empty champagne glass as if it were the most interesting thing in the world. "Please leave."

"Veronica, I don't—"

Her eyes shot up.

"Cole, leave my house. *Now.*"

He raised his hands and took a step back. She thought she saw tears in his eyes. If he started to cry, Veronica didn't know what would happen. Most likely, she would break down, too.

"Okay, okay—it's your house. Can I just grab my—"

"No. Go now. You can get your stuff tomorrow."

Cole left his glass on the table and took a wide berth around her as if fearing she would physically lash out before opening the door and heading onto the front porch.

Once there, he turned.

"Veronica, I'm sorry for whatever I—"

She closed the door, locked it, and rested her forehead against the cool metal.

This wasn't fair.

Veronica grabbed the champagne from the table and drank directly from the bottle.

No, it wasn't fair at all.

But where in the manual did it ever claim to be? Where in the *fuck* did life ever claim to be fair?

Life was raw, unfiltered, hateful, obsessive, painful, and occasionally bright, but never fair.

Never, ever fair.

Chapter 23

DEA AGENT TROY ALLISON WAS right: it took very little effort to turn Steve from Bear County sheriff into a generic, and thus unrecognizable, addict. A little dirt on his face, a soiled hoodie and messy hair, and Steve fit right in.

His hands were jammed into the pockets of his dirty jeans, and in his right, he clutched the small baggie of white pills that Troy had signed out of evidence.

It was complicated to obtain product from the evidence locker via legal means, even when the DEA was involved. Things got especially dicey when their plan was *not* to return said evidence. It was easier because Steve was the sheriff and Troy was with the DEA, but it wasn't *easy* by any stretch.

Dozens of photographs were taken, and forms signed.

Pages of protocols were to be read, of all things.

They skimmed over that part.

Steve had wanted opioids, of course, but Troy insisted that the best way to get in with the crew was to offer Kendrick 'Trigger' Holchester ecstasy. So, that's what he had in his hand now, a bag of ecstasy worth maybe four hundred dollars.

A trade, that's the story that Troy had armed him with. Trade the E for some H, see if the product has the insignia on it. If it does, they intended to up the stakes. Try to work on trading larger quantities.

McVeigh had wanted more details, develop a deeper back story, but Steve had decided against it. He didn't want to sound too rehearsed.

Now, though, as he was forced to duck into alley after alley to avoid being seen by what felt like a Greenham cop on every corner, Steve began to reconsider their hastiness.

A tarp flapped in the wind, and he realized that he'd worked his way back to the crime scene he'd stopped in front of earlier that day.

That was another minor detail that they'd neglected to consider while discussing the undercover operation: the fact that someone had just murdered a junkie and torn his lungs out.

A junkie who, in all honesty, didn't look all that different than Steve did now.

This should have been front of mind, but it wasn't.

As of late, Steve's focus had become singular in nature and chemical in desire.

"You looking to score?"

The voice came out of nowhere and Steve jumped. That was okay—that was in character. When junkies weren't high, they were on edge. It was the chemicals that smoothed them out.

Just past the place where Bunky had taken his last breath, a dark shadow leaned against the wall.

"Trade," Steve said, intentionally making his voice sound raw and distressed. "I want to trade."

The man pushed off the wall and stepped into the light. It wasn't Trigger or Toots, but a sleepy white man wearing a T-shirt at least four sizes too big for him. He had a rose tattoo on the side of his neck, which stood out on his pale skin.

Steve made note of the ink as he continued forward.

"A fuckin' trade?"

Steve pulled his hand out of his pocket and held up the bag of E.

"Pharma grade, man, good shit. Got so much of it, I-I can't move it, you know? I want to trade it for something else."

The man eyed him up and down.

"It's good, I promise. I got this source, he—"

The man snatched the bag from him. Steve had been holding it lightly, and it was gone before he could tighten his grip.

"Hey!"

He reached for it, but the man pointed at his chest, his hand shaped like a gun.

Steve backed down.

"Don't fuckin' move."

This was another risk: Steve being robbed and beaten. Probably not killed, but it wasn't outside the realm of possibility.

Sinner.

"I just thought that Trigger might want some, you know? Like, to trade?"

The man, who had been looking into the bag as he shook it, suddenly glared at Steve.

"How you know Trigger?"

"I don't, I just heard."

The man sucked his teeth and reached into his pocket. Steve surreptitiously slid his hand behind his back, not quite reaching for the pistol tucked out of sight, but getting ready, just in case. But instead of pulling out of a weapon of his own, the man in the giant T-shirt withdrew a small white pouch about the size of a book of matches.

Steve recognized what it was immediately, but his junkie persona did not.

"What's that?"

"Shut the fuck up."

The man took one of the white pills and dropped it into the pouch. He then proceeded to squeeze and massage it.

After about only ten seconds, the liquid in the pouch turned a dark purple and then, a few seconds after that, black. Steve had used many a Marquis reagent test during his days as a State Trooper during roadside stops. They were used to determine whether a drug was real or not and occasionally to identify an unknown compound that was suspected to be controlled. The tests were notoriously inaccurate, and these results were often thrown out in court, but they were enough to slap the cuffs on.

"Shit, you ain't lyin'. Where you say you got this from, again?"

"I didn't."

"Huh. Stay here."

"My—" *Shit*. The man was gone, moving quickly down an alley and then out of sight, leaving Steve to just stand there, wondering if he'd been robbed after all.

Fuck.

Five minutes passed. At around seven, a slow-moving cop car turned down the street and Steve became one with the shadows.

They must have increased patrols, he thought. *Trying to find out who killed Jake. Or to deter another attack.*

Steve didn't even hear the man coming.

He felt a hand on his shoulder, but this was just a distraction. By the time Steve spun around, the gun had already been pulled from his waistband.

"Nice piece." It was Trigger. He cut an imposing figure with broad shoulders and a thick chest. His afro was larger than in the mugshot Troy had shown him, and he appeared to have a word tattooed above his left eye, only it was too dark to read it.

Steve held up his hands.

"Give my fuckin' gun back, man."

Trigger turned the pistol on its side and pointed it at Steve.

"You ain't in no position' to make demands, nigga."

Steve's heart was beating fast, but he didn't let his cop instincts take over; he had to remember why he was here in the first place.

"Fuck, man, I wanted to trade, man. Your fuckin' boy jacked my shit. Good shit—and-and-and I can get more."

Trigger squinted one yellowy eye.

"What's your name?"

"Steve."

Shit, his first slip. He should have come up with something else.

"Alright, *Steve*." Trigger tucked the gun into the front of his pants and held up the bag of ecstasy. "Where you get dis from?"

Steve just shrugged, a pained expression on his face.

"Alright. I respect dat. Ain't goin' tell me even wit' a gun on ya. My man said you can get more?"

"I can." Steve licked his lips. He was agitated but he wasn't sure he was acting anymore. He was close. Really close. Usually, around this time he'd already taken his daily vitamin shot, but Steve had decided against it tonight. Not only would it have been logistically difficult with McVeigh and Troy around, but he had to keep his wits about him. Sometimes, his nightly dose hit hard, knocked him out completely. "Every week, I get about the same. But-b-b-but I-I could get more. Like lots more."

The way Trigger kept staring at the bag of ecstasy confirmed what Troy had said. He was desperate to pop one or maybe two of the chalky white discs into his mouth.

"I can give you cash. This about—"

"I wanna trade. Trade for some smack."

Trigger just stared at the drugs. Then he grabbed Steve's gun and pulled it out again.

"Nigga, you come into my house and want to deal your shit?"

"N-n-n-no." Steve shook his head. "Not deal, man. I-I just want to trade."

Trigger angled the gun again.

"What the piece for then?"

"Fuckin' protection, man!"

Steve really hoped that the thug chose another time to earn his nickname.

"I'm keepin' the gat. That's the tax, nigga. I'ma give you... five beans a pill. You got like two hundred—"

"Two-fifty."

"—two-hundred pills." Trigger looked skyward. "That's worth twelve bags."

Even though Steve knew he was getting absolutely hosed—his E was worth in excess of five hundred bucks on the street, and twelve bags was worth about two hundred, give or take—but he wasn't in any position to negotiate.

"Okay. Okay."

Losing the gun was a nightmare, too. But thankfully, McVeigh of all people had suggested that they swap out his service pistol for something untraceable.

Steve gestured for the drugs, but Trigger wasn't ready to give them up just yet.

"No selling in Needle Point."

"I know, I won't. I just—"

"No, nigga, hear what I'm sayin': no sellin' in Needle Point. I catch you sellin' anything, I'ma drop you. That means your Molly or my gear, got it?"

"Yeah. Yeah."

"Next week, if you want more, bring me more, *Steve*."

"Yeah, I will."

Trigger had a mean stare and he used it. Steve was so locked in that he barely picked up on the man's nod. He did, however, see the twelve small bags of heroin that came out of the darkness and littered the ground.

Then he dropped to his knees and started to pick them up because that's what fiends did.

When he'd finally collected all of the bags, Trigger was gone, and Steve found himself alone.

But his heart was still racing. He wasn't sure if this was a result of having a gun pointed at him by a man named Trigger, or if he was just excited.

Steve tried to calm himself by inspecting one of the bags. The strange thing was, every bag that he'd ever bought from Bunky was blank—no logo, no words, nothing. Yet, Troy had said that Jake was the man who was moving this new stuff out of New York or Colombia or wherever it was coming from.

Steve knew this couldn't be true. Unless, of course, Bunky was rebranding his gear. And why would he do that?

It made no sense. Not only was it a lot more work, but Troy asserted that this new stuff was cheaper and better.

Fentanyl problems notwithstanding.

But this stuff? Trigger's stuff? Every single bag had a stamp of the snake eating the eyeball on it.

The plan had been for Steve to make a connection with Trigger or Toots. If things went well, and this definitely qualified, gun issue or not, then Steve would walk to Meadowbrook and meet up with Troy who was standing by. Under normal situations, the DEA would swoop in and immediately pick Trigger up the second the trade was made and get both the E and H off the street. Then they would squeeze Trigger.

But Troy had already told him that this wouldn't work. Instead, he wanted Steve to forge a relationship with Trigger. See if he could trade up. Get to Toots, go from there. Their main goal was to find out where this new shit was coming from and how it was getting into Oregon.

Steve flicked the powder in one of the bags.

That had been *their* plan—mostly Troy and Steve with a little bit of McVeigh sprinkled in.

But *his* plan? Steve's plan was slightly different.

Without consciously thinking about it, he had slunk deeper into the alley in the direction that Trigger had disappointed. Then, before he knew it, he was pulling out a syringe, a spoon, a lighter.

He had to try it. He *had* to.

He *needed* to.

It was easily explainable—hell, he could even use the whole gun thing to his advantage if he got caught.

Trigger stole my gun. Said he thought I was a cop. Told me I had to inject to prove that I wasn't. I know it could be tainted! I know! But… but, like you said, people are dying out there. What was I supposed to do, anyway? He had my gun. I couldn't just say hold on a second and give you a call. I… I had to do it.

And he did.

Steve shot the heroin into his forearm and then he waited.

Waited for that rush, that numbness, that—

Normally, he had a moment to remove the needle before it hit him. This time around, Steve had no time at all. The drugs hit him so hard that his eyes raced to the back of his skull.

It was good—no, it was great.

Until it wasn't.

Steve felt his lungs suddenly expand so large that he feared they might break his ribs.

Then he collapsed and started to seize, his head making a dull thudding sound each time it bounced off the cracked pavement.

Chapter 24

VERONICA'S PHONE RANG INCESSANTLY, WORMING its way into her dreams, but she didn't wake. She didn't even stir when the pounding on her front door first began.

But then the two sounds mixed together, and she was finally dragged from her slumber.

What the hell is going on?

Bleary-eyed, Veronica rolled over and grabbed her phone just as it went to voicemail.

It was two-thirty in the morning.

Bam, bam, bam.

Veronica swung her legs over the side of her bed and tried to sit up. A bout of nausea struck her, and she closed her eyes until it passed. Then, still lying down, she looked at her phone.

Four missed calls, all from Freddie.

Even hazy as her mind was, she could only think of one reason why her partner would be calling her at this hour.

"Fuck."

Veronica slowly sat up, rose to her feet, and then made her way downstairs, all of which took longer than it should have.

Unsurprising, the man who was still banging on the door with the ball of his hand was Freddie.

When Veronica opened the door, Freddie had been looking off to one side and nearly fell into her.

"Shit, sorry," he grumbled.

"What's going on?" she asked, even though she already knew.

"We have another one. Another sinner."

Veronica pulled the skin beneath her eyes down.

What had the captain said again?

Something along the lines of not wanting another victim before going to the media?

"Okay." She released her face, but her skin didn't seem to want to rebound. "Give me five."

Veronica left Freddie standing in the doorway while she rushed upstairs, popped a few Advil, and took a quick shower. She stood under the icy water for a full minute, trying to clear the alcohol-induced fog. When she was done, Veronica figured she was twenty-percent drunk and ten-percent hungover.

"Here." Freddie handed her a coffee, but she had no idea where he'd gotten it from. It wasn't in his hand when he'd been trying to break down her door. Had he gone to the store when she'd been in the shower? Or had he had it all along in his car?

Either way, she was grateful.

"Thanks."

"You want to drive or...?" Freddie gestured toward his car.

Veronica wanted to drive—she'd gotten used to driving herself around during Freddie's leave of absence. But she couldn't. If she got pulled over, Veronica figured that the chance of her blowing over the limit was sitting at fifty-fifty. And there were a lot of people who would relish the opportunity for her to slip up and wouldn't hesitate to use it to finally cut her loose.

Now that was a PR nightmare that the city of Greenham and herself, perhaps, might not recover from.

"You can drive."

Veronica's second surprise of this early day—the first being rudely awoken—was considerably more pleasant: the interior of Freddie's vehicle was clean.

There were no balled-up fast-food wrappers littering the back seat, no twenty-ounce soft-drink cups jammed into the holder, there weren't even any stray French fries on the floor.

It even smelled okay. Not good, *per se*, but *okay*. And that was a considerable step from what she was used to.

Veronica took a large gulp of her coffee.

"Alright," she said with a sigh. "What've we got?"

"Officer Furnelli responded to a tip of something going down in an alley in Needle Point not far from where Jake Thompson was killed. By the time he arrived, it was too late. Another victim, similar to the others, with SINNER written in blood."

"Shit," Veronica cursed. "Any idea who the victim is?"

"Not yet."

"Another dealer?"

"Don't know. They're running his fingerprints, but I haven't heard if they've gotten a match yet."

Veronica went to drink more coffee only to find her cup already empty.

"Captain Bottel's not gonna be happy about this," she muttered under her breath.

"Nope."

They actually passed the dirty tarped area where Jake had been killed before stopping about a mile, mile and a half south. They were still technically in Needle Point, but near the border of Cedar Heights.

They parked in front of a Greenham squad car and got out. Officer Furnelli greeted them.

"Do you ever sleep?" Veronica asked.

"Do you?" the man shot back, a grin on his face.

"I try."

"So do I, but I was never good at it."

"Me neither." He started walking and Veronica and Freddie followed. "I don't know if Detective Furlow told you, but this one's a bit different than the other two."

"How so?"

"It's probably best if I just show you."

Veronica shook out her hands as she walked. The coffee had done its job.

She was now ten percent drunk and twenty percent hungover. The crime scene was destined to sober her up entirely, only Veronica wasn't sure if that was what she wanted.

Another alley—it seemed that if someone were to design a haven for drug dealers, criminals, and junkies, Needle Point would be the blueprint.

Furnelli lifted a ribbon of yellow crime scene tape with the blade of his hand to allow Veronica to duck under. No tarp this time, no chair either. But as she neared the body, her synesthetic reaction was the same: reds, oranges, and yellows flitting across her vision like watercolor motes.

The victim, a male, in his early forties to mid-fifties, wasn't lying with his back exposed. He was slumped against a wall, legs splayed, hands open at his sides. His wrists had been slashed in long vertical strokes. Above his head, written in blood, was a single word: SINNER.

The man was shirtless, but it was difficult to see his back with his body pressed against the wall. Veronica moved to get a better angle. His skin appeared scratched, but that might have been from rubbing against the coarse brick.

"No wings this time?" Veronica asked, a little stumped.

"I don't think so. Haven't touched the body, though—was waiting for you guys and the coroner."

Veronica pulled her sleeve over her hand and moved the man's body away from the wall.

"No wings," she confirmed. Veronica scratched her chin. "What do you think happened? Our unsub was rushed? Didn't have time to finish the job?"

Like her, Freddie was staring intently at the body.

"Maybe. But why the wrists and not the throat this time?" He pointed at the multiple gashes on the man's skin. "Throat would be more efficient, and wrists seem like a de-escalation, if anything."

Veronica shrugged and looked at Court.

"Is Kristin bringing Dr. Thorpe this time around?"

"Unfortunately not. Dr. Thorpe had to head back to Portland."

Veronica glanced around the crime scene. Light was weak in the alley, but the victim wasn't all the way at the back. If someone had the correct angle, they might just be able to see him from the street.

To test this theory, Veronica backed up, ignoring Court's curious gaze.

Yeah, you can see him. Maybe not his upper body, but his legs for sure.

And if you *could* see something in Needle Point, then someone had. Because there were eyes everywhere.

The streets were poorly lit on account of neglected streetlamps, but Veronica still spotted some movement half a block away.

Veronica squinted and started in that direction. The person's outline was familiar and unmistakable.

Thankfully, they didn't run this time.

"Hey!" Veronica called, waving her hand above her head.

The man was standing in front of an alcove of what might have been a barbershop. As she approached, he moved onto the sidewalk.

"Hi," Veronica said softly. "Do you remember me?"

The man nodded.

"Police... police... police..."

"Right. I'm with the police. Did you see anybody out here tonight?"

More emphatic nodding, sending his chins flapping, which reminded her of the old Freddie.

"Good. Do you know what they look like, or—"

"Midnight blue... midnight blue... midnight blue..." The man pointed away from the murder scene.

"Wait, the same car? The same one as the last time? When you saw the monster?"

The word 'monster' made the man stop nodding.

"Star... star... star..."

That was enough confirmation for Veronica.

"Show me." When the man didn't move, Veronica repeated the order. This time, he slumped his shoulder and started to walk.

"Veronica? Where you going?" Freddie called out.

Recalling how the man in the Oregon State sweatshirt had reacted negatively to Court's presence the last time they'd approached him, Veronica hollered over her shoulder, "It's fine, stay there. I'll be back."

"Back... back... back."

The man led her down the street, took two turns, and stopped abruptly.

"Car... car... car..."

Veronica's jaw dropped. The vehicle was indeed midnight blue, but she quickly realized that the man repeating 'star' had nothing to do with the sky or her badge.

There was a star on the side of the car.

It was Sheriff Steve Burns' car.

"The man who owns this car, have you seen him?" Veronica grabbed him by the sweatshirt and pulled him close. He reeked of urine. "Where is the man who owns this car?"

"There... there... there..."

Once again, he pointed, but even though he started to move, Veronica knew that something was terribly wrong, and she didn't wait.

She broke into a run, glancing down every alley she passed without slowing.

Where are you, Steve?

Desperation crept into her thoughts.

Where are you?

Five minutes... she'd been running for five minutes and nothing —

Black boots.

Veronica spotted a pair of black boots. They were the only thing that she could see in a particularly dark passage — a thruway, perhaps, or maybe it was another alley. If the toes of these boots hadn't been routinely polished, she would have missed them.

"Steve!" Veronica shouted as she turned and sprinted toward the fallen man.

It was Steve.

He was lying on his back, his eyes closed. His entire body was blue, but Veronica couldn't tell whether this was because he was sweating or if this was the actual color of his skin.

The foam in the corners of his mouth suggested the latter.

Veronica dropped to her knees and only then did she notice the needle sticking out of his arm. She pulled it out and tossed it aside before putting her ear to his lips.

He wasn't breathing.

"Help! I need help!"

She moved her head to his chest.

Still nothing.

"Help me!" Veronica screamed as she started CPR. "Help! I need Narcan! *Narcan!* Freddie, *help!*" She pushed even harder on his chest. "Don't fucking die on me, Steve! *Don't fucking die on me!*"

Chapter 25

OFFICER FURNELLI ARRIVED FIRST, AND he came with Narcan in hand. Veronica grabbed the pre-loaded needle from him and jammed it into Steve's shoulder. For a heart-stopping moment, nothing happened. Then, Steve gasped, sputtered, and his eyes flew open.

"Thank God," Veronica whispered, holding Steve's head as he gulped air. "Thank God."

"What the hell? Veronica, what the hell happened here?" Freddie had arrived at Court's side. "Is that... is that Steve?"

Tears streamed down Veronica's cheeks and even though she wanted to answer, speech was impossible. She overheard Court confirm that it was the sheriff, and her partner called it in.

Things slowly started to happen around her—Court was examining the scene, Freddie was backing onto the street, waving someone over—but Veronica just cradled Steve's head in her arms.

What happened? What happened to you, Steve?

Even though the man was breathing now, his eyes were still glazed over.

"I'm sorry." That was the only thing Veronica could manage to say. She choked out a sob. "I'm so sorry."

"Ambulance will be here in two minutes," Freddie exclaimed. Veronica kept her eyes locked on Steve as she brushed his hair from his forehead. "Spoke with Deputy McVeigh, said he'll meet us at the hospital with the DEA."

Veronica sniffed again and was finally able to look at her partner.

"DEA?"

Freddie shrugged.

"I don't know... McVeigh said he would fill us in there." Freddie bit his lower lip. "Veronica? What the hell happened here?" He looked down and to his right, his eyes lingering on the syringe that Veronica had pulled from the crook of Steve's elbow.

"I—" she began but was interrupted by a flood of memories. Of Steve standing in her loft bedroom, fury on his face. Shouting at her for his drugs. Drugs that she'd just flushed. "Fuck." Veronica sobbed and looked skyward as tears spilled down her cheeks.

Freddie immediately dropped to her level.

"It's okay," he said, rubbing her back. "It's okay. Whatever happened, Steve's alive. We'll get through this."

They remained this way, with Steve's head in Veronica's lap and Freddie squatting while he gently massaged her back, until the ambulance arrived.

Even then, it took two EMTs to coax Veronica to release her hold on Steve. They loaded him onto a gurney and hooked him up to some monitoring equipment.

"Is he going to be okay?" Officer Furnelli asked. Veronica was fairly certain that the question was directed at her, but one of the EMTs took it upon themselves to answer.

"BP is stable," the man said as he used some sort of thick leather straps to tightly secure Steve's wrists to the metal gurney.

"Wh-what are you doing?" Veronica asked.

The EMT ignored her and continued to speak to Court.

"But if this is his fourth or fifth overdose, things might get dicey."

"Fourth or fifth..." Veronica was trying to wrap her head around this when the EMT moved to Steve's legs next. Like his wrists, the sheriff's ankles were also slipped into leather straps. "What are you doing? Stop."

"Ma'am, this is for our protection. Sometimes when Narcan is administered, these addicts can get fast-tracked into withdrawal. They can be violent and—"

"Stop!" Veronica yelled. She grabbed the EMT's hand and forced him to let go of Steve's ankle.

The EMT looked to Court for help but everyone, including the officer, was so taken aback by the scene that they did nothing.

"Ma'am, please do not—"

"This isn't an addict!" Veronica spat. "It's the fucking sheriff!"

"The sher—"

The EMT leaned closer to Steve and observed his face. Then his eyes widened.

"Oh, shit, I didn't know."

"And she's not ma'am. She's a detective," Freddie said, finally finding his tongue.

The EMT backed up.

"Look, I'm sorry. This—I—what—" he finished this incomplete sentence with a series of mouth sounds.

Veronica had already unstrapped Steve's ankles and was now working on his wrists.

"He's not an addict," she repeated softly.

A hint of gas entered her nostrils and, unwilling to accept what this meant, Veronica held her breath.

"I really… the sheriff…"

Freddie put a strong hand on the rambling EMT's shoulder.

"Just get him to the hospital."

"Yeah, right, of course." But the EMT still didn't move.

"Now!" Freddie snapped.

The EMT finally sprung to action, looking at his partner who had said and done practically nothing—*Do ambulances have Uber drivers now?* Veronica wondered incoherently—since arrival. Even now, in the height of the confusion, he just shrugged and got behind the wheel. It was on Court to help the EMT load the gurney into the back of the ambulance.

All the while, Veronica refused to let go of Steve's hand.

"What about the body?" she asked when the EMT started to close the rear ambulance doors.

"Don't worry about that," Freddie replied. "Just worry about him."

"Thank you."

The doors closed and the lights flashed.

***

"Do you think he's going to be alright?" Officer Furnelli asked as both he and Freddie watched the ambulance drive off.

Freddie wasn't sure. He wasn't even sure what the fuck just happened.

The sheriff dressed in a dirty sweatshirt, his face covered in filth, overdosing in a Needle Point alley?

What the hell?

He'd been gone for a while and had expected some changes but…

"I hope so."

And he did. But there was nothing they could do for Steve now.

"Let's get an officer here to collect evidence of… well, to collect evidence while we go back to our vic. Yeah?" He couldn't remember sounding this uncertain while on duty, but he couldn't remember anything like this ever happening, either.

Steve? Overdose on heroin in an alley?

"Sounds good."

Freddie had to pinch himself to make sure he wasn't dreaming.

"Coming?"

He shook his head.

"Yeah."

The crime scene that he'd only briefly examined served as a formidable distraction. As Veronica had pointed out, it was different from the others. So different that if it weren't for the word 'sinner' written in blood, he would've thought it unrelated. This was Needle Point, after all, home to the highest concentration of overdoses in Greenham. Also, the highest concentration of murders.

A copycat?

Highly unlikely. To Captain Bottel's dismay, they had yet to release details of any of the crimes to the public.

Was Veronica right? Was the killer rushed?

Freddie grabbed a flashlight and a pair of gloves from Officer Furnelli.

Three deaths in three days.

Whoever was behind this was hell-bent on wreaking havoc.

Or punishing sinners.

"Detective Furlow?"

"Yeah?" Freddie was in the process of raising one of the victim's wrists to get a better look at the wounds.

"I think this is his wallet."

Freddie raised an eyebrow and looked at the cop. He was indeed holding a wallet between gloved fingers.

"Well? Open it."

"Right." Court opened the wallet and looked inside. "Aaron Decker. Lives in Meadowbrook."

"Get someone to look him up in the system," Freddie ordered as he turned back to the body.

Blood coated the man's jeans and thigh. The cuts almost looked self-inflicted, with no hesitation marks or signs of struggle. Freddie checked the man's nails and was surprised, and disappointed, to find them clear of blood or debris.

Freddie studied the man's face. Aaron's expression was calm, serene. If it weren't for his pallor from blood loss, Freddie might have thought him sleeping.

Or dead from a drug overdose.

How did you get here? What were you doing here?

Freddie stood up straight and tried to take in the scene as a whole. The body, the blood, the lettering.

The lettering...

There was something different about that as well. It took Freddie a few seconds to figure it out.

"Hey, Court? The other scenes... sinner was written in all caps, wasn't it?"

"Yep."

"Not here—the 'e' is smaller case here."

Court wandered over.

"No shit. Why—"

"Detective Furlow? What happened?" Both men turned to see the Bear County coroner hustling over to them, a black case in one hand. "Someone said that Sheriff Burns was in some sort of accident?"

Fuck.

The news was already getting out.

"I don't know. I really don't know," Freddie replied. "I just hope that he's going to be okay."

"What the hell? Did he—"

Freddie cut Kristin off.

"I don't know."

Kristin was clearly confused, her gray eyebrows nearly touching at the center, but she detected something in Freddie's voice and decided not to ask again.

"Alright. What do we have here, then?"

"Aaron Decker, forty-four years old. Lives in Meadowbrook," Furnelli said, reading from the man's wallet. "On his red cross card here, says he has a wife, Sylvia Decker. And... it looks like he sells cars for a living...?"

"Rap sheet?" Freddie asked.

"Don't know."

Kristin pulled a telescopic stage light from her bag and set it up. Freddie squinted and shielded his face. When his eyes adjusted, he took another look at the body. Now, Aaron looked dead.

The man wasn't just pale, but his skin looked waxy and devoid of any color at all. Freddie was about to look away when something that was partially covered by one of the man's legs reflected the light. He reached beneath Aaron's thigh and used a gloved hand to pick it up.

It was a razor blade.

"Looks like our guy got sloppy," Freddie said, holding the blade up to the light.

"Finally, some good news."

The second the words left Court Furnelli's mouth both Kristin and Freddie knew that he immediately regretted them.

There was no good news.

Not on a day like today.

Not with Aaron Decker dead and Sheriff Steve Burns in the hospital.

Chapter 26

EVEN BEFORE HE HEARD THE bear, Steve knew it was behind him. It was a feeling, like when you sensed someone staring at you even when you couldn't see them.

Then he heard it: a deep, throaty growl, a snort, followed by a blast of hot air in his ear.

He ran.

Steve ran as fast as he could, his arms pumping, lungs burning.

The animal was behind him, gaining on him.

The recurring nightmare was always the same. And Steve was all too familiar with overwhelming fear and anxiety that was like poison coursing through his veins.

Just when he felt the bear's rancid breath on his neck, Steve turned.

And there was no bear at all.

In its place was his wife, Julia Burns.

"Why did you do this to me, Steve? Why?" She held her hands out, displaying the ragged slices across her arms, running vertically and horizontally like a patchwork of stitches.

"Why? *Why?*"

***

Veronica glanced at her phone, hoping that it was Freddie calling but it wasn't.

It was Cole.

She didn't answer.

As she put the phone away, her eyes drifted to Steve in the hospital bed.

He was dead. The man's eyes were open, and he was staring blankly at the ceiling. For some reason, this didn't shock Veronica as much as it should have.

Then Steve blinked and Veronica, who hadn't realized she was holding her breath, inhaled sharply.

Steve's eyes drifted to her, and his face twisted into a mask of confusion.

"Where... where am I?"

Veronica sobbed once—just one solitary sob—and then she grabbed Steve's hand and squeezed it. The doctors had said that his heart was going to be fine. What they were really worried about was his brain.

When Veronica had found him in the alley, he'd been blue from lack of oxygen. There was no way of telling how long Steve's brain had been deprived.

But the fact that he was speaking was definitely a positive sign.

"In the hospital, Steve. Can you... can you remember anything?"

Steve blinked and swallowed dryly. Veronica brought the straw jutting out of a cup of water to his lips and the sheriff drank greedily.

"I was in Needle Point," he said after swallowing. "I was in Needle Point when—"

The hospital door blew open and Deputy Marcus McVeigh entered with a big bald man whom Veronica didn't recognize in tow.

"Detective Shade," McVeigh said with a nod in her direction. He looked past her to Steve. "Can we have a moment alone with the sheriff?"

Veronica curled her upper lip.

"No."

"Detective—"

"It's okay," Steve croaked. "It's fine—she's okay."

"Sheriff, we—" McVeigh was interrupted by the bald man who roughly pushed by him and moved toward the bed. He reeked of cigarette smoke and didn't so much as acknowledge Veronica.

"Who gave you the hot dose?" he demanded. "Was it Trigger? Did Trigger do it? I'll fucking strangle that prick."

"He just woke up," Veronica protested, but her words went unnoticed.

"I don't... I don't remember."

Veronica thought she smelled gas when Steve answered but couldn't be sure because of the cigarette stench.

"It was probably that prick Trigger." The bald man turned to look at Veronica. "When you found him, did you see any drugs around him? Any baggies? Baggies with a snake and an eyeball on them?"

Veronica stared at the man in disbelief and then finally came to her sense.

"Who the fuck are you?"

The man didn't skip a beat.

"Troy Allison, DEA. Did you find any drugs on the sheriff?"

Veronica glared at Troy.

"He almost fucking died. I don't give a shit about the drugs he might've had on him." She swiveled her head to face McVeigh. "What the fuck happened?"

McVeigh licked his lips before replying.

"Sheriff Burns went undercover, trying to find out how this new supply is getting into Greenham."

Veronica wasn't sure she'd heard correctly. An undercover operation wasn't unusual but having the sheriff himself go undercover? That was like a CEO of a waste management company rooting through the trash.

It didn't make sense.

"*What?*"

McVeigh turned nearly as pale as the victim in the alley.

"Yeah. This new supply—"

"It was my idea, Veronica," Steve said.

Veronica looked at him and then at the DEA Agent.

No, I don't think so. I think it was your idea, she thought, eying the much bigger man.

"It doesn't matter whose idea it was," Troy said. "What matters is that we find out who—"

"Give it a fucking rest," Veronica ordered.

"Who the hell are you?" the man shot back, repeating her words from moments ago.

"A detective with Greenham PD. And last time I checked, Needle Point is in Greenham. Running an undercover operation in my city without—"

"Stop it," Steve said. He broke into a cough, drawing everyone's attention. "This is my fault… this is my fault. And yeah, Troy, the drugs had the same emblem you showed me, a snake eating an eyeball. Trigger's selling them."

"I fucking knew it."

Veronica didn't like Troy Allison. She'd known the man for a grand total of only five minutes but was certain she didn't like him.

She'd dealt with people like him before, people who cared only about their agenda.

In a way, he reminded her of Ken Cameron.

The door opened again.

"Gentlemen, you can't be in here," a doctor said as he tried to squeeze into the small room. He spotted Veronica. "Nobody can be in here."

"DEA," Troy stated.

The doctor was unimpressed.

"I don't care. You can't be in here."

McVeigh nudged Troy and the two men reluctantly exited the room.

Veronica didn't move.

"I'm sorry, but that means you too," the doctor said.

Veronica tightened her grip on Steve's hand.

"I'm staying," she said forcefully. "I don't care if you call security or get the SWAT team in here. I'm staying right by his side."

Like I should have done back at my house instead of kicking him out, Veronica thought but lacked the courage to say.

Chapter 27

THE DOCTOR GAVE STEVE SOMETHING to help him sleep, reassuring them both that more than likely, he would make a full recovery. Although they were still waiting for the toxicology report, the doctor also said there was a high likelihood that the heroin he'd been injected with was spiked with fentanyl.

He added that Steve was lucky to be alive.

The medication took effect quickly, and Steve was asleep before any awkward conversations could ensue. As he began snoring softly, Veronica kept a tight grip on his hand.

After McVeigh and the DEA's visit, she was stuck with more questions than answers.

Steve going undercover explained what he was doing in the alley while why he had gone undercover remained a mystery.

Steve being unconscious and not breathing was a result of heroin laced with fentanyl. How the drug got into his system was unknown.

If six months ago they hadn't had a big blow-up, Veronica could easily come up with the most realistic scenario that had put Steve in the hospital.

She knew that some dealers were paranoid. Perhaps this 'Trigger' that the DEA agent had mentioned had sold undercover Steve the drugs. But, thinking that he might be a cop, Trigger forced him to shoot up before leaving. And Steve was just stubborn and dedicated enough to do it.

That's when things turned bad and Trigger scooped up his product and fled, leaving Steve to die.

It was possible.

Unusual, irresponsible, but also possible.

Then there was their fight to consider: Veronica flushing the pills—his pills?—and Steve exploding in rage. And even before that, he'd been acting irrationally and short-tempered.

This reminded her of someone else.

Someone obscenely tall who had once been an addict and was now wiling away in a prison cell waiting for Veronica to do something.

Undercover or not, if Steve really was an addict, and all signs pointed to this being true, maybe he'd bought the drugs and decided to test them on his own accord.

Veronica slid her hand from Steve's and stared at his chalky complexion.

Her phone rang again, and she moved toward the door and answered softly.

"Hello?"

"Detective Shade, it's Kristin."

"Hey, what's up?" Veronica wasn't sure if the coroner was calling about Dylan or the crime scene.

"Just wrapping up here... victim's name is Aaron Decker, forty-four, wife, no kids, lives in Cedar Heights. Detective Furlow found a razor blade at the scene. Likely the murder weapon."

Both Cooper Mills and Jake Thompson had been killed with a knife—a kitchen knife, probably the same one.

Since finding Steve, Veronica hadn't thought about the case at all. But now, she remembered all the inconsistencies.

Including this new bit of information shared with her by the coroner.

"No injuries to his back?"

"Nothing substantial. As with the others, I'll do a tox screen on his blood. Dr. Thorpe is going to be difficult to reach in the next few days, but I don't think we'll need her." Kristin paused. "There's… there's another reason why I called you."

Steve was sleeping soundly, and Veronica slipped out of the room.

"What is it?"

"It's about our mutual friend, Dylan Hall."

Veronica looked through the glass at Steve and was once again struck by how bad he actually looked.

His cheeks were sunken, his eyes recessed, and his beard was longer than she'd ever seen it before.

"Yeah?" Veronica asked hesitantly. She knew this wasn't going to be good.

"The DA passed the case onto the assistant district attorney. I have a bit of a history with her."

Or maybe it was good news.

"And?"

"I managed to get them to offer a deal. To be honest? It's not bad, either."

"A deal?" Veronica rubbed her forehead aggressively. "No, no deals, Kristin. They weren't his drugs."

"Be that as it may, I have to run it by him, Veronica. They're offering sixty months in a medium-security prison. He might even be able to do it at Bear County Correctional. With good behavior, he'll be out in less than three years."

Veronica groaned.

"Three years?"

"It's a good deal, and I'm required to offer it to him. And, between us, if he asks—if Dylan asks my opinion, I'm going to suggest he takes it."

"What?" Veronica was incredulous. "Kristin, he didn't do it. They're not his drugs. I thought we were on the same page here."

Kristin fell silent for so long that Veronica took the phone away from her face to make sure the call was still connected.

"Kristin, he can't do three years for drugs that weren't his. He can't."

Dylan was a wreck. He'd done time before, lots of time, but Veronica suspected that he'd been high going in and was probably high while inside, too.

And three years... three years for something he didn't do?

"Veronica, we're out of time and out of options. We've gone over this, if this goes to trial, Dylan's looking at ten to fifteen. And if it goes to trial, he will be convicted. No jury is going to buy that he was set up. I know it's unfair, but those are the facts."

Veronica exhaled loudly.

This couldn't be the end of the road. This couldn't be it. She had to come up with something.

Fuck.

But with a murderer on the loose and now Steve...

Veronica closed her eyes.

"When?"

"I'm sorry?"

"How long before you have to bring the deal to Dylan?"

"Usually, twenty-four hours," the woman admitted. "But I can stretch that for another day, after all, I'm busy with these murders. I don't think the ADA would balk at that."

Veronica exhaled. She liked Kristin Newberry. The woman was smart and knew how to play the game.

"Thanks, Kristin."

"You're welcome. But if I don't hear anything from you, I'm going to bring the deal to Dylan. And I'm going to suggest he takes it."

The coroner knew how to play the game, but she was also a lawyer. And by all accounts, a good one.

"I understand," Veronica said. "And thanks again."

She hung up the phone and watched Steve's chest slowly rise and fall.

The murders… Steve… Dylan.

Ethan.

Freddie.

As much as she wanted to take care of everything herself, it simply wasn't possible.

Veronica needed help.

This… is a mistake, she thought, even as she dialed a number on her cell. Her call was answered on the first ring.

"I… I need your help. Can you meet me at my place?"

Chapter 28

COLE WAS WAITING OUTSIDE WHEN she arrived home, which Veronica thought strange considering that he had a key.

"Before you say anything, I just want to apologize," Cole said the minute she got out of her car. It wasn't even seven yet, but Cole, not a morning person by any stretch, appeared sharply coiffed and dressed.

He looked timid, which was also new.

And cute. She hated that he looked timid, nervous, and cute. Mostly because it just made her feel worse about how she'd treated him.

"I get that this is a big deal—I know that—and I shouldn't have put all that on you, Veronica. I didn't mean to. I was just excited. I'm sorry."

Fuck you, Cole, for being so damn good all the time.

"No, it's my fault. You did nothing wrong. Things with me are... complicated."

Cole cringed, and Veronica felt his pain.

Complicated? God dammit, you sound like a Spanish soap opera.

"You can go in and get your stuff."

Veronica didn't think that she could feel any worse, but she could.

Cole's expression made her feel like utter shit.

She'd been deliberately obtuse on the phone, and she could see, in a round-about way, how her words had been interpreted like her wanting to try and work things out. And judging by how crestfallen Cole was, that's exactly what the man thought was going to happen.

"Shit, I'm sorry, Cole. I really need some time by myself."

"I understand." His sudden professionalism stung her. "I'll just collect my things."

Even with permission, Cole still waited politely for her to open the door and enter first. The man immediately went upstairs. He hadn't come with any bags, so he just scooped up all his neatly arranged clothing in his arms. It was as pathetic as it was heartbreaking.

Veronica gave him a garbage bag. A fucking garbage bag. They'd been together for almost six months, practically living together, and she didn't even offer him a decent suitcase to move out with?

What's wrong with me? She chided herself. *What in the hell is wrong with me?*

After five minutes, the garbage bag was full of Cole's belongings, and he slung it over his shoulder. And then he gave her a sly grin because of course he did. He looked like an oldtimey pilgrim heading off to war in some desolate country.

Even though he'd been insulted and pretty much emasculated, he still had the audacity to have a sense of humor.

And to top things off, *she* was about to ask *him* for a favor.

"Cole, I'm in a bind, and I could really use your help." The smile vanished. "I know—I know this is fucked up. Like, really fucked up. But it could work out for both of us, you know? You're getting your first PI case, and I'm helping out an old friend."

It was clear by Cole's expression or lack thereof, that he wasn't sure whether she was being serious or not. This hurt Veronica too because if he thought she was joking then he also thought she was capable of being cruel.

Veronica sighed and Cole eased the tension by saluting her with his empty hand.

"CB Investigations open for business. You know, I pictured my first client meeting being a little different than this." He shook the garbage bag.

"Yeah, I bet you did—I bet you pictured yourself sitting in a smoking office and a pretty lady in a red dress comes in begging for your help."

"All that's missing is the red dress."

Veronica shrugged.

"I deserved that."

"Naw, not really. What can CBI do for you?"

"CBI? What kind of name is that? Sounds like a venereal disease."

"Work in progress. Anyways, I charge by the hour, so…"

Veronica spent the next five minutes telling her now ex-boyfriend about Dylan Hall and his predicament. It felt good to tell another person. Sure, she'd spoken several times to Kristin Newberry about the case, but the woman looked at everything through the lens of the lawyer, as she should, considering she was representing the man.

Cole listened intently, only once shifting his heavy garbage bag to the other shoulder. His features remained stoic throughout.

"What… what do you think?" Veronica asked, surprised at how nervous she felt. This was Dylan's last hope.

Cole sighed loudly.

"So, let me get this straight, for my first case, you want me to investigate a DEA case against a man who already has dozens of drug convictions? A man who had a kilo of heroin in his possession? Essentially, you want me to do the impossible?"

"Not impossible, but yeah, it'll be tough."

"And what timeline are we looking at, Veronica?"

Veronica felt the muscles in her neck tighten.

"One day. Maybe two."

Cole threw his head back and laughed.

"Wow, you must really hate me."

It was an offhand remark, just Cole being Cole, but Veronica took it seriously.

"I don't hate you, Cole."

"Oh, I know." The man suddenly grew serious. "You don't hate me, you hate yourself, Veronica."

Veronica immediately grew defensive.

"What? What the hell are you talking about?" The lack of sleep and the stress of the day, early as it was, not to mention her resurfacing hangover, had put her on edge.

"Don't get mad at me. I'm just calling it the way I see it. Just… forget it. I'll do my best to help Dylan."

He tried to slide by her, but she blocked his path.

"No, don't do that. You said it—now, tell me what you mean."

If last night hadn't happened, Veronica knew what Cole's reaction would have been. He would have made a joke, nuzzled her, kissed her, and that would have likely led to sex. But not today. Today, Cole was—rightfully—angry.

"Fine, you really want to know?"

In Veronica's experience, whenever someone said something of this nature, it was best to plug your ears and run.

Too bad Veronica pretty much did whatever was contrary to common sense. That was her MO.

"Yeah, tell me. What do you mean by, I hate myself?"

Cole took a deep breath before answering—another bad sign.

"Well, you forgave Steve—yeah, I heard about him going to the hospital and you joining him there. You forgave Freddie—he was there, too. And I know that you will, eventually, forgive your dad. Dr. Jane Bernard, as well. But there's one person that you will never forgive, Veronica: yourself."

EENIE, MEENIE, MINEY, MO.

"And it's really, really sad. I'm being serious. I care about you, whether we're together or not. You need to forgive yourself."

Once a killer, always a killer.

Veronica wiped tears from her eyes.

"I'm sorry, I didn't—"

"Just go."

"Veronica, I'm—"

Veronica went to the door and yanked it open.

"Just *go!*"

Chapter 29

"Mr. Decker had alcohol and lorazepam in his blood," Kristin remarked as she typed on her computer with one hand. In the other, she held a half-eaten breakfast sandwich wrapped in plastic. When she took a bite, Freddie couldn't take his eyes off it.

"Lorazepam?"

He couldn't remember the last time he had a breakfast sandwich. Two months ago? Three?

A long time, but he could still feel the texture between his teeth, the burst of fat as the sausage patty exploded on his tastebuds.

"Yeah." Kristin swallowed. "Basic sedative."

"Recreational?"

"Nope." She took another bite of her sandwich. "Helps you sleep, maybe. But in this case? I'm guessing the person who wanted him to sleep, didn't want him to wake up."

Freddie rubbed the back of his neck.

"So, he was drugged then. He had alcohol in his system, as well? Maybe someone slipped the sleeping drug into his drink?"

"Impossible to know for sure. But... probably. He died of exsanguination—bled out—like the others."

"Any chance his wounds were self-inflicted?"

"Can't tell for certain. I managed to send some images to Dr. Thorpe, and she couldn't confirm, either. She did, however, say that it was unlikely." Kristin zoomed in on images of the slits on Aaron Decker's wrists. "Notice anything different about these cuts?" She indicated first the left wrist and then the right.

"They look about the same," he said with a shrug.

"Yep, that's kinda the point. Let's assume he was right-handed and cut his left wrist first. These cuts are deep—he would've bled out hard and fast. Then he'd have to switch the razor blade to his other hand and then slice his right wrist. I would expect some of these cuts to be shallower as he lost energy, but they're all pretty much the same."

"You're saying he was murdered."

"Well, unless he got a nosebleed and used that blood to write on the wall before he decided to slit his wrists, then, yeah, I'd say so."

"Good point."

Kristin closed the image and finished her sandwich. Freddie felt almost remorseful that it was gone.

"I'm going to mark the cause of death as exsanguination and manner of death as a homicide." The computer pinged and Kristin smiled. "And we have a suspect!"

"Sorry?"

"Found a partial on the razor blade and put it in the system. That ping? That was a match." Kristin finished typing her report and then switched over to CODIS. "This here, Detective Furlow, is your primary suspect."

Freddie extended his chin as he moved his face closer to the screen. The man in the black and white photograph looked more like a car salesman than Aaron Decker. He was a spitting image of Bill Paxton from True Lies.

"Bobby Harvey? Who the hell is that?"

"Looks like he's a bit of a scumbag, at least according to his rap sheet. Multiple assaults and batteries, mostly with his ex-wife. Beat her up pretty bad... here... yeah, here's a photo."

Kristin clicked a button and an image of a woman with a badly bruised face appeared. This one was in full color and in graphic detail.

"Jesus. What is with these douchebags? Can you print that out—not the ex-wife, but the Bobby Harvey guy's sheet?"

"No problem."

A few seconds later, Freddie had a stack of papers in his hands, and he was sitting in his car.

Bobby Harvey… a serial wife abuser. A lot in common with Cooper Mills, actually. Only one was a victim and one was the perpetrator.

Except nothing in Bobby's past suggested a progression this… violent.

Well, he thought, *Captain Bottel wanted a suspect and now we have one.*

They also had another victim, but the captain didn't know that yet. Or, if he did, he hadn't said anything.

Freddie called Veronica, half-expecting her not to answer. She looked rough this morning when he'd woken her up, and he wouldn't have been surprised if she'd fallen asleep at the hospital with Steve.

But she answered and sounded wide awake.

"Veronica? How's Steve?"

"He's going to be okay. It's a long story. What's up?"

A long story, indeed.

Freddie still couldn't chase the horrible image of Steve lying on his back, Veronica pumping furiously on his chest. He would never say it, but his first thought was that the sheriff had been killed by the same person who had taken Jake, Cooper, and Aaron's lives.

"We found a razor blade at the scene, and it had a fingerprint on it. Belongs to a real scumbag, Bobby Harvey, who likes to beat up women. I'm thinking we should pay him a little visit." Freddie looked at the time on the dash. It was just after eight.

"Maybe we'll catch him sleeping. Unless, of course, you want to stay with the sheriff. I can call Court and—"

"No, I need to be there. I *want* to be there. Can you swing by and pick me up?"

"At the hospital?"

"No," Veronica replied hesitantly, "at home."

"Not a problem. I'm just leaving Bear County Morgue. I'll be there in fifteen."

Freddie hung up the phone and tapped it on his palm. Being out of the scene for as long as he had, Freddie wasn't up to date with Veronica's love life. Not that it was any of his business, but when it involved the Bear County sheriff it had the tendency of affecting their work.

He'd heard rumors that Veronica was dating Cole Batherson of all people, but the way that she'd reacted in the alley?

They'd all been stunned and shocked, but Veronica had been *ruined*.

She still loved him, that much was clear.

Steve and Veronica back together, Freddie and Veronica partnered up.

It was like old times.

So much so, that on the way to Veronica's house, Freddie stopped at McDonald's and grabbed two double cheeseburgers. He ate one in three bites, tossed the wrapper onto the floor of the backseat, and then started on the second.

Chapter 30

VERONICA CAUGHT A WHIFF OF grease the moment she entered Detective Furlow's car. Perhaps it was because the last time that she'd gotten in she'd been surprised at how clean it had been, or maybe it had been a while since she had smelled it and had grown sensitive. Either way, it only took her a few seconds to find the wrapper in the backseat. She tried not to stare too long, attempting to pass off her search for the source of the smell as a casual curiosity rather than judgment.

After all, she was in no position to judge anyone.

"Just a minor setback. I'll run an extra mile tomorrow," Freddie said, noticing her roaming eyes.

Figuring that this was his own personal justification, Veronica didn't bother commenting. Instead, she fell into thought.

Cole… forgive myself? What did he know, anyway? What did Dr. Patel know?

Everyone had an opinion about her, but they didn't *know*. They didn't know what she'd been through. They couldn't.

They wouldn't.

And, besides, she hadn't forgiven Steve, her father, or Jane. Maybe Freddie, but that was about it.

Forgive myself. How in the hell can I do that?

No, Cole didn't know anything.

Veronica had Freddie's laptop open on her lap and she used it to distract herself from her own toxic mind.

"So, this is the guy who killed Aaron Decker?"

"Sure seems that way."

Veronica twisted her lips.

"I can't find a single connection between Bobby Harvey and Cooper Mills or Jake Thompson." She scrolled back to Aaron Decker's socials. As one might predict from a car salesman, he had a lot of activity on many different sites. So far, nothing connecting him to either of the other two victims.

"Me neither. I didn't get a chance to look that deep yet, though."

"Why the MO change, you think? He went from these elaborate blood eagles—"

"Death Angels."

"Whatever, anyways, he goes to these elaborate lengths, but then this time he doesn't bother? Not only that, but he changes his murder weapon *and* leaves the razor blade with a fingerprint behind?"

Freddie grunted in frustration.

"I don't get it either. Doesn't seem... well, none of this seems right. Or normal. He had to have been spooked... I think?"

The image of the man in the Oregon State sweatshirt and the wide-set eyes flashed in her mind.

Monster... monster... monster...

Veronica shrugged.

"Yeah, maybe he was spooked."

"And yet, he still had time to write on the wall," Freddie said, challenging his own theory.

Veronica didn't reply this time.

There had to be a link between the victims. They just hadn't found it yet.

But the harder she looked, the more distant a possibility this became. There were no connections. Not only that, but Aaron didn't seem to fit the profile, as sketchy as it may be. Despite being from different walks of life, Cooper and Jake had criminal records.

Aaron did not.

Undoubtedly, he was a sinner—the man was a car salesman, after all—but so far as Veronica could tell, Aaron hadn't beat up his wife. He hadn't been arrested for tax fraud and she found no evidence of drug use, either.

Veronica sighed and closed the laptop.

"Nothing," she remarked. "I can't find a connection between any of them."

"Maybe we are dealing with something completely random," Freddie suggested. This wasn't the first time that this idea had arisen and wouldn't be the last.

But Veronica didn't like it.

Gloria Tramell had killed women whom she perceived had flirted with her husband because of the man's previous infidelity. Dante Fiori had killed people who associated with Veronica because he was obsessed with her, and jealous that even though they were both orphans, only she had been given the opportunity to live a normal life.

Their motives were undoubtedly twisted and bizarre, but they weren't random.

And Veronica was well aware of the strange dichotomy when it came to how people perceived violence and the risk of violence. People were both terrified and fascinated by random killings, especially when they involved serial killers. These were never completely random—most victims fit a profile, albeit occasionally obscure, like body shape or hairstyle—but the victim rarely did anything to incite the killer's wrath. The reality was that these types of murders were exceedingly rare. The vast majority of violent crimes were perpetrated by someone the victim knew, more often than not a family member or romantic partner. But people didn't find this fascinating or terrifying. Veronica surmised that this was probably a prime example of cognizant dissonance—after all, what were the chances of a good night's sleep if you couldn't stop thinking about the fact that the person most likely to smother you with a pillow was lying beside you?

"This is it." Freddie pulled over and parked outside a permanent trailer home. The interior appeared dark. "You want to take the front or the back?"

Veronica peered down the side of the cream-colored trailer. The lattice work that was intended to cover the cinder blocks propping up the trailer was mostly broken, giving a clear view beneath the trailer as well. It was packed with garbage.

"Back."

"Sounds good."

Both detectives exited the car, drawing their guns as they did. Veronica watched Freddie head to the front door while she hunkered down and proceeded down the side. A small, wooden back porch, worn and weathered, led to a neglected white door with a large inset window.

Veronica moved slowly up the steps, wincing at every creak. When she reached the top, she peered through the door. The trailer was so small that she could almost see out the other side.

The interior reminded her of the shitty hotel, The Phoenix, that Captain Bottel had set up Freddie and Veronica in when Dante was after her: old wallpaper, dated bedspreads, a maroon and green color scheme.

As Freddie knocked on the front door, a sound Veronica heard from around the side of the trailer as well as through it, she pressed her face against the dirty glass to get a better look inside.

She detected no movement, but that didn't mean Bobby wasn't in there. As Veronica continued to scan the interior of the trailer, she spotted something sticking out of the garbage. It was fabric, a sweatshirt maybe, dark in color, but darker in some spots.

It could be anything. Could be a kitchen towel with grease stains.

But it could also be the shirt that Bobby Harvey was wearing when he slit Aaron Decker's wrists.

Freddie stopped knocking and Veronica tried the door.

It was locked.

Veronica tapped the glass with the butt of her gun. It was cheap and weak. One hard rap, and it would—

"What are you doing?"

Veronica was startled and turned around, unaware that she was leading with her gun. Freddie, now more agile, quickly ducked out of the way.

"Jesus."

Veronica lowered the gun.

"Sorry."

"What were you doing?"

Veronica was too embarrassed to say outright that she was thinking about breaking the window.

"Look, this guy might have murdered three people. We have more than enough probable cause to—"

"Maybe. But think about it, Veronica. Bobby's not inside and if he comes home and sees a broken window and a bunch of cops tearing through his shit? He's going to run. We're better off just calling someone out here to watch the place and putting out an APB on him."

That made sense. It made much more sense than breaking down the window, going inside, and hoping to find something like a calendar on Bobby's fridge saying exactly where he was right now.

Maybe they'd get really lucky and find out that Bobby was so nice that he put Aaron's murder on the calendar while he was at it.

Veronica tucked her gun back into the holster on her hip.

"You're right. Let's go back to the car."

Once there, Freddie did just as he'd suggested, putting out an APB for Bobby Harvey. He left it up to Veronica to get an officer stationed outside, and she knew exactly who to choose.

Of course, Officer Court Furnelli was awake, or at least he sounded like he was, and he was more than happy to set up shop outside Bobby's trailer.

That left only one thing for them to do, something Veronica thought they couldn't push aside any longer.

"I think we should probably go see Sylvia Decker," Freddie said, reading her thoughts.

"Yeah," Veronica said dryly. "We probably should."

And, for the second time in as many days, they were about to live the worst part of their job: let a woman know that she was now a widow.

***

Unlike Bobby Harvey's place, Sylvia and Aaron Decker resided in a high six-figure home. It wasn't a palace, but it was large, with an impressive front yard and a stone façade.

They'd performed this routine many times before, too many times, and didn't need to clarify their positions. Freddie asking her if she wanted him to take the lead at Molly Mills' place had been an act of sheer politeness.

Falling back into their roles was as easy as an alcoholic picking up a drink after years of sobriety or a man who nearly died from fast-food addiction to devour at least one, and maybe two, burgers only six months after his coronary.

Sylvia Decker, a woman in her late forties who aimed to look like she was in her mid-thirties, answered the door. She was wearing a long white slip and while her hair was messy, her eyes appeared clear.

"My name is Detective Furlow, and this is Detective Shade with the Greenham PD."

"Aaron? What happened to Aaron?" The woman's voice was desperate. This didn't reach her eyes, but Veronica suspected that Botox, and not genuine lack of concern for her husband, was the cause.

"Can we come in?" Freddie asked.

Veronica expected Sylvia to agree, but instead, the woman just stood there, blocking the door, and shaking her head.

"Tell me what happened to Aaron." Part plea, part demand.

Freddie shot eyes at Veronica, signaling for her turn to take over.

"Mrs. Decker, I think it's better if—"

"He's—" Sylvia gasped. "Oh my God, he's dead, isn't he?"

"Please, just let us come inside."

Sylvia still refused to invite them in, but Freddie maneuvered his body in such a way that either they bumped chests, or the woman backed up. She chose the latter and once the invisible barrier was broken, Sylvia Decker allowed them into her home.

Veronica made sure to close the door behind them.

"Is there somewhere we can sit?" she asked.

"I don't want to sit!" Sylvia shook her head, sending her messy hair falling to her shoulders. "Just tell me what happened to my Aaron!"

With her increased agitation, Veronica suddenly became more aware of her surroundings and deliberately focused on her synesthesia. At murder scenes or while questioning notorious liars, her condition was impossible to ignore.

That wasn't always the case. Sometimes the impact was subtle. Sometimes Veronica had to focus to pick up the tells constructed by her subconscious.

Not now, however. Now, her synesthesia was silent.

No colors, no smells.

No sounds.

It had been a long time since she'd heard her brother's voice singing *la, la, la, la, laaaaa, laaa.*

It seemed to have vanished along with the man.

And she was glad it was gone.

Veronica hated that song, even back then.

"Mrs. Decker, I regret to inform you that your husband is dead."

"No!" The woman dropped to her knees. "*No!*"

She reached down and helped Sylvia to her feet, then guided her deeper into the house. Off to the left, Veronica identified a sitting room. She lowered Sylvia onto the couch and sat beside her.

Freddie chose to stand.

"What happened to him?" Sylvia managed between sobs.

"He was murdered, Mrs. Decker. I'm really sorry."

Sylvia wailed and threw herself into Veronica's arms.

Though uncomfortable, Veronica held her. There had been a time when she would have masterfully finagled her way out of such a consoling gesture, but that part of her at least appeared capable of change.

"I know you're hurting, Mrs. Decker, but we're hoping that you might be able to help us find who did this," Freddie said. "Can you tell us the last time you saw your husband?"

"Tonight. Jesus... I saw him *tonight.* He's... he's really dead?"

Sylvia pulled back from Veronica and wiped at her tear-streaked face.

"I'm sorry," Freddie said. "Do you know where he went?"

"Aaron said he was going out for a drink."

"Do you know where? Or with who?"

Sylvia shook her head.

"I don't know. I don't know." Her voice was barely a whisper now. "He's... gone... Aaron's gone..."

"I know this is hard, but can you tell us some of Aaron's favorite spots to go for a drink? And maybe some friends that he likes to go out with on a regular basis?"

"I can't believe it."

"Mrs. Decker, please."

"I don't..."

Veronica rose from the couch and stood next to Freddie. They weren't going to get anything more out of the grieving woman tonight—they would have to circle back in a day or two when she'd settled down.

"Mrs. Decker, is there someone you can call to be with you tonight? A sister, or friend, someone like that?"

"My friend Tonya."

"I suggest you give her a call. Tell her to come over, keep you company. An officer will come by in the morning with more details. Again, Mrs. Decker, we are truly sorry for your loss."

"Will you find out who did this? Who did this to my Aaron?"

Veronica nodded firmly.

"We will. And we'll see ourselves out. Please, call your friend."

Veronica was three-quarters of the way to the door when she felt a sudden compulsion to ask one final question.

"Mrs. Decker?"

The woman had taken her phone out and looked up from the device with bloodshot eyes.

"Yes?"

"Do you know anybody named Bobby Harvey? One of your husband's friends, maybe?"

Beside her, Freddie tensed but Sylvia didn't react.

"No, I don't think so."

This answer was uttered in the same tone as every other one that the new widow had given them.

Only something about it was different. Because all of a sudden, all Veronica could smell was gasoline.

Chapter 31

AT TWENTY-FIVE YEARS OLD, COLE Batherson had dated plenty of women. More than most had by the time they reached forty if they hadn't settled down by then.

Most of these had been fleeting encounters—women he met during basic training, came across while working in internal affairs, or online.

Others he met in bars.

In his younger days, college girls had been his thing even though he'd never formally attended.

Cole had numerous partners, both sexual and romantic.

But none had ever lasted.

In truth, the six months or so that he and Veronica had been seeing each other, which had become more serious over the last two and a half, were the longest he'd ever been in a relationship.

And he wanted it to continue. He enjoyed his time with her, appreciated her uniqueness, and liked that he couldn't outwit or deceive her as he had a habit of doing with previous partners. She kept him honest.

Kept things real.

And added a much-needed element of both spontaneity and excitement to his otherwise mundane life.

Love? Cole didn't know about love. But what he felt for Veronica was more than just like, that's for sure.

Speaking of like, no one liked internal affairs officers—they were perceived as snitches with badges. Or worse: completely and utterly irrelevant.

Most of Cole's assignments were similar to the one he had just completed. Stealing underwear from a coworker wasn't always the focus, but it was a surprisingly recurring theme.

Or had been, he reminded himself. It *had* been a common theme in his work.

It wasn't anymore because Cole was no longer an internal affairs officer.

It felt strange. Stranger still, he already had his first case.

Whoopee!

Not officially, of course. They hadn't discussed payment or anything. Pro bono work... not the ideal way to start a business endeavor.

So why did you agree? Cole asked himself. *You don't owe Veronica anything. Is it to curry favor with her with the hopes of getting back into that sexy red thong she likes to wear on the weekend?*

Maybe.

Probably.

There was another reason, too: not only were most IA assignments incredibly boring, but bureaucracy turned the simplest of tasks into a forty-eight-point checklist requiring more signatures than the Declaration of Independence.

He'd taken the case because the compressed timeline made it thrilling, and the stakes made it exhilarating.

Cole had called the job impossible, but it wasn't—*Nothing's impossible! Yeah? Jump off a tall building and flap your arms as fast as you can. Good luck*—it was *near* impossible. And he didn't even know where to start. His options were limited, given that he hadn't officially obtained his PI license. The only thing working in his favor was that he'd quit so recently, and so quietly, that Cole doubted many people knew about him leaving IA. And hated as IA officers were, they were still cops. Cops with a special ability to make anyone else's life miserable.

Porting what he learned from IA, the first step Cole took as a PI was to delve into Dylan Hall's past. He was already somewhat familiar with the man from the Ken Cameron case, but he thought it best to refresh his memory.

Dylan Hall had been in and out of the disaster that was Renaissance Home since a very young age. Adopted three times, he seemed to have the worst luck imaginable. It was unsurprising that he became an addict and started a life on the streets.

And then, as of about a year ago, he seemed to have cleaned up his act. After being falsely accused of stalking Chloe Dolan, Dylan hadn't been arrested for six months, the longest stretch of his adult life.

Then everything changed.

Cole decided to start from Dylan's most recent arrest and work his way forward, which led him to the Matheson Police Department.

He knew that what he planned on doing was probably illegal, but he was still *kinda* a police officer.

And *kinda* was a legal term… wasn't it?

"Hi there," Cole said to the secretary. He raised his IA badge dangling from the gold chain around his neck for the plump woman behind the desk to see. "Cole Batherson, Internal Affairs. I'm working on a case and need access to certain files."

"What kind of files?" The woman was young and moderately attractive. This didn't matter as much as the fact that the precinct was fairly empty.

Most officers were probably out to lunch—figuratively and literally.

"The case against Dylan Hall. Drug possession, charges filed about six months ago, going to trial in a few days." Cole spoke quickly to avoid dwelling on the details of the case or allowing her to do the same. "According to my notes…" He opened the folder that he'd brought with him that just happened to be completely empty and tilted it so that she couldn't see. "There was an anonymous call that led to his arrest. Would you happen to have the call logs for that?"

"Six months ago?"

"Give or take," Cole said with a grin. He knew how to put on the charm, and while he wasn't proud of using his looks to get what he wanted... well, pride was a sin, wasn't it?

Besides, he was on the clock here.

"Let me check."

She was cute, with short blonde hair and an upturned nose. A bit on the plumper side, most likely from sitting behind a desk all day, but in the past, Cole wouldn't have turned her down, that's for sure.

As the secretary began typing on the keyboard, Cole placed his elbow on the desk and leaned forward, getting close to her but not uncomfortably so.

"No, I don't see it here. Are you sure it was six months ago? And Dylan Hall? That's his name?"

"I'm sure. There was no anonymous call logged to Matheson PD?"

"No... there was a call from a... a DEA Agent Troy Allison? Yep, it's right here." She tapped a manicured nail on the monitor. Cole leaned further and with a smile of her own, the woman tilted the monitor to give him a better look.

The call from DEA Agent Troy Allison was logged at 1:30 AM and was placed to a Detective Jacob Tinkler.

Tinkler? Give me a break.

"Can I see the details of that call? Are they recorded?"

"No, not like recorded, recorded. But I should be able to pull up Detective Tinkler's notes." More typing, then she started to read out loud even though Cole had already finished reading what was on screen in his head. "DEA Allison called; said he got an anonymous tip about a considerable stash of heroin—new product—in Dylan Hall's possession." The address followed and Cole committed it to memory.

"Thank you. And this Detective *Tinkler*, is there any chance he's around?"

"No, I'm sorry. Detective Tinkler went up to Washington. He's working in the White House, I think?"

Not ideal, but not the end of the world, either.

"Thank you so much for your time, sweetie. I owe you one."

"You're welcome."

Back in his car, he took a Sharpie out of the console, bit off the cap, and scribbled Dylan Hall's address on the outside of the empty folder.

Although the trip wasn't a complete waste of time, what Cole had discovered wasn't heartening.

Dealing with a Matheson Detective was one thing—*Tinkler? Really? Shouldn't he have been a mall Santa or something?*—but the DEA?

Once, Cole had investigated a case of stolen identity that had links to the DEA of all things.

Nope.

DEA Agents were built like brick shithouses and spoke as much as them, too.

Sure, Cole *could* just lower his shoulder and blow through cinderblocks if he really wanted to.

But wouldn't it be more fun to just start removing brick by brick and peeking inside?

He cracked his knuckles and then started his car.

Who's up for a little masonry, huh?

Cole pointed both thumbs at his chest and said, "This guy, that's who."

Chapter 32

"THAT WAS A BIT ODD, no?" Freddie asked.

This was an understatement—Sylvia Decker's behavior had been more than a little odd. Veronica was well aware that grieving reactions were as varied and individual as hairstyles, but something in particular stuck in her mind.

"She never asked how, did she? I mean, when we told Sylvia her husband had been murdered, she never once asked how he was killed?"

"No, I don't think so."

"Huh."

"Was she... lying?" Freddie asked uncomfortably. They didn't talk about her synesthesia—nobody did. It had somehow been relegated to a taboo subject, as was the case with most things that people just didn't understand. And Veronica was fine with that. If it were up to her, it would've remained a secret until the day she died. And the less they talked about it, the more people tended to forget. There was the New York Times article Cole wrote about her, of course, and that would undoubtedly come up anytime someone searched her name, but the mention of her synesthesia therein was succinct. Not only that but it was located somewhere in the middle, which was like writing a preamble before a recipe. It was simply never read.

First and last paragraphs, only.

But now that Freddie had brought it up...

"Yeah—when I asked her if she knew Bobby Harvey and she said no? That was a lie."

Freddie snapped his fingers and pointed.

"I knew it—I saw your nose crinkle a little—just a little—and I *knew* it."

Veronica smiled.

"Is it that obvious?"

"No, not really. I was just looking for it. Why was she lying?"

Veronica raised one eyebrow.

"It doesn't quite work that way—I wish. I can tell if someone's lying, but I can't read their minds, Freddie."

"*Ha*, I know, I was just thinking out loud."

"What if Sylvia was sleeping with Bobby?"

Freddie grimaced at her 'what if' scenario but he went along with it.

"And what if Bobby killed Aaron to have Sylvia all to himself?"

"Maybe Bobby Harvey *also* killed Jake and Cooper because Sylvia was sleeping with them, too?" Veronica joked. "Kidding. I mean, maybe you're onto something? Doesn't explain the other two murders, though. If the man only came home, we could ask his sorry ass."

"No update from Officer Furnelli?"

"No. Nothing. Still all quiet in the trailer."

"Then we wait," Freddie said with a shrug.

"I hate waiting."

"Me, too. You want me to drop you off somewhere or do you want to come back to the station?"

"And feel Captain Bottel's wrath? No thanks." Veronica suddenly grew serious. "You think you can take me to see Steve?"

"Yeah, of course. I'll let the captain know where you are."

"Thanks."

They fell into silence. An awkward silence. Veronica could see Freddie's face twitch as if he was preparing to say something, but he stopped himself at the last second.

This was maddening. If they were going to be partners, they had to be able to trust one another.

You forgave Freddie...

Veronica grunted.

Fuck you, Cole.

"What's that?"

"Nothing. Listen, Freddie, it looks like you want to say something. Please, just say it. I hate this awkwardness."

"I—well, it's personal and I don't—"

"...Freddie..."

"All right, well, I heard that you and Cole were together. It's not my business, but I was just curious and—"

"Cole was writing that article about me, and we hit it off. Dated for a while, got pretty serious," Veronica interrupted. "Steve and I had already broken up by then. Simple as that."

You forgave Steve...

Veronica sighed.

"Maybe... maybe it wasn't that simple."

People often said that verbalizing your feelings made them more real, but that wasn't true. What it really did was force you to think about your feelings in a cohesive and understandable way instead of them just existing as infinite versions of Schrödinger's cat inside your head.

"I think Cole's a great guy—Freddie, I was completely wrong about him, and you were right. He's smart, funny..." Veronica chuckled. "God, I sound like his hype girl."

Freddie laughed, too. For the first time since getting back together, his laughter seemed unrestrained.

"If you say you just weren't compatible, I'm going to vomit."

Veronica smirked.

"He wasn't the one," she said jokingly. "But seriously, I think maybe he was too good for me."

Was—past tense.

Even though their break-up was less than twenty-four hours old, it didn't seem foreign to her. Did that mean that it was the right decision?

She didn't know.

"Veronica—"

"No, don't do that either. Don't patronize. The fact is, I didn't love Cole. Sounds cheesy, I know. But I didn't. So, I cut it off because that isn't fair to him."

You don't love yourself, Veronica.

It was Cole's voice, but he'd never said those words. Still, the man taking up residence inside her head received her wrath anyway.

Fuck you, Cole.

"I understand." The seriousness of Freddie's voice made Veronica put a hold on mentally bashing her ex-boyfriend.

"Go on…"

"Naw, it's just… I want to apologize, Veronica." She knew that this wasn't what Freddie wanted to say—rather, it wasn't what he was referring to when he'd said, 'I understand'. But she'd cut him off once already when he'd tried to apologize and regretted it and wasn't about to do that again. "I'm sorry for the way I acted that day in the car. I should never have said that stuff to you. It was messed up. I'm… I'm sorry."

Veronica didn't need to say, 'I forgive you,' 'That's okay,' or 'Don't let it happen again.' All she had to do was give the man a sincere nod.

That bastard Cole was right: she'd already forgiven Freddie. But there was one last issue that she needed to resolve before moving on completely.

"Freddie, what happened that day? The day you met with Agent Keller? After that, you got serious—more serious than usual."

More serious than a heart attack?

Too soon, Veronica decided.

Freddie quickly looked away.

"I can't. I know this is going to seem unfair, terribly unfair, what with your secrets coming out—but that was by accident. I just—" He was really struggling now, and Veronica felt bad for even asking. "One day, I'll tell you... I'll tell you everything. But—"

"Not today."

"Right. Because today is Tuesday."

"It's Thursday," Freddie corrected.

"Whatever. But okay, Freddie. One day. I'm going to hold you to that."

"I'd expect nothing less, Veronica." Freddie looked sad and all Veronica wanted to do was hug the big man. "And thank you."

"I aim to please."

"In that case... you hungry? Because I could go for a double whopper right now."

Veronica leaned over and punched Freddie's shoulder.

He was smiling now.

"No way. Kale only, got it?"

Chapter 33

VERONICA DIDN'T SEE THE DOCTOR who had tried to kick her out before, but she did see a nurse. The woman informed her that visiting hours were over, but all it took was a stern look and the nurse backed down.

Steve was sleeping on his side, mouth open. The IV fluids that had been pumped into him gave his skin a slightly puffy look, but overall, he looked better than when Veronica had seen him outside of Jake Thompson's crime scene.

Definitely better than when she'd found him in the alley.

Veronica removed her gun and holster and sat in the chair beside the bed. She thought about putting her piece on the table but then recalled the previous incident at the hospital when her gun had been stolen and used to kill Marlowe Lerman.

Veronica decided to tuck it out of sight behind one of the larger pieces of medical equipment just in case she dozed off. Then she took her keys, badge, and phone and put them on the table to get more comfortable.

Just in case... within moments, she was asleep.

Sometime later, Veronica was awakened by the sound of a scream.

Steve's eyes were wide, his face glistening with sweat. The man's mouth was agape and even though he was looking in her direction, he wasn't seeing her.

Veronica got to her feet so quickly that the chair banged against the wall behind her.

"Steve!"

The man screamed again. It was a haunting sound.

"Steve, it's me! It's Veronica!"

She reached for his hand, made contact with his cool, clammy skin, and Steve immediately pulled back. He was shaking, and as a shudder traveled through him from head to toe, he suddenly became lucid.

"Veronica?" The door burst open, and the nurse rushed in.

She hurried to Steve's side, ignoring Veronica completely.

"How're you feeling?" The nurse's eyes darted to the monitors before returning to Steve's face.

"Like shit," he said through gritted teeth. "Like absolute shit."

The nurse offered him a half-smirk, and Veronica silently slipped her hand back into Steve's. He didn't pull back this time.

"That's to be expected. But trust me, things will get better. Just give it time. Two days, no more."

Steve tried to sit up only to immediately collapse back into his sopping pillow.

"Two days..." he grumbled.

"Can we get him a new pillow? This one's soaking wet," Veronica asked. She was feeling a little useless.

The nurse's smile faded.

"Of course."

The woman performed one final check of Steve's vitals, which Veronica suspected was just an attempt to assert her authority, before leaving the room.

When the door closed behind her, Steve squeezed her hand, and his eyes met hers.

"You're here?" He sounded confused.

"Yes, I'm here, Steve. I'm here."

Steve sighed with relief, then closed his eyes. He became so still that Veronica thought that he had fallen back asleep. Then he started speaking, with his head still aimed at the ceiling and his eyelids firmly closed.

"I'm in Hilltona." His voice was husky, dry. "I'm running, I think… I think there's someone ahead of me. Maybe it's the girl, maybe it's Angie Caulfield, but I don't know because I never catch her. But it's not about the girl; it's about running away from something. The bear. The bear's behind me. I can hear it, I can smell it, I can feel it. But no matter how fast I run, I can't get away." Steve indicated the back of his neck. He was becoming increasingly agitated and was squeezing her hand almost hard enough to make it hurt. "I can feel its breath, its rancid breath. Then I turn—I turn…" Steve's eyes opened, and he looked at her. "Veronica, it's not a bear… the thing behind me *was* a bear, but it's not anymore."

Veronica's phone rattled so loudly on the side table, jangling her keys, that she jumped. Had it been in her pocket or anywhere out of sight, and had it not made that noise with her keys, she wouldn't have looked at it. And if she hadn't looked at it, she wouldn't have seen who it was, she definitely wouldn't have answered, and she would have allowed Steve to finish his story. In fact, if it had been anyone other than Officer Court Furnelli calling, and maybe Freddie, she would have allowed Steve to continue.

But it was Court. And Court was watching Bobby Harvey's trailer.

"Shit, I'm sorry… I have to get this."

Steve nodded, understanding, but there was a deep sadness in his eyes. Veronica let go of his hand. Her palm was so moist that she had to wipe it on the front of her pants before answering her phone.

"Detective Shade?" Court sounded excited.

"Yeah? Did you find him?"

"Yeah, we found him all right. At a bar, of all places. We're bringing him back to the station now. You want me to—"

"Wait. Don't do anything. Don't say a single word to him. Put him in a holding cell and wait for me and Freddie. You understand?"

"Got it."

"Good." Veronica hung up, and then immediately dialed Freddie's number. "I'm sorry," she said to Steve as she waited for her partner to answer.

"Veronica? Everything alright at the hospital?" Freddie asked.

"Yeah, fine. They found Bobby Harvey. Court's bringing him in now. Think you can swing by and pick me up?"

"Of course. Captain Bottel is pissed, wants us to go live ASAP. But I'm guessing he'll be okay with waiting if we have a suspect in custody."

"He'd better be."

Veronica hung up. Her mind had gone from bears in Hilltona to suspects in a bar and she hadn't noticed that Steve had fallen back asleep. She wanted to hear the end of the story, and knew that *he* wanted her to hear it, but Veronica wouldn't wake him.

He needed his sleep. After silently collecting her things—her gun was still there—she exited the room.

The nurse joined her by the door as they both looked at the sheriff.

"He'll recover," the nurse said, unprompted.

"Two days," Veronica said, repeating the woman's words from earlier. "And the fentanyl disaster is over."

The nurse turned to her.

"The fentanyl's already out of his system."

Veronica frowned.

"Doesn't look like it."

Steve was puffy but somehow also frail.

"Well, the fentanyl's gone. What you're seeing," the nurse pointed with her chin, "is withdrawal."

The word hit Veronica like a ton of bricks. Deep down, she must have known that this was the case. She must have known when Steve had started acting erratically all the way back to before *Marlowe* that he'd had a problem.

But she'd ignored it.

And then, when she'd flushed the pills and he'd blown up? Instead of offering Steve the help he'd needed, Veronica buried her head in the sand and pushed him away.

Goddamn it.

"He's strong," the nurse said reassuringly. "He'll get through it."

"Yeah, he will."

Veronica's phone rang again.

"Five minutes out," Freddie told her. "Meet me outside."

"Will do."

Veronica turned to the nurse and offered a tired smile.

"Thank you for everything."

"No problem. We'll get him up and running again, but once he leaves the hospital? That's a different story. I've seen patients worse off and better off than him go back to old habits. The better the support system he has, the better the chance of success."

"Yeah, I know." It was true. This is what every psychiatrist Veronica had ever been to had told her.

The more support, the better the chance of overcoming your issue. It didn't matter if you were dealing with grief, loss, depression, or drug abuse.

But Steve didn't really have support. His closest 'friend' was Deputy McVeigh, and that man was out for his job.

All he had was her.

Veronica took one last look at Steve, whose face was now pinched.

I won't let you down this time, Steve. I won't.

Chapter 34

BOBBY HARVEY'S CLOSE-SET EYES WERE red with alcohol, and his average-sized nose was paired with a slightly larger chin, which gave him a bit of an underbite. His dark brown hair was pushed away from his face, with most of the medium-length strands tucked behind his ears.

He wore a white T-shirt that was damp in the armpits.

Veronica could see the blue waves of sweat coming from the crown of their suspect's head.

"Did he say anything when you brought him in?" she asked Court.

The officer looked exhausted—they all did.

"Nothing, really. Yelled something about knowing his rights, but he didn't even ask what he was being brought in for. He's scared."

Veronica looked back at Bobby through the one-way glass. He was grinding his teeth now.

"How did you find him, exactly?"

"I didn't," Furnelli corrected. "One of my guys spotted someone matching his description at a bar after you sent out the APB. I went over there, confirmed the ID, and brought him in."

"And he really didn't ask why he was being hauled in for questioning?" Freddie said.

"Nope. And for all of his jibber-jabber about knowing his rights, he hasn't requested a lawyer yet."

"Good—thanks. Great work. Go home, get some sleep," Veronica suggested.

Officer Furnelli shrugged.

"I want to see this through."

"I hear you."

Veronica took the folder that Court had prepared with the photographs she'd requested inside and then glanced over at her partner.

"All right, let's get this started."

As per their plan, neither Veronica nor Freddie said anything to Bobby when they first entered the room.

"Hello? *Hello?*" Bobby Harvey had a screechy, annoying voice. "*Hello?*"

Instead of answering, Veronica began laying out pictures of the first two victims on the table in front of the man.

Jake Thompson, the drug dealer with the word 'sinner' written in blood above his head, his lungs pulled out of his back. Cooper Mills, lying on his stomach by his car, pants on but back bare. Lungs exposed.

"Jesus Christ. What the fuck is this?" Bobby made a face. "What the fuck is this shit?" The man reeked of alcohol, but his words were only partially slurred.

"Bobby, do you like Vikings?" Freddie asked, his voice devoid of any emotion.

"What?"

"Vikings. You know, tattoos, braided hair, that sort of thing?"

"What the fuck are you talking about? Fucking Vikings?" He flicked a hand at the photos, but Veronica noticed he was trying his best to avoid looking directly at them. "What is this?"

"Why don't you start by telling us why you're here?" Veronica suggested.

The man's eyes shot to her.

"What? I'm here because you guys dragged me in here."

Veronica stared at Bobby, purposefully making him as uncomfortable as possible.

"I-I don't know why I'm here," Bobby stammered. The room suddenly reeked of gasoline.

"You know, most people who get dragged out of a bar in the afternoon and hauled down to a police station for questioning usually ask why. I mean, I'd wanna know why?"

"Well, y-yeah. Why am I here?"

Veronica leaned away from the table and Freddie took her place.

"Do you like Vikings, Bobby?" Freddie asked, completely ignoring the man's question.

Bobby exhaled loudly.

"What is this about Vikings? No, I don't like Vikings." Bobby crossed his arms over his chest defiantly.

"What about sinners? What do you have to say about them?" Freddie asked.

The smug look fell off Bobby's face.

"What? I-I don't know what you're talking about."

Veronica pulled out another photo, this one of Aaron Decker.

"I'm talking about Aaron Decker. You know him, right? You were at the bar with him?"

Bobby's mouth twitched but he didn't answer. Veronica knew that the man's mind was working a mile a minute trying to figure out if they were just fishing or if they knew this to be fact. And if so, how he could finagle his way out of the situation without being caught in a lie?

"Aaron Decker... you were at the bar with him. You gave him a drink laced with lorazepam to put him to sleep. But before he went dodo, you brought him to an alley. There, you slit his wrists and wrote 'sinner' on the wall in his blood."

Bobby's exaggerated shocked expression was almost comical.

"I-I-I have no idea—"

"All because you were sleeping with his wife, isn't that right, Bobby? Sylvia Decker?"

Freddie raised an eyebrow. This wasn't part of their script, but Veronica could see by the way the blue aura of sweat had increased dramatically that she was barking up the right tree.

"I get it. You didn't learn how to share. But what I don't understand is why you killed these other men. Were you sleeping with their wives, too?" Veronica tapped Jake's photo. "No, that can't be it, because Jake Thompson didn't have a wife or girlfriend." Now, Veronica tapped her chin. "And Cooper Mills? I don't think his wife was your type. I'm thinking—wait, did I forget something?"

"You are. Hold on." Freddie grabbed the folder now and removed the final photograph. "The razor blade."

"Ah, yes. The razor blade. We found this beneath one of Aaron's legs. It had a fingerprint on it... wanna take a guess at whose fingerprint that was?"

Bobby licked his lips and swallowed hard.

"No? Okay, fine. Well, surprise, surprise, it was yours."

"N-n-n-no."

"Y-y-y-yes," Veronica mocked.

Another look from Freddie.

"I'm going to be honest with you, Bobby." Veronica popped her Bs. "I don't think you killed Jake or Cooper."

"I didn't!"

No gas this time.

"But I know you killed Aaron."

"I—"

Veronica held up a hand.

"But you know what the media is going to say, right? Two of the worst words someone like you wants to hear: serial killer. Because serial killer almost always means the death penalty."

Bobby gagged and his cheeks puffed. Veronica took another step away from the table.

"You might be thinking that there's been a moratorium on executions, but that's what Trent Alberts thought, too." Veronica lowered her voice to a whisper and tapped the inside of her left bicep. "And he got the needle."

"Oh god—oh god, I'm going to be sick. I—"

Bobby Harvey vomited onto the photographs. It was mostly liquid, beer, probably, and it splatted on the high-gloss images. A little landed on Veronica's shirt and she cringed. Neither she nor Freddie made any attempt to clean the vomit either off themselves, the photos, or off Bobby Harvey.

The man wiped his mouth with the back of his hand. There was snot hanging from his nose and his eyes were watering.

"I'm not a serial killer. And it wasn't—it wasn't my idea." He belched, but nothing came out. "It wasn't even my drugs. It was *hers*. It was *her* idea."

With this, Freddie leaned out the door and asked Court to fetch some paper towels and a glass of water.

"Why don't you tell us about what happened, Bobby?" Veronica said.

The words came fast and furious, the words of a man who was terrified and even disgusted by what he had done.

A confession about murdering Aaron Decker, his relationship with Sylvia Decker, a promise of a life together, of a windfall of an insurance policy.

An ill-conceived, not overly original, and poorly executed plan.

Court returned with the supplies, and he gave Veronica a knowing nod. He was going to go pick the woman up.

"I-I-I'm not a serial killer," Bobby sobbed. "I didn't even want to kill him, you know?" He was begging for sympathy, but Veronica gave him none. "It was all her idea."

"Freddie."

Freddie nodded, read the man his rights, and cuffed him.

"I'm... I'm sorry."

"Yeah, I'm sure you are." Veronica was about to leave when several things occurred to her. "Why did you write the word *sinner* on the wall?"

Bobby licked his lips again.

"'Cuz he was a sinner, you know?" The man's eyes continued to dart nervously.

"Right. And why'd you leave the razor blade, Bobby?"

Something close to a moan exited Bobby's mouth.

"I-I just—I saw someone, something, I dunno. I saw a monster. I saw a monster and I knew it was coming for me. I dropped the razor and ran. That monster is the one who killed those other people. Not me. A fucking *monster.*"

"Yeah, a monster," Veronica grumbled as she left the room.

These were the ramblings of a desperate, guilty man. Veronica knew this.

But she also knew that they were the truth. Or, at least, Bobby Harvey was convinced that they were real.

That the monster was real.

Chapter 35

"As I said on the phone, she's gone."

Veronica looked past Officer Court Furnelli's broad shoulders and through the open door to Sylvia and Aaron Decker's house.

"Shit. Did you go inside?"

Court nodded.

"Warrant was fast-tracked, but there's no one here. And judging by the fact some of her drawers are still hanging open? I'm guessing Sylvia Decker packed up and left."

Veronica cursed under her breath.

"Put out an APB for Sylvia Decker. Contact border control, make sure she doesn't leave the country." Veronica let out an exasperated sigh. Something told her that finding Sylvia wasn't going to be as simple as going to the bar at the end of the street. She looked at Freddie. "Did I mess up here? I knew she was lying when we told her about her husband. Should we have put someone outside her house as we did with Bobby?"

Freddie gave her a look—*that* look.

"No. You couldn't possibly have known that she was involved. One lie doesn't make her a suspect, Veronica."

Except, she had known, hadn't she? At least, Veronica had known that Sylvia was involved when they'd been interviewing Bobby.

Why else would she have brought up the woman's name?

"I mentioned Bobby's name when we were here," Veronica continued. "Maybe that tipped her off. Maybe if I hadn't said anything, she'd still be sitting in her living room."

"What if you had?"

Veronica shot Freddie a look. *What if* was her game, not his.

"What if this was all part of her plan?" It was Court who picked up the ball when Freddie just stared at her. "Maybe Sylvia Decker was sick of her husband and her boyfriend. Maybe she didn't even like Bobby, just knew that she could manipulate him into doing what she wanted. And what Sylvia wanted, was to get that handsome insurance policy handout and start fresh somewhere else."

When Freddie and Veronica didn't say anything, Court immediately started to backpedal.

"I'm sorry if I overstepped. I know I'm just here to lend a hand, and I don't have nearly the experience—"

"No," Veronica stopped the man mid-sentence. "I think you might be right. Makes sense."

Sylvia had lied to her face about not knowing Bobby Harvey. What else could she have lied about? Lying came easy to most people, they'd been doing it their entire lives. But it was considerably more difficult in the midst of the apparent throes of grief.

Yeah, she could be a master manipulator.

But if she was, why hadn't Veronica picked up on it?

"Court, dig into Sylvia and Aaron's bank accounts, would you? If she planned to leave and start somewhere new, we should see large sums of money being withdrawn over the past few months. Also, let's look a little harder at the insurance policy."

"Sounds good. Just…"

"What?"

Court scratched his chin.

"If Sylvia didn't kill Jake or Cooper, who did? I mean, how did they even know the MO—Sinner written in blood on the wall? The details haven't been released and there have only been… what? The two of you, maybe another cop and the coroner who have been at the scenes. That's it. So, how did they know about the writing?"

There was one more person who was present at every scene, Veronica couldn't help but think. *You.*

Veronica stopped herself before she said anything offensive.

Court was a good cop who was doing everything he could to help out on this case including foregoing sleep entirely. What could he possibly stand to gain from leaking information about their crime scenes?

Besides, Veronica fundamentally refused to believe that the only male cop other than Freddie who didn't despise her was a bad seed.

"I couldn't find a direct link between Sylvia Decker and Bobby Harvey," Freddie began, pulling out his phone, "but maybe I can find something common between them…"

"How's the sheriff?" Court asked as they waited for Freddie to finish his search.

Veronica pictured Steve in the hospital bed, eyes wide, mouth open, that horrible scream coming from his throat.

"He's…" She was about to say that he was hanging in there, but then she remembered her promise. "He's going to be okay."

"Good. I've always liked Sheriff Burns. He's a good man."

"Yeah, he is."

"Hey, guys?" Freddie was holding up his phone for them to see. "You are not going to believe what I found."

Veronica looked more closely at the image.

"No way." Someone had taken a picture at Cooper Mills' crime scene. Only the man's bare shoulder was included, but the word 'sinner' was clearly visible on the car, as was the pool of blood beneath it. "Where was that posted?"

"Instagram—I already reported it," Freddie replied. "And guess what? The guy who posted it? Both Sylvia Decker and Bobby Harvey follow this guy."

"Really? Wait—wait a second." Court looked pensive. "Do you think maybe Sylvia and Bobby were planning on offing her husband and when they saw this, Bobby got the idea to try and stage it to look like Cooper? Like a, I dunno, copycat?"

It made sense—it made a lot of sense. If Court's theory was true, and if all Bobby had to go off was that photo, then he wouldn't have known about the lungs. Hell, maybe if he had, he would have opted for something different.

But he would have known about the bloody word.

"You might be right," Veronica said. "Freddie, who posted it?"

Freddie fiddled with his screen and Veronica's jaw fell open.

"You've got to be kidding me."

"Who is it?" Court asked and Veronica stepped aside. "No way."

"Yeah, it's him," Freddie said.

"You're telling me that the geriatric security guard who couldn't even operate a goddamn computer has an Instagram page?"

"Yep. Looks like he posts a lot, too—weird things that happen in the office building. Has a decent following. The photo of Cooper Mills? It has nearly two-hundred likes. Like I said, I reported it, and eventually, it'll be taken down, but who knows when."

This was beyond frustrating.

"Looks like Captain Bottel got his wish," Veronica muttered. "This thing's already gone public. We need to try and get ahead of this. Well, not get any further behind, anyway."

Freddie nodded in agreement.

"How do you want to do this? If we think that Aaron isn't related to the other two, do we even mention him? Or Bobby Harvey, for that matter?"

"You know what the captain's going to want," Court said.

They all did. He was a politician after all. He would want them to say that there had been three murders and that they'd already arrested the man responsible: Bobby Harvey.

Bobby's big plan to make Aaron's murder look like it was part of a string of killings? That had the potential of backfiring horribly.

If the monster who was actually responsible for the angels could stop, and with the right pressure from the right people, Bobby might just find himself on the hook for three murders and not one.

This made Veronica think.

"Does the captain know about Bobby Harvey, yet? About the confession?"

"Not sure," Court offered. "I know he had some big meetings all afternoon. I know I didn't say anything, but someone else at the precinct might have mentioned it."

"So, maybe he doesn't know?"

Court shrugged.

"Maybe not."

"Then let's do this—" Veronica was interrupted by Court's radio, and he excused himself. "—quickly. I say we don't mention Aaron or Bobby. Just keep it on the down low, for now. You know what's going to happen if we say that we have three murders, right?"

"Of course," Freddie said. "Serial killer will be in the mouths of every person in Oregon in a matter of minutes."

"Yeah, and we'll never hear the end of it. Every—"

"Guys?" Court had been serious before, but now, with his dark eyes and the gloomy late afternoon lighting masking his features, he looked almost ill. "That *was* the captain. Patrol just found another body."

"Well," Veronica said, her voice husky, "there goes that idea."

"Serial killer it is," Freddie said ominously. "And the monster is still out there."

Chapter 36

FALLING ASLEEP HAD NEVER COME easily for the boy. Not since his mother died. But now that their uncle had moved in with them when sleep finally blessed him, it didn't last long, either.

Every night, he would wake up at least once. The first few times this happened, the boy called for his dad. But his father was a notoriously heavy sleeper and never came. Neither did his uncle. So, the boy just lay there in the dark, staring at the shadows that his mind morphed into shapes, figures, and finally monsters.

In the morning, he'd asked his dad for more lights in his room. His dad had obliged, setting them up in a way to try and minimize the number of shadows. But no matter how many lights they had—*Icarus, you'll be like Icarus if you have any more lights in here*, his father had joked—the darkness always found a way to sneak in.

Sometimes when he woke up, the boy had to pee. But he was so terrified that he couldn't force himself out of bed. He'd either hold it until morning or change his sheets before anyone noticed he'd wet the bed.

He was too old to be wetting the bed.

After nearly a week of this, the boy decided that things had to change, and he opted for a more proactive approach. He put his favorite baseball bat under his bed, just in case one of the shadow monsters decided to reach out.

This helped him for a day or two.

But then the insomnia returned, and the shadows mocked him.

Don't fall back asleep, boy, they warned. *Because that's when we'll grab you. That's when we'll take you to a better place… a place where you will sleep peacefully.* Forever.

The words were familiar and haunting.

No, sleep was out of the question. But everyone had their breaking point, even a young boy who was scared of the dark. And this was his. He couldn't sleep and he refused to lie in bed any longer.

He decided, instead, that he would sneak outside and walk. Of course, he knew that leaving in the middle of the night by himself was dangerous.

But that didn't matter.

Because the monsters out there couldn't possibly be as scary as the ones in his head.

Or so he'd thought.

But then he'd seen a monster—a real one—and everything changed.

He still walked, but not alone anymore.

Tonight, the boy didn't even get the chance to leave his house. Tonight, it wasn't the shadows that woke him, either.

It was a sound.

A bang?

Yeah, some sort of bang.

And while his eyes couldn't be trusted, his ears were different. It sounded like something had bumped into a chair or table.

Every part of his body told him to just stay still, to lie there until the sound went away. But then what? Would he be afraid of the dark and noises? The dark only existed at night, but sound was everywhere… during the day, too.

No, this was it. He would go and confront this beast.

He *had* to.

And then whatever happened, happened.

He'd either be off to the better place to sleep forever or he'd be cured.

Trembling, the boy forced himself to rise. Steering clear of the shadows, he grabbed his bat from beneath the bed and gripped it tightly in both hands.

"Dad?" he whispered.

His father's door was open a few inches, but the sound hadn't come from that direction.

"Dad?"

Still no answer.

The boy looked toward the couch next, where his uncle slept, but the man wasn't there.

I made it up, he thought. *There was no sound.*

But then it came again—metal, like the garbage bin in the kitchen opening and closing.

The boy, breathing heavily, took one step, then another, then peered around the corner and into the kitchen.

Unlike the shadows, there was no doubt in his mind that the man he saw now was real.

The heavy figure appeared to be trying to shove something into the garbage, something dark and wet... a towel?

His back was to the boy, shoulders hunched, and he was breathing heavily.

It was the same breathing the boy had heard in the alley.

The same breathing he'd heard when he saw the monster rip that man apart and play with his blood.

That wasn't real, was it?

No, it couldn't have been.

Was *this*?

Even though he had the bat, the boy knew it wouldn't help him against this beast. And all the courage, all the whatever happens, happens attitude was suddenly gone.

The boy backed away, slowly, careful not to make a single sound. If the monster turned, he'd swing the bat. Or he'd drop it and run.

But the monster didn't, and the boy made it back to his room without incident and crawled beneath the sheets. Gripping the bat to his chest, he lay there in the dark, waiting for the monster to come for him.

But it never did.

As time passed, he started to convince himself that what he'd seen in the kitchen was like what he saw in the shadows.

A figment of his imagination, fuel for the drawings he loved to make during the day. Nothing more, nothing less.

None of it was real.

And what wasn't real couldn't hurt him.

Could it?

PART THREE: SINNERS

Chapter 37

UNLIKE WITH AARON DECKER, DETECTIVE Veronica Shade knew instantly that whoever had killed this man had also killed Jake Thompson and Cooper Mills. The MO was nearly identical, and on top of that, her synesthesia blazed.

Jake Thompson had been murdered in an alley in Needle Point while Cooper Mills' life had been taken from him outside his office building technically in Meadowbrook, but not far from Jake. The third victim, as of yet unidentified, was killed and partially eviscerated in the quiet suburb of Cedar Heights, approximately three miles from where Cooper was found. This victim wasn't quite as large as Cooper Mills, but he was more muscular, more rugged looking with a thick black beard tapered to a point. SINNER was written on the wall in his blood. Like with Jake Thompson, this victim was seated, but not in a chair. He was on the ground propped up against the brick wall of a middle school, his head flopped forward so that it was nearly resting in his lap.

The man's throat had been slit and his lungs had been crudely pulled out of his back.

By the time Dr. Thorpe arrived—nobody could manage to rouse the coroner, Kristin Newberry—the sun had almost started to rise. It was in these few moments before dawn that Veronica usually felt most peaceful, on the rare occasion that she was awake to witness them. Not today.

Today, she felt like a walking zombie. If the killer had a type, she had no idea what it was. Jake Thompson had been a drug dealer, waif-thin, wasting away. Cooper Mills had been an overweight accountant. If she had to guess, the latest victim was someone who worked with their hands, a mechanic, maybe. All men, all between the ages of twenty-five and forty-five.

All sinners?

Yeah, that was a given.

Jake Thompson had been a drug dealer. Cooper Mills had been arrested several times for domestic assault.

Veronica crouched down and stared at the dead man with his throat slit, his bare, muscular chest covered in dried blood.

What did you do? She wondered. *What was your deadly sin?*

As she rose to her feet, Veronica glanced over at Freddie, who was conversing with Officer Court Furnelli. She overheard them talking about the person who had called in, someone who had heard shouting echoing off the schoolyard and thought it was perhaps a vandal. Unlike the other crimes that were reported anonymously, this person left their name. Reporting a crime in Cedar Heights didn't hold the same stigma as in Needle Point.

She doubted that this would lead anywhere.

"What did you do?" Veronica whispered, this time out loud. Another question popped into her head.

How did he know?

Veronica shook her head and made her way over to her colleagues.

"Any idea who the victim is yet?" she asked when there was a lull in their conversation.

Court frowned.

"Ran his fingerprints—he's not in the system. Might take a while to figure out exactly who he is."

This surprised Veronica. Evidence of Cooper's and Jake's sinning ways had become evident with a simple search. Even if they didn't have this man's name, they had fingerprints, which should've led them to any sort of criminal past.

"You sure?"

"Yeah, ran it through the Greenham database. Nothing. The lab said they're trying CODIS next, should be an hour or two before we hear back."

While Veronica mulled this over, Freddie spoke up.

"What are you thinking?"

Veronica wasn't used to verbalizing her unpolished thoughts with anyone other than just Freddie, but Court was proving himself not just useful but also insightful.

She decided to bring him into the fold. Not much else was a secret with her, not after *Marlowe,* so what did it matter?

"I know that we joked before about everyone being a sinner and how our unsub is likely punishing these men for their sins, but Jake's and Cooper's crimes weren't your run-of-the-mill white lies. I'm assuming that this new guy has a troubled past as well. So, to answer your question, I'm wondering how our unsub knew? If this new guy had sins on Jake's or Cooper's level but isn't in the system, how would our guy know? Assuming, of course, all of these murders aren't just random attacks by a madman."

"I know we said before that practically everyone is a sinner, and that this man could just be getting lucky. But maybe he's not. I mean, with Jake Thompson, he probably knew he was a sinner because, well, where he was and what he did for a living. That was pretty obvious. Cooper Mills? Not so much. This guy isn't even in the system, and if we find out that he is one of these 'sinners,' how the hell would he know about them?"

Freddie didn't appear to have anything, but Court looked uncomfortable.

"I'll ask you the same thing," Veronica said. "What are you thinking?"

Court took off his hat and ran his hands through his black hair, pushing it away from his forehead.

"A cop?"

Veronica cringed.

"What do you mean?" Freddie asked.

"Well, I mean, a cop would have access to Jake's and Cooper's histories." Court pointed at the corpse, which Dr. Thorpe was now inspecting carefully. "What if the cop came across this guy doing something sketchy? Maybe it wasn't enough to charge him or... you now... there was a... 'mix-up' with evidence and he slipped through the cracks."

"That's all we need," Veronica grumbled. But Court was right. It *could* be a cop. "It's worth checking out, but let's not limit it to police officers. Look into Cooper's and Jake's arrests and trials. See if they have anyone in common—a cop, judge, lawyer, anyone, really." Veronica considered this for a moment, looking at Court's drawn features. "But not until after you get some sleep, Court."

The man straightened.

"I'm good. I'll look into it right away."

Then he left before Veronica could turn her suggestion into an order.

"What do you think about the rent-a-cop from Cooper's work?" Freddie asked out of the blue.

"What do I think about him? I think he has a hard time taking a piss, not sure how he'd be capable of overpowering any of these men, including Jake."

"And I didn't think that he could operate a calculator much less have a following on Instagram," Freddie countered.

"Good point. Worth looking into, I guess."

The two of them just stood there, saying nothing, for several seconds. Then Veronica yawned.

"You should get some sleep too," Freddie suggested.

She shot him a less-than-accommodating look.

"Just saying, just saying."

It had been a hellish forty-eight hours, and the only sleep Veronica had gotten had been either disrupted by alcohol or by one of Steve's nightmares.

But Veronica couldn't sleep now. She had to go back to Steve, check up on him.

She also had to speak to Cole.

But first and foremost, she had to find out who the hell was behind these brutal murders before they struck again.

"Looks like I'm going to have to go in front of the camera," Veronica said reluctantly.

"Let the captain speak to the press," Freddie said. "I'm sure he'd love that."

"Yeah, that's exactly why I want to do it." Veronica cocked her head. "Screw the captain."

She thought Freddie would chastise her for the comment, but he didn't.

Instead, he smiled.

"Yeah, screw the captain."

Chapter 38

"Your EKG looks good, and electrolytes are all within range," the doctor said. "I think you're almost ready for discharge. We'll keep you here for another twelve hours or so, just to make sure, but if everything stays this way," he tapped his pen on the clipboard, "you'll be good to go."

Steve wasn't sure how to feel about this. On one hand, he was glad that he was getting healthier, and that he was going to make a full recovery. That was a plus.

The downside was that once he left, he'd have access to drugs again. Or if not direct access, he'd know where to find some.

Could he resist?

For the first time in about four months, he didn't really feel the urge to use. Didn't feel like he needed opioids to get through the next few hours. Steve was no expert, but he attributed at least part of this cooling-down period to the fact that he'd nearly died. But he also knew that like the alcoholic who has a nasty hangover and says they'll never drink again, this was fleeting.

Memories of pain were like farts in the wind.

They came, they fouled up the place, but then they were gone and soon thereafter forgotten.

"Doc, I think I need help," Steve said quietly, too ashamed to look at the man.

The doctor tapped his pen incessantly until Steve was forced to raise his eyes.

"Right. I thought it might come to this. To be honest, Mr. Burns, the best thing that you can do for yourself at this point is counseling. I know it's difficult for you, given your position and an obvious desire for secrecy. Group sessions have been shown to be the most effective in overcoming addiction and trauma, but I'm guessing that that's out of the question?"

"You guessed correctly."

The doctor nodded.

"Well, I think the next best thing is private counseling. There is one psychiatrist I always recommend." The doctor flipped to a blank page, scribbled a name, then tore the paper off and handed it to Steve.

He shouldn't have been surprised by the name, but he was: Dr. Jane Bernard.

Steve carefully folded the paper into a small square.

"I can also give you a prescription for methadone if you're still experiencing physical withdrawal symptoms."

"No—no more drugs."

Steve was adamant.

"Then I suggest you give Dr. Bernard a call. I'll be back in a few hours to check up on you again. Try to continue to get some rest, Sheriff."

"Thanks."

The doctor left, and Steve lay on his bed holding the paper in his hand, debating what to do with it. He knew of Dr. Bernard, knew what Veronica thought of the woman now. He also knew how she considered the psychiatrist before learning about Dante Fiori.

Talking about his feelings wasn't something that got him excited. He'd tried therapy for a short while after Julia had gone missing.

Steve hadn't gotten much out of it other than feeling guilty that he was doing something *other* than looking for his wife.

But the doctor was right, he had to do something. He couldn't go on like this. He *wouldn't* go on like this.

The next time he shot up, Veronica might not be around the corner to save him.

With a sigh, Steve reached for his phone. His intention was to call Dr. Bernard, but he was distracted by a text that he received moments ago while the doctor was speaking to him.

It was from Chief Deputy McVeigh.

Detective Shade is on the news. Thought you might want to know.

Steve felt his heart skip a beat.

McVeigh had been kind enough to leave a link and he clicked on it.

And then he saw her.

Detective Veronica Shade, once again stood in front of a podium and addressed the media. She looked tired, there was no denying that. But she also looked fierce and imposing. Not bad for a woman who was all of five-foot-five and maybe a hundred and ten pounds. It was her eyes that gave the impression she wasn't someone to mess with. Light brown irises speckled with strange gold flecks.

She was talking about another serial killer, and Steve clenched the paper with Dr. Jane Bernard's name in his hand as he watched and listened.

It was a recording from not quite half an hour ago and ran a total of only three and a half minutes.

Veronica was asking for help, asking if anyone had seen three men in and around Nettle Point over the last few days. Images of the men appeared on screen, one of which, Jake Thompson, Steve recognized immediately.

He didn't know the other two.

After her plea for help from the public, there was a brief pause, and a reporter asked a question. Veronica's eyes flicked directly toward the camera. The look only lasted a second, but Steve felt like she was looking right at him. It was almost as if she was saying, "I'm not giving up, Steve. I won't let this one go."

He swallowed hard, feeling a mixture of guilt and gratitude. She was fighting, trying to keep her town safe, while he was stuck in a hospital bed, wrestling with his own demons.

Her town, his county.

I should be out there helping. I should be talking to the media, not her. Me.

The press conference ended, and Steve looked down at the crumpled piece of paper in his hand. He took a deep breath and unfolded it, smoothing the wrinkles absently. It was time for him to fight, too. For himself, for Veronica, and for Bear County.

Determined, he dialed Dr. Jane Bernard's number. He knew this wouldn't be easy, but it was a start. And sometimes, that was all it took.

Something strange occurred to him as he waited for someone to answer.

Sheriff Steve Burns couldn't remember the last time he'd thought about anything other than his next hit. For the better part of six months, his focus had been singular in nature and chemical in desire.

Not anymore.

Chapter 39

COLE BATHERSON WATCHED THE BURLY DEA agent he suspected was Troy Allison get out of his car and walk towards the small strip mall. He made his way toward a grimy door and tried to open it, but it appeared locked. Frustrated, Troy slapped his pockets.

No keys.

The man banged on the door with a fist hard enough that even though Cole was parked across the street and down a quarter block he could clearly make out each resounding thud. The door opened, and another man peered out. Cole had no idea who he was, but judging by his frame and the fact that he was sporting the same black T-shirt as Troy, he'd bet every dollar he had that it was another DEA agent. If this was the case, then this decrepit building was a DEA office.

Made sense.

Cole knew that the DEA liked their reputation as grimy, feet-on-the-ground people, and often used this to separate themselves from the likes of the FBI and other acronyms that wore fancy suits. Including IA.

Cole sunk deeper into his car seat. He knew that asking the DEA for any help at all, in this case, was going to be a non-starter. Not with Agent Baldy and Agent Biceps.

Which put him back near square one.

And he wasn't about to drive up to Washington to speak to Detective Tinkler. Not that the man could give him much.

It was Troy Allison who had received the anonymous call that led them to Dylan's place and the subsequent arrest.

If Dylan had been framed as Veronica was certain of—her synesthesia at work, no doubt—then the person who made the call was the primary suspect.

And anonymous was rarely anonymous.

Access to Troy's phone records would be telling. Even if the call was made from a burner phone, there were methods to narrow down who the caller might be.

But that wasn't going to happen.

Even if Cole could imagine a scenario whereby it was possible to intimidate the DEA agent, that wasn't going to pay dividends moving forward. Sure, he was helping Veronica out on this case and would do the best job possible. That was just who he was. The number one underwear thief investigator in all of Greenham.

If he really wanted to make a career out of being a PI—which he did—he would have to foster relationships with the cops and other agencies. They would have to work together.

Synergistically.

Ah, business buzzwords. How far you have fallen, Cole. One day and you're already speaking the lingo.

Smirking at his stupid self, Cole craned his neck and looked around the neighborhood. The DEA really picked a sweet spot to set up. Dingy, dirty. One convenience store half a block away.

No ATMs, no CCTV.

Except...

Cole was practically crawling over the passenger seat now to get a better look.

There was a stop light not far from where he was parked, and there appeared to be a red-light camera mounted on top of it. It was angled strangely as if someone had struck it with a rock.

Maybe it could see the DEA parking lot?

Maybe...?

It was something to do at least.

Cole tried logging into the camera system on his laptop, only to find that he'd already been locked out.

"Shit."

He was decent with computers, but far from a hacker.

Not that he'd hack into the city's camera system even if he could.

But...

A couple of months back, his password and login for almost everything had been hacked—yeah, it happens to cops, too—and he'd used a colleague's username and password to access the system.

Maybe it was still... *saved*.

A grin formed on Cole's face. All he had to do was start typing and through the magic of the browser, the information auto-filled. Just a quick and easy confirmation that he wasn't a bot, and Cole was in.

Now, where am I?

Cole looked out the window again and then typed in the cross street.

Voilà.

"Wow."

He was staring at his own car in real-time. The picture quality was amazingly clear, and he was overjoyed to see that the image captured not only his side of the street but the DEA parking lot, as well. It almost—*almost*—showed the dirty front door.

This was better than expected.

Cole spent the next few minutes orienting himself with the software, which he'd only used twice before. For a government program, it was surprisingly intuitive and streamlined. He was able to rewind the footage with just a click of a button and saw Troy arriving, and then, twenty minutes before that, Cole watched his own car pull up.

Confident now that he wouldn't accidentally crash the system or delete everything, Cole typed in the date and approximate time that Detective Tinkler claimed Troy called and passed along the information about the tip. He wasn't sure what he was looking for—maybe Troy looking directly at the stop light as he made dramatic and easy-to-read lip movements? The agent scribbling information in obscenely large letters on a notepad revealing the 'anonymous' caller's name?

Nope—no such luck.

Nothing happened. Literally nothing. Not a single car passed through the lights, and nobody opened the DEA headquarters door.

"Okay…"

Knowing that the raid at Dylan Hall's house occurred around two in the morning, Cole scrolled forward to that time.

"Okay."

DEA Agent Troy Allison stepped out of the building with a couple of his colleagues in tow. They got into separate cars and drove off, presumably to meet up with Detective Tinkler in Matheson before heading to Dylan's. Cole thought that he might be able to follow the agents' cars by jumping from red-light camera to red-light camera, but not only would that take time and a lot of trial and error, but he also wasn't sure what that would accomplish.

He already knew that Troy had been there when Dylan had been arrested.

Instead, Cole let the footage run at four times speed. Troy didn't return until the next day. And then he smoked. My god did the man smoke. Cole counted Troy coming outside for no less than fourteen cigarettes before something substantial happened.

Two new men stepped into the frame. One was huge, morbidly obese, the other in decent shape.

"What the hell?" It was Freddie Furlow accompanied by a man Cole didn't recognize. "What are you doing here?"

The two unlikely colleagues approached the DEA stronghold and then disappeared into the blind spot near the door. A second later, the skinny man reappeared and crossed the street. Even though his face was clearly picked up by the traffic camera, Cole still didn't recognize him.

Nothing happened for about ten minutes, and then Freddie exited the building. He looked flushed and there appeared to be sweat on his forehead as he hurried across the road.

"Okay..."

Cole nibbled on his lip as he once again fast-forwarded the footage.

Less than forty-eight hours later, after Dylan was arrested, Freddie returned. Only this time it was night and Troy was waiting.

And smoking.

After a short, heated conversation, Troy retreated to pull someone from the building. This man was skinny, frail, and young—younger than the stranger who had accompanied Freddie the first time he'd arrived.

Freddie and this newcomer embraced, conversed, and then the big man promptly collapsed.

This was the moment the detective had his heart attack.

Cole wished he had some popcorn. It was like watching a silent film, one with intrigue, mysterious characters, and, of course, danger.

After the ambulance left with both Freddie and the young man inside, Agent Allison went back to smoking.

Cole paused the footage and grabbed his cell phone. He scrolled through his contacts and pulled up the number of an acquaintance who worked at the hospital.

The man answered on the first ring.

"Hey, Junior."

"Cole, what's up my G?"

Cole rolled his eyes. Monty 'Junior' Sillapse was a twelve-year-old trapped in a forty-three-year-old's body. He'd worked as an orderly in the hospital for nearly a decade and had zero desire to move up, and absolutely no career ambitions. So long as Junior made enough cash to afford to spend all of his spare time streaming video games online, then he was more than content.

In a way, the simplicity of the man's life was something to be envied.

The only drawback that Cole could see was that a prerequisite for such a life required you to speak like a human meme at all times. Meaningful conversation wasn't just difficult, but it was practically shunned.

"Need a favor."

"Low key, you always need a favor."

"You say you always have time for your subs."

"Yeah—and you're one of the OGs."

"Got me my fourteenth-month sub badge just a week ago."

"*Dayumm.*"

"And I'll tell you what, you do me this solid, and I'll drop a few gifted subs next time you go live."

"A few?"

Cole considered.

"Three."

He could almost hear Junior smile through the phone.

"You got a deal."

"Great—now, I need to know who came in with Detective Freddie Furlow about six months ago." Cole glanced at the video footage on his laptop to relay the exact date. "Detective Furlow came in with an apparent heart attack, and I need to know who accompanied him in the ambulance."

"All right, give me a second. I'm cleaning a bed—some woman hopped up on meth shit herself three times last night."

"Just—"

"Hold on, I said. Damn Boomers don't got no patience."

Cole listened to the flapping of a sheet and then Junior's breathing as he walked somewhere. Finally, he heard the characteristic whine of a computer fan starting up.

"A Detective Freddie Furlow, you said?"

"Yep. Fred Furlow."

"Okay."

Junior typed on the work terminal keyboard.

"Okay, I have them coming in at around midnight, EMT was Lucas Hood... here it is: Fred Furlow was accompanied by Randall Byers. B-Y-E-R-S."

Cole frowned. He had never heard of Randal Byers.

"Any relation listed?"

"Nope. Just the name."

"Thanks, Junior. I'll hit you with those subs next time you go live."

"Nice. Later, G."

Cole hung up and turned his attention back to his laptop. A criminal records search for Randall Byers came up negative.

"Hmm... who are you?"

When a second search yielded nothing of substance, Cole decided to change tactics and looked into Freddie's past instead of Randall's.

This proved much more insightful.

A grin formed on Cole's face, and he leaned back, proud of himself.

Maybe I will be good at this whole PI thing. Goated, as Junior would say. The greatest private—

A knock on his car window caused Cole to jump nearly high enough to hit his head on the roof. He was so shocked by the intrusion that his bladder let go and a little drop of urine soaked the inside of his boxers.

Troy Allison grinned at him around a cigarette, his thick knuckles still resting on the glass until Cole rolled it down.

"You can't be here."

Cole was pretty sure he could, this being public property, but arguing didn't seem like the best course of action in this situation.

"My bad, just hacking the Pentagon."

"What?"

Troy squinted at him, and ash fell from the end of his cigarette. Cole was already gone before the spent tobacco even struck the DEA Agent's dark T-shirt.

And for once, Cole knew exactly where he was going.

It was time to have a chat with Randall Byers, a.k.a. Randall Furlow.

It was time to find out why Freddie Furlow's son had changed his last name.

Chapter 40

"**Well, that went about as** well as expected," Veronica said as she stepped into the precinct.

She was sweating and so was Freddie.

Captain Bottel, on the other hand, was calm and collected.

Officer Court Furnelli fell somewhere in between.

They'd made a simple call to the public, asking if anyone had seen anything suspicious on the night of the murders. Asking if anyone had seen the victims.

Speaking to the public with the media as the intermediary was always a crap shoot. The press refused to just relay the message, they had to flavor it with their own insight. They *had* to. And this invariably affected the nature of the calls they received.

Most were meaningless. Some were deranged.

But rarely—very rarely, a tip came in that led them to something. Most often, these were issued by reluctant individuals who were convinced that what they'd seen was irrelevant, but a friend or family member had convinced them to call in anyway.

In essence, a call to the public was an act of sheer desperation.

But there was no denying that's exactly what they were: desperate.

They had nothing. Three mutilated bodies, a specific and horrific MO, but no links between the victims.

No suspect.

And, to complicate things, there was also Bobby Harvey and Sylvia Decker who had teamed up to murder the latter's husband in a warped and frankly poor attempt at a frame job.

The calls would soon come in, but filtering through them was a job for the junior staff—not Veronica and her team. And they couldn't count on their plea accomplishing anything other than Captain Bottel's desire to be seen as the man in charge, even if it had been Veronica who had done most of the speaking.

"I cross-referenced the names of everyone involved in Jake Thompson's arrests with Cooper Mills and also looked into Frank Klarno's social media presence like you asked."

Veronica stared blankly at Court. All of them had taken a two-hour hiatus between discovering the new victim and the press conference. Veronica had spent half of that time napping and the other half trying to make herself look halfway presentable.

Judging by their change in appearance, she suspected that Court and Freddie had done something similar.

Yet, she felt more lost than before the rest and icy shower.

"Frank who?"

"Oh, shit, my bad," Court scratched the back of his neck. "While you were—"

"Who's Frank Klarno?" Veronica interrupted.

"The third victim. I managed to get into his phone and ID'd him from that."

"Frank Klarno," Veronica repeated out loud. It didn't ring a bell. "You were saying something about a connection?"

Court looked uncomfortable.

"I wish—nothing. Frank is a woodworker, Jake a drug dealer, Cooper an accountant. No real links, so far as I could tell."

"And Frank has no record?" Veronica asked, recalling that the man's fingerprints hadn't pinged any database.

As they spoke, Veronica led Freddie and Court further away from the captain, who was still staring out at the last few reporters who were packing up their things.

"No record."

Something in Court's voice made her stop and look at the officer.

"But?"

Court shifted weight from one foot to the other.

"But Frank was no saint, that's for sure. I found a lot of pictures of women on his phone. A *lot*."

Veronica cocked her head.

"Underage women? Snuff films? Rape? Torture?"

She was rattling off everything she could think of, but with each word, Court just shook his head.

"No—no, nothing like that. Actually, most, if not all, of the pictures were sent by the women themselves. That's what it looks like, anyway. Everything appears completely consensual."

"I don't get it then."

"Frank was married, Veronica," Freddie spoke up. "And infidelity is a sin."

In her mind's eye, Veronica saw the word 'sinner' written in blood on the side of the school.

"Damn. Alright, who knew about this, then? Who knew about Frank sleeping around?"

Neither man had an answer.

"His wife? A friend of his wife? Could still be a cop. Or a PI," Veronica offered. She was just rambling now. "Stalker? No, that doesn't make sense. Who would know about all these men's sins? Who would want to punish them for it?"

"A priest?"

Veronica looked at Court. More like glared at him, judging by how he reacted.

"Sorry," the man said. "I just thought—

Freddie broke the tension by exhaling loudly.

"Maybe—but I don't know. I'll tell you what, it's not the rent-a-cop, though. He's clean. The security guard just likes to post about his job. Mostly of overworked people and their fancy cars. Just got lucky with Cooper."

That was a strange way of putting it, Veronica thought. *Not so lucky for Cooper.*

She ground her teeth. Usually, she was good at keeping her frustrations at bay.

But usually, they didn't have a fucking psycho turning sinners into angels on the loose in Greenham.

"What in the actual fuck, Freddie? Who is this guy? And what does he want?"

"I think he wants to punish people." Court again. The man had a habit of saying what they were thinking, but he wasn't adding anything productive.

None of them were.

They were just waiting for the unsub to strike again and hoped that he screwed up this time.

Or that the killer decided to call Captain Bottel's tip line and confess.

Yeah, sure. Like that was going to happen.

Veronica let out a long, prolonged sigh. She closed her eyes and placed a cool palm on her forehead.

"I guess… I guess there's only one thing to do now." She opened her eyes and looked first at Court then Freddie. "Let's go tell another woman that her husband has been murdered. And that we have no *fucking* idea who killed him."

***

To his credit, Officer Court Furnelli offered to break the devastating news to Karen Klarno. Deep down, Veronica wanted to say, "Thanks, go right ahead," but this was her responsibility—hers and Freddie's.

They were the lead detectives on this disaster of a case.

The odd thing was, Karen behaved almost identically to the way Sylvia Decker had, even though the latter had orchestrated her husband's murder.

That was grief for you. Unpredictably predictable.

This time, Veronica stayed well back from the woman, not wanting to be another shoulder to cry on.

She didn't want to share the woman's grief.

Freddie filled this void, which was more typical of their arrangement. Still, he looked shaken.

No matter how many times you dealt with death, you never became comfortable with it. Maybe if you were a mortician, maybe if you dealt with bodies day in and day out, but not if you were a cop. You could depersonalize as much as you want, but, at the end of the day, the body was still a person.

Had been a person.

Freddie, running on no more than a couple of hours of sleep, clearly hypoglycemic, was having a rough go of it. It didn't help that he'd been out of the game for six months and this was what he returned to.

After her multiple hiatuses, the department had eased Veronica back into the fold—or at least they'd tried to.

Not so with Freddie.

Veronica wasn't sure if she should be grateful or insulted.

"Frank was a good man," Karen whined between sobs.

Was he, though?

Frank had dozens of lewd images from other women on his phone. And while there was no universal litmus test for the goodness of a man or woman for that matter, this didn't seem to be a good starting point.

A good man? Probably not.

As if reading her mind, Karen's eyes drifted over to Veronica. Perhaps she saw something in the detective's face, or perhaps she only wanted to associate with a woman, hoping that they could relate on some genetic level.

Sorry, Karen, you picked the wrong broad.

"Before you say anything," Karen began, her voice strangely calm, "I am aware of Frank's indiscretions. And even though adultery is a sin, he was seeking absolution."

It took all of Veronica's will power to keep a straight face. The last photo, a woman doing squats wearing nothing at all, had been sent to Frank's phone just two days ago.

"I'm not here to judge," Veronica said. "We just want to find out who did this. Can you… can you think of anyone who would want to hurt Frank?"

A laundry list of potential suspects appeared in Veronica's mind: and every woman who sent a photo, every potential husband or boyfriend of said woman, was at the top.

In total, Court had counted seventy-eight photographs from sixty-three different women on Frank's phone.

Sixty-three.

Including significant others, which pushed the number of people that they had to talk to to well over a hundred.

"I don't. I don't know who would want to hurt Frank. He was a *good* man."

The woman's conviction was odd. Was she being defensive? Trying to protect her husband's name? Or was she embarrassed?

"Did Frank receive any threats?"

"Threats?" Karen started to cry again as she shook her head. "No, no threats."

There were so many more questions that Veronica wanted to ask, primarily related to Frank's potential relationship with either Jake or Cooper, but she couldn't bring herself to do it.

She had a sudden urge to get out of there.

"I'm very sorry for your loss."

"If you think of anything, please give us a call," Freddie said, sensing Veronica's urgency. He offered Karen a card, but she was too distraught to take it.

He placed it on the table and then together they saw themselves to the door. Veronica reached for the knob and then stopped.

Something was niggling at her.

Something that Karen had said was stuck in her brain.

"Mrs. Klarno?"

Karen turned slowly. Freddie, who had been behind her, slid to one side. In the past, she would have to walk around her partner to see, but not anymore. It was a testament to how far the man had come.

"Yes?" Karen wiped her face.

Veronica hesitated, and then it came to her.

And even though adultery is a sin, he was seeking absolution.

"Are you religious?"

As if Veronica had just blasphemed, the woman felt the need to cross herself before answering.

"Yes. I'm Catholic and so is Frank."

Is *not* was.

Veronica's pulse quickened.

"May I ask which church you attend?"

"Grace Community. It's not far from here. Why are you asking about my church?"

"Looking for a new parish myself," Veronica lied.

Karen's mood lifted.

"Oh, Grace is fantastic. And Father Murphy is a very kind man."

"Thanks."

Freddie looked at her, but Veronica didn't meet his gaze.

Instead, she turned her thoughts inward.

And to the word that had appeared above each of their victims: SINNER.

Jesus, why didn't we think of this before? It was staring us in the face all along.

"What's up?" Freddie asked once they were outside.

"I think I might have just found out the connection between our victims," Veronica said. This revelation should have felt good. But it didn't. It made her feel dirty and Veronica frowned deeply. "I hope you're ready to confess, Freddie, because if I have to do it, we're going to be at Grace Community for a week."

Chapter 41

COLE OBSERVED THE BYERS' RESIDENCE from his car window. Inside were three occupants: the young man from the red-light camera footage, his mother, and another young man who appeared even more on edge than the first.

Susan, Randall, and Kevin Byers—all of whom had gone by the last name 'Furlow' for a time.

Freddie's ex-wife and two estranged children.

Cole's research revealed that both of Freddie's sons had petitioned to change their surnames to their mother's maiden name about ten years ago. The reason for this change intrigued him, but for now, Cole's priority was to exonerate Dylan. He still wasn't sure how all these pieces fit together, but the timing of Dylan's arrest and the interaction between first Freddie and the DEA Agent and then with his son was intriguing, to say the least.

Perhaps even 'coincidental'. And years in Internal Affairs had taught Cole that coincidences—*true* coincidences—were exceedingly rare. If someone in the precinct reports a pair of panties missing and the next day you catch a lieutenant sniffing underwear?

What were the chances that they were his? That he was just obsessed with his own musk?

Randall left the house about half an hour after his mom. Sporting a neatly pressed polo shirt and gray slacks, Cole would bet his designer shoes that the young man was off to work. Randall left on foot, and mindful not to tip off Kevin Byers of his presence, Cole waited until Randall was out of sight of the house before following him.

"Excuse me!" he called out, waving an arm. "Randall? Randall Byers?"

The jumpy young man turned, tensing as if preparing to flee.

Cole put on his most soothing expression, a skill he'd honed over time when dealing with people who were naturally suspicious of his intentions and position.

"Hi—it's Randall, right?" Cole displayed his badge, which hung from his neck. "I'm a friend of your father."

Randall's face shifted from fear to concern.

"Is he okay?"

"Oh, yeah, sorry, didn't mean to alarm you—he's fine. In fact, Freddie's lost a ton of weight. That heart attack was probably the best thing that ever happened to him."

Now, Randall's expression hardened.

"Then I have nothing to say to you." He turned to leave but Cole, still smiling warmly, grabbed his arm.

"I'm sorry, I just… I have a few questions about what you were doing with DEA Agent Troy Allison the night your dad had his heart attack?"

"I have nothing to say to you."

Randall squirmed, but Cole squeezed the man's thin triceps even harder.

"Right, I understand you're late for work and I don't want to hold you up. Really, I don't want any trouble. I just want to know why you were with the DEA when your brother has a history—"

Randall snarled and instead of trying to squirm free, the man flipped the script and grasped Cole by the collar of his shirt.

"If you want to know about my family, why don't you ask Detective Furlow? Me, my mom, and my brother have nothing to say to you."

Randall shoved Cole. It wasn't particularly hard, but Cole let go and stepped back.

"I'm sorry," Cole said, maintaining his calm expression. He raised his hands. "I didn't mean to bother you."

"Stay away," Randall warned.

Cole watched the man go, making no attempt to follow. While he generally didn't like judging a book by its cover, Randall's behavior was suggestive of something.

Had he hit a nerve? Maybe. Probably. But what had he said that set Randall off? Was it the DEA comment? The mention of his father?

No, that's not it, Cole conceded.

When Randall was out of sight, he returned to his car parked outside the Byers' home.

It was his brother—Randall got squirrely when I mentioned his brother.

Kevin Byers was taller than his younger sibling but also leaner, which was saying something. He had the look of someone on the verge of addiction, if not already there.

Strung out.

Anxious.

Kevin left the house at 9:22, scanning the quiet suburban street as if expecting someone. At 9:34, that someone arrived.

A black Mercedes with tinted windows so dark that it was impossible to see inside—even the front windshield was blacked out—pulled up to the curb.

Again, Kevin's eyes darted up and down the street, this time most likely searching for cops.

Personal experience shaped their expectations of what police looked like. For a man like Kevin Byers who grew up with his father as a detective, he had his own assumptions. If he noticed Cole at all, with his dark, neatly styled hair, square jaw, trimmed beard, and handsome features, he didn't see a cop.

He saw a lawyer, actor, or businessman.

But not a cop.

Kevin got into the passenger seat of the Mercedes and the car drove off. A few minutes later, Cole followed. As their destination became clear—Needle Point—a hypothesis about what had happened to Dylan Hall began to form in his mind.

Still circumstantial, no doubt, but the circumstances were far from ideal.

In fact, they were downright terrible.

Especially when considering Detective Freddie Furlow's involvement in Dylan Hall's increasingly complex case.

When Veronica asked him to do whatever it took to exonerate Dylan, she likely meant working long hours, spending cash, greasing wheels, pulling favors. That's what most people meant—work hard, spend money, do some digging. Get the job done.

The problem was, once Cole Batherson started digging, he wouldn't stop until the hole had been completely cleared out.

"Fuck," he whispered.

He was beginning to suspect that this hole wasn't hiding gold coins or crypto keys. Cole was slowly starting to think that this hole was actually a grave. And if he kept digging, nobody was going to be happy with the bones he unearthed.

Least of all, Veronica Shade.

Chapter 42

"**What if... what if you** stopped doing that, Veronica?"

Veronica raised an eyebrow.

She wasn't sure what was more confusing, the fact that her partner was using her what-if strategy, one he openly despised, or what, exactly, Freddie wanted her to stop doing.

"What do you mean?"

"I mean, you walking away, acting like you're about to leave, only to stop at the last second and then turn like Columbo." Freddie put on an accent. "'Just one other thing, Mrs. Klarno...'."

Veronica laughed. It felt strange to laugh, and probably a little inappropriate considering what they were investigating, but it was funny. And true. She had pulled a Columbo. But it hadn't been by design, some egotistical production ensuring she was on center stage. Veronica simply hadn't put the clues together yet.

She blamed this on fatigue.

"I was giving you the chance to speak up," Veronica said with a grin.

"I was too busy consoling the woman."

Veronica rolled her eyes.

"Right."

"But you know what? You might be onto something."

"Don't sound too surprised."

Freddie chuckled.

"If our unsub isn't a cop, PI, or psychiatrist, he could be a priest. People like to talk to priests."

Veronica thought about the photograph she kept in her wallet, the one of her brother and Dante posing while at Renaissance Home.

And then she thought about Father Cartier. She'd never met the man, but she knew all about the terror he'd unleashed on the orphans, including Benny.

Officially, the priest had died of a heart attack. Unofficially, Dante Fiori had beaten the man to death. His right hand, Sister Margaret, who had facilitated Father Cartier's abuse, officially died by suicide. Unofficially, she'd been hung by at least one but probably by a handful of the Renaissance boys.

Although she would never say it out loud, Veronica hoped the unofficial versions were what really happened to those disgusting and vile individuals.

"Let's try to keep our minds open," Freddie said without prompting.

Veronica's disdain for priests and churches in general must have been plastered all over her face.

"Are you a religious man, Freddie?"

"I was, once. Not so much anymore."

The finality in her partner's voice discouraged further inquiry. Her partner's attitude reminded Veronica of how he had reacted to her asking about what he and Agent Keller had spoken about outside the precinct that day.

"Well, I'm not making any promises, Freddie," Veronica admitted. "But I'll try to keep an open mind."

Grace Community Church was technically located in Cedar Heights, but it was within a half mile of the wedge-shaped Needle Point with Meadowbrook looming just on the other side. Although Veronica was fairly certain that these borough distinctions came about after the church was built, it seemed to share characteristics with all three of these very different districts.

The grass out front was Needle Point: burnt, littered with refuse, and mostly patchy. The building itself was all Cedar

Heights: an imposing two-story brown brick structure with a peaked front and a stained glass window depicting a giant brown cross. The walkway to the front door was Meadowbrook: it was well maintained, and someone had put effort into making it look nice. But it was the fact that this effort was obvious that kept it from claiming the same prestige as Cedar Heights.

Veronica had had every intention of keeping an open mind, but that just simply wasn't in the cards. Seeing that large brown door reminded her of Renaissance Home, and she imagined the screams that it kept trapped within the building's walls. With a half-scowl on her face, Veronica's pace slowed, and Freddie got to the door first. He politely held it open for her, but Veronica indicated for him to go first.

And then her partner did something she hadn't expected.

Once inside, he knelt on one knee and crossed himself.

Freddie hadn't explicitly stated that he was non-religious—*not so much anymore*—but this action just seemed wrong. They were working a case. They shouldn't be praying or doing whatever... *that* was.

"You okay?" Freddie asked quietly.

Veronica realized that she was clenching her jaw and forced herself to relax. Then she inhaled twice in succession before letting all the air out of her lungs.

"Fine. Since you seem to be the expert here, you want to find out who's in charge?"

Freddie frowned but let the comment go and Veronica looked around.

The church was well lit and the abundant use of light-colored wood—pine?—only made it seem brighter. The layout was typical, with arced pews flanking a center aisle leading to the stage. The raised area consisted of a classic lectern containing a single metal microphone with a bent arm. Behind that was a large rectangle covered in a white cloth adorned with gold-stenciling. High above the stage, in front of the largest south-facing stained-glass window, was Jesus hanging from the cross.

Veronica looked away from the half-naked man. To the right of the pews was a series of confessionals, which looked to her like oversized and overpriced high-school lockers.

As she watched, one of the doors opened and a plump man in his early fifties with a kind face and thin brown hair brushed to one side stepped out. He was wearing a black smock, and even though he looked nothing like the late Father Cartier, the simple idea of him was similar enough to incite a twinge of anger deep in Veronica's gut.

She was about to elbow Freddie to indicate the priest, but her partner was already starting toward him.

"Father," Freddie said with a polite nod. "My name is Detective Furlow, and this is my partner Detective Shade."

He flashed his badge and Veronica did the same.

"Father James Murphy, but I prefer James." The priest smiled warmly. "You're too young, and I'm too old to be your father. How can I help you, detectives?"

Up close, the man's kind features and demeanor were even more evident. But rather than comfort Veronica, they only seemed to make her angrier.

"Is there someplace quiet we can talk?" Freddie asked.

The pious man held his hands out, indicating the pews. There were only a handful of people in the church, none of whom had even noticed the two detectives.

"Okay, here's fine," Freddie said. "Do you know a man named Jake Thompson?"

Father Murphy nodded.

"Oh, yes, I know Jake. He's a parishioner at Grace Community," Father Murphy replied, cocking his head. "Or was."

"What do you mean, was?" Veronica snapped.

They hadn't released Jake's name to the public. They had shown his picture, but what were the chances that this man even owned a TV?

"Well, I haven't seen Jake in a while—in about two weeks. I fear he may have fallen prey to his old habits."

If the priest was insulted by Veronica's tone, he didn't show it.

"Which were?"

Father Murphy held his hands out.

"It is not my place to say, detective. However, I presume that because you are here asking about him, you know what Jake's weaknesses are."

Veronica soured.

Now it's *are*. Present tense.

Does he know that Jake is dead?

"How about you don't presume things, Father, and just answer our questions? Does that work?"

Try as she might, Veronica couldn't stop superimposing Father Cartier's face over James Murphy's. And then she pictured this hybrid of a man walking down the hallway of Renaissance Home, the orphans in their rooms gripping their sheets hoping, praying—yeah, a lot of good that did them—that Margaret unlocked any other door than theirs.

"I'm sorry, Father," Freddie intervened, stepping between them. Normally, this would completely cut Veronica off from the scene, but given his recent weight loss, she could still see Father Murphy and the effect was less pronounced. "It's been a very taxing day. We are looking into Jake Thompson's activities over the past few days."

"Well, in that case, I'm sorry I can't help you. Like I said, I haven't seen Jake in at least a week but more like two. Is he—is Jake okay? Did something happen to him?"

"What about Cooper Mills?" Veronica blurted.

"Cooper Mills? Yes, I saw him last Sunday, actually."

"He's a member of this church, too?"

"Yes. Detective... Shade, is it?" Veronica nodded out of habit and the priest took this as a cue to continue. "If you were to tell me what, exactly, you were—"

It wasn't.

"What about Frank Klarno?"

"Yes, I know Frank, as well. Please, if—"

Veronica slipped out from Freddie's shadow.

"You know them by name alone?"

Father Murphy remained stoic despite Veronica's aggressive challenges.

"Detective Shade, I try my best to get to know every one of my parishioners by name. I believe that to be an important part of my job."

"Right, right, then you must have known that all three men were sinners, correct?"

Freddie finally interjected.

"Detective Shade, perhaps you should get some fresh air?" Even her partner addressing her by her professional name, something that usually indicated she was stepping over an invisible line, didn't work on Veronica this time.

"Naw, I'm good. Father? Would you consider all three men sinners?"

"Veronica, please!" Freddie looked personally offended now.

"No, it's fine, it's fine. Here, walk with me, detective."

"I'm good right here."

Out of the corner of her eye, she saw Freddie reach for her, and Veronica preemptively stepped out of range.

Father Murphy's face finally changed. He wasn't mad, but he no longer seemed completely unaffected by Veronica's aggression.

"Every man sins, detective. Every woman, too. We are born out of sin."

Veronica's eyes narrowed.

"I'm not talking about that. I'm talking about... listen, let's just cut the shit, alright?" Freddie's hand extended further, and this time Veronica pushed it away. "Jake Thompson was a drug dealer, Cooper Mills liked to use women as punching bags, and Frank was a serial adulterer. That's the truth. That's their sins. And they weren't born with them, were they?"

Father Murphy licked his lips. Deep down, Veronica wanted this man to become enraged, for his facade of tranquility and composure to come crumbling down.

But he refused to take the bait.

What's worse was that Veronica's synesthesia hadn't picked up anything even remotely violent about this man or even a hint of a lie coming from his lips.

"As I said earlier, I won't speak negatively of any of my parishioners but suffice it to say that everyone who steps through my doors is seeking help for one thing or another. That includes you, Detective Shade."

"Fuck you."

"Woah, woah!" Freddie held his hands out, blocking Veronica. "Father, I'm very sorry for my partner. As I said, it's been a long day."

Veronica had stepped over the line and knew it. The words had just slipped out of her mouth. Another consequence of fatigue?

Maybe.

"Yeah, you're right. I'm sorry," she grumbled, then turned. Freddie's apology to the priest followed her through the pews and out the front door.

As soon as her shoes touched concrete, the pressure that weighed on her shoulders began to lessen. This continued until Veronica was back on the sidewalk, staring up at the huge stained-glass window.

The pressure was gone, but her anger remained.

And the urge to scream was strong. To make fists with both hands, bend down, and just shout at the top of her lungs, like they do in bad horror movies.

Veronica forced herself to do a double-inhale instead.

She'd honestly thought she'd be able to keep at least a partially open mind. But seeing that man... seeing Father James Murphy and listening to his pious speech was too much. As unfair as it was, Veronica couldn't stop picturing Father Cartier in his place.

Without conscious thought, Veronica had pulled her wallet out and removed the photograph of her brother with Dante.

I bet Father Cartier spoke to you in a calm, even voice, she thought. *I bet he even tried to make the orphans he raped and abused feel special.*

Dante Fiori's words suddenly resonated inside her skull.

"Father Cartier would make us—his special orphans—strip naked and jump in the freezing water. Then he would tell us to swim across. He would stand here and watch us, with a grin on his fat fucking face. He made us a promise: if we swam all the way across, if we got to the other side, he would leave us alone."

A tear spilled from her eye, and she swiped at it.

Five, six, I crossed the River Styx.

"That went well."

Veronica sniffed and quickly tucked the photo back into her wallet. Freddie was coming toward her, a stack of papers in his hand and anger in his eyes.

"You were too soft on him." Veronica pointed at the church. "Too soft!"

Freddie stopped cold and squinted at her.

"And here I was thinking that you'd be waiting with an apology."

"An apology? I—" Veronica caught herself. Father James Murphy didn't deserve her ire—not yet, anyway—and Freddie especially didn't. She threw up her hands. "I'm sorry, all right? But this... he knows about their sins, Freddie. He's the link between all of our victims."

Freddie started moving again, and he indicated for her to follow him further away from the church.

"We don't have anything, Veronica." Freddie's teeth were clenched. "We have an idea, maybe, but we don't have anything concrete. No evidence."

"He's the link!" Veronica protested.

Freddie had knelt and crossed himself... was he too blinded by faith to see the connection?

"Veronica, did your synesthesia tell you that or are you just projecting your anger from what happened to your brother?"

Now, it was Veronica's turn to stop cold.

"That's not right."

"No, I'm being serious. I'm asking you. Did something about the church or Father Murphy trigger your synesthesia?"

Veronica glared at her partner. Unlike when he'd blown up in the car six months ago, Freddie appeared genuine now. He was honestly trying to understand her.

And it was a valid question.

She'd considered that Freddie was blinded by his faith, but never had it crossed her mind that it was her experience that was coloring her judgment.

"I didn't see anything," Veronica admitted softly. Her face started to get warm.

Did I actually just tell a middle-aged priest to fuck off?

"Okay, look, I'm not saying that the church or Father Murphy had nothing to do with our murders, but before we go down that road, we're going to need some hard proof. And in case it has nothing to do with him, we have to explore all options." Freddie held up the stack of papers. "Father Murphy was kind enough to put together a list of all people that volunteered at the church over the past year or so. I figure that if our victims were revealing their sins in confession, maybe someone overheard. An altar boy or, I dunno, electrician or something. What do you think? Is it worthwhile looking through these?"

Freddie gently flapped the list. He had a kind, caring look on his face. One that was not unlike Father Murphy's expression.

No, his judgment isn't jaded. It's mine that's the problem. I'm the one who's fucked up.

Veronica shook her head.

Once a killer, always a killer.

"I think... I think I need to go see somebody. Can you cover?"

Freddie nodded.

"Of course—I'll go through these names, give you a call if I find anything. Just... just take care of yourself, Veronica."

"Thanks, Freddie," Veronica said, wiping her face again. "Thanks."

And then she turned and left, not even considering looking back at the church or her partner.

Chapter 43

"I'M SORRY, BUT YOU CAN'T go in there."

Veronica ignored the secretary and opened the door to Dr. Simon Patel's office.

"I need to—" she paused. Dr. Patel was sitting with his legs crossed, iPad in his lap. Across from him was a woman who was dabbing at her nose with a tissue. "—talk."

Dr. Patel looked at her, then at the sniffling woman, and then at the secretary who appeared behind Veronica.

"I'm sorry, Dr. Patel. She barged in."

Dr. Patel waved the secretary away.

"That's quite all right, thank you, Tina." He turned his attention to the woman across from him. "Mrs. Tucker, I'm very sorry for the interruption but our time here is almost up. Do you mind if we continue our discussion next time?"

The woman gave Veronica a seething look, but she eventually nodded.

"I'll see you next week, Ms. Tucker. And thank you."

The woman balled up the tissue in her hand and then left the room.

"Shut the door, please."

Veronica ignored Dr. Patel.

"I need help," she said flatly.

"Shut the door," Dr. Patel ordered again, this time more sternly.

With a furrowed brow, Veronica closed the door, then repeated her request.

"You can't just barge in here, Veronica. I don't know how you did things with Dr. Bernard, but that's not how it works with me."

Veronica was taken aback by the man's demeanor. Last time she met with the psychiatrist, he'd been clever, but demure.

He was anything but now.

"Sorry, but it couldn't wait."

Dr. Patel wasn't quite leering at her, but his look was far from friendly.

"I understand. But I don't run a walk-in clinic. I'll see you today but if you barge in again, you will no longer be a patient of mine. Do you understand me?"

Veronica made a face.

"Yeah, I understand. Can I..." She indicated the chair.

"Please, sit." Veronica did. "To be honest, I'm surprised to see you back here at all, after how things ended last time."

Ah, yes, another man I told to fuck off.

This was becoming so commonplace that Veronica was tempted to start a journal to keep track.

"Sorry about that."

"Happens." Dr. Patel shrugged. His demeanor had once again become calm. "What can I help you with today?"

"I..." Veronica was suddenly tongue-tied. She'd rushed over here directly from the church, angry at Freddie, at Father Murphy, and pretty much everybody. But now that she was sitting in this chair, what was she supposed to say?

I almost ruined an entire investigation into a serial killer because I couldn't compartmentalize my distaste for the church? That my boyfriend—ex-boyfriend—said the exact same thing you did? That I can't forgive myself for what happened when I was young, but I can forgive everyone else?

That I'm really messed up, and I need serious help?

That I killed two people and I'm worried that I'll kill again?

"Remember, nothing you say to me will ever leave these walls."

"Yeah, I've heard that before," Veronica muttered under her breath. This wasn't exactly fair assessment of Dr. Jane Bernard. As far as Veronica knew, it was her father who had shared information with her ex-psychiatrist and not the other way around. Still, Jane kept things from her. Important things about her past that might have—no, *would* have helped Veronica understand her condition.

Her *behavior*.

"I saw you on the news early this morning," Dr. Patel said, changing the subject. "Does your being here have anything to do with the missing persons you mentioned?"

"They're not missing persons. They're dead. Three of them, murdered. So, yeah, it's about that... and about a lot more."

As psychiatrists were apt to do, Dr. Patel said nothing; he just stared.

"Why do you guys do that?" Veronica demanded. "Why do you guys just look at us and expect us to open up?"

Dr. Patel shrugged.

"Well, I don't know why 'us guys' do it, but I know why I do it."

Veronica took a page out of the psychiatrist's book and simply looked at the man. After a few seconds, the corners of Dr. Patel's lips turned upward ever so slightly.

"Well, two reasons, really: the first is exactly what you suggested. Silence can make people a little uncomfortable and encourage them to speak; and two, I don't want to bias you in any way. If I suggest what to talk about, we might miss what is really on your mind. Does that answer your question?"

"It was mostly rhetorical, anyway." Veronica paused and looked at her hands. She was once again rubbing them back and forth in an attempt to feel burn scars that were no longer there.

"I—I need help. You touched on something last time. Forgiveness. I-I need to... I need to learn how to forgive myself." Her voice cracked, and her eyes became unexpectedly moist. This sudden outpouring of emotion was nearly impossible to stem. "I killed them... I killed my family. Then I killed Gloria and then Dante and... and... and I'm afraid I'll kill again."

When Dr. Patel still didn't say anything, Veronica rubbed her eyes and finally looked up. Her ears were hot, and she wondered if she'd made a mistake.

Dr. Patel's face gave nothing away. He was stoic, unaffected by her damning confession.

The man cleared his throat and adjusted the iPad on his lap, the screen of which Veronica saw was dark.

"There's a lot to unpack there, Veronica. *A lot*. I'm familiar with your file, of course, and I know what you went through as a child was extremely traumatic. You ask me to help you forgive yourself for what happened, but I don't need to do that. Nobody does. I don't want to diminish your feelings, but what happened to your family was not your fault. You didn't choose anything. Those men... they chose *you*. You can't blame yourself—"

"But that's the thing—I *do* blame myself. Because I was bad before. I hurt people before Trent and Herb broke into my house. Everyone says that they selected my house randomly, but what if they didn't? What if they picked me because they knew what I was capable of?"

Veronica's mind turned to what Dante Fiori had shouted at her on Donovan's Bridge. That Benny had told him that she'd cut her dad's finger off. That she'd tried to poison her mother with bleach.

Veronica had no recollection of these events. This, in and of itself, wasn't surprising—much of her memory of her childhood was clouded.

But the fact that she couldn't definitively say that these two things hadn't happened was telling enough.

Wasn't it?

Veronica had searched high and wide for any sort of record of these events, going as far as to look into hospital records for incidents involving her birth father, Trevor Davis.

Nothing.

There was nothing.

But that didn't mean that it hadn't happened. Veronica knew firsthand that there were ways to change one's name, to redact pertinent information, and to just make things disappear.

"I can't speak to what happened or didn't happen in your past, because I wasn't there," Dr. Patel said suddenly. "The point is, however, that while there is no denying that our pasts shape us, only the past itself is indelible. The future is undecided. Now, I don't want to belittle the impact that your trauma has had on you, Veronica, but you must realize that you don't have to do today what you did yesterday. You don't have to *be* who you were yesterday. The person that we project onto others and even the way we consider ourselves can change from day-to-day, week to week, even moment to moment. We just need to be careful and precise with our actions."

Dr. Patel had said a whole bunch of words, but all Veronica heard was Peter Shade's voice.

The past is boring; it's already happened. The future is far more interesting.

"I've tried, though," Veronica protested. "I've tried to stop myself, but I can't. And that... that scares me."

Dr. Patel stared at her for an uncomfortably long time before saying something wholly unexpected. Something that surprised Veronica so much that she instinctively sniffed the air to determine if the man was lying.

She detected not even a hint of gasoline.

"When I was eleven, I was diagnosed clinically as a psychopath. Now, we don't like to use that term anymore; we prefer antisocial personality disorder. But back then, that's what they called me: a psychopath. Basically, they did some tests, and they found out that I had a region in my brain that doesn't light up normally when I'm bombarded with sad or violent imagery. I don't feel empathy, and because of this, it can be challenging to interact with others."

Veronica's shock must've shown on her face because Dr. Patel held up his hand.

"Don't worry; I'm not violent. Never have been, in fact. The movies and books might portray all psychopaths as being aggressive, but that's not the case. There are triggers, of course, and if I don't control my actions, I may inadvertently hurt someone because I don't understand their pain. This scared the hell out of my parents, but it's also probably what drove me toward this profession. I'm not ashamed to admit that at least part of my motivation as a psychiatrist is to better understand people so that I can fit into society. But my disorder provides benefits to my patients, as well. For instance, I am almost painfully unbiased, and I can speak as bluntly as I need to, to get my point across. No social grace hurdles to overcome—and, yes, they typically exist, even within the walls of a psychiatrist's office."

"That's... sad," Veronica said.

Dr. Patel shrugged.

"If you say so. And maybe it is, I don't know. But the way I look at it, I can't miss something I never had." Veronica opened her mouth to speak, but Dr. Patel wasn't done yet. "I know what you're thinking, Veronica. You're thinking that you might be a psychopath, too. But I can assure you, you're not."

"How can you know? I've only spoken to you for—what? A half-hour?"

"Because you're here. It's as simple as that. I know that your previous session was mandated, but this one isn't. And you must be aware that I didn't report you for leaving the way you did last time and not finishing the session." Dr. Patel leaned forward. "Veronica, you came here because you want help. Someone with antisocial personality disorder wouldn't seek help."

"But it doesn't help." Veronica was aware of the fact that she was whining but thought nothing of it. "It… it doesn't."

"Just showing up isn't enough. You've gone through terrible things in your life, and understanding, like healing, takes time."

"But I've been going to a psychiatrist since I was a kid."

"Right. Well, a person who wants to stay in shape has to keep going to the gym for their entire life," Dr. Patel countered. "And with your history, you're like Sisyphus pushing a boulder uphill. You make progress one day and the next your line of work exposes you to more grief. This reignites feelings inside you, mostly of guilt, and before you know it, you've crested the hill and the boulder is racing down the other side. And then it's like you're starting all over again. Veronica, these feelings you have won't just disappear on their own. Let me guess, when things get bad inside your head, you start drinking a little more?"

Spot on, Veronica thought but didn't say anything.

"Sorry to break it to you, but that doesn't help—it won't help. You need to keep talking about it. You need to work these things out. I know Dr. Bernard, well, know of her, anyway, and I know she's good. But I also know that you guys were close. Sometimes, closeness can be helpful. Sometimes it can hinder how open and honest we are."

"That's a pretty damn good sales pitch, Dr. Patel," Veronica joked.

"It's not a pitch—it's based on my experience."

Dr. Patel was stone-faced.

"Riiiight. Well, I—"

There was a soft knock on the door and the secretary peered in.

"Dr. Patel? Your next patient has arrived."

"Right. Give me just a moment, would you?"

"Sure."

The secretary closed the door and Dr. Patel addressed Veronica.

"I'm sorry about that, but this meeting was impromptu."

Veronica rose to her feet.

"No, I understand."

"Should I have the secretary book you another appointment?"

Veronica considered everything the man had told her since she'd burst through the door unannounced. Like her being able to project a different person into the world. Like being able to change who she was from moment to moment.

Was that possible?

Veronica didn't know.

Then there was the man's odd confession about being diagnosed as a psychopath. Dr. Patel claimed that he wasn't prone to violence, but others with his disorder definitely were.

Veronica sucked in her bottom lip.

The psychiatrist across from her had also admitted that he used these sessions to learn about how normal people behaved in an attempt to mimic them.

An idea began to form in Veronica's brain, one that centered around a more reciprocal relationship.

Maybe even a symbiotic one.

If he can learn from me, maybe I could learn from him.

"Yeah, you know what? I think I would like another appointment. I'll be back to push that damn stone up the hill."

Dr. Patel nodded but his overall expression didn't change at all. If he was happy about her decision, there was no way for Veronica to know.

Yeah, he had a lot of learning to do.

"And I'll be here to try and stop it from rolling down the other side."

Chapter 44

COLE'S PI SKILLS WERE DEFINITELY lacking in one very specific department: tailing a suspect. Or person.

Essentially, just following someone in a car.

He lost Kevin Byers and the black Mercedes after less than ten minutes. Cole drove around Needle Point looking equal parts junkie and narc for perhaps twice that long, before giving up.

Instead of wasting any more time, he grabbed a coffee and sat with his laptop in the parking lot.

Then Cole spent the next three hours scouring video footage from pretty much every camera he could access in Matheson: traffic lights, ATMs, even some unsecured footage from outside several local businesses he got into by just guessing the password.

Everything he saw, which, granted, wasn't much, supported his theory regarding what really happened to Dylan Hall. There was only one piece to the puzzle that he was missing. One final piece of evidence that he needed to assuage any doubt in his mind.

Cole picked up his cell phone and scrolled through his contacts.

"Hey, Lily, it's Cole. How're you doin'?"

"Oh, you know, livin' the dream," a female voice replied. "How're you? Sittin' on a beach somewhere now that you're retired?"

Cole grimaced.

"You heard already, hey?"

"I heard? *I heard*? Of course, I heard. An ex-partner of mine goes all rogue, spits directly in the man's face? Bucks big corporate to go solo? Damn, boy, you're livin' the dream."

Cole rolled his eyes.

"Right. I mean, after the boss broke us up, I just couldn't handle it, you know? Just wasn't the same without you."

Lily Chen laughed. Cole always liked Lily's laugh. They'd worked together for just under two months until budget cuts and rampant misconduct—likely related—inspired a departmental reorg, and the two had been separated. But during their short time together, Lily's laugh had managed to keep things light, almost palatable.

"What're your plans? And don't hold back on the details—I need to live vicariously through you."

Well, first up, I'm an unpaid, unofficial private investigator working for my girlfriend who threw me out. I'm investigating an ex-con named Dylan Hall who was caught with a kilo of heroin. The thing is, Lily, he was set up. And the best part? You're not going to believe this...

"Well, I've started a PI firm." A little white lie. "And, you know, times are tough. Need a little help to get things off the ground, you know?"

"Like using my name and password to access red-light camera footage?"

Cole's jaw tightened.

"You know about that?"

"What can I say? Maybe I'm a natural PI?" There was an airy silence. "This time only, okay, Cole? I don't have a backup plan, and if brass finds out—"

"I understand. I'll delete your username and password. But... but there is one favor I need to ask."

"One *more* favor."

There was that laugh again.

"Yeah, one *more*. I don't have access to video footage from inside Matheson PD." Cole let this sink in. "Specifically, their evidence locker."

No laugh from IA Chen this time.

"I know, I know," Cole continued, anticipating her response. "But this has nothing to do with Matheson or Greenham PD." A not-so-white lie. "It's about the DEA, so it won't blow back on you if—"

"The DEA? Cole, what the fuck? Those guys are pricks, and you know that. Assholes who hold a grudge and—"

"I know, Lily. Trust me, I know. But this..." Cole sighed. "I don't want to ruffle feathers. And, if I do this right, I think I can make sure that no one gets plucked. But I need footage from inside the Matheson evidence locker. That's the missing piece I need."

"Oh, right, *just* that?"

"*Just* that."

Cole heard what sounded like Lily Chen working her mouth, probably chewing the inside of her cheek the way she always did when she was mulling over a problem.

It was cute... she was cute. They'd had a fling when they'd worked together, nothing serious, just a one-night thing after a particularly stressful day at work. They hadn't pursued a relationship because they worked together and then when they didn't, they'd already moved on.

"Okay, fine. Tell me the date and time. Last time, though, okay, Cole? I mean it. And delete my damn password."

Cole smiled.

"I will. And, yeah, last time. Promise."

After giving Lily the date range he wanted footage from, she told him she'd send it his way as soon as possible.

While he waited, Cole looked at the montage video he'd put together with just basic video editing software. It was disjointed and jumped around, switching from color to black-and-white, but he thought it was good enough.

The video started with Randall Byers being escorted into the Matheson police department. The cop who had cuffed him was carrying a brown package in one hand. Time skipped ahead about thirty minutes and that's when DEA Agent Troy Allison arrived and retrieved Randall from the Matheson police. The red-light camera outside the DEA headquarters picked up Allison and Byers shortly thereafter.

Fast forward several hours and Freddie Furlow is seen visiting the DEA stronghold. He leaves alone, empty-handed.

The following day, Veronica and Freddie were spotted outside Matheson PD. They entered the building and spent about three hours inside. If Cole hadn't been paying such close attention to Freddie, hell, if Freddie hadn't lost so much weight and he was marveling at how large the man used to be, he might not have noticed it.

The odd square bulge amongst many round ones.

When Freddie got to his car, he turned and it looked like there was an object tucked beneath his shirt, at the back, two corners of which jutted oddly against the already taut fabric of the detective's white shirt.

Cole let the rest of the video montage play out, except he stopped it right before Freddie had his heart attack.

Don't let me down, Lily.

Satisfied with his work, and not wanting to watch it again, Cole called Veronica.

There was no answer, and he opted against leaving a message.

With time to kill, Cole decided to dig a little deeper into Detective Freddie Furlow. He may have promised Lily to delete her credentials from his laptop, but neither of them actually thought he would do it.

Come on… if Lily really cared that much, she would have changed her password herself.

And she hadn't.

The problem was that the Matheson PD evidence locker footage wasn't posted online for obvious reasons: if a hacker managed to gain access and saw a cop roll in with a massive drug bust, they might be inspired to attempt to rob the place.

Rob a police evidence locker?

Yeah, it had been done. Successfully, too.

So, figuring out who, exactly, Detective Frederic Almonte Furlow was, was on the agenda. And an hour after he'd first started looking into the man, doing a deep dive into the detective's history as Junior would have called it, Cole leaned back from his laptop and whistled.

"Goddamn, I'm good," he said out loud, his lips curling into a grin. "Cole Batherson, PI of the motherfucking year."

He'd figured it out.

He'd figured out why Susan, Randall, and Kevin had changed their names from Furlow to Byers.

But this wasn't the most shocking part. The shocking part was how everything—*everything*—was related.

Chapter 45

BY ALL ACCOUNTS, FATHER JAMES Murphy was a stand-up guy. Everything that Detective Freddie Furlow could dig up about the priest indicated as much. Born fifty-two years ago in Greenham, James Murphy was only fourteen when he left for a religious summer camp in Idaho, a life-changing experience, evidently. At eighteen, he entered seminary school in Washington. Even though Oregon's population was predominantly Protestant, there was still a strong community of Roman Catholics. Father James Murphy returned from his studies at twenty and started working at Grace Community Church alongside the previous pastor, Father Tobias Chesterfield. Ten years later, Father Chesterfield retired, and Father Murphy took over.

There were numerous reports over the years of Father Murphy being an exemplary member of the community. But Freddie had been a detective for far too long to think that a simple search could reveal all of a man's demons.

Or sins.

Case in point, Father Cartier, who on first blush also seemed to be an upstanding member of the clergy. Deep down, however, the man was a sadistic rapist piece of shit.

Once news of what Father Cartier had done to those boys in Renaissance had broken, dozens of reports materialized out of nowhere. The proverbial dam had exploded.

Freddie managed to identify several altar boys who used to work for Father Murphy. He even managed to find a phone number for one of them and the boy, now a man, only had glowing things to say about the priest.

He is a true savior—he helped me through dark times, taught me that there was always a light at the end of the tunnel. Even if you couldn't see it, it was there. That light is the lord.

Two other queries went unanswered, but they both appeared to be contributing members of society.

If their lives had been tormented anything like Dante's, Dylan's, or Benny's had, this would have been nearly impossible.

Normally, Veronica's intuition was spot on. Freddie had learned to trust his partner's 'feelings' even before he'd learned about her synesthesia. But this time, it felt different.

She was convinced that Father Murphy was punishing the victims for their sins, but Freddie got a very different vibe from the man. He was, however, cognizant of the fact that while Veronica's perception of the church was negatively influenced by what had happened to her brother, the opposite was true for him.

Years back, he remembered going to church with his family. It wasn't *really* his thing—Susan was the one who insisted on it, and Freddie had seen enough evil in this world to know that God didn't exist—but it was a nice time.

Family time.

Time he missed.

Freddie spent the next half hour going through some of the names from the list of employees/volunteers that Father Murphy had given him.

Nothing really stood out and his mind soon started to wander.

He leaned back in his chair and tapped his pen on the desk.

It's quiet in here, he thought, too *quiet*.

With Cole Batherson no longer hanging around, Veronica meeting with her shrink, and Pierre Bottel doing whatever he did to gain additional political favor, Freddie found himself alone in the precinct.

Alone and hungry.

"Ah, shit."

When he was busy, it was easier to ignore the hunger.

Freddie sighed and decided to move onto something else. Any distraction was welcomed at this point.

He found himself thinking about the sheriff, of how he'd gone undercover and nearly died from a hot dose. This, in turn, reminded him of the package of heroin that his son Randall had been picked up with.

The one adorned with the logo of a snake eating an eyeball.

Remembering that DEA Agent Troy Allison had told him that that product featuring that insignia was initially being brought into the US through New York, he started his investigation on the east coast.

And then he kept digging, unearthing an unbelievable story of corruption and addiction. Of power.

One name kept popping up over and over again and, on a whim, Freddie picked up the phone and called the NYPD 62nd precinct.

"Detective Damien Drake? Ah, no, he doesn't work here anymore," a Sergeant Yasiv informed him.

"Did he move to another precinct?"

"No, he doesn't work for the NYPD." The sergeant's tone suggested that there was more to this story, but Freddie didn't press.

"Any way I can get ahold of him?"

"What's this about?"

"We found some heroin in Greenham and think it might be linked to product from the East Coast. The package has a snake eating an eyeball on it." Freddie's comment was met with dead air. "Hello?"

"Yeah, sorry—you sure? I thought Anguis Holdings was dead and gone."

"Anguis Holdings?"

"Detective..."

"Furlow."

"Detective Furlow, is this an official investigation? Because if—"

Freddie's phone beeped indicating that he had another call.

"I have to go. Thanks." He switched to the other line, expecting to hear Veronica's voice. "I dug into Father Murphy, and it looks he's clean—can't find a speck of dirt on him."

"Umm... hello? Is this... Fred?"

The voice was unfamiliar to Freddie. He straightened.

"This is Detective Furlow. How may I help you?"

"Fred, it's Susan."

Freddie's eyes went wide.

"Susan? Susan, is everything all right? Is Randy okay?"

"R-Randy?"

"You're... wait—what's going on?" Freddie was on his feet now, one arm already in his jacket.

"Randy's fine. So is Kevin."

His heart was racing, and he tried to calm it, thinking that if it sped up any more, he might find himself back in the hospital.

And this time, he might not come out.

"Are *you* okay?"

"Yeah, I'm fine. Is this a bad time? I can just call back or..."

Freddie was nearly at the elevator, and he forced himself to stop and take a deep breath.

"No—no, it's fine. Sorry. What can I help you with, Susan?"

There was an uncomfortable pause and Freddie fought the urge to break it with small talk.

He tried to remember the last time he'd spoken to her.

Three years ago? *Four*?

"I've... look, I've spoken with Randy. Fred, I think..." It was clear that whatever she was thinking was extremely uncomfortable for her. Freddie gave her time and eventually, she blurted, "Do you want to come over for dinner?"

The tightness in his chest was almost definitely a heart attack now.

Dinner? Did my ex-wife who I haven't spoken to in years just invite me to dinner? Impossible.

"I-I don't mean tonight, but this weekend? Just dinner. Randy will be here, I'm not sure about Kevin. It'll just—"

"Yes," Freddie gasped. "Yes, I would love that." The tightness abated, but only a little. "I would really love that, Susan."

Chapter 46

"HEY! EXCUSE ME!" COLE SHOUTED as he darted across the street. "Excuse me!"

The burly man with a cigarette dangling from his lips didn't even turn.

"Agent Allison?"

This got the imposing man's attention. He stopped and looked at Cole, pinching the smoke aggressively between two fingers as he inhaled.

"What do you want?"

Cole was unsurprised by the man's attitude.

"I'm—"

Troy's eyes drifted to Cole's shoes, and he exhaled sharply.

"I don't talk to reporters."

"I'm not a reporter," Cole said, his voice friendly, a smile on his face.

"Who the hell are you, then?"

"My name's Cole Batherson, and I'm—" he hesitated, "—a private investigator."

The sneer on Troy's face grew even more pronounced.

"I don't talk to the media, and I definitely don't talk to private investigators." Troy flicked his spent cigarette, and it landed within inches of Cole's right toe. Then the big man spun.

"But you talk to cops, right?"

Troy kept walking, and Cole, feeling bold, followed.

"Detectives, in particular? Like Detective Freddie Furlow? You talk to him, right?"

Troy didn't stop, but his gait changed a little. His strides were tighter, more labored.

"Detective Furlow? You don't know him?" Cole pestered. He'd brought a folder of photographs, stills from the video footage of the Matheson evidence room that Lily had gotten him, as well as traffic light camera footage from very near where they were standing now, but he didn't think he needed them.

Troy knew Freddie, that was no secret, but what Cole didn't know is how deeply they'd collaborated.

"Maybe," Cole came right up next to Troy, "Maybe you need something to jog your memory. Freddie Furlow used to be real fat? Like heart attack fat? No? Okay, how about this: Detective Furlow stole evidence to frame an innocent man to keep his son out of prison?"

That did it.

Troy stopped cold and slowly trained his icy eyes on Cole.

The man had a stare, there was no denying that, and Cole tensed. He was no pushover, and he hit harder than his lean stature suggested he was capable of.

But Troy Allison was a big man.

A big, intimidating man.

He also had a gun on his hip.

"You better be very careful about what comes out of your mouth, dick." The DEA Agent's voice had dropped several octaves. Years of smoking had made the man's tone gravelly, which served to reinforce the notion that he wasn't somebody you wanted to fuck with.

But Cole had a timeline and, besides, Troy had nearly damaged his monogrammed shoes.

No real man could let that pass.

"Weellllll.... I can be more specific if you'd like? How about this: Matheson PD picked up Randy Byers carrying a helluva lot of smack. The detective, not wanting to deal with this mess, gives you a call and is more than happy to pass the buck. Then you and Detective Furlow have a little chat. Surprise, surprise, two days later, Dylan Hall is pulled in for possession of... you guessed it... the exact same amount of heroin that Freddie's son was being charged with. Similar story, right? The difference is, only one of the two men get to go home."

Small vertical lines appeared on Troy's lips.

"What are you saying?"

"Weellll... I'm saying that you and Freddie worked together to—"

For such a big man, DEA Agent Troy Allison was surprisingly fast. His right hand shot out and he grabbed a fistful of Cole's shirt.

"Don't you ever fuckin'—"

Yep, he was strong, too.

Cole had no chance of breaking free, let alone somehow besting the man in any sort of combat.

Troy twisted his fist into Cole's shirt, pulling him closer.

"I don't know what you're talking about."

Cole raised his hand, but not in an aggressive way. Instead, he pointed at the traffic light to their right.

"Careful now, somebody's watching."

Troy's mustache twitched as he worked through what Cole had just said.

"The red-light camera," Cole whispered, helping the man out.

This revelation didn't have the impact that Cole had expected it to. At least not right away. If anything, it only enraged Troy further. The man's hand was pulling so hard on the front of Cole's shirt that had it been constructed from cheaper fabric, it might have just given up and burst at the seams.

"Who hired you?" Troy's breath was ninety-percent cigarette smoke.

"I'm not at liberty to say."

"It can't be that pissant Dylan Hall, 'cause he ain't got no money."

Cole pointed at the camera again then his shirt.

Troy finally let go, but not without a strong shove that sent Cole stumbling backward a few steps.

"It doesn't matter who hired me." Cole tried, and failed miserably, to massage the creases out of the front of his shirt. If nothing else, he hoped the action made him look calm. Because inside, he was shitting bricks. "All that matters is that you drop the charges against Dylan Hall. Otherwise," somehow, Cole still held the folder in his hand, and he held it up, "I might drop this in the mail. Then there'll be a lot of media-types asking you questions."

Troy grinned, which was even more sinister than his scowl.

"I can't do that."

Cole cocked his head.

"Why not?"

"'Cause DEA handed that case back to Matheson PD. They're the ones pressing charges. I ain't got nothing to do with it."

This was a surprise but not terribly relevant.

"That sounds like a you problem, Mr. Allison. To be honest, I don't care how you do it. Just get the charges dropped—all of them—or I'll drop these photos in the mail."

Pissing off a DEA Agent while investigating his first case was a shitty career move. Pissing off and challenging someone with connections, someone high up in the DEA who also happened to have the restraint of a four-year-old was going to make Cole's career and maybe even his life very difficult moving forward.

But he made a promise to Veronica.

Okay, it was far from a blood oath, but now that Cole knew Dylan was set-up, he had a moral obligation to see this thing through.

This wasn't the time to back down.

It was the time to *double-down*.

"One more thing: this wasn't your first interaction with Detective Furlow, was it? I mean, the DEAs?"

"What are you talking about?"

"Braden Byers? Ring a bell? No? Well, Braden Byers just happened to be Detective Furlow's brother-in-law. And now he's serving fifteen years in a federal prison for heroin possession. Wanna take a guess at who found said heroin on Mr. Byers?"

Troy glowered at him but remained silent.

Cole shrugged.

"You guessed it: Detective Freddie Furlow. It seems that this whole heroin thing likes to follow the man around. Bit weird for a homicide detective, right? Right?" Cole shrugged again. "Just drop the charges against Dylan. Drop 'em, or..." he wagged the folder obnoxiously, pointed at the red-light camera with his empty hand, and then turned around and walked away.

By the time Cole made it to his car, the smile that had begun as a simple curling of the right side of his mouth had grown to Cheshire proportions.

Hot damn I'm good at this PI thing. Forget what Veronica said, I should have quit months ago.

Chapter 47

VERONICA WATCHED SHERIFF STEVE BURNS as he slept. Even though much had changed between them, this felt like the right place to be.

This felt good.

It felt right.

Steve opened his eyes.

"I'm sorry," he said.

Veronica rubbed the back of his hand.

"You said that already."

Steve's pallor was better, but he was still pale. There was a thin sheen of sweat on his brow, reminding her that while he was in the hospital because of an accidental overdose, he was genuinely ill. The nurse had suggested that Steve was strong enough to recover from his addiction, but it would still take work.

The man swallowed hard.

"I know. I know. It's just—I haven't told you everything." Steve closed his eyes and took a deep breath.

Veronica, feeling uncomfortable with the sudden change in tone, decided to make light of the situation.

"If in that dream you turn around and see another woman, I'm not going to be mad."

Steve's jaw slackened.

"How did you—"

Like the last time that Steve had tried to explain his dream, he was once again interrupted. It was as if the universe was conspiring against him telling his story and Veronica didn't know whether that was a good or bad thing.

A red-faced DEA Agent bursting into the room, on the other hand, was less ambiguous.

"Where's your partner?" Troy asked, his voice like gravel on a metal chute.

At first, Veronica wasn't sure who the man was speaking to.

"Excuse me?"

Troy sneered at her.

"Your partner. Where is your partner?"

"How the fuck should I know?" Veronica let go of Steve's hand and stood up. "What are you doing here?"

Troy's sneer intensified.

"Looking for your partner, Detective Furlow."

Veronica looked around dramatically.

"Well, he's not here. Did you try calling him?"

"Troy, what's going on?" Steve did his best to try and make his voice authoritative, but it was weak and easily ignored.

"When you see your partner, tell him I'm not going down for this. Tell him, he fucked up."

Veronica just blinked.

What the hell is this psycho talking about? How does he even know Freddie?

"Calm down, Troy." Steve cleared his throat. His voice was only slightly louder now. "What's this about?"

Marcus McVeigh entered the claustrophobic hospital room now and Veronica was struck with a strong sense of déjà vu.

Don't these guys have anything better to do than to harass a sick man, sheriff or not?

McVeigh was perfectly capable of handling things by himself. And, if the rumors were true, being handed the reins, even under such bizarre circumstances as these, was something that the chief deputy should have relished.

Then Veronica recalled that they weren't here for Steve. At least Troy wasn't.

"What do you want with Freddie?" Veronica asked.

Troy's eyes were red with anger now and even though she stood her ground, she felt her heart start to beat like a snare drum.

"You just tell him. Tell him what I said."

The spell was broken when Troy turned.

"I don't work for you," Veronica said sharply. It wasn't the best or most confident comeback, but it was all she could muster.

It didn't seem to affect Troy and the man left in as big a huff as he'd arrived. Some of the hot air followed him out of the room.

"What the hell was that all about?" The question was on Veronica's mind, but Steve was the one to ask it.

"No idea."

Veronica felt her face redden a little when she realized that the question hadn't been directed at her but at McVeigh.

"We, *uhh*, we had two more overdoses last night," McVeigh replied hesitantly.

"Really?" Veronica tried to stop the image of Steve lying in the alley from moving to the front of her mind.

It was an impossible task.

"Yeah, both appear accidental, no evidence of foul play. Except..." Once more, the chief deputy looked to the sheriff for permission to continue.

"Go ahead. You can say anything in front of her."

There was a snarky remark on the tip of her tongue, but Veronica resisted the urge to say it.

"Right." McVeigh licked his thick lips. "Well, looks like they were fentanyl overdoses. We found baggies at both scenes—they had that logo on the package, the snake eating the eyeball. The same stuff that put you in here."

There was an odd lilt to the man's tone that was somehow accusatory. For the first time, Veronica considered that perhaps she wasn't the only one who knew about Steve's drug problem, that the real reason he was in here wasn't *just* because of his accidental undercover overdose. This might explain McVeigh's attitude, but not Troy's. The DEA Agent had barely noticed Steve. He was looking for Freddie. And when the bald man hadn't found the big detective, he'd lashed out at Veronica.

What the hell does any of this have to do with Freddie?

"Coordinate with Greenham PD, talk to Matheson, too. We need more officers on the street," Steve said. "People are dropping like flies out there."

Veronica furrowed her brow.

"Nearly every available officer is already out there looking for this killer as it is," Veronica stated. Her phone rang and she pulled it out of her pocket. "Shit, gimme a sec." She turned her back to the men and answered.

"Detective Shade, it's Officer Furnelli."

"What's up, Court?"

"We've got—well, that press conference of yours might have done some good after all. We got a call from someone who claims to have witnessed Jake Thompson's murder."

Veronica's heart rate had returned to normal after Troy's exit, but it rebounded just as quickly.

"What? Are they—"

"Yeah, they're on their way to the station now," Court said, predicting her question.

"Good. I'll be right there. I want to interview them."

"Sure... but, I gotta warn you?"

"What? What is it?"

"Detective Shade, the witness... I thought you should know. The witness is an eleven-year-old boy."

Chapter 48

THE TWO CHILDREN COULDN'T HAVE been more different. Beverly Trammel had pigtails and loved to play with her yo-yo. She was outgoing and gregarious.

Her parents had been murderers.

Max Taylor, on the other hand, was a blond-haired blue-eyed boy hunched over a sheet of paper, tongue pushed into his cheek as he colored. Even before speaking to him, before meeting him, Veronica could tell that Max was a quiet and reserved child.

"Like I said, it's probably nothing." David Taylor's resemblance to his son Max was uncanny. He had the same slight stature, same hair, same eyes. "I was watching the news when Max came in. I was just about to turn it off when he pointed and—"

"You did the right thing by coming in," Veronica interrupted. Like crime scenes, she liked to go into interviews with as little bias as possible. "Since your son is a minor, David, it's probably best if you join us."

Though David nodded, he appeared uneasy.

"This isn't an interrogation," Veronica assured him, hoping to alleviate his concern.

"No, I understand. It's just... well, Max has quite an imagination."

"That's a good thing," Veronica said warmly. She briefly touched the man's shoulder before letting him enter the room first, followed by herself and then Freddie. Veronica had every intention of confronting her partner about what Troy had said back at the hospital, but that would have to wait. When they'd met at the station—Court had called Freddie after speaking to her—not only had David Taylor been present, but the man was uncomfortable and jittery.

They couldn't afford Max and his father to walk. The tone of Court's voice had suggested that the officer was doubtful that the boy had anything of value to offer, but Veronica knew that sometimes the least likely witnesses provided the most valuable information.

And they had nothing else to go on at this point.

"Hi, Max," Veronica said softly. She lowered herself, and Max looked up from his drawing. She was struck by just how blue the boy's eyes were. "My name's Veronica and this is my partner, Freddie."

"It's okay, Max. You can talk to them. Just tell the detectives what you told me," David encouraged.

Veronica sat across from Max, intentionally blocking his father's view.

"Do you like drawing?"

Max nodded vigorously.

"Can I take a look?" The boy nodded again and slid the paper closer to her. Veronica spun it around and held it up. Max had drawn a rather intricate old-fashioned boat complete with a massive helm and oars protruding from the sides.

"This is amazing," she said, genuinely impressed. "You must draw a lot."

"Any talent he has, he got from his mother," David chimed in.

Veronica was beginning to regret her offer of letting the man sit in on the interview. His interruptions, well-intentioned as they may be, were a distraction that served to pull Max's blue eyes away from Veronica.

"Well, I think you are an excellent artist." Veronica switched gears and lowered her voice. "Now, Max, I want to ask you about what you saw a couple of nights ago. Your dad mentioned that you sometimes like to go out at night for a walk. Is that true? Now, you're not in trouble in any way," she clarified. "And your dad says you're not in trouble, so long as you tell the truth."

Max glanced at his father, who gave him an encouraging head nod.

"Sometimes, I can't sleep," Max whispered, forcing Veronica to lean even closer to ensure that she didn't miss a word. "Dad says I shouldn't go out after dark, but I—I just... I just can't sleep, so I go anyway."

Veronica subtly sniffed the air as Max spoke, which felt wrong, but habits were hard to break.

She detected no signs of deception from the boy.

"Believe it or not, I used to do the same thing when I was a girl." Unlike Max's words, this was a lie. While it was true that Veronica would often go on late-night walks, they were always accompanied by her father, who liked to walk and smoke after dinner. And even accompanied by her police officer dad, they would never go near a place like Needle Point. "A couple of nights ago, did you go out then?"

"Yes." As he spoke, Max grabbed another crayon and began drawing on a fresh sheet of paper. Veronica wanted the boy's full attention but if her time with Dr. Jane Bernard had taught her anything, it was that sometimes a distraction could actually be helpful. It could loosen you up, keep you calm while describing an otherwise stressful situation. "And where did you go?"

Max shrugged.

"Somewhere with sheets hanging from the sky."

The white tarps hanging from the building where Jake Thompson was found came to mind.

"Was this far from your house?"

"Not too far. Maybe… I don't know. Thirty minutes? I'm not sure."

"And did you happen to look behind those sheets, Max?"

As much as Veronica desperately wanted a break in the case, the idea of this eleven-year-old boy seeing Jake Thompson sitting on that chair with his throat slit and his lungs pulled out, seemed like a hefty price to pay.

"Yes." The single syllable came out more gasp than word and everyone in the room held their breath.

"And what did you see?"

Max continued drawing and just as Veronica was about to repeat the question, the boy lifted his picture to show them.

"A monster," he whispered. "I saw a monster behind those sheets."

Chapter 49

COLE BATHERSON HADN'T BEEN EXAGGERATING when he'd told Troy Allison that the circumstances surrounding Dylan Hall's arrest were eerily similar to those involving Detective Freddie Furlow's brother-in-law, Braden Byers.

Dylan was discovered with a kilo of top-notch heroin after an anonymous tip-off. An anonymous tip also led to the discovery of a large amount of the Schedule I drug in Braden's possession. The difference was that Braden had been driving his car at the time and not sitting at home.

The man, who, also like Dylan, had a significant rap sheet, received a fifteen-year sentence for possession and intention to distribute.

Cole hoped that his intervention would prevent Dylan from a similar fate.

Perhaps the most striking commonalty between the two cases, separated by nearly a decade, was Freddie Furlow's involvement in both. Now, Cole knew that Troy Allison was too smart to keep his phone records, so not even a subpoena would reveal that Freddie had placed the 'anonymous' tip about the drugs in Dylan's apartment. But he'd bet his bespoke double monk shoes that that was the case.

And the man who had arrested Braden Byers? Well, that was none other than his very own brother-in-law, Detective Furlow.

This dichotomy—feeling such moral compunction that you'd arrest your own brother-in-law and yet have no apparent qualms about framing an innocent man—was the only real confusing thing to Cole.

The good news was that a similar dichotomy existed when it came to people's understanding and perception of Internal Affairs. They fucking hated them, sure, but because they knew how shitty IA could make their lives, a measure of respect was often levied.

And Cole had gotten around. He'd worked cases that involved Greenham PD, Matheson PD, even Bear County Sheriff's Department. Rarely, *very* rarely, Cole had even dealt with the feds. This department whoring paid dividends and would continue to do so until news of his resignation made its rounds. And as luck would have it, the man Cole dealt with on those very rare interactions just happened to be working the desk at the Federal Corrections Institute, Sheraton.

This guard didn't even ask for Cole's badge, which, of course, he didn't have. He addressed Cole by name and granted him a meeting with inmate 990767 without question.

They even gave him quick access to Braden Byers' visitor log.

It came as no surprise that the man's sister, Susan, visited him on a regular basis. Suspiciously missing from this list were both Freddie and his sons, Kevin and Randall Byers.

Cole didn't know what to make of this. Because Braden had taken a plea deal—a terrible one, one that should have been summarily rejected by even the greenest articling student—the details of the case were difficult to come by.

"I just need five minutes," Cole told the guard.

"Yeah, sure."

"Should I be worried?" Cole mimicked having handcuffs put on.

The guard chuckled.

"With Braden? No, no way."

If appearances meant anything, then Cole had no problem taking the guard's words at face value. Mr. Byers' hair, sandy brown, brushed to one side, not only looked clean but recently styled, as well. He had dark eyes, but they weren't hardened, a square jaw, and an average build. Cole saw a resemblance to Susan Byers, which wasn't unexpected. They were twins after all—fraternal, not identical—but still.

"Mr. Byers, my name's Cole Batherson," Cole said, sitting across from the unshackled convict.

"Yeah, I know. They told me you were with Internal Affairs. What do you want with me?"

Cole let his reputation precede him.

"This case I'm working, it's a bit different than the usual."

True.

"What do you want, Mr. Batherson?"

"I want to help you," Cole replied flatly. Braden's orange jumpsuit rustled as he crossed his arms over his chest. No, the man wasn't hardened. But nobody spent ten years in a federal prison and didn't harbor just a little paranoia. It was pretty much required for self-preservation.

"I just want to understand your case. I want to know why you took the plea deal."

Braden sucked his lower lip into his mouth before speaking.

"Who are you working for?" There was a surprising amount of anger in the man's voice.

"Would you believe that this case is pro bono?"

Braden frowned.

"Internal Affairs working pro bono?"

"You're right." Cole showed his palms. "Look, I just want to get your side of the story."

"There is no 'my side' of the story. I got pulled over with heroin and now I'm in here, doing my time."

Braden was surprisingly cavalier about his situation. It could be that he'd found Jesus or something like that. But this deal? The one that put him away for real time? This was the only deal he'd accepted. That was exceedingly rare.

And it didn't make much sense.

"I mean, to be arrested by your own brother-in-law? The man married to your twin sister?"

Braden might not be hardened, but he had a hard streak in him all right.

"What the fuck do you really want?"

"Why are you getting angry with me?"

"Who sent you?" Braden flexed his hands flat on the metal table between them.

"Nobody." Cole shrugged. "The thing is, though, your brother-in-law—no, no, I can't say that. Let's just—can I ask you a hypothetical?"

"I don't want anything to do with this. I just want to do my time."

Cole continued, unperturbed by the man's comments.

"What if... what if the drugs weren't yours, Braden?"

"They were mine," the man countered from between clenched teeth. "They were *my* drugs."

Angry or not, this was a curiously adamant assertion. One that gave Cole pause.

So, what you're telling me, Lieutenant, is that this underwear that you've been sniffing when your office door is closed are yours?

Absolutely! They're my underwear! I swear!

"Right. Well—" Cole stopped mid-sentence.

They were mine... they were my drugs.

Cole recalled the visitor sheet. It wasn't who was on the list who was important, he realized, but who *wasn't*.

"Fuck," he whispered. Then Cole snapped his fingers. "They weren't your drugs at all, were they?"

"They were!" Braden said, his voice getting louder. "They were mine!"

Cole pictured what Veronica might see—*or smell? Was it smell when someone was lying? Yeah, that was it, smell.*

He inhaled deeply, imagining his nostrils filling with the stench of gasoline.

"No, no, they weren't yours."

When Braden shouted this time, the guard opened the door and hurried into the small interview room.

"Leave it alone!" Braden warned. "Just... leave it alone."

"You okay?" the guard asked Cole.

"Yeah, I'm fine."

"Just take it easy, Braden, someone'll be here for you in a moment." Once outside, the guard turned to Cole and said, "What did you say to him, anyway? He never gets upset."

"I just asked him if the drugs were his, that's all."

"Really?"

"Really."

They were nearly at the front doors when Cole thought of something else.

"Let me ask you something—Mr. Byers' commissary, it's always full, isn't it?"

"Yep." The guard confirmed. "He's got everything he needs in here."

"Right, figured as much—he looked pretty comfortable. Who fills it, by the way?" Cole tried to make his interest seem conversational and not investigative. "His commissary, I mean? Wife? Girlfriend...?"

The guard scratched the back of his head.

"No, no, not a man. Some—ah, what do you call it when the first few letters of the first and last name sound kinda the same?"

"Alliteration."

"Yeah, that's it. F-f-f—"

"Fred Furlow?" Cole helped him out.

The officer beamed.

"Yeah, that's it. Fred Furlow—he makes sure that Braden Byers' commissary is always full, that the man doesn't want for nothin'."

Chapter 50

MONSTER...

It wasn't the boy's words that echoed in Veronica's head, but those of the homeless man in the alley.

Monster... monster... monster...

Veronica stared at the image that eleven-year-old Max Taylor had drawn. Unlike the boat with the oars, this image was disproportioned.

Unmistakably humanoid, but with a bulging brow and thickened cheekbones conspiring to hide pinpricks of red glowing eyes. The lips stretched far wider than anything remotely natural, and they were thickened at irregular intervals.

A shudder ran through Veronica. This wasn't just a child's drawing, but nightmare residue. And nightmare residue had a way of clinging to the vestiges of reality like embers that continue to flit upward even after the fire of their origin had long since been stamped out.

"My boy, he has a, *uhh*, a vivid imagination," David Taylor said from behind her.

Veronica couldn't seem to take her eyes off the picture, and Freddie picked up the slack.

"Sure seems that way. So, Max, this is who you saw behind the sheets?"

In her peripheral vision, Veronica picked up on a subtle nod.

Or maybe it was just a tremor.

"Did you..." Veronica tore her gaze away from the terrifying picture and stared into the boy's pale blue eyes. "Did you see the monster writing anything on the wall?"

Max nodded again and reached for the paper. Tongue rooted firmly in his cheek, the boy hunkered over the page. A few seconds later, the boy stopped scribbling.

He had written one single word in all capitals at the bottom of the page: *SINNER*.

All caps.

The boy had been there, all right. And if this monster is what Max saw, then this is what Max saw.

"Max, did you notice anything else? Anything that might help us catch this monster?"

The boy shook his head. Just once, back and forth.

"What about on any of your other walks? On another night?"

The boy didn't move.

"It's okay; you're not in trouble," Veronica reiterated. "You did nothing wrong. And no matter what you say, you're not getting to—"

"I-I think I saw someone with a bloody shirt."

"Max..." the boy's father began as a warning.

Veronica resisted the urge to shoot the man a scathing look. The only thing that stopped her was not wanting to break line of sight with the boy.

"It's just—look, it's a stressful time at home," David continued. Veronica clenched her jaw, wishing that the man would just shut up and let her talk to Max. "That's why I was hesitant to bring Max here in the first place. I mean, I was a little embarrassed that he snuck out and went to Needle—sorry, Nettle Point of all places, you know? But, anyways, my brother recently moved in with us. He was just—well, he just finished serving his time and needed a little help getting his feet under him. Not-not dangerous, not at all. Just—well, anyways, sometimes it gets too quiet at home and my brother Alex says that in prison when it's quiet, that's bad, right? Something bad is going to happen when you don't hear anything. So, Max probably just saw him in the middle of the night. And Max has these nightmares, too…" David let out a sigh that was so exasperated that Veronica was finally forced to look at him.

The man's eyes were beady and his forehead slick.

So far as she could tell, however, he wasn't lying, wasn't trying to cover things up. David was just… embarrassed. Like he'd failed as a father.

"It's okay, I understand," Veronica said. "Is it alright, though, if we just let Max answer?"

David swallowed, wiped his brow, and nodded.

"Yeah, sure, sorry."

The man clearly just wanted someone to talk to.

But Veronica wasn't that person.

She shot him a placating smile, then swiveled back to face Max. She was surprised that the boy was still staring intently at her and hadn't gone back to drawing, which was clearly his way of coping.

"Max, just tell me what you saw."

There was a silent exchange between the boy and his father, a look and a shrug, and then Max began to speak. His voice was quiet, barely a whisper.

"Last night," Max began hesitantly, suddenly no longer able to meet Veronica's eyes. "Last night, I saw someone in my house. They were putting a bloody shirt in the garbage."

"And did you recognize this person?"

David inhaled sharply but Veronica pressed on.

"Was it your dad? Your uncle?"

A listless shrug.

Yeah, they were very different, little Gloria Tramell and Max Taylor. Very, very different.

"I didn't see."

"Was it the monster?"

"I didn't see," the boy repeated. For the first time since entering the room, Veronica thought she detected a hint of deception.

For some reason, she decided not to press.

"You've been really helpful today, Max. Thank you so much for coming in." She picked up the image of the monster. "Can I keep this?"

When Max appeared hesitant, Veronica pulled a $10 bill out of her wallet.

"Consider it your first sale. The first of many," Veronica remarked with a half-hearted grin. "Because I think you're going to be a great artist one day."

"It's okay, Max. If you want to sell the picture, you can."

Veronica wasn't sure if the boy took the money because he was happy about making a sale, or if he just wanted to be rid of it.

It didn't matter to her.

Veronica folded the drawing and slipped it into her pocket. Then she leaned over and patted Max's hands.

"Thank you. You've really been a great help."

Before they left the room, Veronica heard Freddie whisper to David Taylor, "We're going to need your brother's name, of course."

"Alex Taylor. I'm sorry that we wasted your time."

"You didn't. Thanks for coming forward."

Veronica left the interview room first and then stared through the glass at David as he collected his son.

When they were gone, Freddie joined her at her side.

"What do you think?" he asked absently as they both looked into the now-empty room.

"What do I think?" Veronica parroted. "I think we have a sketch of our suspect, that's what I think."

Chapter 51

"YOU KNOW, I'M WILLING TO go along with you on a lot of things," Freddie said. "But you can't possibly believe that some kind of monster is behind these murders?"

Veronica was driving away from the interview room and toward the location where Jake Thompson had been brutally murdered.

The answer to Freddie's question, rhetorical or not, was no. Veronica didn't believe that a hideous Shakespearean beast was prowling around in the dead of night, punishing sinners by tearing their lungs out to make them look like angels and facilitating their ascent to heaven.

But the intellectually disabled man's mention of a monster in the alley and little wandering Max Taylor's description were more than coincidental.

How much more, and what it meant for their case, was anyone's guess.

But Veronica was determined to dig deeper.

Though she didn't expect it to amount to much, Veronica had put Officer Furnelli in charge of looking into the Taylors, focusing especially on Max's uncle, Alex.

The crime scene had been cleaned up at least to the same degree as the surrounding area. Garbage still littered the ground, but the chair was gone, the word was scrubbed from the wall, and while there was still a stain on the asphalt it was indistinguishable from a myriad of others.

There was no evidence that someone had been murdered here less than a week ago.

As Veronica pushed the white tarp aside, she felt a prickling sensation on the back of her neck. Someone was watching her.

"I think—" Freddie began, clearly sensing the same thing.

Veronica hushed him and slowly turned. Across the street, a man's eye peered from the shadows. Freddie reached for his gun, but Veronica once again stopped him.

"It's fine." She raised her voice and her arm. "Hi, there, it's me."

The man stepped onto the sidewalk.

"Hi." Veronica indicated to Freddie, who didn't have a rapport with this man, to stand back and let her do the talking. "Do you remember me?"

"Cop... cop... cop..." Judging by the man's clothes and the increased grime on his face, Veronica assumed that the man hadn't changed much less bathed since their last interaction.

"That's right," Veronica confirmed, not bothering to correct the man. She wasn't a cop; she was a detective. "When we first met, you said that a monster killed the man behind the tarp, right?"

The man nodded, and his many chins jiggled.

"Monster... monster... monster..."

"That's right." Veronica started to remove a piece of paper from her pocket and the man cowered. "It's just a drawing. I want to show you a drawing. Is that okay?"

The man hesitated, before saying, "Yes... yes... yes..."

"Just a drawing," Veronica repeated as she pulled out the picture that Max Taylor had drawn. Beside her, she could almost hear Freddie rolling his eyes. "Is this—" Veronica didn't need to finish; the way the man's lips curled in a half-sneer made it clear that this was the monster he had seen. But for her partner's benefit, Veronica completed the sentence, "Is this the monster that you saw that night?"

The man nodded, and a stream of drool dripped onto his shirt.

"Max... Max... Max..."

Veronica recoiled.

"What? What did you just say?"

The man jabbed a finger at the picture.

"Max... Max... Max..."

"Are you saying *Max*? Max Taylor? Eleven-year-old boy? Blue eyes?"

The man blubbered incomprehensibly.

"Are you saying that this is Max?" Veronica asked again. She stepped forward, but Freddie stopped her from getting too close.

The man was becoming increasingly agitated.

"I'm sorry." Veronica cursed herself for moving too quickly for upsetting him. There was nothing else he would tell them. Not tonight.

He was confused, anyway. The man couldn't possibly have meant Max Taylor.

This time, Veronica slowly and carefully pulled out her wallet, only to peer into the empty pouch; she'd given her last ten bucks to Max for his picture.

"Freddie," she said out of the corner of her mouth.

Her partner begrudgingly handed her a twenty.

"I don't think I caught your name." Veronica gestured with the money, and the man snatched it up.

"Mark... Mark... Mark..."

"All right, Mark. Thank you, again. I might come back another time to ask you more questions. Would that be alright?" Mark looked at the money and nodded. "Okay, thank you. Have a good night, Mark."

Veronica grabbed Freddie by the shoulder and together they walked to her car.

"I don't know what you think this proves, Veronica. But I don't think—"

"I don't know what it proves," Veronica admitted. "But I don't know what 'SINNER' means, or what's with the lungs, either. And no, before you say it, I'm not going to put out an APB for a monster if that's what you're worried about."

"It wasn't."

"Then—" Veronica was reaching for the door when her phone started to ring. "Damn it."

She answered.

"Hi Veronica, it's Kristin Newberry."

"Hold on, I have Freddie here. I'll put you on speaker."

She heard the beginnings of a protest but was already in the process of pulling the phone away from her face and pressing the speaker button.

"It's fine, go ahead."

She nodded at Freddie.

"Actually, this isn't about the case."

Veronica's brow furrowed.

"What do you mean?"

Kristin exhaled.

"It's about Dylan."

Veronica quickly took the phone off speaker and put it to her ear.

"What about him?"

"I just... Veronica, they dropped the charges."

Veronica's jaw fell open.

"What?" She was incredulous. "What do you mean *they dropped the charges*?"

"I know, I know. I've never seen anything like it. They called me in, then brought Dylan and said that he was free to go. That all charges were being dropped."

"Why would they do that?" But even as she asked the question, an idea started to form in Veronica's mind. Charges were often reduced, but not dropped. Not unless something catastrophic had happened.

"Like I said, I don't know. But—I mean, it's good news."

"Yeah, it is," Veronica said absently. "Thanks. Thanks for everything. I owe you one."

"I'm not sure I did anything, but a nice bottle of Cab Sauv is always welcome. About the other case? No update except that I found no drugs in either Cooper Mills' or Frank Klarno's system. Even did a rare drug panel, but still nothing."

"I figured as much. Thanks again."

Veronica hung up, and no sooner had she slipped her phone into her pocket than Freddie was on top of her.

"What was that all about?" he asked with more than just passive interest.

"It wasn't about our case."

"Yeah, I know, but was it about Dylan Hall?" Freddie's eyelids peeled back. "Was it?"

Veronica frowned.

"Yeah, it was. They let him go."

Freddie, who had probably gathered as much from hearing one side of the conversation, looked shocked.

"What?" the man practically gasped.

"Yeah, weird, right?" Veronica tried to open the door, but Freddie was blocking it with his body. She nodded at him.

"Sorry." Freddie stepped back. "Think you could drop me at the station? There's something I just remembered that I had to do."

***

Less than an hour later, Veronica Shade found herself standing alone outside Dylan Hall's shitty apartment.

Veronica reached up to knock on the crooked door, but it suddenly opened. A man rushed at her, wrapping his long thin arms around her in a tight embrace.

The man, wiry as he was, nearly smothered her. She had to physically push him away after a moment.

"I don't know what you did, but goddamn it, thank you. Thank you, Veronica."

Dylan Hall was beaming.

"What I did?"

He nodded enthusiastically.

"You—it was you, right? It had to be you." Dylan's smile tempered somewhat, but he still appeared overjoyed.

"Maybe we should talk inside," Veronica suggested.

"Sure. You want to... well, I don't have anything to drink. My bad. But you can still come in."

Veronica took one look over Dylan's shoulder then changed her mind.

"On second thought," she said. "Maybe we should just stay out here."

"Ha—don't worry, I'm getting some new IKEA shit soon, now that I'm a free man." Dylan looked more bemused by her comment than offended. "You know, I was going to come see you, to say thanks, you know, but I didn't know where to go."

"It's probably best that I come find you."

Dylan held his hands up and his bright smile returned. This was a very different man than the one who Veronica had visited in prison.

"You know where I live."

"Yeah... listen, I don't..." Veronica sighed, unsure of how to continue.

"Don't leave me hangin'."

She cleared her throat and continued.

"I'm not sure I did anything. To be honest, I was wondering what *you* did." Not exactly true. This was more of a fishing expedition.

Confusion crossed Dylan's features.

"What *I* did?" The man chuckled then he grew serious. "I didn't flip. I mean, they weren't my drugs. Hell, even if they were, I'm no rat." Dylan reconsidered this—he had, after all, been a confidential informant. When he spoke again, his voice was low, reserved. "I'm no rat."

"I know." Veronica put a comforting hand on the man's shoulder and repeated the words. "I know."

I also know that you had nothing to do with this, Dylan. I know it was all Cole.

A smile crept onto her pale lips, which Dylan misinterpreted as directed at him.

"I'm out. This is a good day, Veronica. A good *fucking* day."

"Yeah, it is. And I'm glad."

"Me too." Dylan made a face. "I don't have anything to drink inside, but to celebrate maybe you wanna go to a bar or something. My treat."

"Why? So you can grab my ass again?"

Dylan's face turned scarlet.

"I was high—I didn't—"

"I'm fucking with you. Take care of yourself, Dylan. I'm glad that you're out."

"So am I. And I know you're behind this, Veronica. I don't know how, or why, but I know. Thank you. Thank you, thank you, *thank you*."

Chapter 52

FREDDIE PEELED AWAY FROM THE drive-thru, his eyes on the road as he expertly unwrapped the hamburger and took a big bite. Two more, and it was gone.

The second burger went down in roughly the same number of chews.

And the entire time, Freddie never took his foot off the gas. He kept it depressed as he raced across the city.

This was fucked up. This was *royally* fucked up.

He'd wanted to press Veronica further, ask *why* Dylan Hall had been released, but he had to be careful. Veronica was smart. Veronica would figure things out. And if he tried to lie to her... well, that was impossible.

This was fucked up.

Tires squealed as Freddie wrenched the wheel to the left. He bumped the curb as he slammed on the brakes.

The door to the shitty DEA headquarters popped open before he made it halfway across the equally shitty parking lot.

Freddie had expected to see Troy Allison, but this wasn't him.

It was a DEA Agent, two of them in fact, recognizable by their expressions as much as the vests they wore with their thumbs tucked into the armholes.

"I need to speak to Troy," Freddie said, wondering if their appearance at this moment was a coincidence, or if they knew he was coming. "I need to speak to Troy, *now*."

He continued walking, but one of the agents, a man with slick black hair tucked behind his ears and a unibrow, came forward, his hand moving from his armpit to out in front of him.

"Yeah, I don't think so."

"What do you mean you don't think so?" Freddie took one step, and the man placed his outstretched hand against Freddie's chest and shoved. This aggression was so unexpected that Freddie staggered, but he managed to remain on his feet.

"I need to speak to Agent Allison. Tell him it's Detective Furlow."

"I don't care if you're the goddamn Pope. Troy ain't gonna speak to you."

Freddie snarled.

"He knows? Doesn't he? He knows I'm here." Freddie pointed over the man's shoulder at the building with the dirty door and the grease-smeared glass inlay. "He knows I'm fucking standing right here."

"He ain't gonna talk to you." The lack of denial was as good as an explicit confirmation.

"Agent Allison! Get your ass out here!" Freddie yelled. "Get the fuck out here!"

The DEA Agents just watched, and the door behind them remained closed.

"You done?"

Freddie was not a violent person by nature. Never had been. But he felt the urge to lash out and punch the man with the unibrow. This urge was so great that Freddie actually stepped forward again. He didn't know if he'd actually go as far as to throw a punch, and he would never find out.

Because the DEA Agent beat him to it. The blow might have only been delivered at fifty-percent strength, but it was solid enough that both hamburgers Freddie had just inhaled tried to claw their way back up his esophagus. He tried to swallow them back down, but they were persistent.

Freddie turned his head to the side and vomited. As he did, the DEA Agent who'd struck him stepped back, cursing, mumbling something about his shoes.

The other man came forward.

"Troy ain't gonna talk to you," he said in a low voice as Freddie continued to rid his stomach of processed meat and processed cheese. "But he's got a message for you."

Freddie raised his watery eyes.

"Troy wants you to know that you made a big mistake fucking with him. And if there's one man you don't want to fuck with, it's Troy."

"I didn't—"

—fuck with him, Freddie tried to say, but his abdomen clenched and instead of words coming out of his mouth, it was more partially—mostly—digested food.

Kale this time.

Fuck, I hate kale.

***

Freddie spent the next hour getting himself cleaned up. He took a cold shower, examined the bruise that was already forming on his stomach—thankfully, no broken ribs—and then used his laptop to try to figure out why Dylan had been let go.

Nothing. There was nothing.

Why the fuck did you let him go?

Freddie decided that if he wasn't going to get his answers from the DEA, then he was going to try the next best thing—he was going to go to the district where charges had actually been laid: Matheson.

As he made the twenty-minute drive to Matheson, his stomach began to revolt. Not because of the punch, but because it was empty. And no matter how much fast food he jammed into it, it just wouldn't shut up.

"Hi, my name's Detective Furlow from Greenham PD," he said, putting on his best smile.

The secretary asked him if he had a meeting, and Freddie did his best tap dance routine to avoid the question directly.

"I'm here to talk to someone about the Dylan Hall case. I think the arresting officer was a…" Freddie feigned as if he was trying to recall the name.

The secretary filled in the blanks.

"Detective Tinkler. But he's no longer with Matheson PD. Detective Dutton took that case over. He's here if you want to speak to him?"

"That would be great, thanks."

Freddie took a seat and waited.

And waited. And waited.

Close to an hour later, a portly man with doughy flesh and green eyes came out from a back room. He introduced himself as Detective Jake Dutton.

"What can I do for you, Detective Furlow?"

"Is there somewhere we can talk?"

The corners of the man's lips pulled downward, and he glanced around.

"Here is fine."

This was not a good sign. Jake Dutton appeared conciliatory, but it was a front. The wait, the passive-aggressive denial to speak in confidence. Matheson PD and Greenham PD were usually on good terms. Which suggested that this wasn't territorial but case specific.

Not a good sign at all.

"Sure, well, I don't want to take up too much of your time, but I had a question about a case that you're the lead on?"

"Which one might that be?" Another bad sign. The man's demeanor suggested that he clearly knew which case Freddie was referring to.

"Dylan Hall. He was arrested for—"

"Possession with the intent to distribute, yeah, I know." Detective Dutton's voice hardened a little. "What about it?"

"I mean, the charges were dropped, and I was wondering why?"

Dutton dropped all pretense now.

"What's it to you?"

"I'm not here to step on toes. I just want to know why. The thing is, Dylan Hall is a CI for us in Greenham."

"You'll be happy to have him back then."

Freddie lifted his shoulders and held them next to his ears.

"Our relationship is complicated. As a favor, can you just let me know why the charges were dropped? Was there something wrong with the evidence?" He let his shoulders fall. "A witness get spooked? What?"

Jake Dutton squinted at him with his green eyes.

"I'm not trying to stir shit up, Detective," Freddie implored. "It's just, with Dylan's history and—"

"It's a closed case."

This was going nowhere, and Freddie knew that he had to find some common ground if he wanted to get any answers.

"Let me guess, I bet it's because that asshole DEA Agent Troy Allison with his big old bald head and cigarette-smoking ass came in and made you drop it, right?"

Dutton inspected Freddie even more closely.

"You know Agent Allison?" the man probed.

"I know that he's an asshole. I know that when I asked his goons the same questions that I'm asking you now, they did this." Freddie raised his shirt to show off the fist-shaped bruise.

Dutton winced.

"Fuck, sorry. And, yeah, he's an asshole." Common ground it was. "Get this, Allison serves me up this case, says it's better if it goes through Matheson instead of the DEA, says it's a slam dunk. And, I mean, it is, right? A career criminal and known addict caught with a kilo of smack? Easy. But he just sets me up, you know? Gives me the case and then suggests—naw, fuck it, he doesn't suggest anything, he *tells* me to drop it. Makes me look like an idiot."

"Did he tell you why?"

Officer Dutton chuckled dryly.

"Troy Allison isn't much for words. He just said that there was something wrong with the seizure."

Much like the food earlier that day, Freddie's heart tried to rise in his throat. He was more successful in keeping this organ in check than the burgers.

"But did he—did he say why? Did he say what was wrong with the seizure?"

"Agent Allison is pretty tight-lipped."

"I know, I know. I'm just wondering if—"

"Why are you busting my balls over this, Furlow?" Officer Dutton asked, his demeanor changing once more. "I've seen your partner on TV. You've got that big, high-profile serial killer case going on. Why do you care about Dylan Hall?"

Common ground or not, this was the end of the road and Freddie knew it.

"Nothing—no reason. Thanks."

The DEA wasn't going to help him, and Matheson PD only knew so much.

That meant that the only way to find out what the hell really happened with Dylan Hall was to ask the man himself.

Chapter 53

COLE REFUSED TO TELL HER anything over the phone. Veronica was mildly suspicious that this was just a ploy to see her in person, so she chose the meeting spot.

Daphne's.

The eponymous woman greeted her with a bright smile and a hug. This may have been Sheriff Burns' favorite spot for his afternoon coffee, but Veronica had adopted it nicely as her own.

Not only was Daphne kind and caring, but her diner was the perfect place to discuss private matters in public. Safe, but also discreet.

Veronica's plan was to arrive first, but she was surprised when Daphne directed her to the back, and she found Cole waiting. He spotted her immediately and waved her over.

Veronica was struck again by how handsome he was. Conventionally handsome, stolen directly from the pages of pretty much every romance novel: tall, dark, square jaw, well-dressed…

She didn't regret her time with Cole. But if the man knew the real Veronica, she doubted he would feel the same way.

Because Cole was a kind, good person.

And she was not.

Veronica walked over to Cole, her jaw set.

Once a killer, always a killer.

"I'm not really sure how to greet you," Cole admitted. He stood and performed an air-hug followed by an air-handshake and then an air-kiss.

Veronica felt a smile creep onto her lips.

"Hug is fine."

They embraced, and Veronica felt the familiar tug of comfort and safety that had drawn her to him in the first place.

Did I push Cole away because I have stronger feelings for Steve? Or am I just drawn to chaos?

Like whether Veronica had chopped off her father's finger or if he had played a prank on her, or if she'd put hot sauce or bleach in her mother's ice cream, the answer was unknowable.

The two ex-lovers sat, and Daphne materialized. Veronica ordered a beer and Cole, even though he had a half-empty cup of coffee in front of him, went ahead and did the same.

Veronica was tempted to ask about the folder in front of Cole, but she resisted the urge and said nothing until Daphne returned with their drinks.

The beer was cold and crisp. She took two quick sips.

"That for me?" Veronica asked, nodding toward the folder.

Cole licked foam from his upper lip. For some reason, even though he had done the impossible, which definitely came at the expense of sleep, the man looked fresh. Fresh and *alive*.

"It is," he said. Veronica reached for it, but Cole put his hand on the cover. "You don't have to read it, though."

Veronica raised an eyebrow.

"I don't have to read it?"

Cole took another pull of his beer.

"You don't have to read it. You might not want to."

Veronica wasn't much for games. She pulled the folder and Cole let it go. She didn't open it, however.

"How'd you do it? How'd you get Dylan off the hook?"

Cole smiled but instead of answering he just glanced at the folder.

"Right. In here—it's all in here, in the folder I shouldn't read."

"Look," Cole said, becoming serious, "he's out. Dylan's a free man. That's all that matters. It doesn't matter what's in the folder."

"Just tell me this—if I read it, will I be inclined to arrest you?"

Cole gasped and brought the back of his hand to his forehead.

"How dare you. How dare you think so little of me."

"Cole…"

"No, Veronica, I didn't break the law. I mean—not… not in a way that would involve a homicide detective."

"I also investigate burglaries," Veronica reminded him.

"But not tech crimes, right?"

"No."

"Phew. Then we're fine."

Veronica wasn't sure whether Cole was joking or not.

She decided it was better not to know.

Or was it?

As they drank, Veronica considered her options. Not knowing what had happened to her as a child tormented her.

But would knowing help?

If she found out that she had chopped off her father's finger and tried to poison her mother, would she be in a better place than she was now?

That was in the past. What was in the folder happened in the past.

And that was boring.

Or was it?

Cole smiled and sipped his beer.

"I tried calling you a bunch of times. I know that we left things—"

As if summoned by Cole's very thoughts, Veronica's phone started to ring. It was Court and she excused herself.

"I guess you're screening your calls," Veronica heard him say as she backed away from the booth.

"Court? What's up?"

"Detective Shade, I've been digging into the Taylors, as you asked."

"And? Did you find anything?"

"I think I did. Nothing on David Taylor, the kid's father—he's clean. No criminal record, nothing of the sort. But his brother? Alex Taylor? He has a pretty substantial rap sheet. You know how David said that his brother was just released? Alex Taylor was inside for possession of heroin."

Veronica's eyes went to Cole, then the folder. Her thoughts went to Dylan.

"Really?"

"Yeah. Anything else? Any connection to our victims?"

"Not that I could find." Court sounded dejected. "Alex did have an arrest about six years ago for assault with a deadly weapon. He used a knife. Got into a tussle at a bar, and when somebody smashed a beer bottle and tried to stick him with it, he pulled out a knife. Cut the other man's arm pretty deep, required fifteen stitches."

"I dunno—it's a far cry from dissecting someone's lungs out and pulling them from their body," Veronica remarked. "I just don't—"

"Wait, wait, one more thing," Court interrupted. "Sorry, almost forgot. This fucking case—oh, my bad. Didn't mean to curse."

"It's okay, we're all tired. What else you got?"

"Well, I thought it strange that David mentioned his brother but not his wife or the boy's mom, so I looked into her. Max's mother, LeeAnn Taylor, died six months ago. Car accident—some drunk crashed into her, and she died on the scene."

"Sorry to hear that but—"

"Hold on—I got a copy of the memorial card that was handed out at her funeral. Now, I haven't slept in—well, a long time, but I want your opinion on this. Tell me what you see, okay?"

Veronica's patience was waning, but she owed it to Court to entertain him.

"Yeah, go ahead. Send it."

A second later, Veronica's phone pinged.

It took a second for the image to download and when it did, her heart leaped into her throat.

"Did you get it?" Court asked.

"Yeah," Veronica answered dryly.

"And do you see—"

"Oh, I see it, Court. I *fucking* see it. Great work. Meet me at the Taylor house. Meet me at the Taylor house as soon as you can—no uniform, no squad car. Do not go inside and do not let them see you."

"Alright. I'll—"

Veronica hung up and walked back to the booth. Without saying a word to Cole, she grabbed her beer and downed it.

"Business calls?" he asked.

Veronica burped softly and placed the glass back down.

"Business calls," she confirmed with a nod. "Thank you for helping Dylan. You know," Veronica averted her eyes and smiled sadly, "I was wrong. You're going to make one hell of a PI, Cole. And you're an even better man."

She grabbed the folder, still not allowing herself to look up.

"Veronica, it's not too late. I still—"

"Thank you, Cole," she said.

And then Veronica hurried out of *Daphne's*, every step becoming more deliberate and determined than the last and any hint of sadness or loss soon melted away.

Chapter 54

IT WAS DARK BY THE time Dylan Hall finally returned to his shitty apartment. The entire time that Detective Freddie Furlow had been sitting in his car eating French fries and sucking down Pepsi, he expected the DEA to show up and ram his vehicle.

For Troy to jump out of the armored car, cigarette dangling from his mouth, and to shout, *you made a big mistake fucking with me.*

But the DEA never showed up and Dylan did.

Freddie slapped his hands together, sending salt falling to his lap like dandruff, and jumped out of his car.

"Dylan!" he hollered.

It had taken the gangly man some time to walk to his front door—he was staggering a little as if drunk or, more likely, high. But when Dylan heard his name being called, he sobered up and took up a defensive posture.

"What do you want?"

"I just have a few questions for you."

Freddie stepped into the light, and Dylan craned his long, thin neck forward.

"Detective Fatso?" His face was like a caricature. "What the—where the fuck's the rest of you?"

Freddie took the insult in his stride.

"Dropped it off at the shitter before I came here. Hey, let me ask you something?"

"Naw, I don't think so." Dylan backed up to his door and reached for the rusted handle. "Last time you were here, it didn't end so good for me."

Freddie wasn't sure how to interpret this—was it an accusation?

He thought back to the night that he and Veronica had come here, and he'd left to take a piss.

Dylan was a criminal—he'd made some terrible decisions, mostly terrible decisions, *all* terrible decisions, and Freddie loathed him. He loathed Dylan for groping Veronica in the alley and for dealing drugs.

He deserved to be behind bars.

"Well, I'm going to ask anyway. Why'd they drop the charges against you?"

"This shit again." Dylan looked skyward. "Like I told your partner, I got no idea why they dropped the charges, and I don't fuckin' care. All I know is I'm free—and I should be free. Cuz they weren't my fucking drugs."

"Wait—my partner? Veronica was here?"

"Yeah, asking the exact same thing. But she's smart, not like you. She knows why I was let go. She *knows*."

Veronica knew something all right, more than she was letting on. That's why Kristin called her when Dylan was let go.

But what?

"Did Veronica say—"

"No more fucking questions, Fatso. I'm celebrating tonight."

Dylan pulled the door open and began to turn, but Freddie grabbed him before he could slip inside.

"You sure they weren't your drugs, Dylan?"

Dylan tried to pull away, but Freddie squeezed the back of the man's arm.

"Fuck off."

The ex-con straightened to his full height, all six-foot-nine inches, and Freddie let him go. Dylan was still gaunt but no longer sickly.

"I said, fuck off," he repeated. No longer desperate to be inside, Dylan seemed to be challenging him.

But Freddie didn't want to fight. Instead of throwing a punch that would have likely ended with him having both a sore stomach and sore jaw, Freddie opted to pull out his cell phone. With Dylan watching on confused, he scrolled through years of photographs. Once he found the one he was looking for, Freddie shoved it in Dylan's face.

"The fuck is this?"

"You recognize this kid?" Freddie demanded.

"I don't know who the fuck that is."

"Look closer."

Freddie moved the phone even closer to Dylan, but the man had had enough. He slapped it out of his hand, and it fell to the ground.

Freddie made no move to pick it up.

"Yeah, you do, I *know* you do," the detective said. "He was one of your runners. Just a young kid, whose dad worked too much, maybe, and was rarely home. A kid looking to fit in somewhere. You found him, and you used him. Groomed him to work for you. He was just a fucking *kid*."

Dylan's expression had been hard before but now it was granite.

"Really? You're going to talk to me about what it's like to be a kid?" Dylan let go of the door completely and took a step forward. He towered over Freddie. "You're going to tell me that some fucking silver spoon trust fund little shit with daddy issues who ran drugs is my problem? That I did something to *him*?"

Freddie saw red and pulled his gun. Dylan didn't react.

"Are you sure they weren't your drugs, Dylan?" Freddie wasn't pointing his gun at Dylan, *per se*, but he wasn't pointing at the ground either.

"What are you going to do, Fatso? You gonna shoot me? Yeah? Or maybe you're just going to set me up again?"

Freddie faltered.

Did he know? Did Dylan know it was me who planted those drugs? If he did, why didn't he say anything?

The reality of the situation hit Freddie in the solar plexus harder than any DEA Agent's punch.

What the fuck are you doing? he asked himself. *What the fuck are you doing?*

So much had changed.

He'd been a good cop once. Not a great one, not Peter Shade great, but a good, honest cop. And everything had to fucking change.

That fucking night… that fucking traffic stop, that *fucking* anonymous tip.

Fuck! *Fuck!*

He thought it was going to be easy to get Dylan to roll over. It had been easy with Braden.

But Dylan wasn't Braden. Dylan had been through some shit. Some real fucking shit.

Shit that had changed him, too.

Freddie put the gun back in his holster.

"No," he said dryly. "I'm not going to shoot anybody."

"Then I'm going inside."

Freddie let Dylan go and when he was gone, he reached down and picked up his cell phone. He was surprised to see that the screen had landed face-up and that it wasn't broken.

A young, familiar face stared up at him.

His son's.

Not Randall's, but Kevin's.

Freddie cursed and angrily pressed the sleep button, darkening the screen.

That night, that traffic stop had cost him nearly everything. His brother-in-law, his wife, his kids, his health.

But he saved his son, which made these sacrifices worth it.

There hadn't been a single moment during all the preceding years, months, weeks, days, hours, or even seconds that Freddie regretted that decision.

Until now.

And the question that rose in his mind, made Freddie hate himself: How different could things have been if I'd just done my job and booked Kevin instead of convincing Braden to take the fall for him?

Chapter 55

"**WHERE'S YOUR PARTNER? WHERE'S DETECTIVE** Furlow?" Officer Court Furnelli asked as he slipped into the passenger seat of Veronica Shade's car.

"Can't get a hold of him. Left a message but haven't heard back yet." She looked at the man with a dark beard and even darker eyes. "Thanks for getting here so fast."

Court had been putting in long hours, even longer than Veronica. Yet, while he looked tired, he still somehow managed to give off an air of freshness. One day, he'd make a hell of a detective.

"No problem."

Court informed her that he'd seen at least two figures inside watching TV. At around eight-thirty, he saw one of them retire to what he assumed was a bedroom. Probably Max's room, and while he was fairly certain that the boy had gone to bed, the room was still fairly well-lit.

That made sense; the boy was afraid of the dark.

Afraid of the monster.

While they watched and waited, Veronica examined the image from LeeAnn's funeral that Court had sent her. She compared it to Max's drawing of the monster he'd seen eviscerating Jake Thompson.

"Yeah, it was him alright," Court said, even though Veronica hadn't spoken. "Max drew both of them."

The line work was similar, and although the monster was less realistic, it showed some improvement over the drawing he'd done about six months ago.

The subject, however, couldn't have been more different.

There was the monster with a large, protruding, almost simian forehead, small red eyes, and puffy cheeks. Then there was the angel of sorts, petite and delicate. It appeared as if Max, while a decent artist, was still learning about space and proportion. He had drawn the angel too large, and the wings were slightly stunted compared to the size of the person who was clearly meant to be the boy's mother ascending to heaven.

They were wings not lungs, but if you squinted…

If that wasn't enough, there was the text at the bottom of the page, written in a childish hand: *Freed from her sins.*

"Are you a religious man, Court?" Veronica asked, staring at the two images, side-by-side. This question undoubtedly broke some HR rule—while Veronica wasn't technically Court's boss she was definitely his superior—but she didn't care. If the young officer could overlook the fact that she'd practically accused him of being the department leak, then they were on good enough terms to discuss taboo work subjects.

And if Court minded, he didn't show it.

"I mean, I won't profess to be a devout Catholic or anything like that. But I am Italian, and I go to church on Easter and Christmas. I believe in God, so I guess… yeah, I'm religious. How about you?"

Veronica just scoffed.

Religion…

Father James Murphy came to mind then, his wide face infiltrating her thoughts.

Religion…

She was convinced that this case still had links to the church despite the newest development. For once, it hadn't been her synesthesia that tipped her off, nor her prejudice, no matter what Freddie thought, but her intuition.

Veronica glanced at the Taylor house, her eyes falling on the illuminated front room. According to her partner, Father Murphy had been more than eager to provide them with a list of all Grace Community employees and volunteers.

Where was that list? Freddie had it... didn't he?

And if he had it, which Veronica was fairly certain he did, then Freddie would have looked for the Taylors on that list.

Wouldn't he?

Then again, why hadn't I just asked them if they went to church? Veronica wondered. *I should have asked.*

She nibbled on the inside of her cheek, wondering if she should call Freddie and inquire about the list. A year ago, this would have been a no-brainer and Veronica wouldn't have hesitated. Now, things were different. Their relationship had improved somewhat since Freddie had been reinstated but it was far from perfect.

Would asking him to double-check be taken as an insult?

Veronica shook her head and she scolded herself.

The reality was it didn't matter what Freddie thought. What mattered was making sure that whoever was behind these murders didn't kill again.

Her thumb moved from the image of the angel to her recent calls, and she clicked Freddie's name.

When there was no answer this time, Veronica left a message asking her partner to specifically look for a record of any of the Taylors having worked in the church. She added a curt thank you at the end, just in case.

Silence. As soon as she hung up the phone, the interior of her car was blanketed with an uncomfortable, oppressive silence.

"Just ask it," Veronica said, feeling Court's eyes on her. "Just ask whatever you want to ask."

"I... I feel stupid."

"Do you want to stay a police officer forever, Court?" Veronica said, cringing at her own condescension.

"No—I want to be a detective."

"That's what I thought. And I think you'll make a good one." *Condescending to patronizing in a single sentence. Great. Great work, Veronica.* "Truth is, I'm tired, you're tired. Unless you're going to ask me out, just say it, Court. Wait—you're not going to ask me out, are you?"

Court flushed.

"Hell, no," he said with a half chuckle.

Veronica pressed her back into the seat.

"What is that supposed to mean?"

"Oh, no, I mean—it's just the sheriff and then, like, Cole, you know? I didn't—I—"

Veronica laughed and she struck Court playfully on the shoulder.

"I'm messing with you. You're not my type—too nice. *Way* too nice."

"Oh, yeah. Right."

"You need to lighten up, Court. This job... it'll kill you if you aren't careful." *Condescending, patronizing, now lecturing? Keep it up, you're on a roll.* "Anyways, what were you going to ask me?"

"It's—the boy. On the phone, after I sent you the picture, you sounded..." Court sighed, and he finally spat out the question he'd been meaning to ask. "You can't possibly think that little boy is behind this, do you?"

Veronica understood Court's apprehension, and maybe to someone else, the question would have been dumb.

But not to her.

Was an eleven-year-old capable of slicing open someone's throat? Maybe. Were they capable of pulling the lungs to the back? Probably not.

But were they capable of murder? Were they capable of deciding who in their family got to live and who got to die? Would they grow up and shoot a person in the head when a bullet in the arm or leg or stomach would've been enough? What about shooting an unarmed man on a bridge?

Definitely.

"Detective Shade? You okay?"

"I'm sorry, just tired." She cleared her throat. "I don't know. Probably not, but I don't know."

This time, Veronica welcomed the silence. The two of them sat in the car, staring at the Taylor residence, not saying anything.

Eventually, exhaustion got the best of her, and Veronica fell asleep.

She dreamed of a bear chasing her. Only when it was right up behind Veronica and she turned around, it wasn't a bear at her heels at all.

It was herself.

Chapter 56

AN ELBOW IN THE RIBS awoke Veronica from her slumber.

"Sorry, but—"

"What is it?"

Instead of answering, Court just pointed out the window. Veronica blinked the last vestiges of sleep away.

"The man left through the back door."

Veronica leaned forward, moving her face closer to the windshield. There was a hooded figure moving away from the house.

"Is it David or Alex?"

"Couldn't tell. Too dark."

Whichever Taylor it was, he was walking at a good clip—he was already halfway down the block.

Veronica's eyes darted back to the house. Aside from the front room, it was completely dark.

"Should we follow him?" Court asked.

The answer was obvious. They *should* follow him. They *had* to follow him.

But that would leave one brother behind.

And a son.

"No, *we* shouldn't." Court had a confused expression on his face. "*You* should. Stay close, follow him, but don't interact unless absolutely necessary. I want to know where he goes, what he does. Got it?"

If nothing else, Court was a man of pure professionalism when called upon. He nodded without hesitation.

"Stay safe."

"You too."

Court slipped silently into the night, falling into step behind either David or Alex Taylor. She watched the two men until they dissolved into darkness. And then she wasn't sure what to do.

Sitting in the car was a nightmare. Veronica hated waiting around.

"Fuck."

Why didn't I go? I should've gone instead of Court.

But deep down, she knew why. It was because of Court's question.

You can't possibly think that little boy is behind this, do you?

Veronica had detected no trace of violence when interviewing Max—either from him or his father. But the boy...

The car seat protested as she shifted her weight.

LeeAnn's memorial card was clearly a link. The picture with the stunted wings and the quote.

Not a coincidence, no way.

Veronica was reaching for the door handle, intent on heading inside and confronting whichever Taylor brother was still in the home, when the front door opened.

She froze.

While it was impossible to tell if the man whom Court was pursuing had been Alex or David, there was no question who this was.

Same black hoodie, but it was about half the size.

It was Max Taylor.

Now, Veronica was pressed to make another decision.

Although, this one was much easier than the previous one. It took her all of two seconds to decide what to do.

Careful not to make any noise, Veronica opened her car door and slid out. Shoulders hunched, she followed eleven-year-old Max Taylor in the same direction that Court had gone earlier.

It was a chilly night, and she did her best to cover her ears with her shoulders to keep them warm.

Back in the car, she'd asked Court if he was a religious man. He'd answered in the affirmative, but when the question had been posed to her, she'd refrained.

That answer, of course, was no, unequivocally.

And yet, as Veronica followed Max towards Needle Point on foot, she found herself muttering something under her breath.

Something foreign.

It took her nearly two full blocks to grasp what it was.

A prayer.

Not an official one, not a Hail Mary or an Our Father, but a plea to a higher power none the less. And wasn't that, in essence, all a prayer was? A call for good fortune or luck from an element outside of our control?

Whatever it was, be it a plea, an appeal, an invocation, prayer, petition, or request, Veronica couldn't help herself.

She wanted, above all else, for Max, no matter how improbable, to be completely ignorant of Jake's, Cooper's, or Frank's deaths.

Because, as Veronica knew better than most, once a killer, always a killer.

***

Court liked Veronica. She was strange, no doubt about it, but unlike most of the other Greenham cops, she didn't seem to care whether he was young or fresh out of boot camp. All she cared about was that he did good work. And so far, Court thought he'd done just that.

But while he was pleased with his work ethic, his social graces still needed work. Veronica had tripped him up when she'd joked about going on a date. She was attractive—very attractive—and they were both young, perhaps two of the youngest in the entire department. But Court wasn't interested in her—not like that. He wanted to learn from her, and, in some ways, he wanted to be like her, but he didn't want to be *with* her.

Court wasn't so disillusioned that he thought he could ever be as good as her—he didn't have her particular skill set—but he had one advantage that she didn't, something that Veronica herself had already commented on.

No one would ever argue for a life growing up with a meth-addicted mother. But one thing that Court learned very quickly from this very situation was that there were only really two choices in life: adapt or die. And with his mother living in a constant state of flux, her unpredictable and sporadic behavior a cycle of intoxication, withdrawal, and pursuit, no matter the time of the day, adaptation for Court meant rearranging his sleep cycle. Court only slept when his mother was completely out of it. One, two, at *most* three hours at a time. If he was lucky, over the course of a day, he might have three or four of these sessions. Over time, his body adapted to this segmented schedule.

It wasn't until much later on that Court learned that this had a name: polyphasic sleep. He could rest in small chunks throughout the day, whenever was most convenient, and appreciate the same restorative effects of people who went to bed at eleven and woke up at six.

Court didn't have much to thank his mother for. He didn't blame her for what she did—Ida Furnelli was a sick woman. *Very* sick. But his ability to sleep in short bursts came in handy as a cop.

And it would be even more advantageous when he rose to the rank of detective, which had always been a goal of his.

Court knew he had to put his time in just like everyone else. It just so happened that with his unique sleep schedule, he was able to put in more time than his colleagues. But things were happening slowly—too slowly for his liking. Sure, he'd only just been promoted from babysitting drunks in the holding cells to active beat cop, but when it was announced that Veronica was getting a new partner, he held out just a little hope that it would be him.

It was a long shot, and Court hadn't been overly surprised when his name had been passed over, just like he wasn't shocked to discover that her new partner was being imported from another state. The reality was, many in the department still harbored bad feelings toward Veronica, and that, coupled with her uniqueness, made volunteers to partner with the detective a rarity.

Enter Ethan Blake.

Exit Ethan Blake.

Buh-bye, don't let the door hit you on the ass on the way out.

Following the detective's record-breaking stint as the shortest-serving Greenham detective in department history, Court crossed his fingers that this was his chance.

Nope.

Freddie was brought back into the fold and while Court had fond feelings for the detective, he was a little disappointed by the man's return.

But his time would come. All he had to do was keep working hard and never stop learning.

Ahead of him, he watched as the shady figure, either David or Alex Taylor—he had yet to see their face—dipped into an alley. Court, who was still a good block and a half behind, jammed his hands into his pockets and picked up the pace.

And he was learning from Veronica—at least, he was trying to. She wasn't the easiest person to read—

Court took the corner a little too tight, and, lost in thought, was completely blindsided when someone leaped in front of him. Before he could react, two hands grabbed him by the front of his shirt and roughly pulled him close. Court, whose own hands were still in his pockets, lost his balance and stumbled forward. The two men spun as if partaking in a strange, uncoordinated dance, before finally coming to a stop beneath a schism of yellow streetlight.

Court caught just a glimpse of the man's face before his attacker leaned away and the hood he wore cast shadows over his features.

But it was enough to inspire a single thought: *monster. I'm being attacked by a monster.*

"Why are you following me?" Spit sprayed Court's face and he struggled to break free. "Why the *fuck* are you following me?"

Chapter 57

FREDDIE WAS ABSOLUTELY STUFFED. AFTER sticking to a calorie-restricted diet of around 2800 calories per day for nearly six months, he estimated that he'd already consumed 6000 today alone, all from low-quality, high glycemic carbohydrates, and saturated fats. It made him feel full, sure, but paradoxically, it also made him feel empty. And now, as he stared at the extra-large half-empty soft drink in his hand, it made him feel nauseous, too.

Freddie put the drink down and finally reached for his phone. After his encounter with Dylan, he'd deliberately avoided answering or looking at his messages for fear of what they might contain.

Troy wants you to know that you made a big mistake fucking with him. And if there's one man you don't want to fuck with, it's Troy.

Dylan was out and so was Randall.

And that wouldn't sit well with that prick Troy Allison.

Something had to give.

Freddie's phone chimed, indicating that he had a new voicemail.

"Shit."

Even though he saw that it was from Veronica, it took a considerable amount of effort to play it.

With a heavy sigh, Freddie grabbed his soft drink and sucked on the paper straw that had already started to get soft while the message played.

Hearing the familiarity of his partner's voice didn't make him feel any better. And listening to what she had to say definitely made him feel worse.

He wiped his sweaty palms on his thighs and then rummaged through the fast-food garbage in the backseat, searching for the sheets of paper that Father James Murphy had given him. All the while, Freddie prayed that the Taylor name wasn't on any of them.

He eventually found the stack beneath a hamburger wrapper and stared at that first page.

Like with his phone, he didn't want to read it.

Didn't want to acknowledge that he'd made *another* mistake.

Man up, Freddie. Man the fuck up.

With a trembling hand, Freddie forced himself to scan the list of employees and volunteers, which was oddly organized and in alphabetical order. He quickly passed over the Altmans, other random names, including the Kleinmans, of course, but stopped when he saw Karen Klarno. According to the last column, the new widow helped serve Sunday hot lunch.

He passed Prichard, Ronaldo, and Rungal. When he got to the Ss, Freddie's finger tracing slowed.

Please, don't be there. Please, *don't be there.*

Finding any of the Taylors on the list—be it David, Alex, or even Max's name—was a potential break in the case. It was also the link to the church that Veronica so desperately sought.

Selfishly, Freddie didn't want them to be there, he didn't want the Taylors to have anything to do with Father Murphy or Grace Community.

Because it had been his job to search the list for any potential links or clues. And he'd been so distracted by Dylan Hall and Troy Allison, and to a lesser degree, stuffing his face, that he'd barely even looked at it.

"Damn."

Freddie let out a long, prolonged sigh and he closed his eyes for a few seconds.

Of course, they were there.

"Fuck."

He crumpled the sheet of paper and threw it to the floor with the rest of the garbage. Then he grabbed his phone again and called Veronica. She didn't answer and while pulling out of the parking lot and onto the road, Freddie tried her again.

"Answer the phone, Veronica," he pleaded.

But she didn't. Not on the third or fourth try, either.

There was a knot forming in Freddie's stomach, one that couldn't completely be attributed to the glut of food he'd just consumed.

And when he spotted Veronica's car, empty, a block from the Taylor house, this knot became a pitchfork, twisting and grinding its way into his guts.

Freddie parked beside Veronica's vehicle and got out. Then he stared through the driver's side window as if this act alone would make Veronica materialize.

It didn't.

Freddie turned his face up the block toward the Taylor house. It wasn't difficult to spot; it was the only one with a light on in one of the front rooms. Squinting hard, he thought he saw a flicker of movement from between the partially closed blinds. Then Freddie was almost sure he saw the blinds separate a little, a bottom one being pushed down to allow someone to see out.

The bent blind looked like a smile to Freddie, and this conjured a horrible image in his mind.

Veronica, her head tilted back, her throat open in a similar crescent shape.

Freddie broke into a run. After just a handful of strides, grease and bile started to burn his throat. He fought the urge to vomit and kept going, making it to the Taylor house in record time.

"Veronica!" He banged the heel of his hand against the door. "Veronica? You in there?"

Freddie leaned away from the door and looked at the front room with the lights on. No movement and the blinds were completely straight.

Did I imagine it?

"Veronica!" Freddie pounded again. "Ver—"

There was a response this time. Not a word, *per se*, but a grunt.

He stopped and listened.

It didn't recur, but unlike the blinds separating, Freddie was certain that it had been real.

Now the image in his mind of Veronica changed. Her throat was no longer slit, but she was still in danger. She was tied up and there was someone behind her. They were holding pliers that were digging into her flesh.

Tearing, breaking, trying to gain access to her lungs and set her free.

"Fuck this," he whispered.

Freddie took a step backward, preparing to drive his heel into the door beside the handle, but at the last second, he stopped himself. He tested the knob.

The door was unlocked.

With one, final deep breath, Freddie pushed the door open so hard that it banged loudly on the opposite wall.

"*Veronica!*" he shouted as he rushed inside the Taylor home.

Chapter 58

VERONICA HAD NO IDEA WHERE Max Taylor was headed. She wasn't sure if the boy knew, either. He appeared to be wandering aimlessly, glancing up and down each street as he passed.

Was he looking for something? *Someone?*

A sinner, perhaps?

No, it's not him. Can't be him.

Max was just a lonely boy who missed his mother. A boy who had frequent nightmares and roamed the streets at night to try and clear his head.

But part of this didn't ring true.

Because Veronica was following him at a distance. As much as she wanted to convince herself that this was to make sure that Max was safe—Needle Point wasn't the nicest place even in the day and it was a different animal altogether at night—Veronica was also curious.

Court had asked her if she thought Max could possibly be involved with the murders and her instinct had been no, he wasn't.

But the coincidences had started to add up. And if Freddie found the Taylors on that list? That would be impossible to ignore.

They passed the area where Max had witnessed Jake Thompson's murder, but the boy didn't slow. A half block later, Veronica thought she would have to intervene when a skeezy-looking man started to approach Max. But the boy just kept his head down and continued moving, a testament to his experience.

Then, out of nowhere, Max just stopped. He reached an alley, peered down it, and must have spotted something.

Veronica kept moving, closing the distance between them. When Max started down the dark alley, her mindset began to change. She'd gone from considering Max being the killer to him becoming the next victim.

This caused her to walk even more quickly and to reach for the gun beneath her jacket. Veronica got to the mouth of the alley and stopped to listen.

"Hi."

Max's voice.

"*Max... Max... Max...*"

Veronica was surprised that she recognized the second voice as well.

"I brought you something."

Intrigued, Veronica moved so that she could witness this strange interaction. Max was standing in front of Mark, who was still wearing his filthy Oregon U sweatshirt. The boy handed him something—a baguette? Some sort of bread, anyway—and Mark immediately tore it apart and shoved it into his mouth.

"Thanks... thanks... thanks," the man managed between chews.

There was something oddly beautiful about this scene, something so innocent about an eleven-year-old boy bringing food to a disabled homeless man.

Food *and* water—Max produced a bottle of water and handed that over, as well.

Things slowly started to click into place for Veronica.

Mark, saying Max's name when she'd shown him the picture of the monster, for instance.

Veronica could have watched this interaction for hours, but a car backfired somewhere in the distance and both Mark and Max looked in her direction.

"Cop... cop... cop..."

There was no accusation in Mark's words, he was just addressing Veronica with the name that he'd given her.

"Detective Shade?" Max was confused and maybe a little scared, too.

Veronica tried to assuage the boy's concerns by stepping into the light and holding her hands up.

"Yes, but please just call me Veronica."

"What are you... what are you doing here?"

"I'm just making sure that you're okay."

Veronica moved closer, pleased that while Mark was dripping with a blue aura, no fiery colors were coming from either of them.

"I—I was just going for a walk." Max's voice was meek. "Don't tell my dad. I'll get in so much trouble."

"I won't tell him. But this place—" Veronica indicated the filthy alley, "—is dangerous. You shouldn't be out here alone."

Max made a face.

"I'm not alone. I have Mark. He keeps me safe."

"Safe... Safe... Safe..."

The large man nodded enthusiastically, and he shoved more bread into his mouth.

Veronica grinned, but this expression was short-lived when she remembered that someone had left the Taylor house before Max.

"Max, was your dad home when you left?"

"Yeah, I think so." Max looked confused again. "Why wouldn't he be?"

"It's just—" Veronica stepped forward again and Mark very subtly eased his way in front of Max. "I saw someone leave your house before you did. Out the back."

"You did?"

Another step, this time to test a theory. As Veronica expected, Mark matched her movements.

He really was protecting the boy.

"Yeah, I did. Your room's in the front, right?"

"Yes."

"And when you left, did you happen to look into your dad's room?"

Max frowned.

"No, sorry. I left out the front. I... I didn't want him to see me."

Veronica scratched her jaw.

"Where does your uncle sleep? Does he have his own room?"

Max shook his head.

"No, he sleeps on the couch." The boy's eyes widened. "You know what? I don't think I saw him on the couch. It was dark but I'm pretty sure he wasn't there."

That answers that question; Court was following Alex Taylor. Something else occurred to Veronica.

"Max, when you said you saw someone putting a bloody sweatshirt in the garbage—"

"Dad said that didn't happen," Max interrupted.

"Did it?" Veronica didn't mean to sound accusatory, but the words just popped out of her mouth.

Max sucked on his lower lip.

"I just want to know what you saw, Max. I won't tell your dad and you're not in trouble."

"Trouble... trouble... trouble..."

Max's lip popped out of his mouth.

"Yeah, I saw someone putting a shirt in the trash. I did—but I didn't see who."

"Okay," Veronica nodded encouragingly. It was much easier to speak to the boy without his father interrupting every few minutes. "But when you saw whoever this was, did you notice your uncle sleeping on the couch?"

Max's nose crinkled.

"I was scared. I—I—"

"Scared… scared… scared…"

"I know you were scared. I'd be scared, too. But this is important, Max. Was your uncle on the couch when you saw someone putting the sweatshirt in the garbage?"

When Max didn't answer for a good thirty seconds, Veronica took advantage of the break to move even closer still, subconsciously preparing to sniff out a lie.

"I—I think he was, yeah. Uncle Alex was still sleeping on the couch."

If this was a lie, Veronica couldn't tell.

And that wasn't good—that meant that she and Court had followed the wrong Taylors.

Alex, the ex-con, wasn't their man. Neither was little Max.

It was David Taylor they were after.

David was the monster.

And they'd left him alone, free to kill again.

Veronica felt a lump rise in her throat, and she reached for Max.

"We should go, Max. Come with me."

She'd intended to take the boy by the wrist but didn't even come close to making contact.

Mark intervened.

He lumbered forward and before Veronica registered what was happening, the hulking figure raised a fist and slammed it down on the top of her head.

Everything went dark instantly.

Chapter 59

OFFICER COURT FURNELLI RECOGNIZED THE monster who stood before him.

He knew its name, and it wasn't Alex Taylor.

It was addiction.

And it made the man hideous. Bloodshot eyes, a twisted snarl on his lips, and feverish, clammy skin peppered with hives pulled taut over prominent cheekbones. Fortunately, Court had experience dealing with junkies, having been raised by one. And he knew that while they could be terrifying, they also broke easily.

The hands gripping the front of his shirt were strong, but it was only a shirt and not even a good-quality one. Court lowered the blade of his hand across both of Alex's wrists, simultaneously turning his body away from the man. One hand let go, and while the other held fast, his shirt stretched enough to create some distance between them.

Court raised his foot and kicked Alex Taylor's knee. Veronica had said no uniform, which meant he was wearing running shoes instead of his work-issued boots. That likely saved Alex from months of recovery and maybe even the need for surgery. Court also only used about 50% of his strength. But 50% was plenty.

Alex cried out, then staggered away, gripping the side of his knee, pain etched on his face which now appeared more human than monstrous. He was cursing, too, a string of vile, wet expletives spewed from his mouth.

"Officer Court Furnelli, Greenham PD," Court said, pulling his badge out of his back pocket and flashing it at the man.

"Screw you," Alex replied, then spat.

Court sidestepped the glob of yellowish phlegm. Veronica had instructed him to stay back and follow the man, and he'd botched that plan. Now he wasn't sure what to do. So far, Alex hadn't broken any laws. There was no doubt that he would—this man was out to score, as almost everybody who came to Needle Point in the middle of the night was but hadn't yet.

"Listen, Alex, you gotta get help," Court said. "I know it seems hard, maybe even impossible, to get out of this rut, to break the pattern of addiction. But you can do it. I know a guy named Dylan Hall. Hell, you probably—"

Alex snarled and spat again.

"Dylan's a fuckin' snitch."

"So, you know him?" Alex made a face and the space between his upper lip and nose vanished. "I don't know if he's a snitch or not, but the one thing I know for sure is that Dylan Hall is alive."

"Fuck him and fuck you." Alex tried to put weight on his injured leg but couldn't.

"I'm serious. He might be a snitch, but Dylan's alive. But you know who isn't?" Court thought of his mom then, of the day when he'd come home and found her on the couch, her lips blue, her eyes open and unblinking. "Jake Thompson."

Alex grunted.

"Yeah, I'm guessing by the expression on your face, you knew him, too." These junkies and dealers were a tight-knit group, apparently. One big, fucked-up family. Not that much unlike the Taylors. Or the Furnellis, for that matter. Hell, even the Shades, come to think of it. "I don't know if they said this on the news, but Jake had his throat slit from ear to ear. And then, someone sliced him open, cracked his ribs, pulled his lungs out, and put them on his back like an angel."

"You're lying," Alex said. All the fury had drained from his face, and it had been replaced by something else.

Not fear, not really, but close.

"I'm not lying. Get some help, Alex, while you're still alive."

The junkie looked at him but said nothing.

Court backed out of the alley not sure if his little speech had done anything at all. He hoped it had because he knew the road that Alex Taylor was on.

And it always ended in a dead end.

It wasn't a complete waste of time, though, even if his suggestion to get help was ignored.

Because Court had stared into Alex's eyes.

The man was a fiend, but he was no killer.

Which meant that the monster was back at the house.

Alone with Veronica.

Court Furnelli had been walking slowly out of the alley, but as soon as Alex was out of sight, he picked up the pace.

Then he broke into a run.

Chapter 60

"VERONICA!" FREDDIE SHOUTED AS HE rushed into the Taylor house. It was dark inside and his shin struck a chair or couch or something, and he dropped to one knee.

That's when he saw it.

'It' was the only way Freddie could describe the beast that shambled out of one of the rooms. It appeared half-drunk, bumping into one wall before careening across the hallway and colliding with the other side.

"Stay the fuck back!" he shouted, reaching for his gun.

But if the thing heard him, it didn't slow, didn't react at all.

It continued to shamble forward, and as Freddie was pulling his gun from the holster, he saw its face, and he screamed.

Freddie Furlow couldn't remember the last time he screamed. Surely, when he'd been younger, a kid, he'd been frightened by some horror film and had shouted out in fear, but he couldn't recall a specific scenario.

The sound was foreign, and it compounded the fear he felt coursing through him.

The monster looked almost identical to the picture that Max had drawn. Its face was lumpy and misshapen, like a ball of pizza dough that you'd kneaded with your heels. The brow was thickened and overgrown, so much so that the eyes were almost completely invisible. The cheeks were puffy, and the jaw protruded to an extent that gave the creature a Simian appearance.

And then it moaned. The noise was horrible, inhuman, low, and guttural like someone who was trying to vomit but couldn't on account of their throat closing up.

Freddie finally pulled his gun free, but he was too slow.

The beast was upon him.

It didn't tackle Freddie, who was still on one knee, as much as it fell on top of him. Weight loss or not, the detective was still a big man, but the beast was bigger. It was puffy and distended, but also soft like it was holding excess water.

The back of Freddie's head banged off the hardwood floor and he saw stars. Then the thing leaned close and made another sound. Not a growl this time, but a word, hot and wet on Freddie's cheek.

"*Sinner.*"

***

Liquid moistened Veronica's lips and her eyes snapped open. When she saw two shapes huddling over her, she immediately tried to shuffle backward, only to butt up against a hard surface.

Her vision adjusted and her memory returned.

The two figures were Mark and Max, and the latter was holding a water bottle, which he had just pulled away from her mouth.

"Detective Shade, I'm so sorry. Please don't take my friend away. Please don't arrest Mark."

"Arrest... arrest... arrest..."

Mark held his hands out as if asking her to put cuffs on him.

Veronica's head throbbed and she reached for the water bottle.

"Mark didn't mean to hurt you. He just—he thought you were trying to grab me. He was trying to protect me," Max said desperately.

Veronica still didn't understand their relationship, but she knew now that it went much deeper than just a random meeting in Needle Point during one of Max's walks.

"I won't—" Veronica tried to stand, winced, and slumped back down. "I won't arrest him. Just don't hit me again."

"Sorry... sorry... sorry..."

"That's okay, Mark," Max consoled the bigger man. "We know you didn't mean to hurt her."

Veronica drank from the water bottle and some of the cobwebs in her mind began to clear. She had a nice little bump on the back of her head, but she considered herself lucky. Had she been closer to the wall when Mark had delivered the blow, she might have hit her face on the brick, broken her nose or an orbital bone.

"How long was I out for?" Veronica asked as she tried, successfully this time, to get up.

The lack of anger she felt was surprising. Veronica knew she should be pissed—she'd been assaulted, knocked out, but for some reason, she felt oddly indifferent about the entire event.

Was it because Mark was disabled? Or was the heartwarming scene that preceded the act still affecting her? Turning her synesthesia into a rose-colored film?

And why hadn't her synesthesia tipped her off that Mark was about to become violent?

"Not long," Max said. "A couple of minutes. We put you against the wall because we thought it would be more comfortable."

Or was it because being knocked out was a far cry from having your throat slit and your lungs ripped out?

"You have to go home," Veronica said, holding her hand out defensively and leaning back in case this angered Mark again.

"Home... home... home..."

But maybe home wasn't the best place for Max right now.

Veronica was in a jam. She had to go back, she had to confront David. But she couldn't leave Max alone.

Her eyes darted to Mark. The man's posture had changed again. When Veronica had come to, his shoulders had been slumped. Now, maybe because of the mention of home, or maybe because of her change in tone, the man's chest had puffed a little.

Veronica made up her mind.

"Mark, can you keep Max safe?"

"Safe... safe... safe..."

"Right, safe. I want you to stay with him. I want you to make sure he's safe. I want you to protect him, like you're a cop, okay?"

"Cop... cop... cop..."

"That's right. And if anyone comes near you, I want you to do to them what you did to me."

Mark nodded aggressively and Veronica turned to Max.

"Is that okay with you?"

"Yeah, that's fine," Max said softly. "Mark always looks after me. Should I get him to take me home?"

Veronica thought about this.

"Yes. But not now. Wait an hour. You have a watch?"

"Hour... hour... hour..."

Max held up his wrist showing off a Timex. When he looked at Veronica again, the boy's eyes had unexpectedly softened.

Maybe this isn't such a good idea. Maybe I should just call Freddie or Court or 9-1-1 and have someone swing by and pick them up.

But Veronica had a bad feeling about the Taylor house. And she didn't really know where she was. Some alley in Needle Point? How long would it take to find a cross-street that had signs that weren't defaced so badly that she'd actually be able to read them?

Five minutes? Ten?

Something told her that she didn't have that much time.

And how would Mark react to cops barging into this alley?

Veronica might not be angry with him for braining her, but other cops might not have her patience or resolve. If there was ever a place that embodied the idea that it was better to ask for forgiveness than permission, it was crime-riddled Needle Point.

And if some wannabe alpha beat cop came here and mistook Mark protecting Max as something more nefarious?

That wouldn't end well, it wouldn't end with just a bump on the back of the head, that's for sure.

Veronica clenched her jaw.

"You're going to be okay, Max. Just stay here one hour, then get Mark to take you home. I'll be waiting for you there."

Max nodded and he tried to hide the tears that filled his eyes.

"Veronica, is my daddy a monster?"

Veronica swallowed hard, and she had a strong desire to pull the picture of her brother and Dante out and look at it.

Veronica resisted. Now wasn't the time for nostalgia.

Now was the time for action.

"I… I don't know. I honestly don't know, Max."

Chapter 61

"*Sinner.*"

If Freddie wasn't so familiar with the word, he wasn't sure he would have been able to understand it.

It was garbled, nearly unintelligible.

And it added to Freddie's suspicion that he was, in fact, living a nightmare.

His head ached and nylon ropes cut into his wrists and ankles where they were bound to a chair. The knots didn't feel particularly strong—Freddie found it amazing that the beast with bulbous, swollen hands was able to manipulate the rope at all—but the knife that was continually wagged near his face discouraged him from trying too hard to break free.

The Taylor house was mostly dark with the only light coming from one of the front rooms behind Freddie and off to one side. As the monster jerkily rocked back and forth, the light occasionally caught the side of its face. The misshapen lumps that disguised a brow or cheek or jaw cast thick shadows over the rest of the visage, rending it even more horrifying. Freddie was having a hard time wrapping his mind around what he was seeing. His brain told him that this wasn't real, that it *couldn't* be real, that it had to be a one-of-a-kind prosthetic mask. But the way it moved, and the way it glistened with sweat that he occasionally saw bead and drip into a deep channel between swollen tissues, suggested otherwise.

"Sinner?"

This time the intonation was different; it wasn't a statement but a question.

The creature lunged forward, the blade of what Freddie now realized was a filleting knife coming dangerously close to his cheek.

He closed his eyes and turned his head to one side.

"Sinner?" The thing's breath was strangely sour.

As Freddie waited for the knife to penetrate the soft skin beneath his chin, he found his mind considering this question.

Am I a sinner? Well, I framed two men, one more innocent than the other, I've been living a lie and I ruined my family's life. So, am I a sinner? Yeah, I'm a sinner.

He might as well have said this word out loud because the beast growled and pulled back.

Freddie opened his eyes.

The monster was standing three feet from him now, his feet spread shoulder-width apart, his hands at his sides.

It was the most natural human pose that Freddie had seen it make since pinwheeling out of a side room. And when it spoke next, the voice almost sounded normal.

"Then I will free you from your sins."

An odd calmness fell over Freddie, and he no longer even had the desire to try and break free.

I will free you from your sins.

They'd been looking at this case all wrong. Both he and Veronica had thought that their unsub was punishing the victims because of their sins. He wasn't. In a twisted, sadistic way, he was actually releasing them.

He was atoning for them.

He was turning them into angels and allowing them to ascend to heaven.

"I'm a sinner," Freddie whispered. "I'm a sinner."

It was probably exhaustion mixed with the assault of a massive insulin spike from his horrible diet that clouded his thoughts.

Freddie accepted his fate. He even raised his chin ever so slightly.

I am a sinner, and I will be set free.

The beast growled something that Freddie construed as an affirmation and then it clambered forward, raising the knife as it moved.

Freddie closed his eyes.

Images of his sons flashed in his mind. Images of happy times with his boys and his wife.

A smile crept onto Freddie's face that persisted even as he was accosted by the sweet rank of the beast's breath.

***

At first, all Veronica saw were dark outlines. She made out a large person slumped in a chair and another hovering over them.

What she should have seen were swirls of warm colors.

Because there was violence here.

But she didn't.

Freddie... it was Freddie in the chair.

Veronica was still three feet from the open door to the Taylor house and the closer she got the more she saw.

The more she saw, the less she wanted to.

David Taylor was a mess. With Max and Alex out prowling the streets, this had to be him, but the man was barely recognizable. The thing with the knife nearing Freddie's throat was a real monster, shockingly close to the rendition that Max had drawn.

Monster... monster... monster...

Veronica had seen monsters before. Not literal ones, of course, but she'd seen a monster dressed as a woman who used her daughter to lure victims to their deaths. She'd seen a picture of a monster in a priest's robes who had abused neglected orphans for years.

But this was different. David Taylor was a *real* monster. Why he didn't trigger her synesthesia was a mystery. These runaway thoughts combined with the unbelievable scene unfolding before her threatened to derail Veronica. Setting her jaw and squeezing the handle of her gun forced these thoughts away.

Thinking was often the antithesis of action.

Thinking could come later.

She needed to act now.

"David Taylor!" Detective Veronica Shade shouted as she entered the home. "Lower the fucking knife."

The hooded figure looked up.

Fuck.

David was hideous. He had red eyes and a face that was wet and molten like melted wax.

"Sinner!" he hissed.

Despite the fear that gripped her, Veronica forced herself to take another step. She aimed the gun at the center of David's thickened forehead.

"Drop the fucking knife!" Veronica warned. "Drop it now!"

Freddie bucked as if he'd been unconscious, and someone had waved an ammonia tab beneath his nose.

Was he drugged? Was I drugged? Is this all just a drug-induced hallucination?

"There's something wrong with him!" Freddie croaked, craning his head around to look at her. "There's... something wrong!"

No shit.

"I will set him free of his sins!" the beast roared.

He raised the knife and even though it looked like Freddie was going to be able to break free of his bindings, he was moving too slowly.

"The hell you will."

Veronica had enough of this nightmare.

She braced herself and brought her left hand to the butt of her pistol. Before shooting Gloria there had been a brief moment where everything went quiet. It was almost as if the universe was waiting for one, or both of them, to change their mind. To choose a different, less violent path, perhaps. This happened on Donovan's Bridge with Dante Fiori, as well.

But in both of those cases, nothing had changed.

This was different.

Perhaps aware of its impending doom, the beast staggered backward. The knife didn't quite fall from his hand, but it was no longer perilously close to Freddie's throat.

Then the monster transformed. The eyelids retracted, revealing bloodshot eyes, and the brow thinned rapidly as if it had been a flesh-colored inner tube filled with fluid that had been punctured.

And Veronica confirmed that this was indeed, somehow, inconceivably, but unequivocally, David Taylor.

She didn't know how this was possible. But she also realized that it didn't matter. This thing, this monster that was somehow also David Taylor, had murdered three people. He had slit their throats, and then he had crudely torn their lungs out of the back of their bodies. He'd written the word *SINNER* in their blood.

"It's my turn to set you free," Veronica muttered, and as the knife fell from David's hand and clattered to the floor, she moved her finger from the guard to the trigger.

Once a killer, always a killer.

Then she squeezed.

Chapter 62

COURT FURNELLI DIDN'T UNDERSTAND WHAT was happening in the Taylor home. But years of living with his addicted mother had habituated him in such a way that comprehension wasn't required to react to unpredictable scenarios.

He knew that the person holding the gun was Veronica, and maybe somewhere deep down, he had a moment where he considered the rumors regarding the detective and Gloria Tramell, and to some lesser degree, Dante Fiori.

Or maybe he didn't—perhaps his movements were the result of sheer automation.

Court lunged, intending on striking Veronica's forearm which held a gun aimed at an unarmed man. But the darkness tampered with his depth perception, and he came up short, hitting her shoulder instead, sending her off-kilter.

The gun fired.

The lack of light had sensitized Court's other senses. The sound was nearly deafening and the flash from the muzzle was blinding.

Still, even with his ears feeling like they were plugged with water, he heard a guttural sound as something huge and heavy fell to the floor. This was followed by a wet, slapping noise.

"It's me! It's Court!" he cried out as he tried to will his senses back to full function. "It's Court!"

He was worried that Veronica would turn, think that he was an accomplice of some sort, and fire blindly in his direction.

"I'm *Court!*" He groped around blindly, blinking like a man having a seizure, and felt what he thought was the back of a chair. "Don't shoot!"

There was no second shot and after several seconds, maybe a minute, Court realized that he could see again.

Veronica, who was either less susceptible to the effects of the gunshot in the confined space, or had recovered more quickly than he, was hovering over a fallen form. Worried that she was readying to shoot again, even though Court could no longer see the gun, he scrambled to his feet.

"Veronica?" The detective appeared frozen and hurried to her side. "Veron—" —*ica* stuck in Court's throat.

The detective was still holding her gun, but it was pressed against the side of her thigh. Beneath her was a monster.

It was also Dave Taylor... *sort of.* In some bizarre way, the monster reminded Court of a caricature that an artist at a local fair might draw. It exaggerated all of the unique characteristics of Dave's face. Only, in the worst possible way. Everything was out of proportion—it was a haunted house version of a portrait.

"What's—what's wrong with him?" Court asked in a breathy whisper.

There was a golf ball-sized dot of blood on the man's shoulder, one that was growing as they watched. But this change was the least worrisome.

David Taylor's face was... *deflating.* Within seconds it started to look almost normal. This was so disturbing that Court felt his stomach lurch and he was forced to look away.

"What's wrong with him?" Veronica repeated absently. Court tried to meet her eyes, but unlike him, she refused to take her gaze away from the monster. "He's a murderer. That's what's wrong with him."

Silence—even the sound of David's breathing, which had been labored and wheezy, constricted as if he'd been on the verge of anaphylaxis, had regressed to something inaudible.

Then there was a familiar voice.

"Uhh, guys?" Freddie said. "Can one of you please untie these fucking ropes? *Please?*"

Chapter 63

NONE OF THE THREE OFFICERS understood what was happening. All they knew was that David Taylor was dangerous. After tying his wrists while he was lying down and unconscious, wrists that had shrunk considerably in size since even moments earlier, they used a set of scissors from the kitchen to cut away his sweatshirt. When they pulled off his shirt, they found a pair of thick, hand-held bolt cutters in the center pocket.

Bolt cutters that had been used to cut Jake's, Cooper's, and Frank's ribs, allowing access to their lungs.

Veronica's bullet had embedded itself in the fleshy part of David's shoulder. The wound wasn't serious and most of the bleeding had already stopped. The blood that had leaked from the hole was a deep crimson and stained David's blotchy skin, which was normal and therefore unexpected. With the transformation they'd all witnessed, Veronica thought that dark green or black fluid, perhaps the consistency of thick paste and maybe even roiling with bubbles, would have been more appropriate.

She was still trying to understand what had happened to David and if the change was actually real. The idea that they'd all been drugged was still niggling at the back of her mind. They'd all taken different routes to get to Taylors', making it unlikely that they'd been poisoned before arriving. But what about the house itself? Could there be something in the air? Some aerosolized hallucinogen?

Veronica looked at David. His face continued to deflate and if she hadn't seen him minutes before, she might have concluded that he was just having an allergic reaction of some sort.

Were the drugs wearing off?

The scenario seemed unlikely, but the alternative was even more absurd. The fact that neither Court nor Freddie had said anything suggested that they were having a hard time understanding what had happened, as well.

"He's... he's still breathing," Court remarked.

Was that relief in the cop's voice? Or disappointment?

"What do you think—" Freddie was interrupted by the sound of someone approaching.

Veronica turned, her hand reaching for her holstered gun.

It wasn't one person, but two. The person in the lead was large and Veronica briefly, *very* briefly, thought that it was another monster.

The other was small, diminutive, partially hidden by the much bigger man.

"Who—"

Veronica stepped toward the door.

"It's okay," she told her partner, who was primed for action. "I'll take care of this."

She made her way outside, careful not to move too quickly.

"Safe... safe... safe..." Mark informed her.

"Yeah, you did a great job. You kept Max safe," Veronica said. "Now, I need—"

She heard a siren and then saw blue and red lights reflect off clouds in the distance.

"Cops... cops... cops..."

"That's right, the cops are coming. You should probably go."

Mark nodded and Max squeezed the man tightly.

"Thank you," the boy said.

"Go... go... go..." The word trailed behind Mark as he scuttled away.

When Veronica turned her eyes back to Max, she saw that he was looking by her and into his house.

"It was my dad, wasn't it? He was the monster?"

Veronica did a double inhale, but when she tried to force all the air out of her lungs, her chest rattled, and she sputtered.

She was exhausted. Fully and thoroughly exhausted.

There was something horribly familiar about standing on the porch of a child's house while inside the body of a serial killer lay on the floor. With Beverly Tramell, her mother had been killed. Max Taylor's father was still alive—they had Court to thank for that.

Once a killer, always a killer.

If the police officer hadn't hit her shoulder, she would have put a bullet in David's head. Wouldn't she have?

The truth was no one would have blamed her. But no one had blamed her for shooting Gloria Tramell, either. That didn't make it okay.

That didn't make it right.

"Come with me." Veronica put her arm over Max's shoulder and guided him away from the front door. "I want to show you something." She pulled out her wallet and removed the picture of her brother and Dante. "This is my brother," she said, pointing at the shirtless, unsmiling boy. "I didn't know him well, but he had a... well, he had a rough life. A *hard* life." It was a struggle to get the words out. "It wasn't his fault and..."

She wanted to tell Max that no matter what his father did, he didn't have to follow in his footsteps. He could choose to be different.

But she cracked.

Tears welled and spilled over.

Veronica expected Court to comfort her, or perhaps Freddie, but it was Max who wrapped his arms around her shoulders.

The first officer arrived, a nameless foot soldier, and Veronica continued to cry until he was standing right beside them, wondering what in the fuck was going on.

A tear dropped onto the photo, landing next to Benny's head, and Veronica wiped it away.

"He's in there," Veronica said, her voice hoarse.

"The call was for medical, too—is the suspect still alive?"

Veronica cringed at the word 'suspect'. At least he hadn't said 'monster'.

"He's alive."

Now Max started to cry, and it was Veronica's turn to hold the boy.

Chapter 64

DURING THE REMAINDER OF THE night, David Taylor experienced three episodes. Veronica, who had chosen to sleep in the same room as the man handcuffed to the bed, witnessed the first and third such events.

After transporting him to the hospital, David was sedated and immediately prepped for surgery to remove the bullet from his shoulder. During the time between Veronica shooting him and surgery prep, David's appearance continued to improve until he looked exactly the same as he had during their interview.

Perhaps because of the chaotic circumstances—someone in the media had caught wind of them bringing in a serial killer—Veronica hadn't been able to find anyone to provide her with answers. The media circus had also forced the hospital into lockdown mode, which meant only one of them was permitted to stay in David's room. Her phone had also been confiscated, effectively cutting her off from communicating with Court or Freddie. That was fine by her—Freddie had always been better at paperwork, anyway.

The good news was that others had seen David's transformation—the EMT who had treated him at the scene, for instance, although he only witnessed the tail end of it—suggesting that they hadn't been drugged.

Or maybe that wasn't good news.

Veronica would have to wait to pass judgment on that one.

Following successful surgery, and while David was still sedated, one of the doctors had attempted to subject him to an MRI.

This turned out to be a mistake.

Since no metal was allowed in the MRI room, David couldn't be handcuffed to anything. Chest straps held him in place, but they didn't look nearly strong enough to contain what Veronica had seen down the sights of her barrel. Shortly after the machine started its characteristic *thuck, thuck, thuck* noise as it worked to see inside David's head, he began to change. Unlike the transition from monster to David, the transformation from David to monster was horrifyingly quick. Veronica, who watched through protective glass, could actually see it happening, even though David's face was hidden inside the machine.

His hands were a dead giveaway. David's fingers started to swell and twitch. It was like watching someone inflate latex gloves under a faucet until nearly bursting.

Veronica alerted a tech to this change, and they immediately shut off the machine. With a trio of security guards, they rushed into the room.

David was confused and while the chest straps would have been easy enough for him to break free of, he was too disoriented to do anything but thrash and thrust.

He was sedated and the change—which still nobody could explain—quickly reverted.

The second time David became a monster, Veronica was so exhausted that she slept through the entire ordeal. When she woke to use the bathroom, the doctors informed her about it.

The third time, Veronica was pretty sure she induced the change. As morning approached, David started calling out for his son. Veronica, roused from her slumber, looked over at the man. And then she thought of her and Max, holding each other and crying.

The doctors had warned against upsetting David, thinking that this might be a trigger for what they were unprofessionally referring to as 'the change', but Veronica couldn't help herself.

Despite Veronica showing David the mounting evidence, the photographs of the victims, the knife he'd been holding, the bolt cutters he'd had in his possession, David didn't believe a word of it.

He thought she was lying—according to him, she *had* to be lying, because he had never hurt anyone.

The entire time, during every denial, Veronica failed to detect even the faintest of gasoline smells.

When Veronica told David about how Max had seen him as a monster trying to shove a bloody sweatshirt in the trash the man got angry.

First, David's face flushed. Then his cheeks puffed like a kid who was trying to hold their breath underwater. Only, this puffiness soon spread to his brow and around his eyes.

Veronica, legitimately terrified even though she'd seen this show before, scrambled toward the door. She was afraid that the man's wrists would swell so badly that the handcuff would snap.

Thankfully, a nurse appeared and called in reinforcements.

Sedation calmed David's appearance and mind but Veronica, still not feeling one-hundred percent safe, elected to stay outside the room for the next little while.

As she waited, Veronica realized that she recognized one of David's doctors: Dr. Kincaid, the same man who had treated Sheriff Steve Burns, who was, as far as she knew, still in this hospital, albeit on a different floor.

Steve... she hadn't thought about Steve in a while.

"Dr. Kinkaid? Any idea what's wrong with him?" Veronica asked when the doctor, head down, left the room.

Dr. Kinkaid looked at her with eyes surrounded by dark circles that rivaled her own.

"I'm Detective Shade, I was the one—"

"I know who you are."

"Right, of course you do." Veronica had forgotten all about their interactions while in Steve's room. There was a strange parallel to sleeping in the hospital next to the sheriff and then David, but she didn't want to consider this now. "Any update?" She gestured toward David who was now sleeping peacefully. The dichotomy from the man's rage just moments ago was nearly enough to give her vertigo.

"Can't make a conclusive diagnosis yet," Dr. Kinkaid began. "But we did get some results back."

"And?"

"Well, Mr. Taylor had massive levels of IGF-I in his blood—I'm talking a hundred times what we would normally find. Even stranger is that the first blood test was near normal. I didn't think it possible for levels to fluctuate so quickly, or so dramatically, but—"

"I'm sorry," Veronica interrupted. "IGF-I?"

"Insulin-like growth factor. That, coupled with a dramatic increase in growth hormone, is what we think might be responsible for his dramatic change in appearance."

Veronica had heard of growth hormone before—she'd encountered it in a case a while back in which a bodybuilder had bludgeoned someone to death with a dumbbell at a commercial gym. They discovered he was injecting growth hormone in addition to other steroids. The doctors then had been hesitant about blaming the man's behavior on the injections and had settled on naming them as 'non-insignificant contributors'.

Not enough for a diminished capacity defense, anyway.

But this didn't make sense. David Taylor was thin, drawn, perhaps the furthest thing from a bodybuilder.

"You're telling me that he was injecting growth hormone?"

"No, not injecting."

Dr. Kinkaid opened the folder in his hands and withdrew a series of images. Veronica immediately recognized them as MRI scans—as a child, Dr. Jane Bernard had subjected her to many when they were still trying to figure out the origins of her sensory hallucinations. One of the images showed a colorful overlay indicating strong activity in a region—reds, oranges, and yellows—smack dab in the middle of David's brain.

This reminded Veronica of her synesthesia and the fact that on none of the occasions that David Taylor had become violent had she seen any colors at all.

"We didn't manage to complete the MRI because of the, *uhh*, transformation," Dr. Kincaid said, "but based on the IGF and GH levels, along with this abnormality here in the pituitary, I think we might have narrowed down the root cause."

Veronica still didn't understand.

"What is it?"

"Again, without pathology, we can't confirm—"

"Doc, I'm too exhausted for this. Please, just tell me why this seemingly normal man transforms into a... into a... into a *monster*."

Freed from her sins.

The thought came from nowhere and made Veronica shudder.

"A rare pituitary gland tumor. Best guess is that David Taylor is suffering from a tumor that pumps out abnormal levels of IGF-1 and growth hormone in concert. This is what's causing him to change."

Veronica pursed her lips.

Surely, the doctor was pulling her leg.

"A tumor? A tumor is what turns him into a monster?" She looked at David through the glass and remembered Jake Thompson sitting on a chair, blood on his chest and thighs, lungs pulled out his back. "A tumor made him do *this*?" Veronica shook her head. "No, I don't think so."

"I've seen *something* like this before, but usually these changes are more permanent," Dr. Kinkaid admitted. "I'll have to review the literature, but the transient nature of his transformation might have something to do with him becoming prone. David Taylor lying down could trigger the tumor to pump out abnormally high levels of GH and IGF-1, causing transient acromegaly, and the redistribution of body fluid to his face and hands. Again, just a hypothesis and more tests need to be done, but..." the doctor shrugged and let his sentence trail off.

Veronica struggled to wrap her mind around what the man was saying. She wanted to reject this theory but what else could explain the way that David Taylor had changed before her eyes?

"Okay, well, how come when he stood up and started to walk around and murder these people he didn't change back?" She was trying, and failing, not to sound petulant.

"Well, it could take time. I suppose it depends on how long he was on his feet during the day and how long he was lying down before the pressure inside his head woke him up." Dr. Kinkaid didn't quite sigh but came close. "The truth is, Detective Shade, I'm only giving you a hypothesis of the most likely scenario here. There is still much to learn."

Veronica was weary of being duped—not by the doctor but by David Taylor. Everyone who was even tangentially related to law enforcement knew the legend of the man who was charged with murder and pled insanity. Against the advice of his lawyers, he decided to take the stand in his own defense. Then he proceeded to put his hand down the back of his pants, scroop out a handful of what looked to be shit, and then licked his palm clean.

It turned out to be peanut butter and the man was convicted.

This wasn't as cut and dry a scenario, but it still had an odor of deception to it even if Veronica couldn't smell any gasoline. But despite her strong desire to continue this line of questioning, the expression on the doctor's face suggested that they were getting close to the end of the road.

"Fine," Veronica conceded sharply. In truth, David's physical transformation didn't interest her as much as the mental. "Even if that's true—even if this tumor is making him change—it wouldn't make him kill."

Dr. Kincaid cocked his head.

"You see here how there's no space between the brain and the skull?" He pointed at one of the images. It did appear as if the brain was pressing right up against the bone. "This is not normal—it's caused by something called *pseudotumor cerebri*. It's a condition where there's swelling in the brain, likely a result of the sudden rush of fluid when David lies down. It's known to cause everything from visual to auditory hallucinations, to sweating, to delusions. And based on the sheer volume of fluid that is required to move to his face to cause these incredible physical changes, I would imagine that David might experience any and all of these sequelae—*uhh*, side-effects. And to a fantastic degree. So, Detective Shade, if you're asking me if, hypothetically, this tumor and brain swelling can alter someone's behavior, can turn a non-violent person into someone incredibly violent? Then, yes, I believe that is possible."

"No," Veronica snapped. "Brain swelling didn't make him do this. He's a fucking killer. A murderer."

The way Dr. Kincaid looked at her now suggested that he knew Veronica's medical history. Maybe he did, maybe he was a closet *Marlowe* fan and upon seeing her interview he did a little background research, or maybe Veronica was just projecting.

As fantastical as Dr. Kinkaid's explanation sounded, she couldn't help but think of her own story. How trauma had messed with her brain, causing her to see, smell, and hear things that simply didn't exist. Things that, at one time, she believed to be true, and that even today she trusted more than her real senses. It would also explain why David's denial of involvement hadn't triggered her synesthesia. If what Dr. Kinkaid said was accurate, what were the chances David would even remember what had happened once his brain returned to 'normal'?

But why pull their lungs out? Why write sinner with their blood? Why target people from the church at all?

Veronica conjured an image of the drawing Max Taylor had made of his mother on the funeral card ascending to heaven like an angel.

Did LeeAnn's death and funeral influence David somehow?

"We're going to have to do many more tests to be sure," Dr. Kincaid said. "Like I said, I've never seen anything so dramatic or transient before but it's the best explanation we can come up with right now."

"But it's possible?" Veronica said under her breath.

"Yeah, it's possible."

Veronica's question had been rhetorical.

If it was possible for someone to savagely murder three people and not remember any of it, then it followed that it was also possible to chop someone's finger off or try to poison them with bleach.

Even if these people were your mother and father.

"Fuck."

"I'll keep you posted. I need to see another patient."

As Dr. Kinkaid walked away, Veronica looked at David Taylor again.

Just because something was possible, didn't make it true. Did it?

Once a killer, always a killer...?

Chapter 65

VERONICA WAS STILL STARING AT David when someone approached her from behind.

"Detective Shade?"

She turned and her brow immediately crinkled.

"What are you doing here?"

"Managed to sneak in," Officer Court Furnelli said. "Captain's outside talking to the media, less security now."

Veronica looked skyward.

"Of course, he is."

"I just wanted to let you know that I was digging into Sylvia Decker, and I think I found something."

Veronica stared at Court for several seconds before saying, "Have you even gone home?"

The young officer was taken aback by the question.

"Y-yeah, I showered and got a little catnap in."

There was something odd about Court, something that was just a little off. Not in a bad way, but it made the man difficult to read.

Veronica sniffed the air. No gas, but she still thought that he was being deceptive in some way.

Or maybe she was just running on fumes.

"Sorry—Sylvia Decker?" The name was familiar, but Veronica couldn't place it.

"Yeah, Aaron Decker's wife who was sleeping with Bobby Harvey? The man who killed Aaron?"

"Of course, did you find her?"

"Unfortunately not, but I gained access to her bank records. Bobby's, too. About a week ago, Bobby took out forty-five hundred bucks—every cent he had. Two days later, Sylvia did the same."

Veronica frowned.

"Shit. She *did* plan this. She planned this and got Bobby to do her dirty work. Played him and played Aaron, took off with both their cash."

Court licked his lips and nodded.

"Sure looks that way. I gave her name and photograph to all bus terminals, airports, and car companies in the city. Hopefully, someone will recognize her and call it in."

"Hopefully."

But doubtfully.

No one who planned something like this was dumb enough to use their own ID to get on a plane. Chances were, Sylvia Decker had a new identity and was probably in another country. Perhaps she'd fled to Vancouver or gone south to Mexico.

They'd never find her again.

Veronica sighed.

"Good work."

"Thanks."

Unlike Court, Veronica hadn't gone home yet. When she looked down at herself, she saw that her shirt had sweat stains on it and her shoes were dirty from all the walking she'd done in Needle Point.

"No, I should be thanking you," Veronica said softly.

Court raised a dark eyebrow.

"For what?"

She didn't want to say it but thought she had to.

"When you hit me on the arm—"

"You had everything under control," Court assured her.

That was true.

"Yeah, but you hit my arm and if you hadn't, I would have—"

"

Court reached out and put a hand on her shoulder. Normally, a gesture like this would feel patronizing and annoy Veronica but for some reason, coming from Court, it didn't.

It felt kind.

And it did actually comfort her.

"You incapacitated him." The way Court said this left little room for argument.

"Yeah, I guess I did."

She squeezed Court's hand.

"Think you can take over for me here?"

Court cast a glance over her shoulder and into David's hospital room.

"Of course, go get some rest."

Again, no room for argument, but this time, Veronica wouldn't even consider it.

***

There was a car parked at the curb in front of her house, and Veronica's first thought was that it was Cole's. And when she saw a person sitting on her front stoop, she thought it was him, too. But as she got closer, and as dawn's early light cracked open and revealed its golden yolk, she saw that it wasn't Cole.

It was Steve.

He must've been dozing in a seated position because when she came near, he startled and then immediately got to his feet.

"Steve? What are you doing here? I thought you were in the hospital?"

"They let me go. Veronica, I'm sorry. I'm so damn—"

Veronica didn't wait for the man to finish.

She rushed to the sheriff, opened her arms, grabbed him, hugged him, and then kissed him hard on the lips. Steve wrapped his hand around her waist and kissed her back. With their lips still locked, Veronica reached and tried to open the door. It was locked, and she fumbled with her keys, dropping them to the ground.

Steve pulled away just long enough to pick them up and hand them back to her. Then she kissed him again. Once inside, they kissed all the way up the stairs. It was as if they both feared separating their lips for just one moment would cause an impassable chasm to form between them.

By the time they made it to the loft bedroom, Veronica's shirt was off, her breasts bare, and he was shuffling with his pants at his ankles. With a sigh, Steve lowered her onto the bed, and then he was yanking at her pants, pulling them down to her ankles while wriggling out of his boxers. When he entered her, she moaned and threw her head back. Their love was fast and feverish, more passionate than romantic, and while it didn't last long, something happened to her that hadn't happened for a long while.

Veronica found herself not thinking about Dante or Benny or Gloria or David or Max or Beverly or Peter or Cole or Jane or Freddie or anyone.

She thought of nothing.

Nothing at all.

Her mind was clear.

When it was over, she slept.

That night, no bear chased either Steve or Veronica.

Chapter 66

UNLIKE VERONICA, STEVE HAD HAD plenty of sleep over the last few days. Too much, in fact. Which was why, after their frenzied lovemaking, when he shut his eyes, his sleep—dreamless as it was—lasted only a few hours.

He made sure not to disturb Veronica when he woke. Things had gone far better than Steve could have ever hoped. Exceptionally well, unbelievably well.

But he also knew what Veronica had been through and didn't want to push his luck. Sitting in a hospital bed recovering from a fentanyl overdose and enduring opioid withdrawal had given him a lot of time to think.

And a lot of time to stay apprised of Veronica's case.

Not to interfere—no, she had shown time and time again that she was more than capable—but to help her if she asked for it.

Steve wondered if the strange cases, the bizarre, deadly ones found Veronica or if it was the other way around.

There was no way of telling.

But it took a toll on her, that was for certain.

Steve gently stroked Veronica's cheek, wondering how he'd fucked up so badly. She wasn't perfect, wasn't even perfect for him, but she was different, and she was special. And he had nearly let that slip away.

What the fuck happened?

But Steve knew what had happened.

On the advice of his doctor, he'd taken some pain meds. Fast forward six months and he was a full-blown heroin addict. It seemed impossible, but he knew that his situation wasn't unique.

Steve exhaled and for some reason, he started speaking.

And once the words started to come out of his mouth, soft as they were, he found himself as capable of stopping as quitting heroin cold turkey.

"We were having problems, my wife and me. I won't deny that. We still loved each other, but we were fighting more. I was working long hours as a trooper. *Long* hours. And let me tell you, working long hours is one thing... working long hours with Phil Crouch? That's a different beast entirely. And this case... this case was killing me. Missing girls. Lots of them, and we were getting nowhere. Anyway, what made it worse is that, for some reason, Julia likes Phil. I could never understand why because I can't stand him. Every time I would come home after a long day, she'd invite him inside for a drink or a bite to eat. After he'd leave, I'd ask her politely not to do it again, to give me a break, but she insisted. One day, I came home after a fourteen-hour shift during which we discovered the body of a thirteen-year-old girl and Julia invited Phil inside for a drink. I basically told them no—I just couldn't deal with it. Both of them were pissed at me, of course. And let me tell you, neither my wife nor Phil were shy about it. But I just flat refused, went inside, grabbed myself a bottle of my favorite whiskey, and had a drink. Then I had another and another."

Steve closed his eyes not to block out the flood of memories but to fully appreciate them. This was a happy moment despite the context.

Because this was before things went bad.

"Instead of joining me, Julia decided that if I wasn't going to let Phil in, then she was going to the bar with him. There, she had a couple of drinks of her own, I'm guessing because when she came home two hours later, she was half in the bag. By this time, I was really drunk. We got into an argument. Nothing extraordinary, not really. I crashed on the couch that night, slept for maybe four hours when I heard a bang. To be honest, I'm surprised I even woke up, given how wasted I was. The first thing I did was call out my wife's name. When she moaned, I went upstairs and found her in the bathroom. Julia didn't remember what happened, but I think she slipped—that's my best guess. Slipped and cracked her head on the ceramic sink. Split her open pretty good. I called an ambulance, and they came to pick her up. Despite all the blood, it didn't end up being that serious—just a few stitches and some aspirin.

"The real problem started when Phil showed up next. He wasn't supposed to be there. But you know how it is—a woman bleeding and her husband is drunk? Someone's going to do an investigation. As they should. But Phil? My partner? How the fuck is that not a conflict of interest? I'm not sure how he arranged it, probably just annoyed someone until they just agreed to get rid of him. And even though Julia never claimed I was violent to her, Phil thought differently."

Steve's tone had increased a little, and Veronica stirred. He waited for her to calm down before continuing.

"He thought I did something to her. The guy that I had been partnered up with for the better part of a year thought I actually hurt my wife. Ridiculous. But you've met Phil, V—sorry, Veronica. He's a different sort of man. I don't know if it was because of the fall, or because I wouldn't let Phil in that night, or maybe they were sleeping together, but things broke down between me and Julia. I moved out shortly thereafter. Not that it made a big difference, I was so deep into the case of the missing children that I was barely home anyways. And when I was, I was drinking a lot.

"But the thing is, I was still teamed up with Phil. Unbelievable. I can't tell you how uncomfortable that was. I tried to keep personal feelings out of things for the sake of the investigation but that proved almost impossible. And this case..."

Steve sighed. This part, he didn't want to remember.

"Three days after I moved out, I went back to get some things. During the day, of course, knowing that Julia wouldn't be there."

Steve could feel his pulse throbbing in his neck. He also felt the subtle tingling in his hands and an itchiness on the inside of his arm.

No, he told himself. *You're done with that. Never again.*

"There was blood everywhere, Veronica. A trail of it leading from just inside the door all the way to the kitchen. There it pooled, and in that pool was a knife. I don't know what I was thinking. Truthfully, I wasn't. I was running on empty, and I was scared. I shouted her name as I picked up the knife. Next thing I know, Phil appears out of nowhere—he's inside the house and I'm fucking standing there holding a knife, blood on my hands. He rushes at me, grabs me by the throat, and demands I tell him what I did to Julia. I couldn't because I hadn't done anything. Phil roughed me up pretty good. Maybe he would have killed me, I don't know. But more cops came and then CSU. The blood was hers and while nobody could say for sure that she was dead, I just knew it. There was just—" Steve's voice hitched. "—so much blood."

Tears distorted his vision, and he closed his eyes again.

"I looked for her, though, did everything I could to find her. But Phil... all Phil wanted to do was catch me in a lie, a slip-up. He was convinced I'd hurt her. *Killed* her. But I wouldn't—I would never. Eventually, after three months, it was just too much for everyone—the stress, the pressure. The department was being slaughtered in the media. They couldn't find Julia and the longer I stuck around, the more the pressure to do something increased. I didn't want to leave, but with Phil running his mouth all the fucking time, I knew that eventually, this would come down on me. They wanted to ship me somewhere far, somewhere out of state, but I refused, just in case Julia came back. I held out and then the Bear County Sheriff position was vacated and while I wasn't exactly promised it, they gave me a platform to run on and inroads with a bunch of wealthy donors. I broke, and I took it. I just couldn't deal with everything anymore."

Steve wiped his face and when he looked down, he was surprised to see Veronica looking up at him. This startled him, and he pulled back, but Veronica didn't say anything.

Her lids just slowly closed.

Steve didn't know how much Veronica had heard, and he didn't care. It just felt good to talk about it.

So *damn* good.

When he was confident that Veronica had fallen asleep again, Steve rose, dressed, and headed out to work as the Bear County Sheriff.

What he didn't know was that today was going to be his last day on the job.

Chapter 67

VERONICA WASN'T SURPRISED TO FIND Steve gone when she woke up. Nor was she surprised to discover that it was 2:30 in the afternoon on Friday.

She felt well-rested, but she didn't feel *well*. To get her mood to near-normal levels, Veronica showered and drank about a pot of hot coffee.

After feeding Lucy, who she'd basically neglected for the past two days, she thought about her night with Steve.

It had been amazing. The sex was just good, a little too hasty to be great, but being in Steve's arms was exactly what she'd needed.

What she wanted.

A small smile on her lips, Veronica dressed and did the only thing she could think of: she went to work.

On the way, she checked her messages. There was one from the captain, wishing her well and advising her to take a few days. When she was ready, he needed to speak with her.

Veronica deleted that one.

Freddie was next, mostly repeating Captain Bottel's sentiment. Finally, there was a message from her father. Peter Shade called her, on average, once a week, checking in and always inviting her to Sunday dinner.

Veronica typically erased these messages, but today, perhaps still under the spell of the afterglow of sex with Steve, she had a change of mind.

It had been six months since that day on the bridge with Dante Fiori, which also marked the last time she'd spoken to her father.

Veronica tapped the phone against her palm and unexpectedly thought about something that Cole had said.

You forgive everybody except yourself.

Veronica saved the message as she pulled into the Greenham PD parking lot.

Her smile grew.

"How did you know?" Veronica asked as she approached Freddie. He was standing by the door with a coffee in each hand, a wry grin on his face. "It's 3:30 in the afternoon on a Friday and every logical person would have stayed home until at least Monday."

He handed her a coffee.

"You're a lot of things, Veronica, but logical ain't one of them." Freddie grinned. "Besides, I put a tracker in your car."

"That's not creepy at all."

"The real question is, what *are* you doing here?"

Veronica shrugged and she reached for the door.

"I guess I was just bored." She started to step inside but realized that Freddie was not following her. He was no longer smiling, either. "Uh-oh, what is it?"

Her partner looked at his coffee.

"I thought I was going to have more time to prepare for this."

"Spit it out." For the first time since waking, the smile fell from Veronica's lips.

"Well, DA decided that they aren't going to press charges against David Taylor."

"What?"

"Yeah. The DA and his team had this meeting with a crew of doctors and psychiatrists. You know how they are, won't say anything definitively, only talk in probabilities, but I guess the consensus is that the tumor was making him kill those people." Freddie paused, clearly thinking that she would be upset by this. Veronica was oddly indifferent. "I think the exact words used were, 'David Taylor's tumor and related condition was a contributing factor of the patient's actions...' or something like that. It's also killing him, by the way."

This was a surprise.

"Really?"

Freddie nodded solemnly and sipped his coffee.

"Yeah, inoperable. Apparently, it invaded some other structures of the brain... I dunno. They give him anywhere from a week to a month. That's it."

Despite the gravity of this news, Veronica was no longer thinking about David.

She was thinking about Max.

"You know what?" Veronica said, letting go of the door. "I don't feel like going to work today, after all. I feel like going on a drive. Care to join?"

***

There were more people inside Grace Community Church today than the last time they visited. Many more, in fact. Veronica had heard that there was always a spike of people visiting houses of worship following tragedies like 9/11 or school shootings. She didn't think that the murder of three people, no matter how brutal, qualified, but given the proximity of these crimes to the church, it was possible that this was the reason.

Father James Murphy, on the other hand, appeared unchanged. He didn't even seem bothered by the way their previous encounter had ended. And when Veronica attempted to apologize, half-heartedly, but still, he'd said that it wasn't necessary.

"Yes, I know David Taylor well. He and his son Max would come in on most Sundays and help distribute hot meals to those in need. David also does some work around here, as a handyman of sorts. And after his wife died, this," Father Murphy made a grandiose gesture, "is where they decided to host LeeAnn's funeral. I'm very sorry to hear about his... *condition.*"

Veronica resisted the urge to look at Freddie. If David had been a handyman at the church, then he was definitely on the list that Father Murphy provided. And if he was on that list, her partner should have noticed it.

"Did Jake Thompson use to come for those meals?"

"Sometimes, yeah."

Veronica chewed the inside of her cheek. That explained where David had met Jake, but it didn't explain Frank or Cooper.

"What exactly did David do as a handyman?"

They were once again walking up and down the aisles, which Veronica found particularly annoying, but she went along with it.

She owed the man that much, at least.

"Nothing specific. Just little jobs. After LeeAnn died, I guess he had more time on his hands. And while the Taylors were infrequent visitors before the woman moved on, after her funeral, they had a change of heart." The priest shrugged. "It was a beautiful service, very, very nice. You know what? I think I might still have the card."

Father Murphy moved towards the front of the church, but his pace only slightly quickened. There were a bunch of pamphlets lying on an ornate table by the door for various causes, and he rooted through them before coming up with a white card.

He showed it to her, but Veronica didn't take it. She already had a copy on her phone.

"Max drew it," Father Murphy said. "This is his mother, ascending to heaven."

"I know." Thoughts of Max sitting on the porch of his house, his cheeks wet with tears threatened to derail her, but Veronica pushed these aside. "Did Max ever join his dad when he was doing jobs around here?"

"Oh, yes. He would sit right there, drawing his pictures." Father Murphy indicated another table, this one only a few feet from the confessionals.

A narrative formed in Veronica's head. A narrative of little Max sitting at that table, drawing pictures of angels after his mother died, overhearing others confessing their sins to Father Murphy. Then, at night, the boy would go home and talk to his dad about what he'd heard. Maybe he'd even be holding one of his pictures as he recounted these stories. And then everything, the images, the sins, the names of the sinners, cemented themselves in David Taylor's diseased brain. Then, when he lay down and began to change, David would recall these tales. And then he would lash out, believing that he was setting these sinners free.

Or maybe David, like his son, just wandered around at night, and when he came across members of the church he recognized, he just assumed them to be sinners.

Because we're all sinners deep down, aren't we?

"Father, did you give the sermon during the funeral?" Veronica asked.

"I did."

"And did it include talk of angels? Of sinners?"

The man glanced at his hands, and Veronica waited for him to look up again.

"Yes. Yes, I believe I did. I spoke about how LeeAnn was an angel ascending to heaven after her sins were forgiven."

"And what might her sins have been?" Veronica asked a little more harshly than intended.

Father James Murphy gave her a tired look.

"Right, you can't tell me what was said during confession."

"Correct."

Freddie started to move forward, but Veronica assured him with a look that she was under control.

"Just one last thing, Father, and it has nothing to do with confession."

The priest opened his hand and lowered his head slightly, indicating for her to continue.

"Do you know a man named Mark? I'm not sure about his last name, but he's tall and speaks in threes?"

Father James smiled broadly.

"Of course. Mark helps hand out meals on Sundays, as well. He is a very special man."

"He handed out the meals with Max and David?"

"Yes, the two of them—Max and Mark, I mean—were good friends." Father James Murphy started to walk again, and Veronica had no choice but to follow. "I even recall how they met. A young man who was down on his luck came in here seeking shelter and a warm meal. He was... agitated and impatient. When Mark tried to serve him a meal, the man mocked his speech. Now, Mark is as gentle as they come, and he didn't even react. But Max overheard and immediately came to his rescue. It was... very heartwarming if I do say so myself."

So, Mark had no problem protecting Max but won't raise a finger to protect himself? Interesting.

"I don't mean to overstep, Detectives, but what will happen to poor Max now that his father is so ill?"

"We don't know yet," Freddie said when it was clear that Veronica wasn't going to answer.

Veronica had banished the thought from her mind. She refused to imagine another orphan, another boy twisted by trauma and left to rot in a place like Renaissance Home.

"I need to go."

Without waiting for Freddie, she started toward the entrance.

"Detective Shade, my doors are open anytime. As are my ears in the confessionals. If you would like absolution, all you have to do is ask for it."

"No, thanks," Veronica muttered under her breath.

Freddie met up with her outside several minutes later.

"Sorry," he said. "Took the man up on that offer of a confession."

"Lots of sins, huh?" It felt good to be back to their normal banter. "Too many Big Macs?"

Freddie snorted.

"Yeah, something like that. I think I'm going to take off, that okay?"

"Big date tonight?" Veronica teased.

Freddie became serious.

"Yeah, actually, something like that. What about you? Any plans?"

Veronica was about to say no but then stopped herself.

"You know what? I think I might have dinner plans, too."

Veronica hugged her partner then, marveling at how she was nearly able to interlace her fingers around him now. And then Freddie left.

Instead of getting in her car, she set out on foot. Moving at a decent clip, Veronica arrived in Needle Point in fifteen minutes.

It took another five to find Mark.

"Cop... cop... cop..."

Veronica couldn't help but smile.

"That's right, I'm a cop. Listen, Mark, I was wondering if I could ask you something. A favor."

"Favor... favor... favor..." Mark nodded with each word.

"I'll pay you."

"Pay... pay... pay..."

"Okay, good." Veronica made sure to speak very slowly. "Max is going to be alone soon, and I want you to look out for him. I want you to protect him. Do you think you can do that?"

She was reaching into her wallet and pulling out the money she'd withdrawn for this very purpose: two hundred dollars in twenty-dollar bills.

It wasn't necessary, of course. Veronica could tell by the man's expression that he would look after Max for free.

"Max... Max... Max..."

Veronica forced him to take the money, anyway.

"Thank you."

On the way back to her car, she pulled out her cell phone.

Before Veronica could change her mind, she dialed a familiar number.

Her father answered on the first ring.

"V? Is everything okay? Are you okay?"

Veronica shook her head.

Some things never change, she thought.

"Yeah, I'm fine. I was just wondering about that dinner. You think you can move it from Sunday to tonight?"

"I haven't put anything in the sous vide yet, and—"

"Dad?"

"Yes, of course. I can whip something up."

"Great. Make enough for four, okay?"

"Bringing two guests?" Peter Shade asked.

"No," Veronica replied, shaking her head. "Just one. You bring the other."

Chapter 68

STEVE KNEW THAT HIS RETURN to work was going to be very uncomfortable. He knew this without a shadow of a doubt.

But what he hadn't expected was some sort of ceremony for his arrival.

Marcus McVeigh was standing outside the Bear County Sheriff's Office headquarters, along with two other deputies.

Steve, growing more than a little concerned with every step he took toward the entrance, felt his heart skip a beat when he noticed a fourth man. He was big and bald, and his vest said DEA.

"What's going on? Any update on the case? On the fentanyl that nearly killed me?"

No answer.

"McVeigh?"

Still nothing.

"Lancaster?" The deputy lowered his eyes. *What the fuck is going on?* "Look, I didn't expect a parade, but 'I'm glad you're okay and welcome back' would've been nice."

Confused, and annoyed, Steve tried to circle around the men to gain access to the front doors, but Troy Allison moved to block his path.

"What the fuck are you doing?" Steve demanded.

"Steve, can we... can we talk for a moment?" McVeigh said.

"It's Sheriff Burns," he corrected.

McVeigh put his hand on Steve's shoulder and tried to guide him away from the other men, but Steve brushed him off.

"That's kinda what I wanted to talk to you about."

"I think you should go for that walk with Marcus," Troy said.

Steve shot lasers at him.

"And I think you should mind your fucking business."

The big DEA Agent set his jaw and balled his fists.

"Steve, please." McVeigh tried once more to lead him away, and this time, Steve went, but on his own accord. He wasn't going to be led away like a child.

"What the hell is going on, McVeigh?" Steve asked when they were out of earshot of the other men. Steve was still looking over his chief deputy's shoulder at first his deputies and then Agent Allison.

The latter seemed to be smiling with his eyes.

"Steve, I don't know how to say it, so I'm just gonna: I'm going to have to relieve you of duty."

Steve's eyes bulged.

"What?"

This came out of left field.

"Yeah, I'm—I'm sorry but I'm going to need your badge. And then I'm going to need you to officially step down as sheriff of Bear County."

Steve craned his neck forward until his face was but a foot from Marcus McVeigh's.

"What the fuck are you talking about?"

McVeigh sighed and looked down. Unlike Troy, and now Steve, himself, there was no aggression in the man's tone or posture.

"I think we both know what I'm talking about."

Steve scowled.

Yeah, he knew, all right.

"This is bullshit. I was undercover, McVeigh. I was undercover because you and the DEA thought it was a good idea to send me undercover. And I almost died because of it. So, I don't know what you think you're—"

"Stop."

"No, I won't stop," Steve barked. "I almost died because I was undercover. So, if you think—"

"Stop," Marcus said, louder this time. "Just fucking stop, Steve. We both know that's not why you almost died. You've got a problem. And your problem isn't just your problem when it puts others at risk. You have to step down as sheriff."

Steve jutted his lower jaw and leaned in, now within inches of Marcus's face.

"Fuck you. I won't fucking step down. This is my job, it's my county," he said as he tapped the gold star on his chest.

McVeigh started to fumble with something on his hip, and for an instant, Steve thought he was trying to gain access to his gun.

"You gonna shoot me now?"

"No, I'm not gonna shoot you," McVeigh said. He pulled something out of his pocket, not a gun, but a small USB key.

Immediately, Steve's heart dropped.

"Steve, I haven't shown this to anybody. *Nobody*. And I won't. If you step down right now, I won't show anybody. I promise you."

Steve instinctively reached for the USB key, but Marcus's fist closed on it before he could grab it.

He knew what was on that key.

It was him, of course. It was a video of him stealing Oxy from the evidence locker. And his whole plan, Steve's whole cockamamie plan of making up a story about how he was using the drugs as part of this undercover operation was absolute bullshit.

All someone had to do was look at the dates, and they'd know the truth.

Still, Steve was angry. More at himself than his chief deputy.

He'd been backed into a corner and there was no way out.

But he still had one card to play.

Steve removed the gold sheriff's badge and shoved it into McVeigh's chest so hard the man nearly fell over.

Then he raised his voice loud enough for everyone to hear, including the deputies and especially DEA Agent Troy Allison.

"I hereby step down as sheriff of Bear County," he said, waving a finger in the air. "But before I do—as my final act as sheriff—I'm calling for an immediate election for a new sheriff to be elected in Bear County." Then, with a wry smile on his face, he lowered his voice and looked at McVeigh. "You didn't think you'd get my job that easily, did you?"

"Steve, if you try to run again, I will—"

"No, I have no intention of running. But I know just the person who will go up against you... and they're going to win."

Chapter 69

DAPHNE'S.

It was peculiar how both Veronica's current and ex-boyfriend both loved Daphne's. The owner, her gray hair down for the first time Veronica could remember, greeted her with a warm embrace.

"You look great."

"I do?" Veronica shrugged. "How bad did I look before?"

"You never look bad," Daphne said with a wink. "Come. Your guests are over here." She indicated a booth around the corner. "Beer or coffee?"

"Beer. And did you say *guests*? As in plural?"

"I did."

"Hmm."

Veronica moved quickly through the café and then halted as soon as she turned the corner.

Cole was sitting in the same spot as the last time they'd met, handsome and impeccably groomed as ever. And he was smiling.

The man beside him, who was at least two heads taller, was not.

And while Cole rose to meet her with a hug, the second party opted for just a handshake.

"Thank you," Dylan Hall said. "Thank you, Veronica."

Veronica acknowledged this, then quickly changed her mind.

"Don't thank me, thank Cole here. He's the one who got you out."

Now Dylan smiled.

"Thank you both, then. Shit, I'm just glad I'm not going away."

"I'm glad, too."

Veronica slid into the booth, and moments later, Daphne came with her pint. She brought one for Cole, as well, but Dylan settled for coffee.

"Is this some sort of celebration?" Veronica asked, genuinely puzzled as to why Cole had asked her to meet him here. It couldn't just be so that Dylan Hall could say thank you again.

Cole took a big gulp of his beer and then made a dramatic *'ah'* sound.

"You know what? I suppose it is."

Veronica clinked glasses with both men.

"Well, congrats on your first case, Cole, and to you, Dylan, for not going to prison," she said, still a little confused.

"Oh, I'm done with that shit. Clean and staying clean. Never going back."

"Yeah, but that's not what we're here to celebrate."

Veronica eyed Cole suspiciously.

He was making things awkward on purpose. Veronica hadn't known Cole to be petty, but this sure felt like a petty move.

Veronica let him have his moment—he deserved that much. What Cole hadn't deserved was the way she'd treated him. Mentally, she was okay with the fact that she'd gone back to Steve. No guilt there. That was where her heart truly lay. But the way she'd done it—no, nobody deserved that.

You've got to learn to forgive yourself.

"We're here," Cole raised his glass high above his head, "to celebrate *Redemption Agency*."

Veronica made a face.

"What? What the hell is that?"

Cole grunted.

"That, Detective Veronica Shade, is our—" he indicated himself and Dylan with his beer, "—brand spanking new PI firm."

Veronica wrinkled her nose and took a big haul of her beer. "Seriously?"

"Now, that's just not nice," Dylan said. He looked at her through the steam of his hot coffee. "I'm clean and—"

"No, I'm not talking about you being a PI, Dylan. In fact, I think you'd be a great PI. You've got the street smarts, while Cole has the…"

"Good looks?" Cole offered.

"… fancy shoes. But… the name? Redemption Agency?"

"Well, I thought," Cole began, a tad defensive, "because Dylan's out of prison and—"

"It sounds like some sort of anti-gambling racket."

Both of Cole's eyebrows rose.

"We can do that." He waved his hand, indicating an invisible marquee. "Redemption Agency, we can keep you out of prison, stop you from gambling, and find out who your sleazy husband is sleeping with. We can do it all."

Veronica laughed. It felt good to laugh.

"You know what? I've changed my mind. I kinda like it."

She drank more beer, now finishing half the glass.

"We're going to need your help, though, to get our feet off the ground, you know?" Cole said.

Veronica nodded.

"Yeah, I know, I'll send any work I can your way. As promised. Look, as much as I want to stick around and drink all night with the Redemption Boys, I've got dinner plans. With my father." She said this last part quickly.

Veronica finished her beer, and when she stood this time, she elected to shake Cole's hand, officially making their relationship solely professional. He seemed mildly disappointed, but he went with it, and for that, Veronica was grateful. Then she shook Dylan's hand and started to leave.

"Veronica, there's one more thing... can I walk with you for a second?" Cole asked.

"Sure."

"Did you read that folder I gave you?" he asked when they were away from Dylan.

At first, Veronica wasn't sure what Cole was referring to.

"... folder?"

"Yeah, the folder from..." He gestured with his thumb over his shoulder.

Now she remembered.

"No, I didn't get a chance."

"Well, you know how I said that you might not want to look at it? I think you should. Like, soon. *Really* soon."

Cole was acting strange but that was pretty much par for the course.

"Okay, thanks. And thanks for everything, by the way. I'm—"

Cole smiled as he cut her off.

"—on your way. Detective Shade, it was a pleasure doing business with you."

They shook hands again and Veronica returned to her car. The folder was there in the backseat, and she grabbed it.

But despite Cole's assertion, Veronica hesitated before opening it.

She had dinner plans tonight. Dinner plans that meant a lot to her.

While she might not be able to forgive herself, she thought she could start to forgive her father.

And Veronica didn't want to ruin this. There was something about the way Cole had spoken to her—*I think you should. Like, soon.* Really *soon*—that made her think that if she opened that folder, she wouldn't make it to dinner.

Because what was in that folder was bad.

Very, *very* bad.

Epilogue

HAVING COME STRAIGHT FROM HER meeting with Cole, Veronica met Steve at her father's house. He looked nervous and uncomfortable, but that didn't bother her.

He *should* feel nervous and uncomfortable. If he didn't, it might suggest that Steve had used something to take the edge off.

But he was clean.

And he'd also learned his lesson. This time, he'd brought a six-pack of craft IPAs instead of a bottle of wine.

Veronica, who hadn't had the time to stop, said, "I'll take those."

Steve let her have the beer.

"There's something I need to tell you."

"It can wait."

Veronica knocked on the door.

"No, I don't think it can."

"Yeah, it can. And it will."

An equally uncomfortable Peter Shade opened the door. He looked the same, perhaps a little plumper around the middle, and he was wearing a tartan button-down shirt that Veronica had never seen before. Only the top button was undone and during the few seconds that the four of them—Jane had since materialized behind Peter—stood there, he'd fiddled with the collar on three separate occasions.

"Come here, Dad."

Veronica reached out and embraced her father, still holding the six-pack behind his back. He smelled of cologne, which was strange, but a deeper sniff revealed the unmistakable odor of cigarette smoke buried beneath, which explained it.

Veronica separated from her father and while Peter shook Steve's hand and said hello, she shook Jane's hand and said the same.

Oh, shit, this is going to be uncomfortable for all of us, she thought.

But two or three drinks in and things loosened up a little bit.

Talk was light, as expected, and the food was incredible, also as expected.

Somehow, her father had managed to make homemade ravioli from scratch in the few hours he had to prepare since Veronica switched the dinner date from Sunday. This was followed by a perfectly cooked flank steak topped with roasted garlic and blue cheese compound butter and a tangy chimichurri sauce.

The four of them talked about nothing and everything as they enjoyed their meal.

To Veronica, they all seemed happy. And who was she to ruin that?

Still, on the way to the bathroom, she crossed paths with Jane and as much as she'd promised herself that she'd keep things light this evening, Veronica couldn't help herself.

"Jane," she said softly. "Do you know a Dr. Simon Patel?"

The woman's eyelids fluttered, just once.

"Not personally."

Veronica didn't press—Dr. Bernard's hesitation spoke volumes. But before she could walk away, Jane grabbed her by the arm.

"Be careful," Jane warned.

An odd remark, but Dr. Jane Bernard was an odd woman. Dr. Simon Patel was odder still.

As am I, Veronica thought, as she returned to the dinner table.

As they wrapped up, Steve volunteered to clean the dishes. Rather predictably, Jane offered to join him.

They were giving Veronica and Peter a chance to talk but the latter snuck off. Veronica found her father on the back porch smoking a cigarette.

"I guess some things don't change."

Peter looked at the glowing ember on the end of the cigarette.

"All we can do is try."

Veronica stared out at the evening sky. She was always amazed at how even though they weren't exactly in the country, for some reason her father's house seemed to exist in its own bubble. That's the thing that she liked best about this place.

It was isolated and safe.

"I need to ask you something, Dad. I want to ask you something, and I want you to tell me the truth, okay?"

Peter Shade didn't agree, but he didn't disagree either.

"Do you know anything about my childhood? I mean, before you found me outside my house that night? What I was like? Anything at all?"

Veronica stared at her dad intently, but he couldn't hold her gaze. He took a drag from his dwindling cigarette and then flicked it on the grass. He still didn't look at her when he said, "The past is boring; it's already happened—the future is far more interesting."

Veronica rolled her eyes.

"Don't avoid the—"

The back door opened, and Steve leaned out.

"Veronica? Can I talk to you for a second?"

Good timing, she thought. *Shit.*

Peter jumped at the opportunity to avoid her question.

"Here, take my spot—I was just leaving."

He gave her shoulder a squeeze.

"I tried to tell you earlier," Steve began when Peter was back inside. "I want you to know—"

"I know about the drugs," Veronica said preemptively. "I also heard you talking about your wife."

The pulse in Steve's throat quickened and yet it was clear by his expression that this wasn't what he wanted to talk about.

"I—I—" Redness rose in his cheeks. "I'm not the sheriff anymore."

This, Veronica had not been expecting.

"What?"

Steve cleared his throat.

"I'm no longer the Bear County sheriff. It's a long story, but McVeigh forced me to step down today."

Veronica felt her forehead crinkle.

"Forced you to step down? What do you mean? What's going on?"

"I—I—"

"Steve?"

Steve exhaled loudly.

"I stepped down and nothing can change that."

Veronica was confused.

"Because of what happened? I mean, the overdose? Or—"

"Bit of both, really. But for now, McVeigh is going to be the interim sheriff for Bear County. But the very last thing I did, my last act as sheriff, was to announce an emergency reelection."

Veronica raised her palms.

"I gotta tell you, this is… well, I don't really understand. Are you thinking about running again?"

Steve shook his head.

"I won't be running again. But I don't want Marcus to be sheriff. Don't get me wrong, he's smart, ambitious, maybe a little too political for his own good, but I just think that there's someone who is better suited for the job. And I think this person can run against McVeigh and beat him."

"Who?"

Steve finally looked at her and Veronica waited for a beat, then two.

"*Whaaat?*" she said, drawing out the word. "No—no way."

The left corner of Steve's mouth lifted just a little. It was hard to notice with his new, longer beard, but it moved all right.

"Yes, way," he countered.

Veronica crossed her arms over her chest.

"You're kidding. I just got out of the limelight, there's—"

Steve suddenly grabbed her, pulled her close, and kissed her hard on the mouth. When he was done, he looked her right in the eyes.

"You're gonna run, Veronica. You're going to run, and you're gonna win."

***

Freddie was nearly an hour early, and he felt like a teenager waiting outside of his prom date's house. Only he wasn't young, and he wasn't going to prom. He was going to have dinner with his ex-wife and one, hopefully two, of his sons.

Parked outside the familiar house, a dozen roses rested on his lap, and he held a bottle of wine in his hand. He'd spent much time considering the roses.

Would daisies have been more appropriate? What about a summer mix of peonies and other flowers?

The problem was, what Freddie Furlow knew about flowers could be folded into a blade of grass.

Roses seemed like a good idea, but now he regretted his decision.

"I should've gone with something less... romantic," he said under his breath.

Freddie moved his eyes from the roses to the bay window. He could see Susan inside, milling about, walking to and fro like she always did to blow off some steam before a dinner party.

He could see his son too, Randy, but not Kevin. He hoped that his eldest was there.

Ever since Susan had called him, Freddie had visions of how this night would go.

Visions of things being awkward at first but then quickly falling into the old routine. After dinner, the kids would retire to bed and he and Susan would sit on the couch watching TV as they finished the wine. Then Susan would turn and look at him and —

"Get a hold of yourself, Freddie," he scolded. "It's just dinner."

But it wasn't just dinner.

In fact, Freddie Furlow was fairly certain that there was no such thing as *just* dinner.

Time passed and another thought occurred to him. He was too early, but what was worse? Being early or risking Susan or Randy looking out and seeing him sitting in the car like a stalker?

The latter, he decided. So, after contemplating his choice of flowers for the hundredth time, Freddie took a deep breath, sighed, and then stepped out of the car. As he did, his shirt came untucked, and he did his best to jam it back in by shifting the bottle and flowers to the same hand.

Why did I wear this shirt?

It was a white button-down and because he had been sitting in the car so long, it was now wrinkled.

And with his weight loss, it was too big, too.

I should have bought something new. I'm such an idiot.

Shaking his head, Freddie started toward the door. With every step his heart rate increased.

Then the blinds parted, and Susan peered out the window and directly at him.

Freddie smiled, which felt surprisingly natural, and he gave her a little wave with the roses.

The roses. Why roses, Freddie? Why didn't you go with daisies? Why—

He'd been so focused on Susan that he didn't see the car approaching. It squealed and Freddie, realizing that he was in the middle of the road, took a large step backward. But the car didn't go around him; instead, it stopped directly in front of him. Another vehicle appeared out of nowhere and screeched to a stop behind him, boxing him in. Freddie dropped the roses, and his police instincts, ingrained in him over decades, took over. He reached for his gun, which, of course, he didn't have, and then he crouched down in a defensive posture. The door of the black car in front of him swung open, and a familiar form jumped out.

The man was tall, bald, and reeked of cigarettes.

"Troy? What are you—"

Before he could finish his sentence, someone grabbed his arms roughly from behind, shoving them painfully up his back. The bottle of red wine smashed to the ground, and he felt and heard the sound of cuffs being applied.

Troy grinned as he came right up to Freddie.

"I told you not to fuck with me, Furlow. I *warned* you." Troy's smile grew. "Fred Furlow, you're under arrest, you thieving fuck. I have you on video stealing heroin from the Matheson evidence locker. You're going away for a long fucking time."

Freddie knew that this day was coming the moment charges against Dylan Hall had been dropped and the man had been released.

But today? Did it *have* to be today?

As he was roughly yanked backward and thrust into one of the unmarked police cars parked, he didn't resist.

It was over.

It was all over.

Freddie let his eyes drift back to the bay window of the place he'd once called home.

The blinds were closed now, and Susan Byers was gone.

END

Author's Note

THERE'S AN OLD SAYING THAT no good deed goes unpunished. Well, rarely do bad deeds go unpunished, either. True, some people do get away with murder, but the universe often finds a way of extracting its pound of flesh. The main difference, as I see it, anyway, is that the punishments for good and bad deeds alike aren't always consistent—they tend to vary considerably across the board.

This is something that the residents of Bear County are slowly beginning to realize. Let's face it, life just ain't fair. Do the right thing for the wrong reason and maybe you're spared Karma's wrath. Do the wrong thing for the right reason? Well, you get the idea.

To find out the ultimate consequences of everything, good and bad, that our esteemed residents of Bear County have done over the past year or so, you're going to have to wait until *The Taste of Murder*.

No spoilers, but I promise you this (no, it's not an exact release date—I've learned my lesson): everything has been leading up to the explosive conclusion in the final book of the Veronica Shade series.

See? Good things, good people, and I'm still making you guys wait. Told you, life's not fair.

You keep reading, I'll keep writing.
Best,

Pat
Montreal, 2022

Made in the USA
Middletown, DE
12 October 2024